A CLASH OF

I stared at the tall, fortified walls surrounding the castle. *Why won't they open the gate? Don't they understand me? It cannot be my accent. My Sorvinkian is almost perfect.*

"OPEN!" I shouted one more time. "I am Prince Amir of Telfar. I accompany Princess Eva, the king's daughter. OPEN THE GATE!"

The gate remained closed. I turned my gray mare around and rode back to our caravan. I had reached its first carriage when I heard orders being yelled behind the wall. I looked back at the castle and saw armed men lining up behind the fortification and, *oh dear*, bows being drawn. I felt my stomach drop. I couldn't believe it; they were going to shoot at us. Before I could order Eva's Farrellian guards to take cover, a volley of arrows flew in their directions, piercing their chests and necks.

As the guards fell dying on the ground, the carriage door flew open and Milo appeared in its frame. "My lord, what's happening?"

❋ THE KING'S ❋
DAUGHTERS

The "Prince Amir" Series by Nathalie Mallet:

The Princes of the Golden Cage
The King's Daughters
Death in the Traveling City (forthcoming)

❀ THE KING'S ❀
DAUGHTERS

NATHALIE MALLET

NIGHT SHADE BOOKS
SAN FRANCISCO

First Edition

ISBN 978-1-59780-135-5

Night Shade Books
Please visit us on the web at
http://www.nightshadebooks.com

For my parents, Mona and Eliodore Mallet

ACKNOWLEDGMENTS

Once again, I want to thank my husband, Andre, without his support this book simply wouldn't exist; and my wonderful agent, Jenny Rappaport, for believing in me. Thank you, David Randall, for your precious feedback. My thanks to all the members of my writing group, who were never short of encouragement and advice. Thanks also to Marty Halpern for the copyediting. And finally, a special thanks to Jason Williams and Jeremy Lassen of Night Shade Books for making my dream come true.

CHAPTER ONE

Bitter cold stung my cheeks and transformed my breath into vapor. The snow squeaked under my boots as I walked along our caravan of wagons and carriages in search of survivors. Corpses; so far I had found nothing but corpses. I spotted a column of steam rising from one of our fallen men. I rushed to his side only to discover with much chagrin that the white cloud of steam wasn't coming from his mouth… but from his opened gut. I touched his neck—no pulse. This one was dead too.

"Aiii! What kind of frozen, bandit-infested hell is this?" I cursed aloud in frustration and anger. This was the seventh attack by brigands we'd suffered since we'd set foot in Sorvinka. The elite soldiers who had escorted us from Telfar had long been decimated. We were now reduced to using Eva's Farrellian eunuch guards as our last defense—the eunuchs were a *parting gift* from her aunt, Princess Livia. At first, I did not fancy having them around. Now… well, now was a different story.

I cast an uneasy glance at our dead guards. Their numbers were dwindling fast. At this rate we'd soon be left without defense.

I looked at the frozen, barren landscape. I hadn't been long in Sorvinka, and already I hated this country. Although

I knew it was Eva's home, I couldn't understand why she wanted so badly to return to this frigid, inhospitable land. How could one miss this miserable place? *She misses her family, not this ice-locked, sunless country,* I told myself. I understood her desire to rejoin them, yet I wished we had stayed in Telfar, my homeland; warm, beautiful, and safe Telfar. I let out a long sigh and then continued my search for survivors. Even though I was still sweaty and warm from having fought in a battle, I tightened my kaftan around my body knowing that in a moment I would be shivering from the cold in this gray morning air.

"Aaah... Your Highness." The lament came from my left. I turned toward it.

Clutching his bloody side, Ely, one of Eva's eunuch guards, was trying to stand. I rushed to his aid and grabbed him just as he was about to fall forward.

His eyes widened. "Your Highness, behind you!"

I spun around. First, I saw the brigand coming at me; then I saw his blade aimed straight at my chest. With my own sword sheathed and my arm circling Ely's convulsing body, there was no way I could block his blow. The man was already on me.

Gritting my teeth, I braced myself for its impact. But just as his blade was about to plunge into my flesh, the brigand was rammed sideways by one of Eva's guards. With two efficient swipes of his sword, the tall eunuch easily dispatched the assailant. I didn't question the identity of my rescuer for an instant; it was young Milo. I recognized him immediately, not only by his unique swordplay—which was without flourish and done with an economy of movement—but also by his wispy blond hair. All the other eunuch guards had the bright red hair most common to Farrellians; while Milo's only had the slightest touch of copper. If one looked closely, one could spot freckles of the same hues dusting the bridge of his nose.

This was the second time Milo had saved my life; although I was glad to be alive, a small part of me disliked being indebted to the young eunuch. I didn't like being indebted to anyone for that matter. Still, I knew these were unreasonable, if not irrational, feelings, and that I should be thankful for the young eunuch's presence with us and for his swordsman's skill, especially now that we had so few guards left.

Hiding my discomfort at having been saved again, like a damsel in peril, I commended Milo for his bravery. "Well done, young man. I wish we had more guards as talented with the sword as you... well, I wish we had more guards, period." To my relief, three more surviving guards came round the caravan and joined us.

Relinquishing Ely to the care of the other guards, I made my way to Milo's side.

Looking proud of himself, Milo bowed to me. With his lean athletic body and long limbs, Milo reminded me of a young colt, a bit clumsy yet very powerful, an unusual look for a eunuch... and a deceiving one too. And when one added his square jaw, aquiline nose, and overall masculine facial features to the mix, all that was left to betray his physical condition as a eunuch were his light airy voice and smooth, beardless cheeks.

"How many guards survived? Do you know?" I asked.

"Seven, counting myself, my lord. Three are gravely wounded though. Those men won't be able to fight if we're attacked again."

I aimed my sight to the gibbet still visible on the horizon. "Sorvinka is known as the land of the thousand gibbets. If you ask me, they would do well to double that amount. I haven't seen that many ruffians in all my life." I shook my head. "This country will be the death of us."

"Yes, my lord," Milo said, while stomping his feet and beating his side for warmth. "And if the brigands don't get us, the cold will."

I looked at the shivering Farrellian. Milo was on the skinny side for a eunuch. Without this protective layer of fat, he tended to get cold quickly.

I patted his shoulder. "You fought well today, Milo."

"As did you, my lord," he replied with a bow. When he straightened, I saw that he was beaming with pride. "I am pleased to have served Princess Eva as well as expected and, more so, not to have disappointed you." Milo paused, as if unsure if he should continue.

I gave him a nod of encouragement.

"I know that many… no, actually, most people don't consider us eunuchs as… true men, capable of doing true men's actions. I… I am overjoyed to have been able to prove myself to you, Prince Amir." On this Milo bowed at the waist.

His show of gratitude made me uncomfortable, and I was glad when Eva poked her head out of her carriage.

"Amir! Amir!" she called. "Are you hurt?"

"I'm fine. Please stay inside the carriage. It's safer there. We'll join you in a moment." I turned to Milo. "You'll take Ely's place beside Eva."

"It will be my honor."

Rubbing my short beard, I inspected the young eunuch's clothes. His costume, a red and white mock copy of the Farrellian military uniform, was torn and stained with blood. "Do you have a spare?"

"This *is* my spare."

"Come with me," I said, "I think I have something that might fit you."

I made my way to the wagon containing my belongings. When I opened the back door, I caught a glimpse of my reflection in a polished bronze mirror propped against a chest, and flinched. I didn't recognize myself; for a brief moment, I thought I was looking at a ruffian. All I could see were piercing brown eyes and sharp cheekbones. Then I recognized my flawless profile with its perfect straight nose—the trademark of my family, the Ban—yes, that was me all right. I didn't look my best. I had lost my turban in the battle, and my short, thick black hair was all tussled. Also my beard was clipped too close to the skin for my taste, looking more like a shadow then a true beard.

Eva likes it this way, I told myself as a consolation. It was a pain to maintain however. After a quick search in my garment trunk, I found a loose beige tunic and a dark green kaftan with sleeves ample enough to cover Milo's long limbs. Although he was clearly sad to part with his mock uniform—I had noted how proudly the young eunuch wore the garments—he took the clothing I offered him with good grace.

Leaving the eunuch to change, I made my way to Eva's carriage. I wasn't surprised to see that Eva was outside. She never followed orders... especially mine. She was staring at the horizon, her black mink cape hanging loosely over her blue velvet dress, as if its addition had been an afterthought. For some reason, she seemed unaffected by the ambient cold. Petite and finely built, Eva had golden curls, warm brown eyes, and a peachy complexion. Despite her ethereal look, my beautiful ice princess was not a delicate creature. In the course of this trip, I had discovered that Eva was as robust as a peasant girl and as headstrong as a mule. I found this new knowledge a little disconcerting, yet I let none of my feelings show.

"You should've stayed inside the carriage," I said in a tone of reproval. "It's not safe for you outside."

"Hush!" she whispered, and then closing her eyes she took a deep breath. I watched a content smile stretch her lips. "Hmmm," she made, as if she could taste the air. "I love the smell of spring in the air."

"Spring!" I stared at the snowy landscape with its naked, dead-looking trees, then at the depressing gray sky. "If this is spring, I dare not imagine what winter is like."

Eva burst into laughter. "You would love it," she said amidst billowy clouds of vapor breath. "You complain, but I know you would love it."

I smiled, but quite frankly, I doubted I would ever get used to this miserable cold, let alone enjoy it. Setting my gaze on the road ahead of us, I said, "I hope we can reach your father's castle before nightfall. I fear we may not survive another attack."

"Oh stop worrying. We're almost there. In a few hours we will be warming ourselves in my father's court." Eva's attention slowly glided to the yellow-covered wagon behind us. "Maybe then I will finally get to see all those mysterious gifts you've brought." Her nose wrinkled a bit, a sign that she was annoyed. "I don't understand why you have to be so secretive about them."

"What! And spoil the surprise?"

Eva rolled her eyes. "Fine!" This settled, a brilliant smile lit up her entire face, and she squeezed my hand. "Oh, Amir, I can't wait for you to meet Father."

My stomach clenched painfully—as it always did at the mention of my forthcoming meeting with her father.

"Amir, what's wrong? Why is this dreadful look on your face?"

I shook my head. "I fear… (Sigh). What if your father doesn't see me as a good enough prospect for you and denies me your hand? What if your father dislikes me on sight?"

"You worry too much, Amir. It's your biggest flaw, you know. You are very endearing, my prince. Why would my father dislike you?"

"I don't know. Your Aunt Livia despises me… well, let's be honest, she hates me. She never forgave me for refusing the Telfarian crown and making her son, Erik, the Sultan. She wanted him to be the next Sorvinkian King, not the ruler of a small country. I'm surprised your aunt hasn't exacted her revenge on me yet, she certainly threatened me that she would often enough."

Eva gave me a patient look. "Amir, my aunt does not wish you ill."

"Perhaps. But you can't deny that she distrusts me. That's why she surrounded you with eunuch guards, so they'd keep you safe... from me. We've been traveling together for months, and this is the first moment we have been truly alone since we left Telfar. Those guards were never meant to be a *gift* as she said. They were meant to be a barrier."

Displaying a charming pout, Eva ran a finger along my jaw. "Aren't you happy that she did so? As I see it, if it wasn't for my guards, we wouldn't be alive now." Eva's carefree expression morphed into a somber one. She gazed at the grim surroundings, her brow furrowed in concern. "Something has changed. When I last traveled these roads, Sorvinka wasn't the dangerous place it is now. I don't understand what happened to my country. It worries me, Amir."

Throwing her arms around my waist, Eva rested her head against my shoulder. "Let's leave this spot. Leave now. Let's not waste another moment here. I'm dying to see my family."

"Yes. Anything you want, my love," I said, bending down to kiss her.

"Huh-huh," Milo cleared his throat behind me. "My lord."

I turned and was shocked by how a change of clothes could transform someone. Milo looked like a totally different man. The dark green kaftan accentuated the color of his eyes, which were soft green; it also made him seem blonder and gave his shoulders a more squared appearance. As it was right now, Milo could have passed for a young nobleman.

"We are ready to leave, my lord."

"Then we should," I replied.

Eva applauded with enthusiasm. "I cannot wait to see Father."

"Yes... me too." I smiled at her. Deep down, however,

I was petrified by fear, and given the choice I would have rather faced a horde of brigands than her father. *Enough*, I told myself. *The king has no reason to dislike me. Just don't give him one and everything will go well.*

* * *

I stared at the tall, fortified walls surrounding the castle. *Why won't they open the gate? Don't they understand me? It cannot be my accent. My Sorvinkian is almost perfect.*

"OPEN!" I shouted one more time. "I am Prince Amir of Telfar. I accompany Princess Eva, the king's daughter. OPEN THE GATE!"

The gate remained closed. I turned my gray mare around and rode back to our caravan. I had reached its first carriage when I heard orders being yelled behind the wall. I looked back at the castle and saw armed men lining up behind the fortification and, *oh dear*, bows being drawn. I felt my stomach drop. I couldn't believe it; they were going to shoot at us. Before I could order Eva's Farrellian guards to take cover, a volley of arrows flew in their directions, piercing their chests and necks.

As the guards fell dying on the ground, the carriage door flew open and Milo appeared in its frame. "My lord, what's happening?"

"The king's castle has been taken by enemies; I see no other reason for this attack. Stay inside with Eva. Keep her safe. You hear me, Milo."

"Yes, my lord," he said, and shut the carriage door.

Pulling my sword, I pushed my horse toward the front of our caravan. Before I could get there, the castle's gate opened with the loud clicking sound of well-oiled chains, and a small army of soldiers rushed out. Within moments, the entire caravan was surrounded.

"Drop your weapon," called one of the soldiers.

"NO!"

To my surprise, the soldier seemed unsure of what to do. "Obey."

I shook my head.

"Make way," a voice ordered from the back of the troop.

The row of soldiers circling me parted and four knights riding black warhorses approached. Clad in shining armor and black leather, they looked impressive. All four were tall and solidly built, like most Sorvinkians, but the knight riding in front was particularly imposing. He was a good head taller than everyone else.

Ordering the other knights to stay behind, he brought his horse a short distance from mine and stared at me through the slit in his gilded helm. He had vibrant blue eyes, I noted. "In the name of the King, relinquish your weapon," he boomed, his deep voice amplified by his helm.

I stared at the imperial crest embossed on his armor, divided in three sections it depicted a rose beside a black eagle over a bear. Then I looked at the soldiers. They wore the blue uniform of the Sorvinkian army, and they too carried the imperial banner. I was confused. "In the name of which king?"

"King Erik the Fair. Ruler of Sorvinka."

"I don't believe you. King Erik would never allow my men to be slaughtered in such a way. This is the action of a vulgar bandit."

"You tell me so," he said while pulling off his helm. Gray-streaked blond hair fell about his shoulders. I looked at the strong line of his square jaw, at his straight nose, and his blue eyes. There wasn't a doubt in my mind, this was King Erik. I recognized his rugged looks from paintings I had seen of him. I breathed a sigh of relief.

"Prince Amir, your arrogance is quite shocking to me," said the king. "Not satisfied to surround my daughter with Farrellians—Sorvinka's most deadly enemies—and bring them to my doorstep, you have the impudence to call me a vulgar bandit. Kings have been vexed at far less."

I felt my face blanching. "Farrellian enemies? I don't understand."

"Don't you dare blame your actions on ignorance. The fact that Farrell and Sorvinka are at war is well known. News of it had been sent to my sister, Princess Livia, months ago."

"Princess Livia knew of this! But… she…"

The king's eyes narrowed. "Prince Amir, do not try blaming my sister for this either," he hissed through clenched teeth.

I looked at the dead eunuch guards. Princess Livia had handpicked them for their looks, had had special uniforms made for them so their nationality would be unmistakable. *Princess Livia had gotten her revenge after all,* I thought. I could see no way out of this precarious position… except one. I bowed my head. "My most sincere apologies, Your Majesty. The fault is entirely mine."

Apparently appeased by my apologies, the king nodded. He gestured for the knight on his right to approach. The knight moved beside the king while removing his helm. In a clunk of metal hitting metal, the king slapped his gloved hand on the knight's armored shoulder. "This is my nephew, Lars Anderson, Duke of Kasaniov. I'm sure my daughter mentioned him to you."

I bowed my head at Lars. I had certainly heard of him, Eva's cousin—*twice removed;* she always insisted on that detail, as though this made him less of a relative—and the presumed heir to the throne. Fair of skin and of hair, Lars was a robust young man of my age. His eyes were pale blue, his chin pointy, and he had a slightly upturned nose. Despite the constant grimace of disgust twisting his face, as if something stinky was stuck under that upturned nose of his, he wasn't ugly. For some reason, I had expected him to be.

Loud shouts coming from the back of the caravan made

me turn. To my utter consternation, I saw that the king's soldiers had invaded the last carriage where our three wounded eunuch guards were housed. When the soldiers began pulling the wounded guards out, I knew that if I didn't intervene they would be killed. As I attempted to help them, Lars drove his warhorse in front of my mare, blocking my path.

"Stay put, young prince," warned the king.

Feeling powerless and outraged, I could only watch as two of our guards perished at the hands of the soldiers. But when I saw Ely being thrown to the ground, I couldn't stay quiet anymore. "Your Majesty," I pleaded, "he's Eva's most loyal guard. He served her well. Please, Your Majesty, this man poses no threat to you."

Unmoved by my plea, the king nodded to the soldiers surrounding Ely, and, at once, they pierced the wounded guard's body with their lances. When it was all over, and Ely had expelled his last breath, the king turned toward me and said, "Now this man *truly* poses no threat to me."

Biting my tongue, I squeezed my eyes shut. Poor Ely, he didn't deserve this fate. At that instant, my thoughts turned to Milo, who was still inside the carriage with Eva. He too was doomed… then again, maybe not. I turned to the king. "Will you permit me to fetch your daughter?"

The king nodded.

Within moments, I was off my horse and entering the carriage. I was met by Milo's blade and nearly got my throat slit. "Careful!" I said.

"Oh, my prince, you are safe," he breathed in relief, lowering his blade from my neck.

"Sheathe your sword, Milo." I ordered.

"What?" Milo looked at me as if he thought I had lost my mind.

"Amir, explain yourself," Eva said. "Tell me what's happening."

"There is no time." Then turning to Milo, I blurted, "If

you want to live, you will do everything I say, starting by sheathing that blade and unloading my luggage. As for you, Eva, your father awaits you outside."

For a woman encumbered by three layers of petticoats, Eva dashed outside with amazing speed. Milo shot me a sideways look. Right then I knew he wouldn't obey my orders. As a eunuch guard, Milo's loyalty was to Eva, not to me, and it would remain so until he saw her safely under the king's protection. Before I could stop him he was out behind her.

"Oh lord!" I said, and followed in their steps. Sure enough, once outside I found Milo with his back against the carriage and three lance tips pointed to his neck.

"Father!" Eva exclaimed. "What are these manners?"

"Eva, go inside," the king said.

"No! Not until I know what is happening here."

The captain of the soldiers approached Eva and whispered something in her ear. Her face turned as pale as snow, and if not for the firm grip the captain had on her waist, I believe she would have collapsed on the ground.

"Bring her inside, quickly," ordered the king.

Suddenly docile, Eva let herself be carried away without protest.

Having lost my only ally, I turned to the king. "Majesty, that one is my valet. Please, tell your men to lower their lances. He's harmless. Look at him, he's not Farrellian."

Lars dismounted from his horse, marched straight to Milo, and inspected him from head to toe. "I don't know. He looks half-Farrellian to me. That's enough to merit death."

With a hand on the grip of my sword, I stepped forth.

Milo swiftly raised his hand to stop me; his eyes I noted were filled by a mixture of fear and determination. "No, my lord, do not risk yourself for me," he said in his light airy voice.

Upon hearing Milo's voice, Lars's head tilted, his eyes narrowed, and his lips curled into a feral smile. And without further notice, he leaned forth and abruptly plunged his hand into Milo's crotch. "Aagh!" Lars exclaimed, leaping back in disgust. "I knew it! This one's a gelding. How revolting!"

I looked at the king. His face displayed no emotion, yet I thought I saw a hint of disapproval in his eyes. "I thought eunuchs were only used for guarding the harem, and to serve women," the king said.

"No," I immediately rectified. "White eunuchs serve the Sultan... and princes as... as personal valets. None are better."

"And what tasks are these personal valets supposed to perform?"

"Hmm... hmm. They attend to one's grooming needs, baths, daily washing. They help one dress."

Lars let out a loud cackling laugh, while the other men present were more discreet and just chuckled behind their hands.

The king however remained dead serious. After a brief glance at Milo, he turned his attention to me. "Prince Amir, in Sorvinka, men dress themselves. But as you seem incapable of accomplishing this task by yourself, I will permit you to keep your servant. Because you are a guest in my castle, I am obliged to respect your customs, no matter how strange they may appear to us."

"Your Majesty is too kind," I said, bowing quickly to hide the redness of my cheeks.

"Don't thank me yet, I'm not done. One thing must be clear, Prince Amir. Maybe in Telfar a prince can have his servants fight his battles for him, but in Sorvinka servants aren't allowed to carry swords. And as long as you are a guest in my castle, you will live by my rules. Here you'll have to fend for yourself, young prince."

"Yes, Your Majesty."

With obvious pleasure, Lars swiftly disarmed Milo. Then

he slammed the sword on his armored knee several times, in an attempt to break it, I presumed. His efforts were useless—the sword was made of Telfarian steel, hence of too good a quality to be broken this way. Frustrated by his failure to destroy Milo's weapon, Lars shoved the sword into the hands of the nearest soldier.

The king shook his head, then turned his horse around and rode toward the castle. Once he reached the gate, he pivoted in his saddle and shouted, "Oh yes, I forgot. Welcome to Sorvinka, Prince Amir."

I looked at Milo, who was rubbing the sore spots on his neck where the lance tips had dug into his flesh. I looked at the corpses surrounding the caravan, then finally at the stern, hostile face of the king. In my opinion, this was the coldest welcome I had ever received in all my life.

CHAPTER TWO

The castle was a black stone monstrosity—quite frankly I'd seen prison towers that were more inviting. As if this ominous sight wasn't unnerving enough, I had just learned that my friend, Ambassador Molsky, was on a diplomatic mission in another country.

Wonderful! I sighed. Not only did I expect to see him, I thought I would be under his guidance once I arrived. Besides the language, I knew very little about the Sorvinkians' ways. Maybe I should have spent less time refining my accent and more time studying their customs. Well, it was too late now.

With Milo glued to my side like a thistle, I crossed the castle's courtyard. I was shocked by the quantity of soldiers posted there. They all looked alert and on edge, as if fearing a sudden attack. I discovered the same nervous atmosphere inside the castle. Here too, there were guards posted everywhere. These men, however, looked exhausted; the redness of their eyes and constant yawning clearly indicated that they had not slept in a while.

"My lord," Milo whispered in my ear, "something is amiss here. Perhaps entering this castle was a mistake. The reception they gave us was certainly most unpleasant and—"

"Hush," I said, and turned my attention to the guard

guiding us, a tall, pock-faced youth with sleepy eyes. "The king mentioned a conflict between Sorvinka and the land of Farrell."

"For sure, we're at war with those dogs."

"I noticed that the garrison in the courtyard seemed ready for action. Is the Farrellian army marching on this castle?"

The guard spat on the ground. "Those cowards! They don't have the guts to fight men. Those lowly bastards can only kidnap little girls."

"I'm afraid I don't understand what you mean by that."

"You don't know! The king's youngest daughter, Princess Aurora. The sweetest little thing. She was kidnapped three nights ago. Our poor king is beside himself." Lowering his voice, the guard added, "Word is, Farrellians did it."

"Really? There are no other suspects besides the Farrellians?" Blaming the enemy of the kingdom seemed a tad too convenient to me.

"Well..." said the guard as he readjusted the helm on his head—dented on the right side it kept slipping to the left—"a lot of stories are going around. Some say it's the old gods' wrath, their revenge against our king for banning their worship and destroying their temples. Others think that brigands did it. No good scum—the lot of them."

I couldn't agree more, with that part anyway, and nodded vehemently. Sorvinka was certainly not short of brigands, I could attest to that. However, kidnapping a princess, that was too bold a move, even for the worst of them. "What is your opinion on the matter? Who do you think is guilty of this crime?"

The young guard's eyes widened. He was stunned that a prince would ask him his opinion, and just as I had expected he quickly expressed it. "Well, no ransom has been asked yet. Brigands love gold; they would've demanded a ransom. As for the gods, old or new, they're usually content to ignore us. So, I say it's these dogs of Farrellians. Oh, yes! It's them, I'm sure." The guard spat on the ground again. "They're a vile bunch. Can't trust Farrellians, they're all cowards without honor." On this the guard turned left and entered a long, dark corridor.

Curious to see how Milo was taking all those insults, I glanced at him. Besides the paleness of his face, he appeared in perfect control of himself. *Good boy,* I thought, and followed behind the guard.

I was a bit concerned when the guard stopped in front of a black oak door with its big wrought-iron hinges.

"And this?"

"Your rooms, Your Highness," the guard replied, opening the door.

"Ah," I said. I had secretly hoped that this long corridor, with its barren stone walls and smoky torches, was just some alley leading to the castle, not a part of the castle itself. Apparently, this castle was as ugly and as austere inside as it was outside. Surely my rooms would be better, I thought, stepping in. Of course, I was wrong again. *A cave with furniture* was my first impression of my receiving room, gray stone and cobwebs everywhere, wall to wall, and floor to ceiling. Only the stained-glass window added some well-needed color to this depressing grayness. The room was dreadful, yet I was careful not to show my disappointment in front of the guard—one had to be courteous when abroad.

While Milo and our guide brought my trunks inside my rooms, I approached the window to admire its craftsmanship. Without a doubt, this was the work of a master; the rose design circling its frame like a vine was flawless. I touched the frosted glass at the center of the window and sighed. It wasn't frosted glass; it was just… well, frost.

"Lovely," I whispered sarcastically. "It's almost as cold inside this room as it is outside." I shook my head. I wasn't really surprised by this, though. I had begun shivering moments ago. Hugging myself for warmth, I stared at the sparkling white snow outside. I felt confused and lost. This castle was nothing like the magnificent palace Eva had described to me, nor was Sorvinka the genteel fairytale kingdom of her accounts. To me, this land was hard and cruel, and this castle was even worse: it was dingy, cold, and *oh so* ugly. Had Eva misled me on purpose?

Troubled by these thoughts, I traced the rose design of the window with a finger while attempting to reassure myself. Not everything here was bad or ugly. Maybe it was just me, seeing only the dark side of things; it certainly wouldn't be the first time. I gazed at the frozen landscape outside the window. Could I learn to love this land and its people, I wondered, and would these people ever love me in return? The king's severe face formed in my mind—it seemed doubtful. Unable to find any satisfying answers to these questions, I rested my forehead on the icy glass, feeling depressed.

"My lord."

"Yes, Milo."

"The guard has departed and all your things are here. If my lord wishes, after I've made fires in the fireplaces, I could begin unpacking."

I shrugged. "Sure."

"My lord, I… I…"

The strangled tone of Milo's voice made me turn.

Bearing a look of extreme gratitude and devotion, Milo kneeled in front of me and bowed to the ground. "Thank you, my lord, for saving my life. My lord took a great risk on my behalf. My lord will not regret it."

I didn't reply—truth was, I already regretted my action, and for several reasons. First, saving Milo had disgraced me in the eyes of the king. Second, I didn't know how I could redeem myself. I had no idea how to do that, none at all. Lastly, I didn't care for servants, personal or any other kind, and I didn't trust them either. So being stuck with one really displeased me. I threw a resentful glance at the still prostrated

Milo. "Rise," I said.

"Is there anything else I can do for you, my lord, before I begin unpacking?"

I scratched my head, then my beard. I felt dirty; actually, filthy was more accurate. "Yes. Can you find where the baths are located in this castle? I would like to wash all this dust and sweat off me."

Happy to be of service, Milo swiftly ran out of the room. Sometime later, he returned carrying two buckets of water. "My lord, I have unsettling news. This castle doesn't have baths."

I gaped in disbelief. "You're jesting!"

Milo shook his head. "There are no indoor fountains either." He raised the buckets. "These come from an outside well. It was frozen. I had to throw stones in it to break the ice and get to the water."

I stared at the blocks of ice floating atop the water and winced. "Barbaric. Simply barbaric," I said with a sneer. "I suppose we'll have to make due with these appalling conditions."

"I'm afraid so, my lord."

Raising my gaze to Milo, a dark spot on his face caught my attention. I frowned and pointed at the red welt above his left eye. "What's that on your face?"

Milo covered the welt with his hand in a hurry. "Oh this, nothing. I made a wrong turn that's all."

"Someone hit you?"

"No! I fell. My lord shouldn't worry himself with such minute things. I'm clumsy."

That was a lie. Milo wasn't clumsy. Like all well-trained swordsmen, he was agile and light on his feet.

"Fine!" I declared. "I won't question you further on the subject. But from now on, you will not wander in this castle alone. If you're to act as my valet, I will need you to tend to my affairs. So be careful. This place is dangerous. You're useless to me if you're wounded."

"Yes, my lord." Although Milo had kept his voice as neutral as possible, I couldn't help noticing the slight smile curling the corners of his lips. "I will heat some water so my lord can wash."

* * *

Once I had washed and changed into clean clothes, I inspected myself in the long mirror Milo had set up for me. Although I wasn't fond of the soft gold tunic and pantaloon I wore, I judged that with my emerald kaftan and its matching turban it was suitable for this afternoon. The ensemble's overall look was rich yet not ostentatiously so, in my opinion.

Satisfied by my choice of garment, I affixed my rapier—the narrow-bladed dueling sword I favored—to my belt. Now that I was dressed, I decided to check on the many gifts I had brought for the royal family, as they were to be presented to them this evening. Needless to say, I wanted everything to go as smoothly as possible. Most of all, I desperately wanted to see Eva before the evening.

"Maybe my lord should wait for a guard to lead us there… later tonight, perhaps?" Milo suggested.

"No, Eva needs my support now."

A worried expression formed on Milo's face. "Poor Princess Eva. She must be devastated by her sister's kidnapping."

"Come, Milo. Let's go find her. She can use our comfort."

We left my rooms and walked in the direction of the big entrance we had passed earlier today. Once there, I saw that it was a crossroad that went in four different directions. I looked at each of the corridors and chose the broadest. After two bends, we found ourselves outside in the courtyard and had to turn around and return to the entrance. This time I chose the narrowest corridor.

Wrong road again, I thought upon exiting the corridor. I examined the empty square space we were in. Actually, it wasn't totally empty, a circular stone construction stood in its center.

Milo rushed to its edge. "It's an indoor well, my lord." He ran a hand over the well's stone rim and added, "There's a faint carving of a sea monster on it."

I shrugged. "Is there water in it?"

Milo bent over the well. "It's dry, my lord. There's hardly a puddle at the bottom."

Of course, the opposite would have been far too practical. Nothing in this castle seemed to be working properly, if it even existed at all. Everything looked old and rundown to me. My room was a particularly good example of this.

While inspecting the rest of the area, I noted an upward staircase on my left. I doubted this was the way to the throne room; it looked more like the base of one of the castle's towers to me. I approached the steps to take a peek up the stairs.

Upon setting foot on the first step, I froze in place as a wave of tingling coursed through my entire body. I shuddered and backed away. This was a too familiar sensation, one that conjured bad memories. I had felt a similar tingling before… back in Telfar… when my brothers were still alive. It was remnants of a spell. It was sorcery. It was magic.

I approached the steps again and reached out to touch the invisible veil of energy lingering in the air. My fingertips made contact with it and began tingling. Then all of a sudden the tingling ceased and the veil vanished. I found the sudden disappearance of the veil just as alarming as its presence had been. Now I had the feeling that something dreadful had happened here… something foul, something evil. I could swear to it.

"What is it, my lord?" Milo asked.

I let my hand fall to my side. "Nothing," I lied. "Come, let's leave this place." I turned around and froze in surprise.

A group of young noblemen stood a short distance from us with Lars at their head. I immediately knew we were in trouble. No need to be a seer to figure out they were up to no good. The vicious smirks on their faces were a clear indication of their intent.

Once the group got closer, one young nobleman turned to his friend and said, "Will you look at his fancy clothes. He's a dandy just like the other."

"Yes. He's definitively a dandy," agreed the other young man.

Milo and I exchanged puzzled looks.

"What's a dandy?" Milo mouthed silently.

"Pay no mind to it," I said under my breath as I surveyed the group.

"Is he going to marry your cousin?" one of the youngsters asked Lars.

"Hmmm," said a falsely pensive Lars, while giving me a thorough evaluation. "I don't know. I fear he doesn't really measure up to what is expected as a suitor for my cousin's hand."

"Definitely! He's so small," added the young nobleman.

What! I'm not small. Why is he saying that? Insulted, I glared at Lars. My height is average for a Telfarian, you stupid ignorant boy, I wanted to shout in that tall calf's face. *Calm down, Amir. Calm down.* Swallowing my anger, I bowed to Lars. "Greetings, honored noblemen."

Lars stepped forward. "Prince Amir, have you decided to go looking for the baths yourself this time?"

I looked at Milo's bruised face. Now I knew whose handiwork it was.

"I'll save you some time. There are no baths. Here, men wash with cold water or snow."

Or not at all, I thought. So far, everyone I had met, the

king included, smelled of sweat, smoke, and rancid oil. I stared at Lars; he was making that ugly twisted face again. I wondered if it was the smell of his own stench that caused his grimacing.

Forcing a smile on my face, I gave Lars a polite nod. "I'm afraid we are lost. Thank you for offering to show us the way to the throne room."

It took Lars a while to react to my demand; obviously he had not expected me to ask him for help and didn't know what to do. So during that time, all I could do was watch his mouth open and close like a fish out of water. "What!" he blurted out when he finally regained the power of speech. "I'm not your servant to do your bidding. That's the gelding's duty."

Milo recoiled as if he had been slapped across the face.

"Lars," I hissed, "my valet isn't an animal."

"Perhaps. But he's certainly not a man." His chest puffed up, Lars grinned proudly as his friends applauded the cleverness of his retort.

"That's your opinion. Mine differs," I said. I was not going to argue with him, but I wasn't going to agree with him either.

"You're wrong," Lars said. "That thing is a vile perversion, and you are—"

"I'm warning you, young duke. I do not take insults lightly. Be careful of what you're about to say."

It was no use. Lars's eyes narrowed and his grin widened. "Oh, I will say what I damn well please."

"Even if untrue," someone shouted from behind the group of noblemen.

"Who said that?" Lars snapped. "Who dares call me a liar?"

The group split apart revealing a tall, well-built young man with long, dark wavy hair and a dimpled chin. He was dressed in the most garish peach satin outfit I had ever seen.

Moreover, lace was bursting out from every visible opening of this ensemble—collar, cuffs, pockets—and even from around the gathering of his knickers. But what struck me the most about this man was his attitude. There was such an air of nonchalance about him, he looked fearless—to wear such clothes one had to be fearless, if nothing else, I suppose. His crooked, sarcastic smile, the kind that made you think he was laughing at you, only intensified that impression. I thought that the two put together, the attitude and the smile, made for a dangerous combination.

Extending his right foot forward, which was encased in a white high-heeled shoe with a bow on top, the man executed an elaborate curtsey, while waving a lacy handkerchief in the air. The move brought a powerful burst of lavender scent to my face. Tears welled up in my eyes. Lord, this man wore more perfume than all the concubines of my father's harem put together.

Milo leaned to my ear and whispered, "My lord, I believe this man is what they meant by a dandy."

"Shhh," I blew.

Rising from his curtsey, the newcomer sashayed toward us.

"You!" Lars sneered. "I should've known."

"Delighted to see you too, Lars."

"How dare you use my name. I have not permitted you such familiarity."

"I am deeply hurt, Lars. And I who thought we were close friends."

Lars snorted. "We were never friends."

The dandy twirled a lock of his long wavy hair. "Now I'm confused. You certainly behaved in a friendly manner when you came to see me two nights ago."

Lars's friends gasped. As for Lars, he turned bright red. "I've never! You're a liar!"

"Are you denying having met with me? The night's guards

can confirm your presence at my door. Oh, and so can Countess Ivana. She was in my adjacent boudoir at the time. Surely you will not call her a liar too?"

"I was there for a piece of garment—for the ball. The coming ball. For that purpose alone."

The dandy placed a finger on his dimpled chin. "Strange. Somehow I remember it differently."

"I spoke the truth, you know it!" Lars said defensively.

"You spoke, I'll agree to that. As for the truth… were you not caught in a lie moments ago?"

"Sir! You've insulted me. I demand reparation."

To my astonishment, the dandy uttered an excited shriek while jumping with joy. "Marvelous! I just love a good fight."

I turned my attention to Lars; he was just as dumbfounded by the dandy's reaction as I was. A peek at Lars's friends told me that they too shared our feelings.

"I will not spare you," Lars warned the dandy. "This is a true combat. Choose your weapon."

"I choose my handkerchief," the dandy said, twirling the lacy piece of fabric in the air.

His face as red as a brick, Lars stamped his foot down. "A handkerchief isn't a weapon. Choose an adequate one."

"I beg to differ. In this case, my handkerchief is the adequate weapon."

"The man is mad," whispered Milo.

I nodded in agreement.

"As you wish," said Lars. He pulled his long sword, and without further ceremony charged the dandy. This one stayed in place fanning himself with his handkerchief until Lars was upon him. Then he took a slight step to the left, escaping the sword, and tripping Lars with one of his dainty feet.

"Oops," he exclaimed, staring apologetically at the sprawled Lars. "You haven't hurt yourself, I hope."

I had to bite my tongue not to laugh.

Lars leapt to his feet and swung his sword toward his opponent. In a swift move, the dandy twisted his handkerchief around the blade and pulled, ripping the sword out of Lars's hands. Tucking the sword under his arm, the dandy waved his handkerchief at Lars. "I told you my handkerchief was more than adequate for this battle."

Heaving with rage, Lars darted a murderous glare at the dandy. "I won't forget this."

"Oh, neither will I, and nor will your friends assembled here." The dandy produced a brilliant smile. "They'll remember this encounter forever. Detailed accounts of it will be spread throughout the castle and the country for years and years to come… I'm quite certain of this."

Stunned by the devastating repercussions of his defeat, Lars became as still as stone. I watched the blood slowly drain from his face, leaving it a pasty white. Then Lars broke his stillness, and his gaze turned to his friends.

The young nobles were all fighting back laughter as best they could. Some had their hands clamped over their mouths, while others tried to look elsewhere in the hope it would suppress their mirth—to no avail. A loud chuckle escaped from one of them. A few more young men in the group followed his example, and soon they were all bent over laughing. And when Lars turned around and left, with his back as straight as the castle's tower and his butt as tight as a merchant's purse, the noblemen's laughter reached a deafening crescendo.

Once they had regained their composure, which was long after Lars had disappeared from sight, the young noblemen congratulated the dandy on his victory. Then following in Lars's steps, they departed, leaving Milo and me alone with the dandy.

Discarding Lars's sword to the side, as if it were nothing more than a cumbersome piece of metal, the dark-haired man approached us and curtsied.

I bowed.

He rose. "Please permit me to introduce myself; I am Diego Del Osiega, Prince of Pioval. And you must be Prince Amir of Telfar?"

"Indeed, I am."

The dandy prince gave me a thorough examination. "You are exactly as I've imagined you: dark, exotic, and handsome." His gaze moved to Milo standing at my shoulder. "You, however, look nothing as I thought. I always envisioned eunuchs as... fat, ambiguously feminine individuals. Never would I have fathomed such a strapping, masculine young man. You will be very popular here, mark my words, very popular."

Once more Milo and I exchanged puzzled looks.

"Aaah!" Prince Diego exclaimed as if suddenly overcome by emotion. "Prince Amir, I must warn you about this horrid castle. It suffers from a deplorable lack of refinement. And you are quite clearly a very refined man. Our kind is a rare breed in this savage kingdom. Therefore we are destined to become best of friends."

Best of friends—with him! I tried not to cringe too much at that thought.

He stepped closer to me. "Oh, and those clothes you're wearing, they are sublime!" Prince Diego ran a long-fingered hand along the fur trim of my kaftan. "You must show me your wardrobe."

I stepped back.

He stepped forth, his hand still caressing my garment. "I demand to see all your treasures."

"Another day, perhaps," I said, stepping back again. This time, however, I moved far enough to get out of his reach. I couldn't believe the effrontery of this dandy. Quite frankly, right now I didn't know who was worse, my attacker or my savior, Prince Diego. I didn't care for this type of attention. Still, the man had come to my defense, and for this reason

I had to display some gratitude toward him.

"Prince Diego, I must thank you for intervening on my behalf. That was a rather perilous act you just performed."

"Oh please, call me Diego. As for that little tiff with Lars, let me assure you, I was in no danger. The young duke's swordsmanship is rather like his wit, slow, predictable, and, overall, deficient."

"Nonetheless, I thank you. As you know, we've just arrived and this castle is—"

"Gloomy, dark, cold, and, my favorite above all, it stinks as foully as a putrid corpse."

"Hmm," I gave. "I was about to say foreign and confusing." I paused. For the briefest moment I wanted desperately to agree with the dandy. This place was exactly as he had said, if not worse.

"Foreign and confusing! How diplomatic of you." Prince Diego smiled. I noted that his smile did not reach his dark brown eyes, which remained intensely serious. "I would gladly be your guide," he offered. "I know the castle well. Its politics and etiquette even better."

I feigned thinking about his offer. I didn't want to insult the prince by saying no too quickly. It wasn't as if I didn't need the help, it was just that I didn't want his. There was something wrong about his constant joyfulness, something unnatural and artificial. Also, I didn't trust a man who could win a combat with a handkerchief. Or maybe it was just his clothes that repulsed me so. Oh let's be honest, I just didn't want to be associated with him. "I am thankful for the offer. However, I will try to face this castle's perils by myself."

If Prince Diego was disappointed, he didn't show it. "As you wish," he said. "But if you change your mind, the offer still stands." He curtsied, began walking away, then turned back toward us. "Where are my manners? I'm assuming that you are lost. If you're looking for the ceremonial throne room, it's through the long, narrow hall. That way." After having pointed us in the right direction, Prince Diego turned and left.

As I watched him disappear down the corridor, I began thinking about my decision. Perhaps refusing his help had been a mistake. This country and its customs were foreign to me, which could lead to embarrassing misunderstandings. Then again, I had already antagonized the king by arriving with a Farrellian escort. I couldn't do any worse now, could I?

CHAPTER THREE

The king's throne room was not only immense, it was cavernous. The three-story-high ceilings certainly added to this impression of grandeur. Yet despite its ample size, the room was so tightly packed with noblemen and dignitaries from all countries that it left one with very little space to move. It made for a suffocating atmosphere. Not to mention that the smell of unwashed bodies mixed with a myriad of different perfumes was almost unbearable. I tried not to think about it and concentrated on listening instead. At any given moment, I could hear at least five different languages being spoken at the same time. Sadly, I feared I was the main subject of all these conversations. For one, I had never been so stared at in my entire life. Every time I turned I could see eyes darting away. This rude staring made me regret having changed my emerald outfit of earlier in favor of this fancier one. I brushed a hand on the front of my kaftan—it was Eva's favorite. Pure white with gold embroidery, the ensemble had a matching turban adorned with a pearl brooch. *Maybe I should have dressed differently, wore something less… attention grabbing.* Then again, Milo's presence at my side certainly didn't help. He was attracting just as much attention as I was.

"Milo, are the gifts ready."

"Yes, my lord."

"Good."

"My lord," Milo whispered, "why are we waiting here, amidst all these people like this? Shouldn't my lord be waiting in another room instead, and only enter this one after having been formally announced and introduced?"

"In Telfar, that is how introductions to the court are made. Here, obviously not."

"In my opinion, this is highly improper."

I agreed, yet said nothing. Trying to ignore the impolite scrutiny I was submitted to, I occupied myself by contemplating the room's meager decorations. There were a few fine tapestries on the walls. Most depicted hunting scenes. My eyes moved to the raised dais at the front of the room. Two huge thrones made of solid, gilded oak dominated its center, and slightly on the left was a cluster of seats.

The sound of my name being whispered amid a conversation made me turn around fast. I looked about the room, seeking which guests might be talking about me. My gaze met Prince Diego's, who was standing nearby with a stunning young lady on his arm. I must say, I was surprised to see him with a woman—especially one as striking as she. Clad in a red velvet dress that made her pale, flawless skin look like polished alabaster, she was slender yet well formed. The plunging neckline of her dress, exposing the swell of her full breasts, confirmed this fact. Her facial features—small narrow nose, curvy pink lips, and large eyes—were delicate without being weak, which was often the case with such dainty bone structures. In her case, however, the effect was one of such perfect balance; it was a sight to make a painter cry. Her flaxen blond hair shone like the finest silk—an obvious sign of a recent washing. The shiny mane was artistically mounted atop her head and held in place with a tiny jewel pin. The aquamarine tip resembled a raindrop and was the same light blue as her eyes, which sparkled with intelligence. But what truly held my attention was her smile. Without a doubt, hers was the first real friendly smile I'd seen since I had entered this castle, and as a result I found myself smiling back at her. My eyes then settled on the two individuals standing a short distance from her.

Startled by their savage appearances, I flinched. At first glance, they looked like wild beasts. This, I soon realized, was due to the fur caps covering their rough leather clothes, boots, fur-rimmed hats, and… chain mail.

LORD! Those were barbarian warriors dressed for action; they even had bows strapped to their backs. Small in stature—compared to the Sorvinkian's average, otherwise they looked about my height—they both possessed slightly slanted, almond-shaped eyes, high cheekbones, and golden tan skin. Their straight jet-black hairs cascaded down the middle of their backs. The round-cheeked individual on the right surveyed the room with the calm demeanor of someone who wasn't easily flustered. The one on the left, I observed, was more lightly built than his serene companion. His attitude was different too, more intense and jittery. And he had a fierce penetrating gaze that kept burning holes in me, as if I was a strange and intriguing creature which needed to be studied closely. Needless to say, I found those large almond-shaped eyes of his, with their dark-as-night irises, highly intimidating. Although the two barbarians resembled one another very much, there were some noticeable differences between them. For instance, the jaw of the slim, jittery individual was narrower than his companion's; his nose was also smaller, his skin silkier, his lips fuller…

OH! This one's a woman!

Milo nudged me. "My lord, the King!"

Instantly, all conversations ceased. Everyone in the room curtsied, saluted, or bowed to the king.

I bowed. When I rose, I saw that the king and his family were seated in their respective thrones. I also noticed that everybody had backed away from me, Milo included, and that I now stood alone in the middle of a wide, empty circle. The room was deadly silent. Confounded by this sudden and oppressive quiet, I looked around.

Everyone in the room was staring at me expectantly, as if I was supposed to do something.

I looked at Milo.

He shrugged at a loss.

A movement on my left caught my eye. Prince Diego and his companion, the beautiful lady in red, were gesturing for me to move forward, toward the king's throne.

I swallowed hard and took a hesitant step in the direction of the throne.

"HIS HIGHNESS, AMIR BAN, PRINCE OF TELFAR!" resonated through the throne room.

Feeling relief for having been properly introduced, I took a deep breath and made my way to the foot of the dais. I saw that the throne beside the king's was empty. My eyes switched to the four princesses in their soft-colored gowns seated on the king's left side. Eva was closest to her father with Lars standing behind her. Once more Lars had that hideous expression on his face, as if he was suffering from an intestinal blockage, or some other kind of embarrassing ailment. As for Eva, she looked stunning in pale-blue silk, and the smile she was giving me filled my heart with hope and joy. I turned to the king and bowed. "Your Majesty."

"Prince Amir, you are welcomed to Sorvinka."

I rose. "Thank you, Your Majesty."

King Erik extended a hand toward his entourage. "You know my eldest daughter, Eva, and you've already met my nephew, Lars, Duke of Kasaniov. Now let me introduce you to my other daughters. I'll begin with Thalia."

The young lady in a pink dress rose from her seat and curtsied. She was perhaps a year younger than Eva and, despite her excess weight, almost as pretty. Princesses Olga and Mesa, adorable twelve-year-old twins with dimpled cheeks, were introduced next. They wore identical dresses of pale yellow taffeta. Ribbons of the same color were woven through their brown braids. They were the only members of this family who were not blond. The twin princesses stepped down from the dais and curtsied in front of me, then, giggling madly, quickly ran back up.

"Your Majesty, I come bearing gifts, small tokens of my gratitude for receiving me here. Four of our best Telfarian horses."

The king's left eyebrow rose. "Four horses! How generous of you!"

The sarcasm weighing the king's words was so flagrant that it raised murmurs of concern throughout the assembly of nobles.

I nervously wet my lips before speaking. "We left Telfar with twenty. Thieves took some… and, unfortunately, most of the others perished along the way."

"Ah!" The king nodded. "From my experience, warm climate creatures don't fair too well in our cold weather. They either die or run away. I'm afraid this will happen again." The king sounded sure of this, and by the dismissive look he was giving me, I suspected that his remark was about me and not my horses.

"These will not leave, Your Majesty. They are well-mannered, loyal companions. They will stay put. You have my word on this. They won't run away." *And neither will I*, I thought.

The king smiled. The gesture brought some warmth to his otherwise cold expression. "Please go on, Prince Amir. I'm assuming… and also hoping that there are more gifts to come."

The court laughed at the king's good word. Almost instantly the atmosphere in the throne room lightened, and with it some of the tension gripping my chest relaxed a little too. My breathing became easier. I gestured for Milo to advance. He immediately joined me carrying a silver platter. On it were five gold boxes, each one decorated with different colored gems.

"These are for your daughters, the princesses." I took the first box. Rubies formed a rose pattern on its top. "This one is for Princess Eva."

I opened the box. Nestled on a white satin pillow inside the box was a magnificent ruby necklace. To my surprise, Eva rose from her seat and came to fetch her present herself. In Telfar, a valet or a page would have brought it to her. Then again, I wasn't in Telfar.

"It is spectacular," Eva told the assembly.

A hush of approval echoed from the crowd.

"Thank you. This truly is a royal gift, Prince Amir." Her eyes met mine. "You're doing well," she whispered before returning to her seat. It was only then that I saw Thalia standing beside me with her hands clutched under her round chin and her eyes sparkling with impatience.

"Princess Thalia, this one is yours," I said, offering her the box decorated in a sapphire forget-me-not. When I opened the box she let out a shriek of joy so piercing it damn well startled me.

"Heee! Sapphire earrings!"

"Actually, Princess Thalia, these are blue diamonds. They are much rarer than sapphires." I hadn't finished my sentence, yet the twin princesses, Olga and Mesa, were pushing Thalia aside and demanding to receive their gifts. Their effrontery made the entire court laugh. Regardless of their evident disregard toward etiquette, I found these princesses delightful and would've liked to kiss their cheeks for having brought this mirthful interlude to this otherwise nerve-wracking ceremony. But instead I hurried to give them their gifts. Olga received the emerald shamrock box containing a diamond bracelet and Mesa the diamond daisy box with its emerald brooch. As the contented twins returned to their seat, the room became dreadfully silent.

I glanced at the royal family. All joy had left their faces. The king's stare was heavy with sorrow. Why this sudden gloom, I wondered. Seeking an answer amid the crowd, I saw that all eyes were fixed on the last box, decorated with pearl snowdrops, resting on Milo's platter. This was Princess Aurora's gift... and also a painful reminder of her absence. How could I have made such a stupid mistake? And how could I fix it? At that instant, my nerves got the best of me and my mind went blank. I didn't know what to do. I froze.

A spot of red amid the crowd captured my attention. I recognized Prince Diego's companion, the kind lady who had smiled at me before. She was gesturing for me to continue, and so was Prince Diego at her side.

Filling my lungs in one long breath, I faced the royal family. "Your Majesty, this box will be added to the other gifts I brought for the queen: bails of fine linen, rolls of silk, rich damask, and silverware of all kinds. A detailed list of it has been made for you."

Milo handed me a roll of velum, which I placed beside the box.

I looked at Milo.

"It's ready, my lord," he murmured, through scarcely moving lips.

I nodded. "I also brought some exotic goods from my homeland." I clapped my hands once.

Four servants, each carrying a silver casket, made their way to the front of the dais and lined themselves up next to me.

I opened the first casket. "Dates, a delicacy from Telfar."

"WHOO!" went the crowd.

I moved to the second casket. "Figs!"

"AWWW!" gave the crowd.

I flipped open the third one. "Spices," I said, lifting one of the many bottles filling the casket.

Loud cheers rose from the crowd.

I approached the fourth and last casket. "This one holds a special treat for His Majesty—ALMONDS!"

The crowd gasped in horror.

Appalled, the king leapt to his feet and roared, "How dare you bring these despicable things into my castle!"

"I… it's… they're just almonds—nuts."

"NUTS! They are far worse than that!"

"But… but, I was told that those were your favorite. Honestly, I cannot see what harm almonds can do."

The king's face became a twisted mask of anger while scandalized mutterings arose from the assembly. In panic, I searched the crowd for Prince Diego and his lady friend and found them staring at me with genuine concern. Their faces couldn't be any paler, I thought. I watched the lady place a hand on her lips and bow her head. *Yes, my dear, you're right.* I sighed. I knew what I had to do.

Bowing low to the king, I said, "Your Majesty, I apologize for my ignorance. Perhaps if you enlighten me I may come to understand the root of my mistake."

After a period of hesitation, spent staring at me as if I were a scorpion, the king sat back down on his throne and said, "Almonds have been banned from this court, castle, and surrounding villages since someone attempted to poison me with an almond cake. Almond's smell and taste can conceal certain poisons."

I nodded. "Cassava root extract."

"Yes. I believe this was the poison used in the attempt against my life. That day, I was saved from certain death by an ill-mannered hound. Good old Boris snatched the poisoned cake from my plate before I could take a fatal bite. Since then my taste for these nuts has waned."

Lars stepped forward. "Uncle, I will supervise the destruction of these treacherous gifts. The castle will be cleansed of their threat; you have my word on this."

My eyes widened in disbelief. *Destroy my gifts! Surely he won't do such a thing—I must have misunderstood.*

The king made a slight nod. "I trust you to see to it, nephew."

I clenched my teeth hard. *Of course, he's doing it; he's nothing but a savage with a title.* Even though I was boiling with anger, I told myself to hold my tongue. But when Lars motioned for *all* the servants to withdraw from the room, I had to speak. "Your Majesty, only the nuts offend you. The spices and fruits cannot cause you any harm."

"They were stored near the nuts, weren't they," grumbled the king.

"I'm afraid so." I glared at Lars. He stared back at me with a small smile of satisfaction. Oh how I wished I could have wiped the smirk off his face, with my fists preferably. Clearly, Lars was overjoyed by my mistake, and even more by the business of burning my precious gifts. With rancor, I watched him leave the court.

An awkward silence followed Lars's departure. Gathering my courage, I managed to blurt out, "I have a few more gifts for His Majesty."

The king did not respond, which I didn't see as a good omen. So it was with much apprehension that I clapped my hands again. Servants made their way to the front of the court. The two in front carried a rolled-up rug while the third one held a tall obelisk-shaped object covered by a red silk shawl.

"I had these commissioned especially for you, Your Majesty." On my sign, the servants unrolled the rug, revealing that it was in fact the skin of a giant brown bear. Not a peep was uttered by the crowd.

Paying no attention to this unusual silence, I moved to the tall obelisk and pulled on the silk covering unveiling a black eagle in a gold cage. Filled with the hope that I'd redeemed myself, I faced the king. My heart sank. In my opinion, King

Erik couldn't have looked more shocked if I had walked up to him and sat in his lap. I turned my eyes to his daughters. The princesses were staring at me with their mouths agape. I peeked at the crowd. Prince Diego was shaking his head in consternation. His lovely companion, for her part, looked positively stunned.

Oh, what have I done, crossed my mind as I turned toward the king.

Squeezing the throne armrests with white-knuckled hands, the king leaned forward and bored his icy blue eyes into mine, raising goose bumps all over my body. "Prince Amir, as if bringing those poisonous almonds to my keep, for me to ingest presumably, wasn't enough, you had the affront to kill a brown bear, the Sorvinkian symbol of power, and then had this noble animal made into a rug for everyone to wipe their boots on. Worse yet, you caged the black eagle, our imperial emblem, like a vulgar songbird." As the outrage in the king's voice increased, I felt myself shrinking. "What is the message you want us to read in this appalling display? That Sorvinka will be laid flat like a rug?" he spat. "That our dynasty will be rendered as helpless as a caged bird? Young man, are you in league with Farrell?"

"I—NO! Your Majesty, there is no ulterior motive or meaning behind these gifts, I assure you."

"No meaning!" said the king. "Besides being insulting you mean." He shook his head. "And how many more insults shall I bear from you, young man?"

"Er… I have no more gifts, Your Majesty."

"Well, that's a blessing!"

I stayed mute. It was safer; also I didn't want to lie to the king again, as I had just done. There were plenty more gifts. However, at this point, I dared not present them to him for fear of making more mistakes. And by the devastated expression on Eva's face, I couldn't afford to make more, if I wanted to marry her. *I certainly won't win her hand with these gifts.*

* * *

Later that evening, the entire court moved to an adjacent banquet hall where two long tables awaited us. Seated a short distance from the king and his daughters, I tried to concentrate my attention on my placing and not on Lars sitting across from me. He had been watching me all evening. Waiting for some wrong move on my part, I suppose. Well, from now on, I intended to be careful and not make any mistake. The last thing I wanted was to give Lars satisfaction. But to be honest, I thought it regrettable that our first meeting had begun on the wrong foot and that a profound dislike was already growing between us. We hardly knew each other. We didn't have to be enemies. There was no reason for this. We could still be friendly or, at the very least, be civil toward one another.

Determined to prove myself good company, I looked up at Lars. I found him with his finger knuckle-deep in his nose. *Charming!* I thought, trying not to look too disgusted by his flagrant absence of manners. Lars—civil, what was I thinking? I doubted he even knew the meaning of the word. Like good manners and regular bathing, civility and courtesy were foreign concepts here. With this grim notion in mind, I watched a procession of servants enter the dining room. Moments later, they began serving us the first course.

As the smell of food hit my nose, I realized I was starving. That surprised me. After the gift ceremony fiasco, and Lars's disgusting display, I didn't expect to have any appetite at all. Then again, I hadn't eaten all day.

A servant set a white porcelain bowl in front of me. It was brimming with a thick red soup with a spot of cream floating in the middle. I didn't question if I should wait for the service to be completed to begin eating. The slurping sounds rising all around me meant I could safely go ahead.

n. I've heard such good things about her. I must
isappointed by her absence. Will she not join
knew I had made another faux pas before I
y sentence. First, the room had become dead
because everybody had frozen in mid-motion.
Diego had been frantically gesturing for me
ing from the moment the word *queen* came
th. As for Lars, well, if his grin got any larger,
e would split in half. I looked at Eva's quiver-
nd misty eyes; she appeared on the verge of
couldn't be good. Reluctantly, I turned to the
ed.

oked like he wanted to strangle me. His
e two red bruises, his lips were thinned to
s eyes were now reduced to narrowed slits.
ng breath and said through clenched teeth,
alth is far too fragile to attend this evening's
you have her risk her life so you can satisfy

tely not—I—I didn't—" I went on bab-

reath, Prince. I have had enough of your
d for our customs and the welfare of our
d enough!" On this the king stormed out
all.

ped to the bottom of my stomach. I felt sick.
ted. Because right now I was sure that the
permit me to marry his daughter, and by
k on Eva's face, so did she.

I took a spoonful of the mixture expecting some warm, exotic, savory broth to hit my tongue. No such luck. It was cold, viscous, and vile. My first impulse was to spit it right out. I fought back the urge and managed to swallow the horrid brew without gagging. I then slowly laid my spoon back on the table. When I looked up I found Lars staring at me again.

"Why won't you eat? You don't like it? Are you going to insult our traditional meal too?"

"Certainly not!" I seized my spoon again and smiled at Lars. For a moment, I wrestled with the idea of stabbing him in the eye with it. But as tempting as it was, and it was *very* tempting, I knew I had to contain myself. "This dish is new to me. What is it?"

"Borscht. Cold beet soup with sour cream."

"Ah," I said before shoveling a spoonful of borscht into my mouth. Lars watched me eat the soup like a fox would watch a cornered chicken. However, with every spoonful I took I could see his glee diminishing; obviously he had expected me to retch. His expression then lightened, and a smirk curled his lips. This sudden change in attitude made me nervous.

"Try the bread. It's good." He grabbed a round loaf of bread and threw it across the table. The loaf struck the side of my bowl, toppling its remaining contents all over my white kaftan.

"Lars!" Eva snapped. "Why are you so detestable? Apologize to Amir!"

"Sorry," he said in a flat tone.

Meanwhile servants had rushed to my side and were attempting to clean the red soup off my clothes.

"Oh, Prince Amir," Princess Thalia lamented. "It won't wash off. I know it. I have ruined many dresses the same way."

She was right. The stain was huge and too dark, it would

never go away. My outfit was ruined. Yet I smiled as if it mattered not.

"Arr," grumbled the king around a mouthful of bread. "What a fuss over a spot. Men shouldn't wear white anyway."

"Father!" Eva's cheeks were red with embarrassment. "Amir usually doesn't wear such elaborate clothes. He favors much more practical outfits."

The king didn't reply. He just went on chewing.

"Please, don't worry. Your father is right. White is a difficult color to wear. I think I'll have the entire ensemble dyed red."

"That's a brilliant idea!" said Thalia.

I nodded enthusiastically. Deep down, I was fuming. I hated the color red. But not as much as I hated Lars. My only consolation was that now I didn't have to eat cold soup anymore.

While waiting for the second course to be served, I studied the other guests at my table. Prince Diego was seated next to Thalia. The plump princess had eyes only for him and kept giggling, talking, and blushing, while leaning heavily on his arm. She was enamored with him, that was obvious. It was also sad; because the long-haired prince made no effort to hide his lack of interest toward her—his rolling of eyes and heavy sighing were good indications of his feeling. Still, it failed to cool her ardor. Thalia began a long, unfocused and somewhat confusing story about a lost knitting needle. The look on the dandy's face turned from pure misery to utter agony.

Tired of that story myself, I scanned the length of the table. On my left sat an obscenely fat nobleman from Arguta dressed in an overly stretched-out blue silk suit. Then there was a group of stern-looking Minalians in dark gray coats, followed by several courtesans in bright-colored dresses. Some of those courtesans wore strange bouffant hairdos

with feathers jutting out of
headdresses that rose up
And beyond this colorful g
I spotted the two barbarian
stared back at me in a mo
comfortable, and I looked

Directing my gaze to Ev
a sad little pout. She mad
I should speak to the king
try that again and shook

"Something wrong, Pr
seem agitated."

I felt my cheeks burnin

At that very instant I kn
for myself that everyone
me. I supposed they were
inappropriate, again. I n
So I chose to talk abou
of our time together an
the king's nephew. (Ac
was the king's secret so
adventures and of my b
throne of Telfar capti
the king seemed pleas
in what I was saying. I
their eyes twinkling
every word. Even Prin
bored, was engrossed
expression.

"This nephew of
king said, raising hi

"My brother is a

"Indeed," agreed
must be a disappoi

"Certainly not,

meet the que
say I'm a bit
us tonight?"
had finished
silent, mainly
Second, Prin
to cease spea
out of my mo
I feared his fa
ing lower lip
tears. Oh, that
king and crin
King Erik
cheeks were l
nothing, and
He took a hiss
"The queen's l
ceremony. Wi
your curiosity
"No! Absol
bling.
"Save your
blatant disrega
family. I've hea
of the banquet
My heart dro
Worse, I felt gu
king would nev
the shattered lo

CHAPTER FOUR

I spent the following two days under a dark cloud of hopelessness and misery. I stayed in bed almost the whole time, only arising to go searching for Eva. I couldn't find her anywhere, and all the messages I sent to her remained unanswered, which led me to believe that she was purposely avoiding me. Had I disappointed her beyond redemption? I asked Milo if I should have instead given them the tulip bulbs I had brought along with me.

Milo looked at me like I had spoken nonsense. "Pf… my lord should have gifted them soap. That's what they really need."

Even though Milo's comment was amusing, it failed to lift my spirits. Strangely, I felt that the mood in the castle mirrored mine. With each day that passed without receiving a demand of ransom, hope of seeing the kidnapped princess alive lessened. During my last excursion throughout the castle in search of my beloved Eva, I noted that the quantity of guards posted in the corridors had diminished, and that the remaining ones all had a disheartened air about them. Then again, everything seemed depressing and dull to me. I feared that if I persisted in wandering the castle in this pitiful sulking state I would soon be dubbed the moping prince.

I was entering a section of the castle I hadn't visited yet, when from the corner of my eye I caught a glimpse of a fleeting shadow on my left. I turned toward it and saw a dark silhouette vanishing through the stone wall. Baffled, I took a step back. I scratched my head. Had I seen right? Or was it a vision brought on by my melancholic state? My curiosity piqued, I approached the spot where the silhouette had vanished.

The area was more somber than the rest of the corridor. After inspecting the surroundings, I discovered that it was because there were no torches on the wall here. *That's odd.* I touched the cold, rough stones of the wall. Then as I walked along the corridor I noted a rectangular space on the wall where the stones were flatter and smoother than everywhere else. I glided my fingers over this smooth surface and smiled. This was a door painted to resemble stones.

"That's why there are no torches here. Darkness hides many things."

I probed the door seeking a knob or a latch. Under the pressure of my finger, the door popped open. I slipped inside.

"Lord!" I breathed. Dozens of bizarre creatures towered over me. I was surrounded. In the penumbra of the room, I couldn't tell what they were. But as my eyes became accustomed to the surrounding darkness their identities became clear: statues. The room was filled with them. There was also a vast quantity of paintings scattered all around. Most of these portraits depicted fierce-looking warriors and gorgeous nymphs. Well, that was only when they weren't portraits of bizarre and grotesque monsters, like the two canvases at my feet. The larger painting of the two was of a giant bird of prey with the torso of a young woman and the face of a hideous hag, while the other appeared to be of a serpentine creature with powerful arms and a lion's head. I returned my attention to the statues. Not all those were large, some were my height and many were smaller. Some were even tiny enough to fit in my fist. I approached a small round table overflowing with such tiny figures. Sea monsters, wolves, nymphs, all were represented in this format. Could this be a collection of some sort? I wondered. My father had been a great collector of rare objects. He had rooms filled with strange and wonderful things. Was this King Erik's collection? Somehow I doubted it. For one, most of these statues were constructed of vulgar material, like clay, stone, or bronze. While the majority of my father's objects were made of precious material: gold, silver, ivory, and such. There were treasures here, though. The paintings, which were done on wood planks, all appeared to have some precious metal covering on them. Even in the darkness I could distinguish the glimmers of gold and silver emanating from their front. Also some of the statues had gems applied to them.

My attention turned to the mound of shimmering blue silk drapes rising behind the table housing the miniatures. The statue underneath the drape was twice my height. Why was it covered? I wondered. I grabbed a handful of silk drape. I was about to pull it off the statue when I heard the sound of voices coming from further down the room.

Letting go of the drape, I tiptoed in the direction of the voices while careful not to break any statue along the way. The space was so tightly packed with them it rendered my progress slow and difficult. Once I reached the end of this room, I found an open archway leading into a second one.

Less cluttered by artifacts than the first, this new room offered me an unobstructed view of the group of people gathered in its center.

All clad in black-hooded robes, they stood close together in a tight circle with their hands joined and heads bowed, chanting—except for the tall figure in the center. This one stood fully erect in front of a pedestal supporting a small statue. By his height and the broadness of his shoulders, I deduced that the individual under the robe was a man. He began speaking; I could hear his voice, but because of the strange litany the others were chanting I couldn't understand anything he was saying. As for his face, it was, like all the others, hidden under his hood. One thing caught my attention though. The right sleeve of his hooded robe lay flat against his side—empty. This man was missing his right arm.

I was wondering if I should come out of my hiding place and introduce myself, when the circle of hooded people broke apart. Led by the one-armed man, the entire group walked behind the large tapestry that seemed to be dividing the room. I heard some rustling sounds and then nothing. I waited and waited. *What are they doing?*

Tired of this waiting, I stole from my hiding place and made my way to the tapestry. "Aiii," I grumbled upon seeing the door it was hiding. Not wasting one more instant, I hurried through.

I emerged into a corridor, but it wasn't the same dark corridor I had come in from, but a brightly lit one. I looked around, amazed. This was a different section of the castle altogether, one filled with people. I searched the crowd for the black-robed group and thought I saw one of them passing from sight around a bend in the corridor. I was readying myself to give chase when I heard my name being called.

"Prince Amir, Oooh, Prince *Amiiir.*"

I recognized Princess Thalia's playful tone. I turned and watched her approach. She wore a sunny-yellow dress which, by the tightness of its pleated waist and the stress placed on its seams, appeared to be two sizes too small. Although it might have made her waist look narrower, the roundness of her chin and the swells of her arms betrayed her true size. Which I thought wasn't anything to be ashamed of.

Smiling, I bowed to the young princess. "Your Highness."

"Oh, please rise," Princess Thalia said with a giggle. "Nobody here makes such a fuss over me. Call me Thalia."

"Well, they should. You're a princess."

"Eva's a princess. She's exactly how people imagine a princess should be. I'm just Thalia, her fat little sister."

"That is sad," I said.

She shrugged. "Not really. I've grown accustomed to being ignored. Eva's always been the favorite, you know—especially Father's."

"I'm sure the king loves you just as much," I said, feeling sorry for her.

Thalia pouted. "Yes. But he doesn't look at me the same way he looks at her, with pride. Father often says that Eva is smart enough to govern. That's because she's genuinely interested in the kingdom's affairs, politics, and even the military. Eva pays attention to these matters, while I couldn't care less about those things. They bore me terribly."

I nodded, smiling. I too had very little interest in these subjects.

"Enough about this!" she suddenly declared. "Have you seen Diego?"

My eyebrows rose. *Again!* I had met Thalia several times in the course of my searches for Eva and each time she had been seeking Prince Diego. "No. I must say I haven't."

"Oh." Thalia's demeanor took a somber turn. She was disappointed. "He always does that to me."

"Do what?"

"Hide." Thalia planted her fists on her waist. I could swear I heard some seams rip. Face pinched, she declared, "Oh, I will complain about that…" She paused, her face relaxed, and through an outburst of giggling she added, "But not too much. No one likes a nag."

She was so delightful I had to smile.

Thalia produced a little curtsey; then, to my utter dismay, grabbed the bottom of her dress, yanked it up a bit, and took off down the corridor at a dazzling speed. The girl could run like a gazelle.

"Princess Thalia, wait, wait," I shouted. "Princess, do you know where I can find Eva?" I sighed. It was pointless. Thalia was already too far away. I shook my head. These Sorvinkians were all crazy.

So after yet another unsuccessful search for Eva, I returned to my bedroom and went straight to bed. Hidden under the cover of several blankets and crushed by despair, I let myself sink into melancholy. As I lay there wallowing in misery, I completely lost track of time. So when Milo ripped the blanket off me, announcing that it was morning, I was shocked to hear that a day had passed—and more so by Milo's bold behavior.

"What? That can't be right!" I said rubbing my eyes. "I just got into bed. How dare you wake me up this way? I'm your master. I can choose never to rise if I wish."

"No. My lord must rise. You must awaken now."

Milo's insistence seemed strange to me. I glanced at the window at the other end of the room. It took me a moment to spot the black glass square amidst the gray stone wall. "It's still dark outside! Why should I rise now?"

"Something has happened in the castle last night. I don't know exactly what, my lord, but I think you should investigate."

I stared at Milo with narrowed eyes. "How do you know this? You're not supposed to go out alone."

Lowering his head, Milo began wringing his hands. There were no clearer signs of guilt, yet I thought it was too early to chastise my servant. I wasn't in the mood for it right now anyway.

"Forget it," I said, "just get me my clothes."

Shortly after, Milo and I were out in the castle's corridors. We didn't question where we should go; we just followed a group of alarmed-looking guards hurrying ahead. They led us to the narrow corridor where I had gotten lost on my first day at the castle. There seemed to be something on the ground ahead of us, I couldn't see it though. All the guards crammed in this narrow space were hindering my sight. Amid the group of guards, I spotted the pock-faced youth that had served us as a guide on our first day here. I waved for him to approach.

"Young man," I said, "can you tell us the cause of this commotion?"

With a proud look at his companions, the young guard explained, "The ghoul got someone again."

"A ghoul?"

"Yes, the castle's ghoul. It's been here for years they say."

"Hmm." I rubbed the short stubble covering my jaw. To my knowledge, ghouls only roamed cemeteries, eating corpses. Normally, they never attacked the living. "Can I have a look at the victim?"

"Sure. I must warn you, though. It's not pretty to look at." Our guide shouldered the other guards out of the way with the rudeness of one unaccustomed to having power.

A path leading to the corpse opened up. The instant I set eyes on the remains I wished I hadn't gotten out of bed. This was one bloody mess. The man sprawled on his back in front of us had been split open, his guts strewn about. As if that wasn't enough, one of his legs was gone. Actually, the bone was still there; it had just been stripped of flesh.

I winced, realizing that some horrible creature had feasted on this poor fellow. I heard Milo gasp beside me… or maybe he had gagged, I couldn't tell.

Taking a deep breath, I approached the dead man. "Who was he?"

"Don't really know yet," replied my guide. "We think it's a servant."

Careful not to step in blood, I crouched beside the corpse and inspected the gaping cavity in his chest. His heart and liver were missing. If his half-chewed lungs were an indication, those missing organs had probably been eaten. I directed my attention to the man's face. Still intact, it was twisted in a rictus of terror and pain. Gently brushing my hand over his wide-opened eyes, I closed his eyelids. A wave of tingling ran along my hand. The feeling was as light as butterfly wings—then nothing. It was gone. Magic. Sorcery. Was magic involved in this man's death? Was a ghoul guilty of this crime? I really doubted that. To me, this looked more like the work of a pack of wolves. But wolves roaming inside the castle, that was unlikely.

"You said this wasn't the first time the 'ghoul' got someone. When exactly was the other time?"

My guide shrugged.

"The night after the young princess's kidnapping," answered a tall guard with broad shoulders and thick yellow mustache. Stepping out of the fold, he came to stand in front of me. "I remember it well because I was on duty that night and one of the guards who found the bodies."

"Bodies! How many were there?"

"Three. Two guards and a Tuvelian emissary."

"Can you show me where it happened?"

The guard led us to an area between the narrow corridor and the garden's entrance.

"Which one died here?" I asked, staring at the polished stone floor.

"All three, Your Highness."

"What! Together? You cannot mean together."

"Yes."

"All three!" I found this shocking to say the least. "In what condition were the victims?"

The guard's face paled. I watched his Adam's apple go up and down several times, apparently recalling the scene wasn't a pleasant task. Lowering his gaze to the floor, the guard said in a grim tone, "The thing... the thing that killed them... was very hungry that night."

I didn't ask the man for more details. His answer was clear enough. "Thank you," I said, and left.

* * *

"My lord… my lord, where are you going?" Milo asked, while trotting behind me.

"To my room, Milo."

"But… I thought you were going to solve this mystery, like you did in Telfar with your brothers?"

I stopped walking, folded my arms, and faced Milo. "Oh, I am! I'm going to try my best to sort this out. Who knows, maybe ridding the castle of its ghoul will earn me the king's gratitude and Eva's hand."

A wide grin split Milo's face. "My lord will succeed, I'm sure of it."

I sighed. "I wish I could be as optimistic as you are, Milo. Honestly, I'm scared to fail and ridicule myself even more than I already have. Since I arrived here, I've been unable to do anything right. It's like I'm cursed. At this point, Milo, I'm not even sure Eva wants me anymore. She's ignoring me, leaving me all by myself, as if I didn't matter to her." I stopped talking, fearing my voice would break if I continued.

"My lord, with her mother gravely ill and her sister's recent kidnapping, perhaps she needs to spend some time alone with her family."

Milo's words made so much sense that I felt my mood lift and hope returned to my heart. "You're right. I am inconsiderate. I should not jump to conclusions like that. Eva probably has good reasons to—" My eyes had just fallen on a dark spot on Milo's kaftan, right on his shoulder. "Is that blood on your shoulder? Has someone struck you again?"

Milo stared at the stain with surprise. "No!" he said, rubbing his finger on the spot. "It's fresh!"

"You've picked it up somewhere," I said.

We retraced our steps to a fork near the narrow corridor. Specks of blood marred the dark gray stones of the wall. We followed the blood tracks. They led us halfway down a long passage we hadn't visited before, where the tracks abruptly ended. I looked around. I could see that this passage had only one door at its very end, so we pushed on.

Moments later, we both stood in front of a large metal door, staring at it in silence.

I gripped the handle and pulled the lever down. "It's unlocked."

With a nod to Milo, I opened the door. What I discovered on the other side couldn't be more unexpected. "Whooo, what is this place?" I said.

"I don't know, but I love it," breathed Milo.

For a brief instant, we both remained in the doorway, gazing in wonderment at what lay ahead. A lush jungle occupied the space in front of us. I could see palm trees and hibiscus bushes. The entire space was bathed in warm sunlight, and songbirds could be heard singing in every corner. Although I knew this was nothing more than a giant conservatory, for me this felt like paradise, like an oasis amid the frigid gloom of this castle.

"Oh, my lord," Milo said, entering the conservatory. "Can you feel this blissful heat? Can you feel it?"

"Yes, Milo. Yes, I can feel it. Quick, close the door before it escapes."

I strolled along the gravel pathway winding through the conservatory, admiring the plant specimens it housed. I was impressed by its broad selection. Most of all, I was surprised by its existence. From what I had gathered so far, Sorvinkians weren't exactly the most sophisticated of people, and a conservatory like this one had to be a complicated and delicate operation to run. I stopped in front of a small iron stove, the third I had seen so far. I assumed that there were more of these stoves placed throughout the conservatory. On sunless days and cold winter nights, these kept the conservatory warm enough for the plants to survive. A rustling of leaves on my left made me look in that direction. "Milo?"

"Yes, my lord," Milo answered from my right.

I turned left, where the sound came from. For a second I thought I saw a woman staring at me. But when I looked closer I saw nothing there but foliage. Still I could swear I'd caught a glimpse of someone: a pale-faced girl with mousy brown hair, rather plain looking despite her striking green eyes.

My curiosity piqued yet again; I walked toward the area where I thought I had seen her. Cutting through a thick groundcover of fern, I left this artificial jungle and entered a rose garden. A heady tea scent choked the air; it was so powerful that it was nauseating. I tried taking shallow breaths while gazing at the roses. They came in all colors, varieties, and forms. This was a stunning collection. As I was admiring the shrubs, I noticed that the one growing beside the pathway had a broken, dangling branch. This seemed out of place in this otherwise perfectly manicured garden. Once I got closer to the shrub, I saw a fluff of brown fur stuck in its thorns. I heard a rustling of leaves behind me; I turned and watched Milo emerge from the bushes.

"There you are," he said, joining me by the rose shrubs. "What's that—brown hair?"

"You think it could belong to one of the king's hounds?" I whispered, rolling the fur between my fingers.

Milo kneeled down a short distance from me. "My lord, by the size of these tracks it would have to be a very big hound."

I moved to Milo's side and looked down. "LORD!" I exclaimed upon seeing the imprint; it was twice the size of my foot. "What animal can make such a print?"

"A big nasty one," Milo ventured before inspecting the rest of the area. "My lord, I see another track over there."

We both rushed to it. This new imprint was made in softer soil, therefore it was clearer.

Milo placed his hand beside the print. "Look at those

claw marks. They are as long as my fingers. What monster is this?"

"I don't know, but if we follow its tracks we might discover clues about its nature."

A brief search uncovered a third track, then a fourth farther away. However, we failed to find a fifth one.

"My lord, come see this!"

"You found a track, Milo?"

"No, I found a flower garden."

Quickly passing through the bushes where I had been seeking tracks, I joined Milo. In front of us was a neatly arranged little garden. For most people, it probably looked like any common flower garden, but to my expert eyes it was far more than that.

"This is an herbalist's garden," I said, eyes roaming over the vast selection of medicinal herbs growing here: caraway, chamomile, rosemary, and sage, to name a few. This garden contained all the ingredients needed to make cures for a broad variety of ailments. However, some of these herbs were also used to make magical potions and spells. A beautiful stem of mauve flowers captured my attention. *Or to make poison.* I shook my head in disbelief. The king had made such a scene over my almonds, and all this time he had true poison growing inside his keep.

I pointed out the plant to Milo. "See that flower at the back."

"Yes. Pretty."

"Indeed. But also deadly. It's commonly called foxglove. Its true name is digitalis; its essence has a sweet sugary taste that if added to desserts or to sweeten tea is undetectable… and mortal."

"Could the flower be grown just for its beauty?" Milo asked.

"In a different garden I could believe that. In this one—no. Whoever planted this garden only chose useful plants. And as far as I know digitalis's only use is to make poison."

"Maybe we should warn someone about this, my...." Milo's words were buried by the flapping sound of a hundred wings, as all the birds in the conservatory took flight at once. When the birds finally settled down a loud BANG rang throughout the conservatory, scaring the birds once more.

"Right in front! That way!" I pointed in the direction where the sound had come from.

BANG. BANG.

We dashed ahead.

BANG-BANG-BANG.

I ran through bushes and across flowerbeds.

BANG.

The sound was louder. As I pushed through a clump of young palm trees, a cold breeze struck me, sending shivers down my spine. When I finally came out from among the palms I saw that the conservatory's exit door was beating in the wind. *BANG. BANG-BANG.*

Pulling up next to me, Milo pointed toward the left wall. "There, my lord!"

Through the thick vine partly covering the glass, I saw the shadow of a silhouette running outside. In the blink of an eye, I was out of the conservatory and knee-deep in the snow. I looked around, seeking the fleeting silhouette, but saw no one. I saw tracks however, dozens of tracks, old and fresh all intercrossing one another.

"Where did it go?" Milo asked once he had safely closed the conservatory's door and joined me.

"I don't know." I looked at the tracks again. Some went toward the castle's garden door while others wandered further down the garden and disappeared behind a tall hedge of evergreen. "Milo, follow those tracks to the castle. I'll take these."

Milo obeyed without protest.

Plowing through the snow, I studied the tracks as I

advanced. Something huge had come through here a while ago. But what exactly, I couldn't tell. The tracks were too old to be read clearly.

As the tall hedge of evergreen grew nearer, I felt a strange feeling deep inside my gut. It was as though a hand was gently tugging at my entrails. I stopped walking and hastily unsheathed my sword.

Moving as swiftly as possible in this deep snow, I passed around to the other side of the hedge. A second hedge, running parallel to the one I had just passed, rose right in front of me. Upon seeing it, I knew that I now stood at the mouth of a long corridor of evergreen. The tugging in my gut intensified. My eyes raced to the opposite end of this green alley. The two barbarians stood there, staring at me. Taken aback by their unexpected presence, I froze. So did they, becoming as still as two fur-clad statues.

"Stay there!" I ordered, rushing toward them. To my surprise, they obeyed and remained motionless. I was halfway down the alley when the barbarians broke their stillness and passed behind the second hedge, disappearing from my sight.

"Wait!" I shouted. "Wait!" I tried running, but it was impossible. The snow was too deep and too heavy; I was exhausted in no time. I cursed the hedge for being so tall. *Damnation! Hedges should be waist high at best. Not taller than men.* "Can't these people do anything right?" I grumbled. After an arduous trek through heavy wet snow, I finally reached the end of the alley. Of course by then the pair was gone. All that remained of them were tracks in the snow vanishing into the dark forest circling the castle. Feeling frustrated, I stayed there staring at the forest's somber mass until my feet were numb with cold.

I was about to return to the castle when I felt that tugging at my guts again. It was stronger this time, more insistent, painful even. Clutching my belly, I turned toward the forest.

The pain immediately subsided, replaced by the gentle tugging I had first experienced. Then it too stopped.

Gasping heavily, I scanned the forest's edge, seeking the barbarian pair. This was their doing, I was certain of it. And this certitude went beyond a simple gut feeling. I had better find out who they were and why they were here. With this in mind, I headed in the direction of the castle.

I found Milo waiting for me at the garden door. He looked anxious and kept motioning for me to walk faster while dancing from foot to foot.

"What now?" I hissed under my breath, knowing that it could only mean bad news.

"My lord, I'm glad to see you returning. Have you found new clues?"

"I'm not sure what I found, Milo," I replied with a peek over my shoulder. "What about your tracks?"

"I was able to follow them inside the castle. It was easy because the melting snow left a trail of water. Unfortunately, it dried up a short distance between the throne room and the royal wing. After that I couldn't tell which way it went."

"Interesting."

"My lord, on my way back here I encountered Princess Eva."

My heart leapt up right into my throat. "Where? Is she around? How is she? Tell me! Tell me everything!"

"She was looking for you, my lord. Princess Eva seemed well enough, although I must say that she appeared nervous and a bit sad to me. Anyhow, she charged me with this message concerning the coming ball."

"Yes, tell!"

"This ball is a sort of gathering, a celebration. She said that she will meet you there. But until then, she demands that you be patient and also that you prepare yourself for the ball. Apparently there will be dancing involved."

I frowned. "Dancers, you mean."

Milo winced. "Errr… from what I gathered *you*, my lord, will be expected to dance."

"WHAT—NO! You must be mistaken."

Milo shook his head. "I fear not, my lord."

"But—but Telfarian men don't dance. It's not proper for a man to dance."

"My lord, this isn't Telfar."

I sighed. *Right.*

CHAPTER FIVE

I couldn't sleep that night because my mind was buzzing with so many thoughts, it was like a beehive in midsummer. Three days, only three days left before the ball. Three days until I'd see Eva. Only three days to learn how to dance.

I will make a spectacle of myself. Humiliate myself. Ridicule myself beyond repair this time. I knew it. This thought tormented me so that I spent the entire night pacing around the room, and as a result, once daylight filtered through the colored glass of my window, I felt drained of all energy.

"Milo!" I called.

No answer came.

"Milo, can you boil water?"

Nothing.

Throwing a kaftan over my shoulders, I shuffled my feet to the receiving room. It was empty. I checked Milo's room. Nobody there. I was returning to the receiving room when Milo came through the door carrying an armful of firewood.

"You know you're not allowed to go out alone. Why do you persist in disobeying me?"

Milo lowered his head until his face disappeared behind his pile of firewood. "I… I know, but I cannot let the fire die, my lord. I fear we'd freeze if it went out. Or worse, catch

61

some horrible affliction of the lungs."

I sighed. I couldn't really argue with that. I had heard too much coughing since I'd arrived here to question Milo's logic. "Very well then, if you must go out, go. But be careful when you do so."

"Yes, my lord."

I sat down on the couch in front of the fireplace and watched Milo unload his wood and put water to boil. My attention then traveled to the book resting on the side table, a manual of Sorvinkian dance Milo had fetched last night from the castle's meager library. I picked up the book and flipped through its pages.

"Do you wish to try the dancing steps again, my lord."

"Hell no!" I exclaimed. "Our last attempt at replicating these footsteps was enough for me. We'll only end up tangling ourselves in our own feet again and tumbling on our faces. I've got enough bruises as it is." Frustrated, I chucked the dance manual on the floor. "This document is useless. What I need is a teacher. I see no other way to learn these cursed dances."

"Who, my lord?"

I stayed silent. I knew who I should approach for this. I just didn't like the idea of asking for a favor. I'd never liked doing so, too many repercussions. And knowing who I needed to ask made the task ten times worse. "I thought about it all night, and sadly, I came to only one conclusion. (Sigh) I will have to ask Prince Diego to teach me how to dance."

Milo let out a gasp of horror. "The dandy! My lord isn't serious?"

"Deadly so. I see no other option. Plus, he's the only person here who has offered to help me. There is no one else."

"Please, my lord, you must rethink this decision. This prince... How can I put this?" Milo paused, a sudden blush colored his cheeks. Nervously wringing the edge of his tunic, he continued, "This prince has a very... questionable reputation. I've heard such unsavory tales about him on my outings. I think you shou—"

"MILO!" I snapped. "Do not judge a man by the rumors spread about him. I've once been the subject of false rumors myself. So I don't care to hear the rambling gossips of servants or guards. You hear me."

Milo shrunk down on himself as if he was afraid I would strike him. Perhaps I'd spoken too harshly. Then again, I couldn't suffer rumors. Milo needed to learn this. Truth be told, my decision to seek Prince Diego's help had been hard enough to make all by itself. The last thing I needed was to have Milo's doubts added to mine.

"I suppose we should bring him a gift. What do you suggest we give him, Milo?"

Looking less than enthusiastic, Milo shrugged. "I don't know. Do we have anything lacy?"

I frowned at him. "Milo."

"A kaftan would be appropriate. He seemed to have liked yours very much. Dandies are known for their fondness for clothing… so I was told."

"It's settled then. Choose one. I'll dress, then we'll try finding his room."

* * *

Time was now precious to me, so I didn't lose any wandering through the castle, which was an impossible maze, looking for Prince Diego. Instead, I asked a guard to guide us there.

Carrying a small cedar chest containing our gift, Milo slowly shuffled his feet behind me with the enthusiasm of someone being led to the gallows. He was determined to make his disapproval of my decision to seek out Prince Diego's help as apparent as possible.

Ignoring him, I set my sight on the path ahead. The section

of the castle we were entering was new to me. Its hallways were broad and well lit; paintings held within large gilded frames adorned the walls. Tables made of exotic woods were placed along the way, displaying ornate vases and silver candelabras. The floor was a shiny mirror of black marble—a far cry from the roughly cut granite of my rooms.

"What is this area? Does it have a name?" I asked the guard.

"Not really. We just call it the new wing."

"Besides Prince Diego, who else has their apartments here?

"The king's nephew. His close friends."

"Ah, Lars."

"We're here, Your Highness," the guard announced, indicating the gilded door on our right.

"Thank you." I waited for the guard to be out of sight before raising my fist to knock.

"My lord, please, we can still—"

"Enough, Milo!" Taking a deep breath, I knocked. I waited a moment. As no answer came I knocked again.

"Prince Diego!" I called. *Perhaps he's not there,* I thought with some relief. *Maybe it's for the best. Maybe coming here was a mistake.*

I was about to leave when I heard laughter coming from inside the room. I knocked again, louder this time.

The laughter died, replaced by the sound of approaching footsteps. The door swung open and Prince Diego stood at the entrance. Bare-chested and all disheveled, he stared at us with a bemused expression while holding on to his unbuttoned pantaloon, so it wouldn't drop to the floor.

"Prince Amir! What a surprise. I'm—"

Just then a half-naked young lady with long chestnut hair, and an armful of clothes tightly clutched against her body, dashed out of the room. She ran down the corridor and disappeared behind the bend.

I couldn't say I was surprised that he was entertaining, however, the type of company he entertained wasn't at all what I had expected. Somehow this discovery only increased my suspicion toward this foreign prince.

"I apologize for having disrupted your... meeting," I said with a little bow.

One of Prince Diego's eyebrows rose slightly. "Please, do not worry about it. In this cursed place, one must amuse oneself whenever possible. Distractions are somewhat slim here." With a subjective glance to Milo, he added, "One is sometimes forced to make due with what's available." On these words, he gestured for us to come in. "Excuse the disorder of my room. I've been otherwise occupied."

Nodding politely, I entered his room. Even though the place was spacious, it seemed small because of the insane quantity of furniture, cushions, artworks, mirrors encumbering it. No space had been left unoccupied; no decorating style had been forgotten either. This place was a mismatch of everything beautiful, rare or gilded. There were Sorelian rosewood benches, Farrellian tapestries, a pair of Atilian gilded chairs. I even spotted a blue enameled Telfarian urn.

"I see that you fancy Telfarian pottery."

"How could I not? Its lines are exquisite in their suppleness. Its glaze flawless. Your people have impeccable taste." His eyes wandered along the length of my body.

I had to bite the inside of my cheek, hard, to control my expression and not let the distaste I felt for this man's appalling behavior expose itself upon my face. Confident that my expression had remained neutral and did not display any hint of my true feelings, I extended a hand toward Milo and said, "How fortunate. I brought you a Telfarian gift."

Prince Diego eagerly approached Milo, and, to my dismay, he ran his fingers through the young eunuch's hair.

Milo winced, yet he stayed motionless with the cedar chest held firmly in front of him.

"What a superb gift. You certainly know my taste, Prince Amir." Prince Diego's hand glided down Milo's cheek to his smooth, beardless jaw and chin, where his hand lingered. "Soft as a sin. He's a real beauty."

"My servant isn't the gift. The chest and its contents are."

"Oooh, pity." Prince Diego lifted the chest lid and pulled out the kaftan that was inside. Milo had chosen a golden-yellow silk kaftan embellished with black arabesque and black fur.

"Fit for a prince, there are no better words to describe your gift," Prince Diego said, wrapping the garment around his shoulders. "I adore it. However, I'm rather puzzled by this spontaneous act of generosity. Will you enlighten me on its purpose, please?"

"I need your counsel."

The long-haired prince produced a dour pout. "It's a pity you didn't come earlier. Before your disastrous introduction to the court would have been preferable. Some of those gifts where of questionable nature." He cringed so forcefully one could've believed that he had just sucked on a lemon. "*Tsk-tsk-tsk*," gave the prince. "Deplorable faux pas on your part. The saddest part in all this is that it was entirely avoidable. (Sigh) Let's forget that unpleasant event. It's in the past anyway. I'm glad you've decided to accept my offer—even if late. I will counsel you to the best of my ability... on one condition."

My throat tightened. Damnation! Why were there always conditions? Hiding my discomfort, I asked, "Which is?"

Prince Diego smiled ruefully. My body tensed up in response. "Simply, that if we are to become friends, we must do away with all these tedious formalities. Let's forget our titles and address each other as friends do. Let's speak each other's names freely."

Relief flooded me; I had feared something far worse than

that. "Agreed, Diego."

A look of satisfaction crossed the long-haired prince's face. "Amir." He spoke slowly as if relishing in saying my name without its title. Quite frankly, he sounded far too delighted for my taste. "Tell me the reason of your visit," he said.

"I need you to teach me to dance."

"Really!" Chuckling under his breath, he shook his head. "This is not what I expected, but I can certainly do that. Will you permit me to dress first? I wouldn't want to lose my pantaloon in mid-rehearsal."

"Please do," I said. *By all means, spare me the sight of your bare bottom.*

While Diego was dressing in the adjacent room, I inspected the contents of this one under Milo's resentful glare. Paying him no mind, I approached the marble-topped table set under the window. Three swords were neatly displayed on top of it. They were all weapons of the type I despised: bejeweled and gilded, which, although impressive looking, more often then not proved useless in battles. Then I spotted a fourth sword propped against the foot of the table. If the bejeweled swords had been an expected sight, this one wasn't. This sword was out of place in this room, mainly because its decoration was limited to some subtle chasing on its blade, which had been crafted with the best quality steel available. As for its grip, constructed of woven leather, it had a simple yet elegant guard surrounding it.

"Milo, come here. What do you think of this?" I handed him the weapon.

Carefully taking the sword, Milo weighed it, checked its balance, then its handling. A look of astonishment formed on his face. "My lord, this is a very good sword. In fact, I would say it's an excellent one."

"I thought I was supposed to teach you how to dance, not how to fight," said Diego.

I frowned. Unless I had misheard, the tone of Diego's

voice sounded deeper than usual... more masculine. *That was odd.*

"I'm surprised to see that you have a collection of swords. For some reason, I had the impression you fought only with handkerchiefs." I indicated the sword in Milo's hand. "And this is a superior weapon. An expert's sword."

"That old thing? *Pleeease,* I would never carry that!" Diego's voice had returned to its usual high, affected tone. "Forget the sword. The dance lesson is about to begin. As you know there are only three days left before the ball—not much time to learn the Sorvinkian dances."

"Dances! How many are there?"

"Four. But I think you can manage with two. So let us begin."

* * *

Diego proved to be an excellent teacher. Unfortunately, I made a poor student, even though he insisted otherwise. This dancing business was much more difficult than I had believed it would be. I kept confusing the gliding steps of the volka—the slow twirling dance performed by pairs—with the fast hopping steps of the travolesky, which was danced in groups. Consequently, I was often obliged to start over with Diego playing my lead.

In the midst of our dance lesson, our hands were constantly forced to meet. During those brief moments of holding hands, I had noted that Diego's grip wasn't weak, limp, or soft as I had expected it to be. Instead his hands were firm, strong, and... calloused. *A dandy with calluses—that's strange.* Then again, not as much as a dancing Telfarian Prince.

While I humiliated myself with this stupid dancing, Milo watched attentively my every move from his seat by the fireplace. Although he was more fortunate than I, Milo didn't entirely escape my fate, as Diego would often use him as an example while I sat down and watched the two of them dance. In time I came to believe that this exercise was also an excuse on Diego's part to dance with my valet. His constant praising of Milo's physical attributes certainly made me suspect that much. I wished he would just shut up about it. Yet I didn't dare tell him so, for fear of antagonizing my only ally before I learned how to dance. Fortunately, Milo proved a quicker study than I was and the lesson moved on rapidly.

I looked at my valet and smiled. I could have wagered my fortune that part of his eagerness to learn quickly was driven by a will to get out of Diego's clutch. Or perhaps he was just more gifted for dancing than I was. When I declared that I had had enough—my feet were throbbing as if a horse had trampled on them—Diego agreed to end the lesson without protest. However, he immediately set up another meeting for the next day.

Lounging nonchalantly on the couch, Diego said, "Don't return to your room just yet, Amir. I have another type of lesson for you."

Head tilted, I stared at him with some apprehension. "What type of lesson?"

"Court politics and Sorvinkian etiquette. If there is such a thing." Graciously pulling himself to his feet, Diego swung a blue velvet jacket over his lacy white shirt, doused himself in perfume, then with a flip of his long hair said, "Come, follow me. Dinner is the best time to meet everyone in the castle—everyone that matters, that is. You mustn't repeat the blunders you made at your introduction, my friend."

I could hardly argue about that. By now, I knew how sorely lacking my knowledge of Sorvinka's customs was, and that it needed improving. With a sigh, I followed Diego to the heart of the castle. To my surprise, he didn't enter the throne room, but took a different route that led us to a new area of the castle which I had not yet visited.

"This is the drawing room," he whispered to me as we passed its tall majestic entrance.

Amazed, I looked around. The room was quite simply magnificent. It had three light-blue walls embellished with elaborately carved white medallions. Tall mirrors occupied the entire length of its south wall, giving the room the appearance of being far bigger than it really was. It also made it more confusing, because the mirrors reflected the image of everyone present and gave the impression that the room was bursting with people. I liked this place. It had a relaxed atmosphere that put everyone at ease. Lords and ladies were socializing freely in this room. Their conversations were light and animated. Laughter was heard regularly.

"Beautiful, isn't it." Diego said.

"Very." I thought the room was totally unexpected in this rough gray stone castle.

"It's a copy of the famous Vivilany castle's drawing room. Sorvinka has very little culture of its own, it seems. They're content to steal, copy, or reproduce other kingdoms' marvels and advancements," Diego explained as we strolled across the room. According to him, Sorvinka's main accomplishment was in the military domain, which explained how such an unsophisticated group of people had conquered so many countries. But now that they had conquered most of the civilized kingdoms, they were having problems controlling and managing this vast empire.

"That's why all these foreign nobles are here. The majority aren't free to leave, you know. They're more or less hostage of the Sorvinkian crown. Guaranties, of sorts, that their kingdoms will remain loyal."

I stared at the joyous assembly. I was now able to discern some signs of tension on many faces. Discreetly motioning toward the nobles nearest to us, Diego began telling me their names, titles, and stories. There were far too many to remember. I would never retain it all.

As I was scanning the crowd, a tall individual at the back of the room captured my interest. Standing as straight as an oak, the middle-aged man appeared out of place amidst this gathering of idle nobles. Maybe it was because of his clothes, a tall pewter-gray fur hat and a matching short coat thrown over one of his shoulders and held in place with a gold chain. Or maybe because of the black military uniform he wore under his coat. No, I thought after closer inspection, it was because of the serious expression on his broad square face. It was the look of one forced to perform a disagreeable yet essential duty. Clearly, this man was ill at ease in this frivolous environment. He seemed to be enjoying himself as much as a cat in a pond. But that wasn't what had attracted my attention to him in the first place. What did was the fact that he was missing an arm—the *right* arm, to be more specific.

He turned his broad face in my direction. I noted that he had thick black eyebrows which had grown together to form one straight band of hair, like a large, hairy caterpillar, and a strong protruding chin—then I noted his attitude. This man glanced about the assembled nobles with the condescending manner of one who believed himself superior to most people. As he surveyed the room, his eyes glided over me as if I were of no consequence. Part of me was glad not to have aroused his curiosity. Part of me was also insulted by that. He turned to the three young officers standing at his side and spoke to them. Those men had to be his sons, I thought. All three possessed the same bushy, grown-together eyebrows, broad square face, strong chin, and stern, humorless look as his.

"Who's the one-armed man at the back?" I asked.

"Baron Vladimir Molotoff. The man's a talented soldier—Sorvinka's best general. He's also second in line to the throne, right behind Lars. Tread lightly around him. He's not to be trifled with. Even the king is wary of him."

That last statement baffled me. I turned a perplexed eye to Diego. "Why? Can't the king simply… eliminate him? That's what my father would've done."

Diego made a sour face. "Too late for that. Molotoff is now more popular than the king himself, with the population. A suspicious death might bring on a revolt. Instead the king sent him to fight a battle that was rumored to be impossible to win and widely viewed as a death trap. Not only did the man survive, he won the battle and returned to Sorvinka. Minus an arm, mind you, but a bigger hero than before."

"What about the three young officers beside him?"

"His sons. They're just as upright and heroic as the father. Needless to say, they despise me."

Nodding, I returned my attention to the crowd of strangers. Just then I recognized a friendly face at the other end of the room. It was the beautiful lady in red who had been kind to me at my introduction ceremony. A group of attractive young noblemen and ladies, each more stunning than the next, was gathered around her. But in my opinion, she remained the most splendid of all.

"The lady with the pleasant smile, is she a hostage too?"

"Countess Ivana? No, she's a victim of her station."

I frowned.

"She possesses almost everything one could wish for: a title, grace, beauty, and wit. Furthermore, she's also a widow, which isn't a terrible thing when one is as young and as lovely as she is. Being poor, on the other hand, is terrible—especially for a woman of noble birth. And she's dirt poor. Without the queen's good grace, Countess Ivana, like many young ladies, would be destitute and left without a roof over her head. Those penniless nobles are among the few people who are actually glad to be here."

I stared at the gathering of lovely young nobles and nodded.

Diego leaned against my shoulder, engulfing me in an

intoxicating lavender perfume, and said, "Countess Ivana is delightful. So are her beautiful friends, and they're not opposed to washing either, which makes their company most desirable. However, I must warn you, if she invites you to her quarters, refuse. Ivana's evenings are extremely boring. Trust me. People just sit around drinking tea." Diego sounded rather offended by this. "Not at all what I expect of an evening affair," he said in a vexed tone. "She and her friends are far too virtuous; it's highly reprehensible."

I didn't reply. I couldn't figure out what to say to that anyway. I turned my focus to Countess Ivana, who was conversing with a small group of ladies. The tall, skinny girl standing aside this joyous group grabbed my attention. She was so serious one would think she was attending a funeral. Such a grim demeanor was ill suited for this event and also for her age, which I guessed was about the same as Eva's, though this girl appeared older. Her clothes were partly to blame for this. The plain blue dress she wore and her unsophisticated hairdo— mousy brown braids simply wrapped around her head—only added to her air of austerity. Why was I intrigued by her? I wondered. It certainly wasn't because of her gaiety or beauty. This girl wasn't ugly either, but she definitely lacked luster. Her features, straight nose, small square chin, prim lips, were for the most part unremarkable, except for her bright green eyes. I found those eyes breathtaking. *Have I seen those before? They look familiar… actually her entire face looked familiar.* Then it hit me. This was the face I had seen in the conservatory. There wasn't a doubt in my mind. *That's why she held my attention so.* "Who's the stern looking girl in blue?"

"Lady Isabo. The queen's confidante." Lowering his voice to a secretive whisper, Diego went on. "If I heard well, perhaps her successor too, once the queen passes away."

"You mean the king would remarry after the queen's death?"

Diego rubbed his dimpled chin. "I'll believe it when it

happens. The king hasn't officially named Lars as his heir yet, however. Believe me, *that* has people talking. Some think he will remarry and try having sons this time."

A smile made its way to my lips. *Lars must love this.*

"You've mentioned the queen, is her illness something new?"

Diego looked at me sideways, as if I should at least know the answer to that. "Amir, as long as I've been here the queen has been sick. If you ask me, it's surprising that she's still breathing."

"Ah," I nodded. "How long have you been here, Diego?"

"Too long."

"Can you leave or are you a hostage like the others?" I doubted he was a personal friend of the king. I could hardly imagine those two discussing clothes together.

A dejected look cast a shadow over Diego's handsome face. "Yes, I am a hostage of the worst kind."

"What do you mean?"

"Not only am I held prisoner in this horrid castle, I am to be married to Princess Thalia.

My eyes widened, and I had to quickly catch myself to prevent my jaw from dropping. "You're very fortunate. Princess Thalia is a charming young lady. Congratulations!"

Diego glared at me. I thought that if his eyes could have shot arrows, I would have been pierced right there.

"Are you mocking me? She's a silly, fat little girl who won't stop babbling about stupidities. Worst of all, she's utterly enamored with me. It's intolerable." Diego shook his head. The move sent a wave of perfume my way, forcing me to step back. "Perhaps I would love her more if she loved me less. Plus the girl is always too happy, it's most annoying."

Well, obviously, this union was an arranged one. I didn't know who to pity the most, Prince Diego, who felt trapped by this arrangement, or Princess Thalia, who loved a man who had no affection for her. She was worse off, I thought.

I peeked at Diego. The more I learned about this man the less I trusted him.

"Amir, you are one of the few people in the room who can leave this place," Diego grumbled. "You're a freeman... and so are they actually."

I followed Diego's gaze to the two barbarian warriors entering the room.

Closing the gap between us, Diego leaned toward my ear. When he spoke his voice was barely above a murmur. "Although the king has problems maintaining the Sorvinkian Empire whole, the Farrell rebellion is far from being his biggest worry. *They* are his main headache now."

"Who are they?"

"Emissaries from the warring empire of the east. These two arrived six months ago, supposedly to learn our culture."

"Have they?"

Diego shrugged. "Hard to say—they don't speak Sorvinkian, or any other civilized language I know for that matter."

These warriors really intrigued me, so I pummeled Diego with questions: What were their names? What was this empire like? To name but a few. Sadly, he couldn't answer any of my questions. Because of the language barrier, Diego had long ago abandoned all attempts to converse with the emissaries, and he couldn't recall having heard their names either.

"Maybe once, at their formal introduction. That was a while ago," said Diego after much head scratching. Then he added that the bulk of his knowledge was made up of secondhand accounts and rumors, which, in his opinion, no sensible man should take too seriously. That last bit of advice took me aback; I thought this dandy would fancy gossip. Nothing this prince did or said was as I expected. I didn't care for the unexpected. More often than not, it turned out to be unpleasant.

Later that evening, I bid Diego goodnight and left for my

room, but only after having promised him to return the next day for more dance lessons. And, of course, he made me promise to bring my *beautiful valet* with me. Needless to say, neither of us looked forward to dancing with Diego again.

CHAPTER SIX

Even though I had spent the previous day practicing dances with Diego, and all of today dancing with Milo in my rooms, I still felt ill prepared and nervous when I entered the ballroom. I stopped in the entrance in awe at the magnificence of this immense space. The glossy russet marble floor resembled a giant sheet of amber. The gilded decorations embellishing the walls were set ablaze by the light of hundreds of candles coming from the majestic ceiling chandeliers. The entire room resembled an opened treasure chest. And the ladies, in their vibrant-colored gowns, looked like floating jewels amidst all this gold.

I was glad to have chosen an ensemble of shiny gray silk with silver trim. (I would not dare wear pale colors in this company again.) Also, this dark shade had a dignified quality that should please the king. With this in mind, I made my way to the center of the room in search of familiar faces.

"Amir," a voice blew at my back.

I turned. Eva stood in front of me in a stunning lilac satin gown. The low-cut garment exposed her shoulders and a hint of cleavage. Under this light her creamy, flawless skin glowed like mother-of-pearl. She was so beautiful, it took my breath away. I particularly loved the way her blond ringlets dangled all around her cheeks and along her long gracious neck.

"Where were you these last days?" I said, careful not to let my resentment at being left alone for so long seep into my voice. This wasn't the time or the place to quarrel.

"With Mother. Her health is so fragile. And because of Aurora's disappearance, she wanted me to stay close to her. She wouldn't let me leave. I'm sorry for not giving you more news, Amir. However, you must understand that my family's needs come first. And they need me now. Please, don't ask me to choose between you and them. I beg of you, don't put me in that difficult position." There was a clear warning in her tone. It made me uneasy.

"Eva, you know I would never do such a thing," I said with a smile, even though the thought of being second in her heart displeased me. "You've been months without seeing them. I know how hard that was for you. Don't worry about me. I'll be fine."

She expelled a sigh of relief. "I'm glad you understand my situation. The last few days have been difficult for me... as it was for you." Eva took one of my hands into hers and squeezed it hard.

I winced. The strength of Eva's grip always came as a shock to me, even though I had experienced its power often.

"I apologize for my father's rudeness. The man has less manners than his hounds."

I was about to reassure her, and tell her that I wasn't offended, at least not overly so, when she added, "Honestly, it wasn't entirely my father's fault. What made you bring those horrible gifts along? None could have been more inappropriate." She sighed. "If only you had asked me for my advice, this disastrous episode could've been avoided."

"Eva! I didn't come here with the goal of insulting you father. You know this."

An awkward silence settled between us. I felt Eva's grip on my hand loosening, then I noticed the brilliance of her eyes, the sudden pallor of her cheeks, and the slight quivering of her lower lip.

"Don't cry," I begged. "I'm not angry at you. I swear. Please, tell me what's wrong."

She shook her head, sending ringlets bouncing all around her face. "There's nothing you can do."

"Tell me regardless."

"It's Aurora's kidnapping. Farrell denies having committed this act… and… and… Oh Amir, it's killing Mother and driving Father mad with worry." Eva let out a long hesitant breath. Raising her face, she stared silently at the ceiling for a moment. When she finally looked at me again all trace of tears was gone from her eyes.

My strong princess, I thought, too strong to cry. "Perhaps I can help," I suggested.

"How?"

"Well, there are some strange events happening in this castle. Something's roaming the corridors killing people. Some say it's a ghoul. Who knows, maybe those events are linked to your sister's disappearance."

By the polite look Eva was giving me, I could tell that she didn't put much weight in what I had just said, and truthfully, neither did I. I was mainly trying to console her.

"I doubt the ghoul or the castle's ghosts played any role in this, Amir. There are no efreets here. No jinn. No sorcerers, no spells."

At the mention of efreet my stomach twisted in a painful knot. I nodded. She was right. There was no efreets or jinni in Sorvinka, no magic either. This was all part of the past, and I was determined that that was where it would stay—in the past. The knot in my stomach undid itself. A thought then came to my mind. "You know, Eva, whoever kidnapped your sister might have left some clues behind. Do you think your father would permit me to visit your sister's room? Maybe I could find something."

Eva's eyes lit up. "Oh yes, Amir. I'm sure he will." Leaning against me, she whispered, "If you can help us find Aurora, Father will be eternally grateful to you. I'm sure you could ask him for anything you want and he wouldn't refuse."

My heart soared. I knew what I would ask the king for. Seizing Eva's hands, I brought them to my lips and kissed them both. "Would he allow me to marry you?"

"Yes, he would."

"Then I must begin looking for clues immediately."

"No. Later."

Music began playing in the room; I recognized the light rhythmic melody of the volka.

Eva slipped an arm under mine. "Now, we will dance."

We joined the three other pairs of dancers in the center of the room. Volka was always danced with four pairs. One pair was made up of a rather miserable looking Diego and Thalia. The princess was literally heaving with delight. The twin princesses and their partners formed the other pairs. Olga danced with Lars and Mesa with another young nobleman.

To my relief, I remembered the steps. I bowed at the right time, twirled without falling, and pivoted in the right direction. I did stumble once though—but caught myself immediately—and that misstep was caused by the two barbarian warriors. Their sudden apparition near our dancing circle had caught me completely off guard. Quite frankly, it was the piercing looks they were giving the twin princesses that startled me so. The manner in which they were staring at those girls, as if they could see something I could not, made me uneasy, very uneasy. Once more I felt my stomach knotting itself.

Finally, the dance ended. The entire court applauded. I bowed, as one must in such circumstances. When I rose I searched the crowd for the warriors. They were gone. Yet the foreboding feeling they had planted in me remained anchored in the pit of my stomach. These two were up to something—I was sure of it.

* * *

"AAAHHH!"

Upon hearing the uproar, I rushed out of my apartment. A thick fog choked the corridor. It was so dense I couldn't see past my own feet. Walking with my hands in front of me like a blind man, I stumbled toward my brother's rooms. "Jafer!" I called. "Jafer, where are you? I can't see anything."

"Amir, open your eyes, my brother," Jafer said in a tone of urgency.

I turned in the direction of his voice. In two steps I was at Jafer's door. I could see his shadow moving behind his peephole.

"Open your eyes, brother," Jafer said just before his shadow vanished from my sight.

"Jafer!"

AAAHHH!" echoed from his room.

"Hang on, Jafer! I'm coming in." I rammed the door with my shoulder as hard as I could. Once. Twice. On my third attempt the door broke down. I burst into Jafer's room and inexplicably found myself knee-deep in the snow outside the castle. I looked down in shock. The snow around me was red with blood. Oh lord, there was blood everywhere—everywhere.

I sat straight up in my bed, gasping. "Jafer...." For a moment I believed I was home, in my tower, with my brothers, Mir and Jafer, warning me against danger. But when I looked around I realized that this wasn't my tower, nor was it my home. This was not Telfar, and my brothers were still dead.

"My lord! My lord!" Milo's alarmed voice called from behind the bedroom door.

"Yes. Come in."

Milo opened the door, yet stayed in its frame. "My lord, something terrible is happening. I think we're under attack."

I was out of my bed in a heartbeat, fully dressed in two, and at the main door to my rooms shortly after that.

"Stay here," I told Milo. Then, sword in hand, I left the safety of my rooms. Once in the corridor I joined the gathering of guards I could see at the junction.

"What's happening?" I asked.

"We're under attack, Your Highness."

"By whom?"

"Err...." The guard stared at his companions. They all either shrugged or shook their heads in ignorance. Having found no help among his friends, the guard then ventured with some hesitation. "Farrellian? We were told to secure this section of the castle. That's all I know."

A scream of agony echoed in the distance. Without a doubt, it originated from the other end of the castle: the royal wing.

"Eva!" I breathed, and ran in the direction of the scream. When I burst out of the old wing's corridor, I collided with the captain of the guard. The man was in a state of panic, and it was pure luck that he didn't stab me with his sword right then and there.

"Back to your room!" he roared in my face; then catching himself, he added, "Please, Your Highness, for your own safety."

"Damn my safety! What's happening? Tell me!"

"Invaders are running through the castle killing men. So far they've slaughtered at least a dozen."

A bloodcurdling scream pierced the air a short distance from were we stood. At once we all ran toward it.

"In the courtyard," shouted the man at the front of our group. Within moments, we were outside in the cold dawn hours, staring down at the fuming, gutted corpses of the two guards in charge of the gate.

I approached the bodies. A powerful stench of feces, urine, and blood poisoned the air around the remains. Clutching a hand over my nose, I fought back nausea. After some deep breathing, my stomach settled down and I was able to study the corpses without fear of vomiting on them. Both men's throats had been slashed and their bellies ripped open. In spite of what I had said about leaving magic in the past, I found myself extending a hand above the bodies, seeking that familiar tingling feeling. I couldn't tell if it was there or not. My fingers were too numb by the cold to feel anything. *Maybe I've imagined it all. Maybe I've never felt magic here in the first place.* Baffled, I stared at the corpses; they were in such a horrid condition. *That must be it. Magic isn't this messy.*

I turned to the captain of the guard who stood just behind me. "What sort of invader would do something like this? This is the work of wild beasts."

"Impossible! That cannot be," argued the captain.

Kneeling beside one of the corpses, I motioned for him to do the same.

He obeyed, but reluctantly.

"See those four parallel slashes across this man's throat. Those were not made with a sword, but with claws. Look how ragged their edges are. Look at this poor fellow's belly. Tell me, in your opinion, what sort of weapon would do such savage tearing?"

The captain stayed mute for a while, and although his eyes were wide open, I thought the man was refusing to see the truth. "Still," he finally began, "how could beasts roam the castle? That doesn't make sense. Why would they be doing this?"

I scratched my head. "Hounds and even wolves can be trained to do one's biddings. Someone could have introduced them inside the castle."

"Why?"

"Right—why? Why would anyone do such a thing? What's the use of all these senseless and brutal murders? It's—" Then the reason hit me like an anvil. I stood up. "To make a diversion, that's why!"

"A diversion?" repeated the captain.

"Yes! Have we not all chased these beasts here? Now, right

now, are we not all staring at these corpses while..." I turned to the castle. "While Lord knows what is going on inside."

"The king!" exclaimed the captain.

Without further discussion, the entire group dashed back to the castle. Once inside its walls, we followed a bloody trail of corpses leading back to the royal wing's entrance.

"These four men were the first to die," I said. "Look, no vapor is escaping their torn bellies." I stopped to study a paw print beside one of the bloody corpses. *Too big to belong to a hound, or a wolf for that matter.* The print resembled the one Milo and I had discovered in the conservatory. Could it belong to the same creature? *What is this beast?*

As I rose to ask one of the guards if he could identify the print, I saw that they had moved further down the corridor. They were not going any further though. The guards just stood there as if they had reached the end of the trail.

I hurried to join the group.

"The king is safe," whispered one of the guards when I pulled beside him. "He's over there."

Rising on tiptoes, I caught a glimpse of the king. The man looked as though he had just seen a ghost. His face was beyond pale, his eyes wide with terror. I stretched some more and saw Eva clutching a bawling Thalia in her arms. I was so relieved I nearly melted to the floor.

"All is well, she's safe."

The guard frowned at me. "Your Highness, nothing is well."

"But, she's safe. The princesses are safe."

"No. They're missing."

"Who?"

"The princesses."

I looked at Eva and her sister.

"Not them, Your Highness. The twins, they're both gone, missing. You were right, this was a diversion. Now two more princesses have been kidnapped."

CHAPTER SEVEN

After a waiting period, which felt like an eternity to me, the corridor finally emptied itself of guards, and I was able to enter the princesses' room. As I crossed the threshold, violent shudders shook my entire body. This feeling of being cold was so intense that I had to fold my arms tightly around myself to stop my shivering. *A draft perhaps.* No, that wasn't it. The windows were closed. I scanned the room; it had been ransacked. The damage was so thorough one could believe a battle had been waged here. Most everything in the room—beds included—had been broken. The only exception was the small vanity in the far corner. Miraculously this dainty-legged, fragile-looking piece of furniture, with that pitcher of water resting on top of it, had managed to escape destruction.

A piece of pink fabric lying on the floor caught my eye. I picked it up and saw that it was a torn piece of nightgown.

"Poor little girls. What monster would do such a thing?" I consoled myself with the fact that there was no trace of blood on the fabric, or anywhere in this room for that matter. Directing my attention to the bedroom door, I inspected the damage done to it.

Half-broken down, the sturdy slab of oak hung precariously by its last hinges. Something was wrong with that picture. After a thorough examination of the broken door, I came to the conclusion that it had been broken from the inside out. The claw marks scarring the inside of the door proved it. *So they entered the room, took the princesses, and unleashed the beast from here.*

"Hmm, doesn't make any sense." I bent over the broken door and placed my fingers inside the claw marks. A cold jolt of energy shot up from my fingers to the rest of my body, knocking me down on my butt.

"What was that?" I breathed, even though I knew all too well what *that* was. Why couldn't I say it aloud then? Why? *No! It can't be. Not here. Not again—NOT AGAIN!* Visions of my dead brothers flooded my mind. I had been helpless to save them against the efreet. That evil creature had killed them all. *I couldn't stop it. I failed. I failed them all.* Would the same thing happen here too? I couldn't risk failing again. I couldn't fight magic. Magic frightened me too much. And this, what happened here, that was magic. I began trembling. Closing my eyes hard, I hugged myself until it stopped.

"Fine!" I told myself. "Fine! This was no ordinary kidnapping; this one was done with the help of magic." Saying it aloud didn't help me much. I still didn't have a clue who had committed this vile crime and why. One thing was clear to me though, Eva was in grave danger. Of that much I was certain. I opened my eyes. Magic or not, I would not let anything happen to her. I would die first.

* * *

The following two days were spent wandering through the castle seeking clues, and the nights spent chasing the beast with the guards, as it kept returning to the castle and killing more people. The beast didn't seem to care who it killed: guards, servants, ladies, or noblemen. They were all slaughtered indiscriminately. However, the beast seemed to hunt only in one specific area of the castle, the maze of old corridors and narrow passageways near the big entrance. I found this odd—then again, one cannot find reason in an animal's behavior. But even though we were aware of the beast's habit, all our efforts to catch it remained unsuccessful.

On the morning of the third day after the twin princesses' disappearance, I stood once more over yet another dead body, with the captain of the guard at my side. The victim this time was a maid.

The captain kicked dust in frustration. "This is impossible. How can that beast escape being caught—or being seen? How can it come and go through the castle at will like this? It's like this damn animal knows the place."

I suspected that the "damn animal" might be able to smell its way through the place, yet I stayed mute, eyes fixed on the maid's body. At least tonight only one person had died. Unlucky girl, I thought. By the bundle of bed linen lying beside her, she was out to do laundry when she was attacked. Sad ending, I thought; she was simply at the wrong place at the wrong time. I couldn't see any other explanation for her death. Feeling helpless, not to mention totally disheartened, I bid farewell to the captain of the guard and returned to my rooms.

Along the way, I met five of Countess Ivana's friends, all handsome young men with modest clothing and impeccable manners. I observed that they were hauling a huge rolled-up rug.

"We're redecorating," announced the blond youth holding the end of the roll. "It's a surprise for Ivana."

I offered them my help. They politely declined, but promised to invite me to see the final result.

"I would like that very much," I said before we parted ways. Not long after, I encountered Princess Thalia. The poor girl was once again searching for Diego. What a waste of time and energy, I thought; a wiser girl would have understood this and given up by now. Well, if nothing else, one had to admire Thalia's determination to find her prince. I could only wish Eva would be half as persistent in seeking me. I hadn't heard from her since the ball. In spite of her explanation, I found Eva's lack of interest hurtful, especially in view of Thalia's dedication. Feeling a dark cloud of melancholy gathering over my head, I hurried my pace in the direction of my rooms.

I was halfway there when Diego appeared from behind the bend. "Ah! There you are. I've been looking all over for you."

I winced. Right now, I feared I didn't possess the mental fortitude to suffer Diego's exuberant, yet aimless, blabbing without losing patience with him.

"I heard about your interest in this despicable affair and thought that perhaps I could be of some help to you."

I stared Diego up and down and tried to keep a straight face. Dressed as he was, in a vibrant blue-velvet ensemble, complete with white stockings and fancy high-heeled shoes, I had trouble imagining him running around with the guards as I'd been doing lately.

Noticing my scrutiny, Diego's left eyebrow rose. "You don't approve of my garment."

I was too tired to lie. "No. I don't care for it."

To my surprise, Diego smiled. "Neither do I. Now tell me what you've uncovered these last days."

I sighed. "Nothing."

"Oh come on now."

"It's the truth… well, not exactly. We know the facts and little else."

"I don't understand. Please, you must explain it to me."

Why does he need to know this, I thought, annoyed by the dandy's persistence. I wanted to tell Diego to forget about this and go away, but the determined look on his face convinced me it wouldn't work—worse, it would bring on a barrage of questions. So it was with resignation that I explained the situation to him. "What I meant is that we know that a beast, or beasts—sometimes I think there's more than one—is killing people in the castle—that's a fact. However, we still don't know why, what sort of creature it is, or how it was brought here. As for the princesses, we know they've been kidnapped—that's a fact. But by whom, how, and why remains a mystery. I can't even figure out how the kidnappers got in and out of the room without being seen."

"The windows," ventured Diego.

"No. They were locked from the inside."

"The servants' passages."

I frowned. "What servants' passages?"

Diego beamed with pride. "See, I knew I could help. And you doubted me. Come, I'll show you where those passages are."

* * *

The princesses' room had been put back in order; even a new door had been installed. As it was, I hardly recognized the place.

Hands on his hips, Diego scanned the surroundings. "Uh, disappointing."

"I know. It's a pity they cleaned it up. I wish you could've witnessed the damage."

"No, silly. I meant the décor. This is the royal wing, it should be better than this." He waved a hand at the light blue walls.

I shrugged. "I've seen worse."

"True. You, yourself, are lodged in what is commonly referred to as 'Draft Alley.'" Diego's expression took on an apologetic air. "For someone of your rank to be lodged there… hmm, it's a clear indication of the king's discontentment with you."

"Discontentment!" I snorted. "He hates me, you mean."

Diego pouted. "Feelings can change, you know." This being said, he walked to the wall. A long silky ribbon with a gold tassel at its tip hung there. Flicking the tassel with a finger, Diego explained, "This ribbon is linked to a bell in the servants' quarters. Pull it, and a valet or a maid will come running out of that door." Diego indicated the space beside him.

I stared at the blue wall with its white, decorative box moldings. "I don't see any door."

"Look." Diego pressed on the wall and one of the box molding panels popped open. "It's camouflaged to blend in with the décor."

I couldn't care less about the door's decorative function, what interested me lay beyond it. But as soon as I entered the passage, my interest vanished. This wasn't the dark mysterious tunnel I had expected. This was a simple passageway of whitewashed walls. I took a few steps down its length. My foot struck a tiny piece of debris, sending it bouncing off the walls. I picked it up further down the passage. It was a small metal loop the size of my pinky. I showed it to Diego. "Any idea where this might come from?"

"Hmm, looks rough. From a shoe strap maybe? I don't know."

I glanced at my meager find and sighed. "Might as well forget it. It's probably nothing anyway." Dropping the tiny loop in my pocket, I moved on.

Shortly after, we emerged in the servants' quarters. The activity in that room was dizzying. Chambermaids were dashing left and right, valets were rushing past us, while cooks kept barking orders in the background. Yet despite the urgency of their work, every servant in the room took the time to acknowledge our presence by curtseying or bowing to us.

DING-DING.

I jumped, startled by the bell. Right beside the door where we stood a dozen small brass bells were neatly lined upon the wall. A label, indicating to which room it was linked to, was affixed under each bell.

Ingenious, I thought. "I suppose my room isn't amidst the ones listed here."

"No, your wing was built long before this system was put in place."

I smiled—*Good.* I hated the idea that someone could enter my room at will without my knowing. Again, my eyes roamed around the busy room. To my knowledge, servants were on duty day and night, so escaping through this passage without being seen was impossible. In my opinion, there were no better eyes than servants'. Most often than not, the permanence of a servant's position in a house depended *entirely* on his keen sense of observation. (A good servant often knew what his master needed or wanted before he knew it himself.) Determined to test my theory, I asked who was on duty the night of the princesses' abduction.

A mixed group of valets and maids stepped forward. After a brief interrogation, I learned that all servants' passages led to this room and no other—a rapid visit of the other openings proved this—and that nothing unusual had come out of any passages that night. We were back to that same point, which was in total darkness.

"If they didn't escape through these passages, where did the kidnappers go? How did they leave the castle?" I slapped my arms against my sides in frustration. "This is impossible! Did they vanish in thin air? Were they invisible?"

I was rubbing my forehead, trying to make sense of this enigma, when a young maid approached me. She was barely out of girlhood, and her features still possessed some child-like qualities, that ephemeral rosy hue, and that perfectly radiant, moist skin seen only in little children. Right now she was pretty; in a year or two she'd be beautiful.

"Your Highness," she began, locking her large hazel eyes onto mine. "I was not on duty the night the princesses disappeared, so I cannot attest to what may have come out of our passages. But I know people who can walk through the castle without being seen."

"Who?"

"Those strange ones from the east."

Diego and I exchanged intrigued glances.

"Go on," I said.

"Two days ago, I was on my way to clean the princesses' room." The maid pointed to the door we had come out of earlier. "Through that passageway. I was almost there when I realized I'd forgotten something. I turned around and… and…" She paused, eyes widening. "And there they were, right behind me, the two of them, as close to me as you are, Your Highness. I never heard a sound or saw a shadow move. If not for my scattered brain, I would've never known they were there. This has happened to other servants too. These strange ones, they keep appearing and disappearing all around the castle like… like spirits."

The girl was trembling. Clearly, she was still shaken by her encounter with the barbarians.

"What were they doing in the passage?"

The girl looked unsure. "Seeking something on the ground. I'm not sure. They scared me so, I screamed and ran away." Her eyes glistening with tears, she lowered her head. "I wish I could be of better help to you. The young princesses have always been kind to me."

Cupping her chin in my hand, I raised her face. "Don't be sad. You've helped us tremendously."

"Oh thank you, Your Highness." Bursting into tears, she ran away.

I turned to Diego. He was looking at me with an odd little smile plastered on his face, which I didn't care much for. "My, my, my," he said, "what a heartbreaker you could be if only you would expand your interest beyond Princess Eva."

The comment shocked me. Caught in a blend of contradicting feelings, I didn't know how to respond. For one, I badly wanted to wring his neck, while my sensible side was telling me to move on, because starting a fight with a foreign prince, over words, wasn't smart. I chose to ignore the comment and changed the subject. "What do you think they were looking for in that passage?"

"Don't know." Diego played with one of his long black locks. "Honestly, I'm surprised they know about these passages."

"Do you have any idea where they can be right now?"

"No, but I assume we're going to go look for them."

I smiled. "Yes."

* * *

Finding the two barbarians took more effort than I thought possible. However, all that trotting and questioning we did throughout the castle bore fruit; we learned some interesting facts about those two. For example, they possessed the singular ability of being at one end of the castle one instant, then at the other end the next. Finally, after hours of search, the barbarians fell into our sight.

"There they are!" exclaimed Diego. "They're heading outside."

I grappled Diego's arm before he could run after the pair. "Where are you going like that?"

"After them—outside."

I pointed to his feet. "With those shoes… in the snow."

We borrowed boots and coats from the guards' supply room, and then we went out. Diego cursed all the way to the garden wall. Apparently, guards' garments weren't to his taste. For my part, I thought they were fine. The coat was warm and the round fur hat fell low enough on my head to protect my ears from the bite of the cold. The boots were a bit big though.

"Where are they?" I asked, squinting. The reflection of the afternoon sun on the snow was blinding,

Shielding his eyes with his hand, Diego scanned the horizon. "Can't see them anywhere. Let's look around. I'm sure we'll find something."

After a thorough search of the castle's grounds, we uncovered a series of tracks in the snow.

"Goodness!" Diego gasped. "Those are the biggest bear's tracks I've ever seen. The beast's a monster."

These tracks were similar to the ones I had discovered in the conservatory. "Are you sure those belong to a bear."

"Can't you tell?"

"Not really—bears do not wander the desert."

We followed the tracks to the edge of the forest. A second series of tracks, a man's footsteps, were visible a short distance away. From where I stood, I could see that those footsteps were also following the bear's trail. So we were not alone tracking this beast.

* * *

I didn't know how long we'd been gone, but to me it felt as if we'd been wandering through the woods in the bear's footsteps for ages. I was glad when we reached the summit of a hill where we could get a good view of the surrounding landscape.

"The bear went down the hill," I said, indicating the sliding tracks to Diego.

"Yes, looks like it's going toward that village over there."

Rising on my toes, I could see the rooftops of small wooden houses in the distance and the thin plumes of smoke rising from their chimneys. I looked at the darkening sky. "It's getting late."

Diego beat his sides vigorously. "And cold. We should return to the castle. Even the hunter following the bear has given up."

Diego was right. Only the bear's tracks went down the hill, the other's were gone. Quite frankly, by now I didn't know which of the two intrigued me the most, the bear or the mysterious hunter. As I began searching for where the hunter's tracks had stopped, the sound of a frightened horse echoed amidst the trees. The crack of branches breaking followed. That noise was accompanied by the stumping of hooves striking the icy ground.

I scanned the forest, at first seeing only tall, dark pine trees. Then I spotted a rider through a clearing in the dense forest.

"THERE!" I shouted, pointing to the horseman. His silhouette was little more then a dark shadow against the horizon. In spite of the lowering sun shining in my eyes, I thought I saw the edge of a long hooded cloak. I ran toward the horseman. Of course, as soon as I neared the clearing he took off in the direction of the village before I could get a better look at him.

"Amir!" Diego called behind me. "Amir, come back."

I pushed on.

"*Aaaamir,* we have a problem." The panic lacing Diego's tone made me stop.

I turned. The woman warrior stood behind Diego holding a blade against his neck. My hand went straight for my sword.

Diego's eyes became as big as my fists. "*Nooo!*" he yelled as the blade was pushed harder against his neck.

"We mean you no harm," I told the warrior woman. "Release my friend."

In a quick head snap, she flipped her long, luscious black hair out of her heart-shaped face, exposing striking exotic features: small, low-bridged nose, high cheekbones, pouty lips, and eyes as dark as a moonless night. Boring those dark smoldering eyes into mine, she motioned for me to drop my sword.

"No! You drop your weapon."

She replied by yanking Diego's head backward, exposing the white flesh of his neck to the frigid air.

"Please, Amir," begged Diego. "Don't argue with her. She'll slice my throat. I know she will."

Well, she certainly looked determined enough. I scanned the darkening forest. Her companion could be anywhere in those woods with his bow drawn and ready to release an arrow... or maybe he'd just galloped away, leaving her alone here. Maybe she was afraid. I shot one glance at her intense gaze, and I was certain that this woman knew no fear. That worried me. My fist tightened around the grip of my sword. Dropping my weapon was the last thing I wanted to do, yet I feared that if I didn't do it Diego would die. Against my will, I opened my hand. The sword fell into the snow.

At that instant, I thought I saw the corners of her mouth curl slightly. But before I could be sure, I lost sight of her face as she tightened her hold on Diego, pushing him forward, forcing him to walk toward me.

"Why are you doing this?" I said. "Unhand him at once! You can leave safely. I won't attack you."

"She doesn't understand our tongue," Diego murmured through clenched teeth.

I began making signs, gesturing to her that she could go in peace. Well, I hoped this was the message she was getting.

Twisting her pouty little mouth to one side, she eyed me with perplexity. The expression on her face couldn't be any clearer; she thought I had gone mad.

I ceased gesturing like a demented monkey and just backed away from my sword. This time there was no confusion, I clearly saw it; she smiled.

Sure, that was too simple.

Still holding Diego in front of her, she slowly walked toward me. Once only a few steps separated us, she stopped, pulling Diego's head back again.

"Let him go," I whispered while raising my hands, palms up.

What she did next totally baffled me. She shoved Diego to the side and pounced onto me like a panther pounced upon a gazelle. The force of the impact made me stagger backward, and I would have fallen into the snow if she had not sunk her fingers into my coat and pulled me up against her. For the space of an instant, no longer than a couple heartbeats really, our eyes locked—mine were wide with shock, hers burning with an uncanny intensity. It was as though she was trying to look into me, into my heart and soul, as though she was searching for something hidden deep inside me. Then she did the unexpected: she kissed me. I was so dumbfounded that I didn't do anything to stop her; I just stayed there without moving. Almost immediately an eerie feeling invaded me. And for a minute there, I could've sworn that time stood still. My senses suddenly became heightened. I was aware of everything around me. More so, I was aware of everything about her, her smell was a medley of leather, horses, and green grass. Her lips were pillowy soft and cool; her hands on my forearms were like iron shackles. Finally awakening from my state of shock, I tried pushing her, but my fingers got tangled in her chain mail. Then she pulled away.

Although her kiss had been very brief, the feeling of her lips upon mine lingered on my mouth long after it was over. And the sharp pang it had produced deep within my core was rather unforgettable. Never had I felt something alike. I stared at her with my mouth agape. How could lips as lovely as hers produce such a jarring effect?

"Shal-galt," she breathed, and then she ran off.

Stunned, I stood there like an idiot, watching her vanish into the dark forest without moving. "What was that?"

Brushing snow from his coat, Diego dragged himself to his feet. "Well, my friend, I think you have an admirer—and she's ferocious. They're the only kind worth having, if you ask me. Let's hope she hasn't bewitched you though."

Even though I knew Diego was only jesting, I feared there might be some truth in what he had just said. "Bewitched, huh," I said under my breath. *There was something "magical" about her touch. Shal-galt, could that be a spell word?*

"Diego, have you managed to learn their names since I last asked."

"The man's Khuan. The woman's name is Lilloh."

"Lilloh... Lilloh," I repeated, as if saying her name could tell me something new.

"Amir, I know she kissed you, but has she stabbed you too?" Diego asked in a concerned tone.

"No. why?"

"You're bleeding."

I looked down at myself and saw that my hand was dripping blood. "Gah, I must have ripped it open on her chain mail." Sure enough, when I checked my palm one of her chain mail's links was imbedded in my skin. I pulled it out and stared at it for a while. Then fishing the small metal loop we had found in the servants' passage from out of my pocket, I placed it beside the link. They were identical.

CHAPTER EIGHT

That night I was plagued with nightmares, in which my dearly departed brother Jafer kept appearing to me.

"Look to the east," he would say in some of those dreams. In the most unpleasant one, Jafer and I were strolling together in the snow when I suddenly began sinking. Most disturbing in this was that while I desperately fought for my life, Jafer just quietly watched me sink with an air of total exasperation and reproach, as though I was the cause of my own sinking.

"Why are you so stubborn," he said in a frustrated tone. "I cannot do this for very long, you know. Why won't you see? Why won't you open your eyes?"

Clutching the snow, I begged him, "Jafer, help me."

He remained immovable. "Listen to me. The past is hard to bury; it tends to rise up to the surface, and when it does, people die. Beware of the past, brother, if you don't awaken soon, it will kill you."

"*Nooo…*" I sat up. I was heaving as if I had run for hours and my hands were clutching the blankets like my life depended on it. Confused, I looked around. Darkness surrounded me.

Suddenly the door of my bedroom burst open and a half-naked Milo appeared in its frame brandishing an iron pot.

"My lord, are you being attacked?"

I laughed. "No. I had a bad dream."

Milo expelled a long sigh of relief. "Oh thank God! Honestly, my lord, I don't think I could have been of much help to you with this pot. But as I'm forbidden to use a sword, that was the only weapon I could find."

"I'm sure you could have done great damage with it. Now, can you use it to boil water for tea? I won't try sleeping again."

Acquiescing to my demand, Milo left to prepare breakfast.

Once alone in my room, my thoughts turned to my dream and to Jafer. Right at the end of my dream, just before I awoke, the anger in Jafer's voice had been palpable. I had never seen my brother this mad at me before. *Stop it! It is just a dream. It means absolutely nothing. Jafer is dead. And even when he was alive, most of what he said made no sense at all, because he was crazy.*

"Maybe I'm crazy too," I whispered softly. This idea had begun tormenting me lately. Mental instability was rampant in my family. "If I'm going mad, it's partly because of this place." In my opinion, this castle could certainly drive one to insanity. My gaze moved to the window; the early morning light was filtering through its colored glass, making the small rose in its east corner luminesce brilliantly.

"Uh," I rubbed my short beard, while recalling my dream. *Look to the east,* Jafer had said. That village Diego and I had seen last night; I could swear it was east of our position. Maybe I should visit it. With this in mind, I dressed.

* * *

Wrapped in thick fur coats, scarves, hats, and mittens, Diego and I were well prepared for a day outside. Our first stop was at the stables. While we were waiting for the stable boy to bring us our mounts, I inspected the surroundings. I noticed that the fenced corral beside the stable held only two horses, if one could call those small hirsute creatures horses.

With their ears peaked up and their nostrils flared, the small brown horses watched me approach the fence with curious yet suspicious eyes. I clapped my hands once. The horses responded by taking a few quick steps on their agile little feet, but they didn't run. They had evaluated the danger and decided that I didn't pose any real threat... for the moment. I was impressed. Perhaps I had judged them too harshly; their behavior was a clear sign of an intelligent, inquisitive nature. They certainly looked very alert.

"Whose horses are these?" I asked Diego as he pulled beside me.

"Khuan's and Lilloh's mounts. Wild ponies of the steppes; they don't look like much but I'm told that they can run for days on end. Hard as nails, those are."

"Could be true. They look quite rugged." I watched the ponies until our horses were ready; then we rode toward the village.

* * *

By galloping most of the way, we had made good time. And now that the village was in sight, we slowed our horses to a brisk trot, allowing them a bit of a rest. I rose up on my stirrups to get a better look at the village. Made up of about forty log houses and numerous outbuildings, this enclave, seemingly lost in the middle of the frozen forest, had an oppressive air of gloom and misery, as if it was plagued by misfortune. I pitied the people who lived there. When we entered the village, I noted that most of the houses were in good condition—a few others, however, were falling apart. One stone building was reduced to little more than a ruin.

"Charming," I said, as I rode in front of its crumbling stone walls.

We were reaching the square at the center of the village, when a group of peasants rushed out of the crumbled building and encircled us. Dressed in thick wool clothing covered with coats or vests made up of mismatched pieces of leather, fur, or goat pelts, they resembled a pack of wild men. Every one of them, I noted, was armed with a different kind of farming implement: pitchfork, spade, or sickle. The sight of those improvised weapons was unsettling, to say the least.

"Lords, lords!" said the man in front, a gray-haired fellow with sunken cheeks and bright blue eyes. "Finally someone comes to our aid."

Diego and I exchanged intrigued glances.

"What is the matter, my good man?" I asked, careful to be as polite as possible—after all the man was carrying a pitchfork.

Wiping his red bulbous nose on his sleeve, the peasant then grinned broadly, exposing three lonely teeth. Well, that explained his sunken cheeks, I thought. "Noblemen from far-away countries, we're in luck," the man told his companions before turning back to us. "I'm glad you're here. Maybe you can help us. Bears are preying on us at night. Huge beasts. So far they killed four of our people."

"When was the last attack?" I asked.

"Last night."

"Can we see the victim?"

"Yes," said the peasant. "Follow me."

He led us to a nearby house. Inside we found two women busy washing the dead body of an older boy. Weeping could be heard in the other room.

"The mother," whispered the gray-haired man. "The boy's the miller's son, Sergei."

I walked to the table and studied young Sergei's wounds. Claws had sliced open his chest, and the flesh of his throat was all torn up. Without a doubt, this was the work of the same creature that had killed the people of the castle. I directed my attention back to the gray-haired peasant who had guided us here. "What's your name, my good man?" I asked him.

"Dimitry."

"Can you show me where the killing happened, Dimitry?"

"Sure, come along."

Leaving the house, we proceeded in the direction of the ruins. Behind a mound of rubble stood the remnants of two walls; a long block of stone lay near the foot of the eastern one.

"The bear hid there." Dimitry pointed to the space behind the stone block where the snow had been flattened.

I closely studied the tracks. I could see where young Sergei had entered the ruin and where the bear had pounced on him, shook him, dragged him on the ground, and finally killed him. The blood and the tracks told me the whole sordid story of Sergei's last moments. Then the bear had left. I strolled along the remaining two walls of the ruins, studying its construction. This building was old, far older than this village. The timeworn carvings on the wall depicting strange and exotic creatures appeared to have been chiseled out of the stone hundreds of years ago. Something red on the ground caught my eye. At first I thought it was blood—and it was—but I had found a bundle wrapped in a piece of bloody linen. Obviously it didn't come from this kill. Gently pulling the bloodstained bundle apart, I exposed its contents, a small heart, like that of a sheep or a goat. "What's this?" I asked, indicating my gruesome discovery.

The villagers exchanged nervous looks. An uneasy silence settled among this previously noisy group. I watched the men nod at each other. Then as if they had reached a mute agreement, Dimitry stepped out of the group and said, "This ruin used to be a temple. The heart's an offering to the gods."

"Pardon me," said Diego, "but I thought the new god didn't need offerings."

"You're right," conceded Dimity. "In these parts, though, the old faiths are still upheld and the old gods worshiped. Priests and priestesses still come once in a while to perform ceremonies. We thought one might come last night, that's why the boy was sent to the temple with the offering."

I frowned. "I must admit that I'm not very familiar with your gods. Can you tell me to which god this temple is dedicated?"

"Oh, to several of the local ones. Mirekia, Samu, Laki. There are many of them."

"Ah." I nodded, wishing I knew how to change the subject without being impolite or looking uninterested in their beliefs. Perhaps I should ask one more question—for courtesy's sake. "Tell me, Dimitry, do you pray to the old gods too."

He shrugged. "Old, new. I pray to all the gods. It's a good safeguard. Anyhow, the gods did nothing to protect this boy from the bear. Animals usually don't have much respect for temples and gods."

I couldn't agree more. "Well, that explained why the bear hid here. The smell of food attracted it."

I walked along the bear's tracks. At one point they merged with a horse's tracks. "Diego, could these other tracks belong to the mysterious rider we saw last night?"

Diego shrugged. "Hard to say."

"Baba Yaga," murmured a man.

"Yes, it's the Baba Yaga," said another.

I frowned. "Dimitry, what's the Baba Yaga?"

Dimitry spat on the ground. "A witch! She lives in the woods."

I stared at the horse's tracks. "A witch riding a horse?"

"A magical colt. She has three of those," shouted a man on my left. He wore a vest made of white sheep fleece. "I saw her riding ahead of the bear."

"Really! A witch on a magic horse." It took me everything I had not to roll my eyes at such nonsense. "And you saw her, you say. What's she like?"

The man's face paled. "Er… I saw the horse. It was dark… too dark to see her face, but it was her. The legends say she does those things. She rides… she does it for real. The tracks prove it happened."

I walked to the tracks, stamped my foot at different places between the horse's trail and the bear's and declared, "Look. Now the tracks say that a man accompanied them. Or maybe it was the witch's pet goblin who just dropped by."

Dimitry kneeled beside the imprints. "I see what you mean. These tracks could've been made at different times. There's no way of telling." He looked up at me. "Still, this doesn't solve our bear problem."

I peered at a large, flat stone. Some of the bear tracks surrounding the stone seemed older than others. "Has the bear hid there before?"

Dimitry nodded. "Yes, it has. Three times at least."

"Then why not dig a trap there? Chances are good that you'll catch the beast."

"We would, if the ground wasn't frozen. We tried everything else, stalking the beast, setting snares. Nothing works. We're out of ideas."

I stared at the snowy ground behind the stone blocks. Surely there was a way one could dig. The man beside me had I shovel. I borrowed it, walked behind the stone, and tried planting the shovel in the ground. Useless, it kept bouncing off as if I were trying to dig through solid rock. I stared at the snow in frustration. *If only we could thaw this ground, I'm sure that a trap—* "Thaw the ground! We'll thaw the ground."

"The ground won't thaw until much later in spring," said a skeptical-looking Dimitry.

"Fire melts snow and ice. So if we build a big enough fire right behind that stone block and let it burn for a couple of hours, it should thaw the ground, don't you think?"

Dimitry's face lit up. "Yes! It will. Good idea. We'll do that right away."

With all the manpower assembled outside, building the fire took no time at all. Soon flames engulfed the entire back end of the old ruin.

"Once the fire dies off, we'll dig," Dimitry said. "But until then come warm yourselves inside with us."

* * *

Dimitry's home was warm and surprisingly clean, despite the thick layer of smoke floating above our heads. I supposed that was the reason why all the seats in the house were so low to the ground, so we could sit beneath this dark cloud. The smoke had also given the plaster walls its deep amber color, a pleasant welcoming hue, I found. The smell of wood fire and stew which impregnated the air wasn't displeasing either. *It certainly smells better than the castle's rotten stench,* I thought, staring at the cauldron of stew boiling over the fireplace.

Comfortably seated on a low wooden bench at Dimitry's table, and surrounded by a dozen peasants, I felt at ease and relaxed for the first time since I set foot in Sorvinka. I never imagined I would enjoy the company of the common man this much. I even found myself laughing at their crude stories.

"You must be hungry?" said Dimitry.

"A little," I said—I was starving.

"Bring the man food, good woman," shouted Dimitry.

Kathia, Dimitry's wife, a solidly built woman with a round red face that exuded goodness, set a steaming bowl of soup in front of me.

Damnation, it was borscht. The joy I had felt at receiving a meal evaporated.

Noticing my grim look, my host said, "Try it. Kathia's borscht is the best."

I looked at the red soup. At least this time it was hot. I took a sip, smiled, and drained half the bowl. This borscht was sweet, rich, and delicious. It tasted nothing like the horrid brew I was served at the castle. I noted a variety of vegetables in the mix; there were also small pieces of meat. Smacking my lips, I declared, "Dimitry, this is indeed the best borscht I've ever eaten."

"Oh, you're just saying that to be nice," said a blushing Kathia. "I'm sure you've eaten better at the castle."

I shook my head. "The castle's borscht is vile."

Diego frowned. "Mine was fine. Yours must have been tampered with. As I recall, Lars seemed quite determined to see you eat it."

"Now that you're saying it that might be why it tasted so foul."

"*Tsk-tsk-tsk,*" gave Dimitry while lighting a long bone pipe.

As I watched the peasants' reaction, something Dimitry had said earlier came back to my mind. "Dimitry, when we arrived at the village you said that you were in luck because we were foreigners. What did you mean by that? Are the Sorvinkian noblemen unwilling to help their people?"

"No, that's not it. We feared you might be some of the young ones, the duke and his friends. Every time they come to the village it's to do no good. Gallop through our gardens, chase our livestock, threaten our people. They're a bad lot. And the duke is the worst among them. That boy has the temperament of a wild dog. The thought that one day he may rule our country keeps us awake at night." Lost amidst a cloud of aromatic tobacco, Dimitry snorted in disdain. "As for our *noblemen*, most aren't Sorvinkian anymore. So why would they care for us?"

"I don't understand."

"Take our last kings for instance. Their name, Anderson, the name they so proudly want to continue to carry the crown, it's not even a Sorvinkian name. It's Tatilion."

"Really! I didn't know that."

"I'll explain it to you." Dimitry began telling the story of how the Andersons, warlords from Tatilion, an annex province of Sorvinka, came to take the crown about two hundred years ago through war, political alliances, and clever marriages. According to Dimitry, since Sorvinka had become an Empire, the noblemen of this country had become more interested in politics than the welfare of their own people. "There are a few old Sorvinkian names remaining though, the Molotoffs, the Sochskys, the Kauvchneivs. But for the most we're now ruled by Tatilion nobility."

"That's true for most dynasties, Dimitry. My father, the Sultan of Telfar, was only half Telfarian. And the new sultan, my brother, has even less Telfarian blood. (Actually he had none.)"

Dimitry nodded. "We understand that this is a common thing...."

I sensed that there was something else behind his hesitation, something left unsaid... too dangerous to say perhaps, especially for a peasant.

"You mentioned the name Molotoff. Did you mean Baron Vladimir Molotoff, the one-armed general?"

"Yes—that's a good man!" proclaimed a red-cheeked youth from the end of the table.

Dimitry darted irate eyes at the youth, who immediately sunk in on himself.

Mmm... interesting. "Dimitry, do you think the baron would make a better ruler than King Erik?"

The room became dead silent. Looking dreadfully serious, the peasants began glancing at one another with growing nervousness. Dimitry remained calm however. After having pondered over my question for a moment, he said, "The man has commanding qualities besides his Sorvinkian name. He's a good solider, brave above all. He respects our traditions and customs, and is a devoted follower of our old faith. Plus, he has three sons—all fine boys with good heads on their shoulders…" Dimitry paused, then fixing his eyes onto mine added, "But as for would he make a better king, no one knows. Power changes people, even the best of them."

I was truly impressed by Dimitry's careful wording; a skilled diplomat wouldn't have done better. And I, who thought peasants and commoners were less intelligent than nobles. I was ashamed of myself. These people might lack refinement and worldly knowledge, but they didn't lack intelligence—I knew that now. I would never look at them the same way again… with the arrogant sense of superiority of a prince. I bowed my head respectfully at my host. "Well said, Dimitry! Well said!"

Pleased, Dimitry produced a big grin, exposing his three teeth. "I hope you understand that we don't dislike our king, or foreigners."

The man seated on my right slapped my shoulder hard enough to throw me against the table. "We like them well enough," he proclaimed with a loud belly laugh.

"Leonid's right," said Kathia. "The queen is from a foreign country and she's a kind, loving lady."

I watched every head in the room bob in agreement. I looked at Kathia busily washing dishes. "So you like the queen?"

"Yes, very much," she replied, drying her hands on her apron. "When she was well, the queen used to travel to the villages, ours and the others farther west. She'd bring goods for the poor. On the bad years, when the harvest failed, she'd make more trips, bringing food as well as other supplies. Now her ladies-in-waiting are doing her charity work. Lady Isabo and Countess Ivana, fine, fine ladies. They often bring the young princesses along when they come to see us. Still, I wish the queen was in better health." Kathia sighed. "It's a shame that she's so sick."

Dimitry coughed. "What's a shame is that she wasn't able to give the king a son."

"She gave him five lovely daughters," I said.

"Arh, they can't rule. We're stuck with that spoiled duke."

"Have you heard about the kidnapping of the king's daughters?"

"The news got to us. That's a scary affair."

"They say Farrellians did it."

"What! Farrellians! Here, in these parts? I don't believe that. If you ask me there is more truth in the Baba Yaga story."

The man with the sheep vest seated on my right slammed his fist on the table. "The Baba isn't a tale. She exists. She's mean and ugly. Her mouth is huge and filled with big rock-like teeth. She's real, I tell you. My son saw her house in the woods, that thing nearly killed him."

"By that thing, you mean the witch?" I said.

"No," the man snapped. "I mean the house. The witch steals children and kills grownups. But the house kills everyone that comes near it."

"The house?"

The man's face twisted in frustration and anger. I watched his nostrils flare, thinking he might strike me for having dared question his belief in the Baba. Fortunately, no blow came my way; the man regained some control over his temper and continued his confusing explanation. "You see, there are skulls with glowing eyes above the house. If they don't see you, you're safe. But if they notice you though, the house would then trample you to death."

"Ah, I see." I nodded, feigning having understood. I glanced at Diego. He made a drinking gesture with his hand then indicated the man with the sheep vest. *Oh yes, my friend, you got that right,* I thought before turning back to the group. "Have any of you got other ideas about who might have abducted the princesses?"

Several theories were expressed by the men assembled around the table. In my opinion, none made sense, so I came to the conclusion that these peasants knew nothing useful about those crimes. After some more time spent talking and savoring Kathia's hearty, delicious cooking, Diego and I bid the villagers farewell and departed Dimitry's home.

The coldness of the air took my breath away. My nostrils stuck together, and I felt the skin of my cheeks tightening as the frigid breeze stung my face. From the corner of my eye, I could see the glow of the fire still burning in the ruin.

"Are you coming?" Diego asked while untying our horses.

I shook my head. For some reason, I couldn't bring myself to leave the village now. Something was bothering me. "Remember those horse tracks we saw?"

"Yes," replied Diego. "What about them?"

"I don't know." I rubbed my beard trying to recall the image of the tracks in my mind. Slowly, they began to take form. The tracks had come from the hill, passed near the ruin, then moved parallel to the bear's trail, entering the forest. "The more I think about it, the more I believe these tracks belong to the rider we saw last night."

Diego was skeptical, I could tell by his posture: arms folded and nose wrinkled. "That's impossible to prove, Amir."

"I know. However, this rider came down the hill and rode into the forest."

"And?"

I sighed. He was right. It proved absolutely nothing. This affair was far more complicated than I had anticipated. Or perhaps I just wasn't smart enough to figure it out, or simply not looking at the right things. Either way, I was lost.

CHAPTER NINE

That night I had a peaceful, dreamless sleep, and I awoke in the morning feeling refreshed but a little disappointed. Secretly, I had wished to see Jafer again, wished for him to speak to me in my dream, to show me the right path. By his absence, I assumed he wasn't going to help me anymore and that I was now all alone—well, not really, there was Milo.

Stretched out in my bed, I watched him prepare my clothes for the day, then boil water for tea and my daily washing. Honestly, I don't know how I would cope without Milo. Even though coming to his defense had put me in a precarious position with the king, I no longer regretted having saved him. My appreciation of Milo's service was unusual for me. I was never fond of servants—I never trusted them. I always believed that their loyalty was something that could be bought with gold or broken by force. So why did I feel so differently about Milo? I trusted him thoroughly. I didn't question the strength of his loyalty either. That was strange... very strange indeed.

While I was watching Milo pick lint off one of my kaftans, I suddenly realized why I trusted him so much. *Because he's not a servant.* As an imperial eunuch, Milo had been trained to fulfill many functions: valet, confidant, taster, even male concubine (for the sultans who were so inclined). But first and foremost, he was a bodyguard, and as such he was ready to give his life to protect his master. No amount of torture or gold could change that.

"Milo, how old were you when you were made a eunuch?"

Milo stopped fussing over my clothes and straightened as swiftly as if he had been bitten by a whip. Keeping his back to me, Milo answered in a neutral voice, "Eight, I believe."

"Uh, was it done in Telfar?"

"No. In my homeland." Clearing his throat, Milo added, "My lord shouldn't trouble himself with this. It's of no importance for my lord."

I ignored his suggestion. "Must've been hard for you. Do you miss your homeland?"

Milo took a deep hissing breath. "Telfar is my home. And yes, I do miss it."

His answer baffled me. Sitting up in bed, I questioned him further. "You don't miss Farrell?"

Milo swung around; his eyes were abnormally shiny, I thought. "Why should I miss a country that... butchered me and... and then sent me away as a gift."

"What about your parents?"

"They died of the plague. I was an orphan living on the street. That's were they got me. I have only bad memories of Farrell. Telfar, your father's palace, is where I felt safe and valued for the first time in my life. They clothed me, fed me, educated me. I had power there. I was trusted with the charge of protecting your father, of conversing with him."

I gasped. "You served my father! You seem too young for that."

Milo raised his chin with pride. "I replaced Ely for a few months when he broke his ribs at wrestling practice."

I was speechless. I'd never thought, not even once, that Milo could've come in contact with my father, let alone serve him. "How was he?"

"Your father?"

I nodded.

Milo shrugged. "Lonely."

I frowned. That wasn't the answer I had expected. "What do you mean? Father had hundreds of women, sons, and viziers. How could he be lonely?"

"He just was. Well, at least that's the impression I got. True, he spent his nights with Çiçek, his favorite concubine, but his days were spent mostly alone... with us. His meetings with the vizier never lasted very long. We, the white eunuchs, provided the bulk of his companionship. The palace made sure that our education was extensive and as complete as any highborn nobles would receive. Hence our lessons included a broad variety of subjects such as mathematics, art, literature. We had to be able to entertain any type of conversation, play music, read poetry, or play chess. Your father loved chess."

A sudden wave of jealousy washed over me. Why not seek us, his sons, for conversation? Were we not good enough? Why did my father spend all his time with eunuchs? Why choose them over us... unless. A distasteful thought had just formed in my suspicious mind. I stared at Milo with some repulsion. "What other duties were you fulfilling for my father?"

"All kinds. We—" Milo stopped speaking. By the embarrassed look on his face, he'd just realized what I'd meant. "Oh, that! No. Your father's taste was strictly for women."

Oddly enough, this answer brought me no joy, quite the opposite in fact. I had hoped this could have been the reason why my father had favored the company of eunuchs over mine and my brothers'. For a good minute, I chewed the inside of my cheek while brewing dark thoughts. We could have been his companions instead of the eunuchs. I glared at Milo, resenting him for having known my father better than I had.

It's not his fault, I told myself. *Princes cannot be trusted. Eunuchs, on the other hand, are devoted, trustworthy, loyal companions. They would never bury a knife in the Sultan's back as an ambitious prince might have done. That's why Father trusted eunuchs more than us. Father trusted Milo. And so do I. We have that in common.* My resentment evaporated, and I smiled at Milo. "Today, I feel like exploring the castle, and you're coming with me."

* * *

I had left my rooms with no precise destination in mind, but for some unknown reason, my instinct had led me to the foot of the tower's staircase where I had first felt the strange tingling sensation.

Milo didn't hide his disappointment; I knew he had been looking forward to spending time in the warmth of the conservatory. Later maybe we'd go there, but for now I had to verify something here, something that had been gnawing at me for a while now.

I placed my foot on the bottom step and leaned forward. Nothing. No tingling whatsoever. Could it have been a draft I felt that day? Could it have been my nerves? It could have been anything, really. I peered up the steps. Perhaps I should see where these steps led nonetheless.

I climbed up. Soon I reached a square landing where the steps turned before going up again. A door was set there. I touched the wooden door. Nothing; I felt nothing besides its rough wood grain. I grabbed the doorknob and turned it. The door was locked.

"Whose room is this?" asked Milo.

"I don't know, but that person holds no interest to us," I said before moving on. As I neared a second landing, another door appeared further up the stairs. I hadn't reached the door yet, when a familiar smell hit my nose. I hurried up the remaining steps to the front of the door. A thin opened space was visible around its frame. I brought my nose to its edge and breathed in the aroma escaping from the small crack. Herbs. That was the familiar scent filling my nostrils. I recognized chamomile and mint. There was more though, much more. I tried opening the door, and again, I found that it was locked.

Closing my eyes, I breathed in the aroma once more. Amid the rich blend, I was able to distinguish one pungent scent. "Camphor," I whispered, a little disappointed that I couldn't discern the others. I backed away from the door.

"What is it, my lord?"

"This room smells like an apothecary's chest."

"Maybe that's what it is—I mean a room-sized apothecary chest."

"Maybe," I replied, although I had a hard time believing that. Putting this room out of my mind, I stared at the last stretch of steps. Without another word, I climbed up them. Just as I thought, one last door awaited us atop the staircase. This one however wasn't locked like the others, but half-opened. Clanking noises were filtering through this opening. *CLUNK, POINK, TANK* echoed from inside. That blend of metallic sounds accompanied with the resounding *clinks* of glass containers touching together reminded me of the cacophony of a busy kitchen. Here too the air was permeated with odors, bizarre powdery ones, oily ones also.

I stretched a hand to further open the door, but Milo blocked my move before my fingertips could make contact with the door. "This could be dangerous, my lord. Perhaps I should venture in first."

"No—step back!" With a hand firmly grasping the hilt of my sword, I pushed the door wide open. What lay in front of me took me so totally by surprise that, for a long moment, all I could do was just stand there in total awe of my surroundings, while ogling everything inside the room, like a thief might ogle the gold of the imperial treasury. This room was filled with all sorts of scientific implements the likes of which I had never seen before. My eyes traveled to the giant telescope aimed at the window, to the many compasses lining the right wall, then to the mechanical time-device beside the door. Well, I *thought* that's what that machine was. Its balance wheel moving left, right, left, right indicated that much.

Finally, my gaze settled on the long table in front of us. Its entire length was cluttered with bottles of chemical substances, some liquid, some in solid chunks, and some in powdered form. There were also two burners, one was lit and had a glass beaker suspended above its flame with an amber-colored liquid inside. Although this amber brew was not boiling yet, I could see a thin strip of vapor coming out of the beaker's open top, indicating that it was quite hot.

"What is this place?" whispered Milo.

"WHO GOES THERE?" a gravely voice hollered from the far end of the room.

"Prince Amir of Telfar," I answered, squinting to see past the clutter of scientific instruments.

Through this mess, I saw a silhouette coming toward us. It appeared to be a disheveled, gray-haired old man well into his sixties with a big bulbous nose. As he approached, I noticed that he was limping heavily. But what really held my attention was the red scar on his face. Starting above his left eyebrow, this jagged line slashed across his dead white eye, down his cheek, to finally disappear in his beard—which I noted was seeded with the leftovers of a late breakfast. I also noted that his clothes were stained and riddled with tiny burn holes.

Observing me with his good eye, the old man stroked his beard. Crumbs rained down the front of his brown tunic.

"A prince—here?" he said in a tone of suspicion. "That's

unusual. Princes normally care more about pretty girls than my work." A sudden expression of understanding flew across his face. "Ahh, you're looking for the countess and got lost. It's the first door. The one at the bottom of the steps. Now leave. I've got work to do."

Milo and I exchanged puzzled glances. Then I turned to the old man. "Can I ask who you are and what is the purpose of this room?"

The old man gave me a look of interest. "Where did you say you were from, Prince?"

"Prince Amir, from Telfar."

"Telfar... hmm," repeated the man, while stroking his beard again. "I've heard tales of your land. Intriguing tales. Tell me, is it true that in your country a man can die of heat in the day and freeze to death at night?"

The man had not answered my question, and that annoyed me. But even though I greatly disliked conversing with a stranger, I felt compelled to answer his question. "The desert nights are indeed very cold. However, the Sorvinkian nights are far colder." Bowing with respect, I added. "With whom do I have the honor of speaking?"

"You're polite. I'll give you that. I'm Auguste Ramblais, the royal alchemist, and this, as you see—" He waved a hand at the room. "—is my laboratory."

I gazed around in amazement, and then I approached the large telescope. Constructed of narrow wood planks clamped together with brass bands, the instrument's body was easily longer than I was tall and its diameter was approximately the size of my waist. I touched the eyepiece. "May I?"

"Sure, go ahead."

Bending forward, I eagerly brought my eye to the telescope's lens. I breathed in sharply. The forest appeared close enough for me to be able to count each of the trees bordering it.

"This is a powerful instrument. What do you use it for?"

"Astronomy."

"Ah! The study of the stars. What have you learned from it?"

"They move... or maybe we are the ones moving. I'm still undecided on this subject."

I smiled and nodded. I had noticed a similar phenomenon using a less powerful telescope—a small brass one safely tucked away in one of my trunks. "What else occupies your time, tell me? Science has always been my passion."

The alchemist eyed me up and down. By the look of distrust painted on his face, I gathered that I would have to prove myself as a man of science to gain this old fox's trust. But was I *still* a man of science? I didn't know... that was the problem.

Regardless of my doubts, I threw myself into a long narration of my own scientific experimentations. The ones I had made with intriguing stones capable of attracting metal. If rubbed on a piece of iron, the stones would transfer this ability to the piece of metal itself. I talked about the properties of certain elements, which when mixed together would create a third and totally new one. This new element often possessed qualities completely different than the two that had formed it. After a few more anecdotes, I noted that the alchemist was looking at me differently. As if I wasn't an annoying and curious prince anymore, but a colleague.

"I'm impressed, I must admit it," he said. Turning around, he waved for me to follow him. "Come. Come."

I hurried behind him as he made his way to the lit burner. The amber liquid in the beaker above the flame was on the verge of boiling.

The alchemist rubbed his hands together. "Good. It's ready."

"What is it? A new experiment?"

Once again, he looked at me as if he was unsure if I had any business being in this place. "Tea! It's tea! What did you think it was? Want some?"

"Er… certainly."

"Tell your companion to come too. There's more then enough for three."

I called for Milo to join us; then we all moved to a table at the end of the room and sipped hot tea while nibbling on hard biscuits.

"You still haven't talked about your experiments," I said after a sip.

"Are they of a dangerous nature?" rapidly added Milo, his eyes fixed on the alchemist's scar. I could've punched him for his rudeness.

But to my surprise the alchemist burst into laughter. He ran a finger along his scar. "Well deduced, young man. This was caused by the explosion of a glass jar containing some new and very unstable spirits."

"Did it cause that too?" I asked, pointing to his lame leg.

"No. I broke my ankle as a boy. Didn't heal well."

"Oh, I'm sorry to hear that."

"Why? You didn't break it!" Leaning forward, the alchemist slapped my shoulder. "You're too polite, my prince. Far too polite."

I felt myself relax, and for the next hour I listened to the alchemist's account of his travels and experiments. King Erik wasn't the first crowned head he'd served, but the third and most powerful of the three. But according to Auguste, the King of Sorvinka was also the king who cared the least about his experiments. The alchemist's presence here had more to do with fashion and prestige than true interest in science.

I swallowed the mouthful of dry biscuit I'd been struggling with for a while and said, "I suppose that running an empire as large as Sorvinka can occupy one's entire mind."

"Pf… keeping the Empire from breaking apart is the real headache."

"Is the Farrellian rebellion that great of a threat to the

Empire?" I asked.

The alchemist's knowledgeable eye turned to Milo.

The eunuch swiftly lowered his head.

"Fear not, young Milo, I won't tell anyone. Farrell isn't Sorvinka's biggest threat—the eastern hordes are. They'll stay put only as long as the king pays them not to invade Sorvinka. However, he cannot stop them from invading the neighboring countries."

"Savages!" hissed Milo.

"Hmm, I wouldn't judge them so quickly if I were you. True, we possess certain knowledge they lack. But the same can be said of them." The alchemist rose, and after a noisy search around the room, he returned with a small wooden box. When he opened it I saw that the box was filled with a black powdery substance. "A gift from Khuan, one of the eastern emissaries."

"What is it?"

"Thunder dust," said the alchemist. Taking a pinch of powder, he threw it into the fireplace.

POOFH. A blinding tongue of flame shot up into the air. A thick black smoke followed, choking the room with a pungent sulfuric smell which irritated our throats and burnt our eyes.

"This dust is only one of the few marvels they possess," said the alchemist amidst a dark could of smoke.

Coughing, I fanned the air in front of my face, glad that the smoke was finally dissipating. "What's the purpose of this dust... besides making smoke?"

The alchemist's expression took on an air of mystery. "I'm not at liberty to say. It's not ready." He closed the box containing the thunder dust. "In the course of my travels, I learned many interesting facts about the eastern hordes. These *barbarians* have a name. They call themselves the Anchin. I believe it means the hunters. Their clothing may be crude, but their weapons are not. Theirs are far superior to any I have seen so far. Do you know that their emperor moves around in a traveling city? Mmm…" The alchemist smiled in beatitude. "How I would love to see such a thing."

I cleared my throat. "I saw their horses. They look like rugged creatures."

"The wild ponies are the Anchin's most fearsome weapon. It has been said that mounts and riders can travel for days without stopping. The riders sleep and eat on their horses. These unstoppable hordes of light cavalry can overrun a country like a swarm of locusts. Many cities have capitulated without a fight at the sight of these warriors, hundreds of thousands of them riding in tight formation, men and women alike. When people saw them for the first time, they thought the Anchin were demons or evil spirits. It's for the best that they surrendered."

"Really! Doesn't seem like a good option to me."

The alchemist sighed. "With the Anchin, surrendering is the only real option. Those who do are always spared. Those who resist are killed to the last. I think this behavior may have helped spread the myth that they were of a demonic nature."

I smiled. "Spirits, ghosts, and demons are the simplest way of explaining the unknown."

"Not always; when no logical explanation can be found, often ghosts or demons are involved."

Taken aback, I looked at the alchemist with wide eyes. "You believe in ghosts! You—a man of science."

"Who said one can't believe in both."

"I… I… never thought this possible."

The alchemist shrugged. "It is for me."

I thought it best if I didn't speak any longer; I was too choked up by emotions to find anything remotely coherent to say. Somehow, I had always assumed that if I allowed myself to believe in the occult, I wouldn't be able to devote myself to science.

After an awkward moment of silence, the alchemist asked, "You haven't told me the reason you climbed up my tower, Prince Amir. Were you, as I first thought, visiting the ladies that share it with me?"

"What ladies?"

"Countess Ivana and Lady Isabo. Both are annoying. If you ask me, all women are. The pretty one is nosy, with all her entertaining and friends coming and going from her room. And the other, the plain looking one, she stinks up the whole place with her potion-making. She prides herself a potion-maker and a healer, that one. If you ask me she's worse than the other."

I stared at Milo. "So the room that smells of herbs is hers. Alchemist, what sort of potions does she make?"

"Witch's brews by the smell. She makes a decent tonic, I must say. The queen takes it every day."

"How long has she been making tonics for the queen?"

"Oh, years."

"Is that the truth, huh?" *And the queen has been sick for years. Strange coincidence.* "Do you know how one can meet the queen?"

"Certainly. Send her a note requesting an audience. The queen rarely refuses a formal request."

I smiled. I intended to do just that.

CHAPTER TEN

Following the alchemist's advice, as soon as I got back to my room, I sent a written note to the queen requesting an audience with her. The day ended without receiving an answer, and by noon the next day I began worrying. Although I didn't expect to receive her reply that same day, her lack of response made me nervous nonetheless.

"Have you thought of what you will bring her, if she agrees to see you?" asked Milo.

I winced. My talent at gift giving was so disastrous that at this point the idea alone of having to choose one frightened me. Not feeling up to the task, I decided to postpone that dreaded chore and remained comfortably seated in front of the roaring fireplace. Here, at least, I incurred no danger and could rest easy.

TAP, TAP, TAP.

The light knocking at my door was unexpected at this time of day.

Milo was there in the blink of an eye. However, before opening the door, he turned to me and in a voice betraying a hint of apprehension said, "I hope it's not that *perfumed* prince again." His comment didn't surprise me. I had noted that Milo had developed a profound dislike for Diego.

I shrugged. "He's not that unpleasant." Thinking of it now,

I'd grown to enjoy Diego's companionship—if nothing else, he was entertaining. I grinned broadly and said, "Open the door, Milo."

Bearing a look of resignation, Milo obeyed and opened the door. "Princess Eva, what a pleasure to see you here," said Milo with obvious relief.

Upon hearing my beloved's name, I leapt to my feet and made a mad dash to the door. "Eva," I whispered, slightly out of breath, while gazing at her with the same overwhelming amazement as when I had seen her for the first time. She wore a thick blue-velvet hood and cape over her bright yellow dress. Her cheeks were reddened by the cold, her eyes sparkled with excitement, and the gold curls tumbling out of her hood framed her face perfectly. Right then, I found her more beautiful than ever.

"Why have you stayed away from me for so long?" The resentment in my voice was biting. And as I watched her lovely smile fade, I regretted having spoken those words of displeasure.

Her smooth brow furrowed. "Amir! I thought we settled this at the ball. You said you understood my need to spend some time alone with my family. Why are you reproaching me now? "

Gripped by a sudden panic, I seized her gloved hands. "Pardon me, my love. I've been sick with worry about you and your family. I was desperate to see you, but helpless to do so. I hope you understand how upsetting this can be for me."

The furrow on her brow eased, and she smiled at me. "I know. I've left you alone with no friend to speak to for far too long. Although, I've heard that you and Prince Diego went riding the other day."

"He's hardly a substitute for you. I would've greatly preferred to spend that time in your company."

Her gloved hand caressed my cheek lightly. Then Eva rose

on her tiptoes and softly brushed her lips over my chin and mouth. Liquid fire spread through my entire body. I bent down and captured her mouth with mine. Meanwhile my hands went in quest of her waist hidden underneath her thick cape, as I tried holding on to her, so that the kiss would last longer. But she slipped out of my arms before I could gain a good grip.

Sidestepping me, Eva entered the room. "Milo," she said, acknowledging his presence. Then she pushed back her hood, releasing a cascade of golden curls, and stared about the room. An expression of consternation invaded her features.

She clucked her tongue. "*Tsk-tsk-tsk.* Father did this on purpose. I cannot believe it. The man is so stubborn. Gah! That makes me so mad."

I made an attempt at a smile to hide the extent of my distress, but only wound up thinning my lips. "Your father really dislikes me. Eva, I'm afraid he'll never agree to our union. No matter what I do. The man is impossible to please—not by me anyway." I felt my chest tightening, and I had to let out a long sigh just to ease the pressure around it.

Head tilted, Eva turned loving eyes toward me. "All is not lost, Amir. We do have an ally. A very powerful and influential one."

"Who?" I asked with renewed hope.

Eva's nose wrinkled as if she were about to play a trick on someone. "Mother," she breathed in a secretive tone. "She has agreed to see you, Amir. Mother's inviting you to have tea with her tomorrow. If someone can change Father's view of you, it is she. Trust me on that."

Beaming with joy, I said. "I do trust you, my love, I do. What should I wear? Oh, and what should I bring her? I don't want a repeat of my introduction mistakes and insult her with an offensive gift."

Eva's laughter filled my room. "Wear something simple

and elegant. As for the gift. No woman will ever be insulted by jewelry."

I grinned. "When should I go there?"

"Don't worry. Someone will come to fetch you when it's time. Now put on your coat, we're going outside."

I didn't argue; I dressed in a hurry. We spent a good part of the day outside walking in the snow. I was so glad to be with Eva that I didn't feel the cold any longer. She was my sun, my fire; her presence warmed me from the inside out. Well, except for when she shoved a handful of snow in my face and some of it ran along my neck and down my back. I was cold then, but that was a small price to pay for being with her.

Grasping my arm, Eva said, "Come with me, I want to show you something."

We ran through the snow until we were past the stable and nearly out of the castle's garden.

Eyeing the dark line of the trees ahead, I felt a sudden uneasiness. "Where are we going? Not in the forest I hope?"

"No. The place is right on its edge."

I hesitated. "Eva… that's dangerous."

"Please," she coaxed. "I need to show it to you. It's not far, I promise."

"Fine. But it better not be far."

Well, it was farther than she remembered. I stared at the partly collapsed stone building with some confusion. Why did she want me to see this pile of rubble?

Wrapping her cape tightly around her, Eva approached the broken-down building.

"This used to be our playground when we were children. My sisters and I used to spend hours here. It was different then. Those walls were still standing and the forest was further back. This place was sunny and flowers grew everywhere." She sighed. "Too many things have changed lately. Far too many things."

"What was this place anyway?"

Eva sat down on one of the fallen columns that had once flanked the building's façade. "An old temple, an old house. Some call them travelers' roofs. They used to be widespread throughout the country. They were shelters to spend the night in safe from the wolves, and to worship the local gods. Now they are all falling apart… because things have changed. Sorvinka is not as it used to be. I don't like the way it is now." Eva paused and looked around while twisting one of her gloves between her hands. Then she turned concerned eyes toward me. "I spent a lot of time with Father in his council chamber these last days, and I was appalled to learn that my beloved country is now weakened by internal conflicts and divisions."

I frowned, shocked by what she just said. "You! You've assisted at council meetings? I thought—I thought you spent most of your time with your mother."

Eva glared at me. "Why are you so surprised, Amir? I told you about my interest in the kingdom's affairs long ago. You knew Father let me and my sisters assist in those meetings."

"Yes… but…"

Eva's eyes narrowed; her chin rose. "But what, Amir? Did you think I lied, or embellished the truth?"

"No! I—"

Eva shook her head. "Don't bother explaining yourself. I understand. You thought those were meaningless meetings. The sort that deals with the purchase of furniture for one of the castle's new wings. You never really believed that Father would let me participate in any meetings of political importance… because I'm a woman."

I thought it best not to say a word; after all, she was right, that was exactly my thinking.

Nodding, Eva whispered, "This isn't Telfar, Amir. Sorvinka has different rules."

"I'm doing my best to learn your ways and adapt to them."

Eva smiled. "I know you are. I shouldn't lose my patience with you like this. You're certainly not to blame for your upbringing. And my presence in the council's chamber is unusual even in Sorvinkian culture. No woman has ruled Sorvinka since the Black Queen, and that was over three hundred years ago."

"The Black Queen... sounds ominous, I've never heard of her before."

"She wasn't evil, just a widow. She wore only black, hence the name Black Queen. She ruled as regent for nine years until her eldest son was old enough to ascend to the throne." A proud grin illuminated Eva's face. "In the few years she ruled, the Black Queen successfully doubled the size of the country by annexing the provinces of Tatilion and Ukavec. She gave birth to the Empire we have today. Sadly, history books rarely mention her accomplishments. Some even omit her reign completely." Eva kicked the snow with obvious discontentment. "It's terribly unjust, if you ask me."

I agreed wholeheartedly, which seemed to appease Eva's volatile emotions. Her posture became more relaxed and her face took on a calm, dreamy expression. As she appeared lost in her thoughts, I decided to take a closer look at the old temple behind us.

I walked around the side of the building and discovered the remains of an entrance. Some timeworn figures still adorned its sides. They appeared vaguely feminine in form—then again, the stone was so pitted and eroded I couldn't really be sure. Further inside the building, where the roof had fallen in, forming a sloping shelter, was a round bowl set atop a tall stone pillar. With an eye fixed on the collapsed roof, I cautiously stepped inside the building and leaned over the round bowl.

"OH!" I jumped back in horror. A bloody sheep's head

lay in the bowl. I then looked on the ground. The snow was beaten by footsteps. Fir branches were spread out in the left corner not far from the darkened patch of an extinguished fire. I could also see some melted wax on several rocks. This place had been used recently. Someone slept here—on those branches. Were they travelers or bandits? I wondered. Either way, this building wasn't safe, I decided, and made my way back out.

"Eva," I called, rushing to her side. "We must leave now."

She shot me an annoyed glance, the kind that made me doubt she would consent to do so. But after a long look at the surroundings, Eva agreed to leave. I was glad to flee the forest, and this spot in particular. This place made me nervous.

We were emerging from between the fir trees growing at the forest's edge, when two galloping horses almost ran us over. I hardly had time to pull Eva out of the path of their deadly hooves. If not for my swift reflex, I believe Eva, who had been walking in front me, would've been trampled. Once Eva and I had regained our wit, we turned to face the riders.

The two Anchin warriors had stopped a short distance from us. The man appeared relieved to see that we were unharmed. The woman, on the other hand, looked somewhat disappointed. Moreover, she was glaring at Eva with open dislike. Without uttering a single word, they turned their horses and galloped away.

"Savages!" hissed Eva.

"According to the alchemist they're not as barbaric as they appear."

"Foolish ramblings of an old man!" she snapped. "They're savages, nothing more." Furious, she raised clenched fists in front of her face, as if she wanted to hit someone, anyone. Her rage was so intense that for a brief instant I thought she was going to hit me. But then her hands fell to her sides. "Oh, Amir, I'm so tired of feeling threatened all the time. I'm tired of being powerless. I wish I could change things. I wish I could bring Sorvinka back to the way it was before: united, strong, and proud." She stared at the diminishing silhouettes of the Anchin warriors with loathing. "I don't understand why Father is paying them to stay away. I wouldn't."

"Your father wants to prevent a war."

"Why? We're Sorvinkian. They cannot defeat us."

That wasn't what I had heard, yet I chose not to argue with Eva. The searing anger, the irrational wrath, she'd just displayed was new to me. I'd never seen that side of her before. Of course, I thought, with what has happened to her sisters, Eva had the right to be angry. And she wasn't really angry at me anyway—why would she be.

Our return to the castle was in a far less joyous mood than our departure had been. Nevertheless, when Eva bid me farewell, promising that we would meet again tomorrow at her mother's apartments, there was enough warmth in her voice to make me forget her irritable attitude earlier. Thus it was with a light heart that I went back to my rooms. *The queen will love me. She has too. I will be charming. I won't say anything inappropriate.* Everything would go well, I was sure of it. Then again, I had thought the same before meeting the king.

* * *

"How do I look?" I asked Milo for the tenth time.

"Like a prince."

Once more, I turned my attention to the full-length mirror attached to the wall. I had chosen a copper-colored kaftan trimmed with black fur and a matching turban. The tunic and pants I wore underneath were made of the finest black silk and my belt was constructed of gold rings. I flicked a finger on the black pearl brooch embellishing my copper turban. Was it too much? I opened my mouth to speak—

"It's fine. Leave it," Milo said, beating me to the punch.

Knocks at the door brought this nerve-wracking wait to an end. I rushed to open it before Milo could make a move. A guard stood at attention in the corridor.

"Prince Amir, by orders of the queen you must accompany me to her apartments."

"Milo, bring the gift, we're leaving."

The trip to the royal wing took more time than I thought. When we arrived at the queen's apartments, the guards opened one of its tall double doors and stepped back.

Taking a deep breath, I entered the room. Situated on the south side of the castle, this long room's entire left side was made up of a series of tall glass windows. With its creamy-yellow walls and bright sunlight beaming in, the room was a warm contrast from the rest of this dark dingy castle. As Milo and I walked toward the group of ladies waiting further down the room, I studied the decorations. Round white medallions embellished the yellow wall, carved white columns stood between each window like soldiers on guard. The ceiling was painted to imitate an open sky, pale blue with a few fluffy clouds. This architecture and style of décor was totally different from anything else I'd seen in the castle so far. *The queen has taste,* I thought, looking ahead.

Reclined against the backrest of a lounging chair, the queen watched me approach. A sallow-skinned, dainty woman, she looked ill and weak, this in spite of the excess of rouge applied to her sunken cheeks. Even her shimmering rose dress failed to improve her complexion and bring life to her face. Still, her exquisite bone structure remained untouched by illness. This woman must have been a great beauty in her day. My attention then traveled to the queen's entourage.

Looking lovely in her cream dress, Eva stood at her mother's right side. Next to her was the stunning Countess Ivana in a bright blue gown. My eyes rapidly returned to Eva, who I could now see had inherited some of her mother's stunning features. Their eyes, those warm big brown eyes, were similar.

I was almost at their side when a third woman stepped out from behind the countess. With her simple gray dress and mousy brown hair tied back in a stern bun, plain-looking Lady Isabo was quite literally outshined by Eva's and Ivana's radiant beauty. Even the queen was more striking than her. To me, Isabo looked more like a servant than a lady. Her eyes met mine, and I immediately reevaluated that impression. No servant would ever stare down a prince with such fearless arrogance. Also, I had to admit those vibrant green eyes of hers were certainly not plain. Sadly, I thought that the hostility clouding her gaze attenuated the effect of that unusual and striking color.

The queen took Eva's hand into hers. "Can you leave us, my child? I need to speak to this young prince alone."

Reluctantly, Eva withdrew from the room. I watched her leave with regret... and a hint of apprehension.

"Prince Amir," said the queen. Her voice was like velvet, soft, rich, and warm, and the rolling accent she possessed as pleasurable as a caress. I felt some of my apprehension evaporate. "You must forgive me for not rising. My health is not the best. However, I can assure you that I've looked forward to meeting you for a while."

I bowed humbly at the waist before her. "The honor is mine, Your Majesty."

"Please rise. I wish to look at you."

I obeyed.

"Mmm!" she said. "You are indeed very handsome. So what I was told proved to be true—for once."

I felt myself blushing.

The queen smiled. "And modest too. You are full of surprises, Prince Amir. I see why my daughter is so..." She paused and studied me carefully before saying, "...fond of you. A pity my husband doesn't share her view. But we'll see, we'll see."

Her eyes moved to Milo, standing behind me with the ivory box containing the queen's gift in his arms. I was surprised to see that her attention wasn't focused on the box at all, but fixed on Milo's face. The poor boy was as livid as one waiting in line at the blacksmith to have a tooth pulled.

"Hmm…" she gave. The sound twisted my stomach into knots. "I was made aware of your servant's condition, and that his looks were deceiving. However, I did not imagine they would be to this extent. This is quite unexpected." She glanced at me. "What is your servant's name?"

"Milo, Your Majesty."

She smiled. "Milo, just out of curiosity, how many invitations have you received."

Milo paled to such a degree that he looked on the verge of fainting. "Your Majesty, I fear I don't understand—"

"Oh yes, you do. I'm talking about the small notes ladies of the court have been slipping in your palm since you got here. Invitations to join them in their rooms at night, I presume. How many so far?"

Milo swallowed hard. "Four—no five, Your Majesty."

I glared at Milo in shock; it took all of my self-control to prevent my jaw from dropping. Well, I couldn't allow myself to look like some gawking idiot in front of the queen.

Satisfied by Milo's answer, the queen nodded. "I thought so. Don't worry, young man, I won't ask you any other rude questions." The queen turned to Countess Ivana. "See my dear, I was right."

The countess curtseyed. "Indeed you were, Your Highness."

"Ivana overestimated the virtue of our courtesans. With their husbands gone to Farrell, many ladies see your valet as a rare source of entertainment. One without risk and consequence. Please, you mustn't be too harsh with him, Prince Amir. After all he is still a man. Promise me he will be spared your wrath and won't be punished. I would feel terribly guilty if my curious questioning caused this young man pain."

This queen was a talented diplomat, and like all good diplomats she was cunning, yet I sensed no deviousness in her. Truthfully, I found her kind and forgiving. Now I understood why the king loved her so. I bowed to her again, agreeing not to punish Milo. The boy was lucky, because I was so mad at him right now, I could have skinned him alive.

"Your behavior pleases me. Kindness is a rare quality among the nobles. I can see why Eva's attracted to you. Now let's change the subject, shall we. My dear prince, I couldn't help noticing how you were admiring my room."

"Yes—it is beautiful. Its architecture is very unlike the rest of the castle."

The queen became pensive, as if recalling pleasant memories, and for a fleeting instant one could see what a stunning beauty she must have been before her health failed. Then her gaze regained focus. "This room is a copy of my father's sun room in his seaside palace. My father is King Herolio of Carltes. All that is missing here is an ocean view. But enough about this. Please, sit and tell me about you and the wonderful land of Telfar. I'm literally dying to hear about it."

I watched the expression of the ladies behind her turn grim.

"Oh please, don't mind them. They both lack a sense of humor."

"As you wish, Your Majesty. Would you care to see your gift first?"

"Certainly. You will find me far easier to please than my husband."

"I…" Mortified, I turned red. "These are difficult times for His Majesty, the King."

"True. Few people understand how painful it is to have one's child ripped away from one's bosom. To have three is unbearable." The queen's eyes welled up with tears.

Lady Isabo rushed to her side and gripped her hands. The queen leaned against the plain woman. "My dear Isabo understands us. She too had been kidnapped as a girl. She knows the perils my daughters are facing."

Dabbing the corner of her eyes with a handkerchief, the queen forced a smile on her lips. "Please, go on, my dear prince."

I snapped my fingers and Milo appeared at my side with the gift. I took the box and, bending on one knee, presented it to the queen.

Accepting the gift with grace, the queen admired the exquisitely carved ivory box at length before gently lifting the lid. Red velvet lined the inside of the box, and nestled in its center was a necklace of baroque pearls nearly the size of hazelnuts with a huge pear-shaped sapphire pendant dangling from it.

Delighted, she lifted the necklace out of the box. "Prince Amir, this is too generous a gift."

"Please, Your Majesty must accept it."

"I certainly will. No woman can refuse such a magnificent piece of jewelry."

I felt tension leaving my body. At least this part had gone well. For the next hour, I did my best to entertain the queen with tales of Telfar while we drank tea. Periodically, my attention would wander to her ladies-in-waiting. Countess Ivana was one of the most charming women I ever had the good fortune to meet. Although she always appeared well clothed with her hair arranged perfectly, I noted that her blue gown, as stunning as it was, was tattered at the seams, stained and discolored in places. By this, I deduced that the garment was old and had been refitted for her. I also noticed that she wore very little jewelry—if one could consider the three small aquamarine pins, with their tiny gems resembling raindrops, hooked to her lapel jewelry. That surprised me a great deal. I would have thought that a woman possessing the countess's multiple attributes would've been dripping in jewels. When I commented on the pins being... delicate, she blushed, saying that they were a gift from her poor deceased mother.

The queen patted Ivana's hands. "Our lovely countess is a widow. The count left her with a title and little else. She could remarry, but she refuses, preferring to remain poor and destitute."

"I was prisoner of a loveless marriage once. I care not to relive that misery again. New dresses and jewelry don't bring one happiness."

Isabo snorted sarcastically. "How would you know? Your husband spent his entire fortune on wine."

"Yes, that is true." said the countess. "But at least *I* had a husband. So far no man has shown the slightest interest in you, my dear."

Isabo gasped, her hands rolled into fists. Evidently this was a sore spot for Isabo, because she couldn't have looked more outraged by the countess's remark. She was positively incensed.

Glaring at the countess, Isabo asked, "True, you had a husband, but was he a husband worth having?"

Looking hurt and angry at the same time, the countess stayed mute.

"Ha!" exclaimed a triumphant Lady Isabo. "That's what I thought."

The countess sighed heavily. Her eyes lowered to her dainty white hands. "My husband was a punishment I wouldn't wish on any woman... not even you, Isabo." Raising her head, she brought her gaze to me. "That's why I believe that Princess Eva should marry the man she loves. A kind, loving man."

"You truly believe this the right thing to do, Ivana?" asked the queen.

"Yes, with all my heart," said the countess.

"And you, Isabo, what are your thoughts on the subject?" demanded the queen.

Isabo's face hardened. "I'm against it. It's not useful."

"Useful!" exclaimed the countess. "Love shouldn't be useful!"

"A princess has duties and finding love isn't part them. Sorvinka doesn't need a second alliance with Telfar. This prince brings nothing new or useful to the kingdom. Thus, it would be foolish to acquiesce to this fruitless union."

"No—you are foolish!" snapped the countess, face pinched.

"My dear, I'm not the one believing in fairytale romance."

Well, I thought, there was no love lost between those two. Watching the two ladies exchange hate-filled stares and vitriolic words, I suspected that if not for the queen's presence they might have fought like commoners.

Amused by her ladies bickering, the queen burst into laughter. As though by magic, she was transformed by this mirthful act: now tension free, her face looked younger, healthier also, as a flush of pink now colored her cheeks. Then all of a sudden she stopped laughing, clutched her chest, and winced in pain.

Countess Ivana rushed to the queen's side. Not knowing what to do, I stood but remained frozen in place. As for Isabo, she dashed to the armoire in the corner of the room. When she swung its doors open I saw that its shelves were filled with bottles, pots, and carafes. A strong scent of herbs and mineral oils escaped into the air. Isabo began searching frantically amidst all the bottles.

In the meantime, Countess Ivana had unfastened the collar of the queen's dress so she could breathe more easily. Moments later, Isabo was beside the queen with a small glass containing a milky liquid. Between gasping breaths and grimaces of pain, the queen managed to drink the potion.

Within seconds of ingesting it, the tension contorting her facial features diminished. I watched the queen's face relax and at last her hand, which had never ceased clutching her chest, finally loosened.

No medication I know can act this quickly, I thought, and peered at Isabo with suspicion. What had she given to the queen? Doubting that she would tell me if I asked, I turned my attention to the queen again. "How is Your Majesty?"

"Out of danger," replied Isabo. "You should leave. This is your fault. You're tiring her too much."

"Isabo!" breathed the queen in a tone of reproval. "Prince Amir, please forgive Lady Isabo's harsh manners. She's too devoted to my well-being. Quite honestly, without her care I would've died long ago."

"Yes, indeed... she seems to be working magic."

A tired smile crossed the queen's face. "I don't believe in magic. I believe in luck however."

"I fail to see your reasoning."

"Isabo, and Countess Ivana for that matter, had just been promoted to my service when I was taken ill. Without their care I would have died—it's surprising that I'm still alive." The queen's expression darkened. "The end is near though. I know it is coming. I can feel it." The queen lightly tapped her chest. "Here."

"Your Majesty—"

"Oh please, I made peace with death long ago. Only one thing troubles me: the fate of the kingdom, and therefore my family, as the two are linked. (Sigh) If my husband had any sense at all, he would remarry, preferably with Isabo, and produce sons." The queen shook her head. "If he had any sense he would not place Lars on the throne. The boy's too inept to rule."

I smiled at the queen, but couldn't help thinking, *Isabo— why her? Why not Ivana?* To me the countess was a much better choice.

"You're questioning my choice," whispered the queen. "I see it in your eyes." She squeezed Isabo's hand. "My husband needs an advisor as much as he needs a wife, I fear. Roles I have fulfilled until my health prevented me from doing so—with disastrous consequences." The queen produced a resigned smile. "Isabo is the best choice. I trust her to put the good of the country above all else."

"I'm afraid the king loves you too much to ever agree to remarry," said the countess.

"I'm not dead yet, my dear. If it's the last thing I do, I will persuade him to do otherwise. That dear, stubborn husband of mine, he always listens to me in the end."

While the queen and the countess continued to argue about the king, my attention wandered to the armoire, which Isabo had left open. Taking advantage of the ladies' distraction, I made my way to the massive piece of furniture and began a quick survey of its contents. I knew what I was looking for, the deadly digitalis. To my astonishment, I saw that none of the bottles of herbs and essences stored in the armoire were labeled. *How can she know what is what? One has to be very experienced to be able to recognize these substances without their labels.*

Squinting, I focused on the row of bottles containing liquids. One in particular caught my attention. It was almost empty; still, there was enough of the clear syrupy liquid left at the bottom of the bottle for me to think that it could be essence of digitalis. I was about to reach for the bottle, when suddenly my entire body stiffened.

"What are you doing?" a voice snapped behind me.

I turned. Isabo stood a step from me. The aura of magic irradiating from her was suffocating me; I had to back away.

She immediately moved forth and shut the armoire's doors; in doing so she brushed up against me. A tingling sensation invaded my stomach. The feeling was so intense, I nearly gagged from the effect, and I had to summon all my inner strength just to remain upright.

"You are… expert at potion-making," I managed to utter without being sick.

She threw me a hostile look. "I know a few things. Now if you please, I must attend to the queen."

I bowed. I knew she had left before I rose, for the simple reason that my nausea was gone. While I was still bent I noticed a strange brownish-red object peeping out from behind the armoire's foot. I crouched and picked it up. *A root?* I turned it over. Shaped like a deformed human being, I recognized the root immediately. *Mandrake, a spell ingredient of choice.*

I replaced the root before rising and facing the ladies again. Only then did I notice Countess Ivana's persistent attempt to make eye contact with me. I also noticed her nervous fidgeting, her sudden pallor, and her trembling hands. Was she afraid? I wasn't sure, but at the very least she was uneasy about something. The queen's illness, I suppose. I gave her a smile of acknowledgment; then I made my farewell to the queen and left.

* * *

Milo awaited me at the door. I shot him the darkest look I could muster. He lowered his head. The message had passed. He knew what was coming. We needed to talk about those notes, but it would have to wait until we reached the privacy of my rooms, I decided. In silence, we began walking in the direction of "Draft Alley."

I hadn't taken five steps before I changed my mind. I stopped and faced Milo. "Explain yourself."

Milo opened his mouth, closed it, and then after a long thoughtful pause he spoke in a prudent voice. "I never thought they mattered. Two are written in a language I can't read."

"And what about the ones you can read? Can you imagine what would happen if you were caught with the wife of a lord? It's not only your life you're risking, Milo. It's also the honor of my name. As your master, I'm responsible for your misdeeds."

"I responded to none of their advances and invitations. I swear."

"Really. You tell me that all those early mornings when I couldn't find you anywhere, you were *not* with a lady?"

Milo's face turned so red I thought that steam was about to spew out of his ears. Without question, it was the most genuine expression of guilt I'd ever seen. Finally mustering the courage to speak, he said, "Not with any of the ladies who gave me a note."

"Who then?"

"Mirinka. She's a kitchen apprentice."

"A cook!"

"Yes, my lord. She works early in the morning preparing breakfast for the royal family. That's how we met—in the kitchen. I think she likes me, my lord. But if it displeases my lord, I won't see her again."

I stared at Milo, and although I knew I should have told him, *Yes, you better not see her again,* I said nothing. I had promised the queen not to punish him. How much did that promise cover? I didn't know. And how big was his fault really? He hid something from me. I didn't like that. *A cook. All this for a cook.* I was flabbergasted, to say the least. *A cook!* I felt my anger dissipating, and soon I found myself smiling at the whole thing. I would probably allow him to see her again. What harm could it do, really? I peeked at Milo. He looked anxious, awaiting my reply. *Well, he'll have to wait until we're in my room,* I decided. *That will do him some good.*

We were leaving the royal wing when I heard "*Psst…*" behind us.

I turned and was surprised to see Countess Ivana standing

at the corridor's junction. Throwing nervous glances around, she gestured frantically for us to approach.

"Countess Ivana," I began.

She placed a finger over her lips. "Shhhh!"

I nodded. We could be quiet; I still didn't understand why though. Milo and I walked silently to her.

After a careful inspection of the surroundings, she leaned toward us and whispered in urgency, "I'm taking a great risk by being here, so listen carefully. Be at the eastern side of the garden tonight past midnight. Please, be prudent and don't make a sound."

"Can I ask—"

"NO!" Eyes darting around nervously, she added, "We never spoke. I was never here." She began backing away from us; then in a rustling of petticoats, the countess spun around and ran away.

"What was that about?" whispered Milo.

"I have no idea. But one thing is sure; we have to ready ourselves for a night outside."

CHAPTER ELEVEN

For the rest of that day, my mind was occupied with thoughts of the night excursion. I had no idea what to expect. This was probably the reason why I decided to ask Diego to accompany me. Milo, as loyal and as brave as he was, wasn't allowed to use or even carry a weapon. Diego, on the other hand, had already proven his ability—mind you, he had waged battle with a handkerchief. However, I believed that any man who could do such a thing was apt to excel at swordplay.

When I announced my decision to Milo, the young eunuch was disappointed, but nonetheless understood why I'd made that choice. Despite his reasonable attitude, Milo still managed to warn me against Diego. According to him, the long-haired prince wasn't to be trusted. I had an inkling that Milo's dislike of Diego was generated, for the most part, by the prince's indiscriminate preference toward his lovers' gender. To my credit, Diego's tastes had little, if any, bearing on my opinion of him. I liked the man and trusted him… to a point.

As expected Prince Diego responded to my invitation with his usual exuberant enthusiasm. He would make this evening an event, beginning with choosing adequate garments. When he produced a full-length white mink coat,

I slapped my forehead out of sheer exasperation. Now, I regretted having asked him to come along. "You're not wearing that, Diego."

Planting his fists on his hips, he tapped his foot on the floor. "All right! What do you suggest I wear then?" By the sharpness of his tone, I deduced that he was vexed.

"Something black would be best. You know, so we won't be seen so easily?"

"Hmm... black. It's a boring color; I doubt I have anything in it. However, I believe I might have a midnight blue coat."

"Perfect! That will do."

"It's settled then."

"One last thing." I glanced at the sword he kept hidden beside the desk. "Take that sword with you and no other."

A crooked little smile curled Diego's lips. "As you wish, my prince."

* * *

"What's that noise?" whispered Diego in my ear.

"My teeth chattering," I replied.

We had been waiting in the dark coldness of the night for what now felt like hours to me. My feet were numb, my nose was running, and as for my ears, they were so frozen I had lost all feeling in them. At this point, I was beginning to think that this was all for nothing, except perhaps catching our deaths.

Shoving my gloved hands in my armpits, I peered through the surrounding darkness. From our hiding place, crouched in the snow behind a stack of barrels, I had a good view of the entire eastern side of the garden. Besides the stable and its corral, there wasn't much to see here. It was unfortunate, because there was nothing to obstruct our view. Moreover, the torches hooked on either side of the stable's doors bathed the area in a soft golden light, aiding our spying.

"Amir, are you sure this is the right place?"

"Yes. Very sure. Now hush."

"Why? There is—"

"Shhh! Someone's coming."

A shadow was moving nearby. I crossed my fingers, hoping it wasn't a guard again. They had walked by twice already, making their rounds. The shadow stopped, hesitated, then moved on toward the stable. With brisk steps, it cut across the golden light circle of the stable torches, and for the space of a few steps the shadow's features became clear.

A woman? I was more intrigued than shocked by that. Wrapped in a thick brown shawl with a broad yellow stripe running along the bottom, the woman quickly dashed out of the light. Yet, I still caught the fleeting glimpse of a pale cheek and a strand of limp brown hair. That was enough. "Lady Isabo," I breathed.

"What?"

"Shhhh!"

In complete silence, Diego and I watched Lady Isabo walk to the forest and vanish behind the trees. Only then did we rise from our hiding place.

Diego placed a hand on my shoulder. "I suppose we're going to follow her."

"Yes."

* * *

Following Isabo's tracks to the forest proved easy enough. Once inside the woods itself, things changed however. Amid the densely packed evergreen trees, the darkness was near total. It didn't take us long to lose her tracks, and shortly after, we realized that we had gotten lost too.

"Wonderful," complained Diego. "Frozen in the woods is not how I planned to die."

"How did you plan it?"

Diego raised his face to the night sky. "I always envisioned myself being killed by a jealous husband—or a scorned lover. Something in that vein."

I had noticed that since we had gotten lost, most of Diego's affectations had evaporated. Even his tone of voice had changed. It sounded deeper and firmer, I thought. "Why do you play this role, Diego? The one of a frivolous dandy." I asked, expecting him to deny doing so. I watched his shadow shake his head.

A sad chuckle escaped from him. "What we both want in life is so different. You desperately want to impress the king and marry a princess. While I want to disgust him and be free of his daughter. I've tried everything short of slapping the man in the face, that is. Nothing works."

"So I'm right, it's a role you play."

"Oh, don't fool yourself, Amir. I am a dandy and a libertine to boot. However, you are right to say that I'm playing a role. I've put on all these flourished, excessive manners in the hope that it would repulse the princess and the king. Unfortunately, not only did it fail to accomplish its goal, I am now forced to remain in this character I have created… and all in vain. The king is determined to forge an alliance with my father's kingdom, no matter what." As Diego came to stand beside me I became able to distinguish his features in the penumbra.

"Perhaps if you make a plea to your father—"

Diego's stare was so hard it shut me up. "Amir, I have two elder brothers. My father has no need for a third prince." Diego's expression became a mask of bitterness. "And certainly not one as troublesome as I am."

I thought about Diego's problem. Surely a solution could be obtained. "Perhaps you could create a scandal. I'm certain that a number of young noblemen would run to the king with grievances if disagreeable propositions were made to them."

"I thought of this too. Don't get me wrong, Amir. I would really like to be free of this wedding arrangement—but, I would also like to leave with my head still attached to my neck."

"Ah! Yes, that could be an unfortunate consequence of such grievances. Surely there are other things you could do that would solve your problem. Let me think." I mulled over Diego's situation for a moment. Sadly no obvious solution to his problem came to me. "Perhaps, you should just leave—run away. Have you thought of that option?"

"Yes. I could do that, if it didn't mean betraying my father and my country. You can *rightfully* accuse me of having committed many, *many* despicable acts. I will not deny that I am a person of questionable morals. Some people have even gone as far as to qualify me as a depraved individual—and I won't debate that either. But a traitor I am not."

A point of light peeking through the forest in the distance caught my eye. "Diego, do you see that light?"

"No—where?"

I walked left and the light vanished. I pushed further and there it was again.

Following closely in my footsteps, Diego bumped into my back, then looked over my shoulder. "Oh, I see it now. The trees were hiding it."

Without another word, we hurried in the direction of the light. Once we got closer we noticed that the light came from torches set atop long posts circling a small log cabin. As I gazed upon the cabin a sudden uneasiness seized me. Something was amiss here. This house didn't seem right... not right at all. The closer we got to the circle of light bathing the house, the stronger that feeling became. And when Diego approached the torches, that growing feeling of uneasiness morphed into one of imminent danger.

"Wait, wait, wait," I whispered. I grabbed Diego's coat and pulled him backward before he could cross the torches' circle. Toppling him on his back, I pressed my gloved hand over his mouth.

"Shhh," I shushed against his cheek.

Bemused, Diego stared at me with a blank face, then his expression turned to anger and he began struggling in my grip.

"Ssstop…" I hissed under my breath. "I think this might be the witch's house. The Baba Yaga."

Diego went limp. Not taking any chances, I waited until he nodded to me, showing he understood the danger, before releasing my grip on him. Silently rising to kneeling positions, we both stared at the cabin.

Two things were bothering me about this home. First, it seemed detached from the ground, and looked as if it was floating just above the snow. Second, the four skulls set on its roof, two facing front, two at the back, appeared almost… alive. I could swear I had seen red glowing flashes coming out of those empty eye sockets.

Either you're crazy, my inner voice nagged, *or you're becoming as superstitious as a peasant. The peasants!* I thought, recalling our meeting. One of them had said something about the house being able to see.

Crazy! Mad! Mad! Mad! the voice hollered in my head. I shut my eyes, ground my teeth, and plugged my ears with my hands. I remained in that position, telling myself that I wasn't mad, until the voice had subsided and peace had returned to my mind. Then I let out a long sigh of relief. When I turned, ready to move on, I saw Diego staring at me. A look of deep concern twisted his face.

"I'm fine," I whispered before he could ask. I then peered at the cabin again. *Only one way to know if I'm mad or not.* I examined the ground surrounding us. Nothing but snow. Snow would have to do then. I quickly made a snowball, then threw it inside the torches' circle. The snowball plopped on the left side of the circle a short distance from the cabin.

Immediately, the skulls' eye sockets glowed as red as burning coals. With a complaint of twisting planks, the cabin rose into the air on... two giant chicken legs. No matter how much I stared at those yellow scaly skinned legs, with thighs the diameters of tree trunks, I still couldn't believe my eyes. I watched those monstrous chicken legs carry the cabin to the spot where my snowball had landed and viciously stomp and scratch the ground. Once satisfied that nothing underfoot could have survived, the cabin returned to its previous position.

Diego and I exchanged petrified looks.

"I'm not getting near that," he silently mouthed to me.

Turning my focus toward the cabin, I studied its construction. The front door and the back window were right under the skulls' eyes, therefore inaccessible. That left the side window, which had no skulls above it. Yet, I knew they would still see me if I tried to go near that window... unless. I made another snowball and threw it toward the window. Just as I thought, the skulls caught a glimpse of the snowball's shadow as it passed in front of one of the torches.

They didn't see the ball. They saw a change in the torch's light when the ball flew by. "Diego, make snowballs. Make as many as you can."

To my surprise, he obeyed without question. In the meantime, I had made some myself. I pitched my first snowball at the nearest torch post and missed. My second ball hit the post right under the torch. My third struck the torch, extinguishing its fire.

"Smart," whispered Diego, and began throwing snowballs too. We threw snowballs until enough torches were dead to form a dark semicircle on the cabin side. At that point, we stopped throwing balls and waited for the cabin, which had been running madly after our projectiles like, well, like a chicken without a head, to settle down again. Once the cabin had retuned in its original plot, I threw a last snowball. It fell on the ground just under the cabin's side window.

Nothing happened. The cabin stayed in place.

Gathering my courage, I moved ahead immediately, fearing that if I waited and analyzed the situation any further there was a strong chance that I might change my mind and not go. After all, this was totally insane. Then again, maybe I *was* crazy.

Regardless of my apprehension, I made my way to the edge of the torches' circle without being noticed by the skulls. Then, careful not to make any noise, I slowly inched toward the window. It was only when I stood right in front of it that one thought came to my mind. What if the cabin could sense my touch as well as it could see me?

As I was debating what to do next, Diego pulled to my side and, without further delay, grabbed the window's frame and opened it.

Struck by fear, I gasped.

"What?" he breathed, with one leg already through the opened window.

"Nothing. Just hurry in."

In no time at all we were both inside the cabin. A warm orange glow illuminated the room. Most of it came from two old lamps: one placed on a square table and the other resting on a shelf near the door. The rest emanated from the fireplace. I looked around. The room we were in was cozy. Strange, I thought, I didn't expect a witch to have a cozy home. There was a pine table with two stools, and a rocking chair was placed in front of the fireplace. Not much, I thought. I checked the only other room of the house, a bedroom containing a small straw-filled bed and a dresser. My eyes went to the window set between the two pieces of furniture. I crossed the room and peered outside. I could see a fence on that side of the house, a sort of enclosure. What could she be keeping in there? In this darkness, I couldn't distinguish anything.

"What kind of animal does a witch keep?" The villagers had spoken of horses. A clearing in the cloudy night sky allowed some rays of moonlight to filter through. Enough to catch a glimpse of something big, black, and immobile… like the mouth of a cave. The cloud moved back in front of the moon and everything disappeared into darkness again. Not expecting to see anything more, I returned to the main room.

"Well," I said, "the witch is not here."

"The Baba Yaga, you mean," mocked Diego.

"Whatever her name is, she's not in."

"She can't be far, she left her shawl behind." Diego plucked a brown wool shawl from the rocking chair.

I took the shawl from his hands; it looked familiar to me. Turning it around, I found a broad yellow line at its bottom. "That's Isabo's shawl. That's hers. I'm sure of it."

"Isabo was here," Diego said. "Why would she come see a witch?"

"Maybe she's the witch."

Diego's mouth formed a perfect circle. "Oh!"

I squeezed the shawl between my hands. Something didn't fit. Something was missing, as for what exactly, I didn't know.

The *clank* of a cooking pot lid tore me from my thoughts. I looked for Diego and found him with the pot lid in one hand and a ladle in the other, stirring the cauldron hanging over the fireplace. "Diego, leave that alone."

"I am curious to see what she's cooking—Ahh!" Diego jumped back in horror. The pot lid and the ladle hit the floor in a cacophony of metallic clink-clank. "Witch's brew! Horrid witch's brew!" Hiding his nose in the crease of his arm, he pointed to the cauldron. "Go look! You have to see that."

I picked up the ladle and reluctantly approached the cauldron. At first sight, the liquid inside had the thick, rich, brown appearance of a common stew. Taking a deep breath,

I plunged the ladle in the steaming stew. A powerful jolt of energy shot through my entire body. At once all my muscles and nerves became as taut as the string of a bow. Frozen stiff, I watched powerless as the stew transformed itself into a green viscous concoction with what looked like a human ear and a foot floating in it. Before I could recoil in disgust, a white flash of light blinded me. As the light began dimming, an odd sensation invaded my body. I felt so strange, so light; it was as if I had no substance. I looked down and saw myself staring in the cauldron. I saw myself as if I were floating... high up on the ceiling. Panic seized me, and I fought to return to my body, like a drowning man desperately swimming to the shore. I was getting closer and closer to myself. I stretched my hand; I could almost touch my shoulder. In a last ditch effort, I kicked and pulled, then finally my fingertips made contact with my shoulder, and I felt sucked right back inside myself. But as soon as I had reentered my body, another jolt of energy shook me and a series of images flew across my eyes: a sea of riders galloping across a field; a vast stormy ocean; a marvelous city with dazzling white towers; a snow-covered mountain; a small, bald man in a deep yellow robe smiling at me, welcoming me. Then I saw Eva's face. Tears covered her cheeks. Suddenly her image vanished, replaced by the vision of blood—blood all over the snow. And there was that scream. It wouldn't stop.

"*AAAAAH-AAAAH-AAAAAH!*"

"Amir!"

"*AAAAAH....*"

SMACK! My head flew to the side. A burning sensation on my cheek followed.

"Amir, wake up!"

I blinked. Everything was blurry and distorted. Yet, somehow, I knew I was still in the Baba's house. *What am I doing sprawled on the floor?* I thought, confused. As my vision began to clear, Diego's alarmed face appeared above mine.

The next thing I saw was his hand rising to strike me again. "NO—DON'T. Once was enough."

Relief flashed across Diego's face, and he let himself fall back on his heels. "Oh my goodness, for a moment there, my friend, I thought you were going to die."

"What happened?"

Diego brushed a strand of hair away from his face. "You were looking in that cauldron, and then suddenly you started screaming. I tried pulling you away from the damn thing, but you were stuck there. I couldn't move you. I had to ram you down. Amir, I thought you weren't going to wake up."

I cupped my stinging cheek. "Well, clearly you found a way of breaking this spell."

"Was it really a spell?"

I shook my head. "Honestly, I don't know what that was." There was one thing I now knew though. Eva was in danger, terrible danger. And my deepest fear was that I wouldn't be able to return to the castle in time to protect her.

CHAPTER TWELVE

Fortunately, soon after we left the Baba Yaga's cabin, a cold north wind blew away the cloud cover and moonlight beamed down upon us, illuminating our steps and rendering our return to the castle an easier feat. This brought me very little relief. I desperately wanted to be in the castle now, right this minute. I wanted to see Eva safe. This was my main focus. My disinterest for everything else must have been written on my face, because Diego gave me one glance when we began our trip back and kept his mouth shut for its duration. That was rather unusual for him. The man seemed to know every tale ever told. So we walked in silence, me in front, plowing through the snow as fast as my legs could manage, and Diego behind. We moved rapidly and quietly, with only the sound of our heavy breathing disturbing the silence of the night.

Finally, the castle fell into view. I was glad we'd reached our destination because I was exhausted, out of breath, and my legs wouldn't cease trembling. But when I entered the castle, my mood turned sour as I realized that I had no way of contacting Eva. I couldn't burst into her chambers like a vulgar thief. Well, to begin with, I didn't even know where her chambers were. I looked at Diego. *But he knows the way.*

"Diego, can you guide me to Eva's chambers?" I knew his

answer was going to be *no* before he opened his mouth. His furrowed brows and overall expression of horror contorting his face made that clear.

"Amir, there are certain ladies' chambers in this castle that even I won't attempt to enter."

"Please, I must see her. I need to know that she's safe."

"No, my friend. It's too dangerous a venture. If the king gets wind of your presence there… goodness, you'll be killed on sight."

"I'm willing to take that risk."

Diego shook his head. "I can't help you—not for this. You're on your own, my friend."

Fists closed, I glared at him. "How dare you call me a friend if you won't help me? Leave then! You're not my friend at all."

Diego sighed. "Yes, I am. But you're too angry right now to see it. Tomorrow maybe." This being said, he turned and left.

Alone in a dark corridor, I cursed Diego. *That stinking dandy! He's no friend of mine. I should set fire to his wardrobe; that would be a relief for everyone's eyes.* Infuriated by what I conceived as Diego's betrayal, I screamed, I wanted to break something. Finding nothing in the corridor to break, I directed my rage at its meager decoration. I ripped a tapestry off the wall and threw it on the floor. Then I kicked it a few times. It did not make me feel any better, only a little ashamed of myself. "What am I supposed to do now? Ask a guard where she sleeps? That will raise suspicions."

As I was wondering what to do, I heard a *"Psst."* I turned.

Countess Ivana tiptoed out of a dark corner. "I've waited for you," she said in an anxious voice. "Have you found something? Was I right to suspect Isabo of wrong doing?"

"Yes, you were."

"Is she a witch?"

I scratched my beard. "I'm not sure what she is. It's just... I have the feeling something bad will happen tonight."

"Me too!" Countess Ivana looked so relieved it was as though I had pulled a sharp thorn out of her side. "I thought I was mad to think so. I've tried warning the queen and the king about her... strange ways. But they won't listen to me." Slapping her thigh with a fist in frustration, she added, "As it stands now, there's nothing I can do. Nothing!"

She raised pleading eyes to me. "But you, Prince Amir, you can help. I heard the plea you made to Prince Diego. I can lead you to Princess Eva's chambers. At least she will be safe tonight."

My heart soared. "You would do that?"

She nodded. "I must warn you though. This is a very dangerous endeavor."

Taking her hands into mine, I kissed them with all my gratitude. "Danger matters not, Countess. I am willing to face any peril set in front of me. Please, lead me to her."

* * *

As I tiptoed toward Eva's majestic white canopy bed, the irrationality of the situation struck me. Why didn't I just knock or scratch at the door like I wanted? Why did I listen to Ivana and enter Eva's bedroom uninvited like a common ruffian? True, I might have awakened someone else by knocking, as Ivana said. Still, invading a lady's chambers like this was highly improper. Oh well, it was too late to go back now. With this in mind, I crossed the space separating me from the bed.

Slowly leaning over the sleeping princess, I gazed at her enchanting profile, her small nose, her half-opened mouth. Eva looked so peaceful, so lovely amid those pillows of soft white linen. Gently, I brushed gold curls away from her cheeks. The touch of my fingertips on her skin awoke Eva.

Her eyes opened wide, and she stared at me in panic. At that instant, I realized that she was about to scream. Quickly, I covered her mouth with my hand.

"Eva," I whispered, while she punched, kicked, and scratched me like a wild cat. "Eva, it's me. Amir."

Recognition replaced the panic in her eyes. Eva stopped fighting and collapsed into her pillows. She tugged at the hand I still kept over her mouth.

"Shhhh…" I made with a finger on my lips.

She nodded.

I lifted my hand.

"You scared me half to death," she hissed. "What possessed you to do such a thing? I thought I was being abducted."

"That's why I'm here, to protect you."

"Protect me from what?"

"From danger—danger coming from within this castle." I told Eva all I had learned tonight, I told her of my fear, my suspicions also.

"Isabo—a witch! Don't be silly. She's a blessing."

"Eva, I wouldn't make up such a story. Isabo was in that house. Evidence of her presence was there. I saw it with my own eyes. Why do you think I would risk my life coming here? I had to make sure you were safe. I just had to. I couldn't bear the thought that someone might hurt you; it was driving me insane."

"What you're doing now is terribly dangerous, Amir."

I took Eva's hands into mine and kissed them softly. "I care not for my own safety. I care for yours. I love you more than anything in the world, and I would gladly risk my life a thousand times to see you safe."

Pushing back her thick blankets, Eva sat up in her bed. She wore a fairly transparent, lacy white nightgown. My eyes immediately lowered to her small perky breasts with their dark pink nipples, now clearly visible through the thin airy fabric.

Eva cupped my cheeks in her hands and raised my face to hers. "Amir," she murmured against my ear. Her warm breath caressed my skin, sending goose bumps along my entire body. "Is my safety *really* the reason why you're in my chambers tonight? Or have you another motive, a lovelier one?"

Our eyes met, our lips followed. Molten lava shot through my veins, warming my body and soul. My hands glided to Eva's narrow waist then traveled up to her breast. She gasped. My kisses became harder, my tongue plunging deeper into her mouth. We fell back into her pillows.

For a long moment, all we did was kiss, our tongues exploring each other's mouths at length. Then I rose up to my knees and, with Eva's help, I undressed rapidly. Even though the room was cold—the fireplace held only embers by now—I felt burning hot. Slipping under the cover, I began the delightful task of undoing the many little bows fastening Eva's nightgown. I relished untying every single one as if it held some lovely treasure, which they did in fact. They held Eva's young supple body. Her skin was soft and creamy, her belly flat, her hips firm and round. My mouth explored every sensual curve of her body, and my tongue played upon her most sensitive part until she was moaning with pleasure. Only then did I gently lie upon her and, with the greatest of care, pushed myself into her. Eva emitted a small whimper of pain, yet urged me to go on. I thrust myself deeper into her. Keeping my eyes fixed on her face, I made love to her as tenderly as my burning passion permitted. I had dreamt of this moment for so long, I didn't want it to end. And when it finally did end, it was in a glorious climax, after which we both fell back heaving, our bodies glistening in sweat.

I was almost immediately ready to start over. And to my amazement, so was Eva. This time, however, our lovemaking was far less careful. This time, there was a feverous hunger in our kisses and caresses that we had not experienced before, an unabashed passion that brought us to a complete and satisfied exhaustion.

As we lay closely intertwined together in her bed, Eva's back resting against my chest and my arms surrounding her shoulders, she began to sob.

A sickening fear seized me. "Eva, my love, what's the matter. Have I caused you some pain? Do you regret—?"

"NO. I regret nothing. Stop worrying, Amir. I regret nothing. I swear." She took a long hiccupping breath, turned around in the bed and buried herself in my arms.

Totally mystified by her reaction, I hugged her as tightly as I could, brushed her hair back, and kissed her forehead in the hope it would appease her. "I love you," I whispered to her. "I love you more than life."

"I know," she replied in a sleepy voice.

* * *

BANG. BANG. BANG. "Princess! Princess Eva!"

The door…

My eyes flew open. For the space of a breath I didn't know where I was. The room was dark. It was still night or maybe early morning, very early. I glanced around. In spite of the ambient penumbra, I could tell this wasn't my room, or my bed for that matter—it was far too comfortable. Then my gaze fell on Eva still clutched in my arms. As the memory of last night returned to the forefront of my mind, I began smiling. Oh, what a magical night it had been.

A ruckus coming from outside the chamber's door brought me back to reality.

"Eva, answer!" a voice boomed behind the door.

My stomach flopped. That was the king's voice. The stomping of heavy footsteps followed. By the sounds of it, there were at least a dozen men on the other side of that door.

"Eva!" I murmured, shaking her awake. "Eva, your father is at the door."

At those words her sleepy face turned into a mask of fear. "Grab your things, Amir. Hurry, hurry," she begged, while slipping into her nightgown.

I was already on the floor, gathering my scattered clothes, when I heard the king shouting, "BRING THAT DOOR DOWN!"

Without further thinking, I rolled under the bed, bringing my clothes with me. Lying naked on the icy marble floor, I watched the door burst open and armed men pour in.

"Father! What is this intrusion?" Eva exclaimed in false outrage. It was a good bit of acting, I thought while shivering from cold under the bed.

"Eva! Oh my dear daughter, you're still here." The king sounded extremely relieved.

"Where else should I be, Father? What is the meaning of this? What happened?"

"It's your sister, Thalia." The king paused, as if the words were too painful to say. "She... she's been kidnapped."

"NO! PLEASE NOOO!" Eva yelled. She fell down on the bed, crying.

Stuck under the bed, I felt awful. I wanted to come out of my hiding place and comfort her. But I knew this was impossible—and I doubted that my getting killed right then and there by the king's men, which was sure to happen, would've comforted Eva very much.

Grinding my teeth, I stared ahead. What I saw then made my blood run cold. My turban, the darn thing was still on the floor beside the bed. I had forgotten to pick it up. I was doomed. It was just a matter of time before someone spotted it, because there were far too many people walking about this room not to. Holding my breath, I watched a pair of blue satin high-heeled shoes walk straight to my turban—*Diego?*

"Your Highness, I have a suggestion," said the person with the blue shoes.

I'd guessed right. It was Diego; I recognized his affected tone. I watched his feet move into a flourished curtsey, and in the process the left one kicked my turban under the bed.

"Yes, Prince Diego," said the king.

"Now that we know that the princess is safe, perhaps we should give her some privacy."

"No. I want guards with her at all times."

I winced. I couldn't stay under her bed forever.

The king cleared his throat, paced around the room, then added. "I want every corner of this room searched."

I let my face drop onto my turban and sighed. Now it was certain. I was dead.

As the guards began spreading throughout the room, a high-pitched shriek echoed in the nearby corridor. Then I heard Diego shouting, "Your Majesty, the beast, the beast!"

"Where?" roared the king.

"Running down the corridor... I think it was going toward the garden door."

I silently thanked Diego for creating this diversion. It was a daring initiative—Diego was braver than I thought. The man kept surprising me. *I owe him an apology. He is truly my friend.* I heard the footsteps of the guards as they rushed outside the room, and then Eva's face popped upside down at the edge of the bed.

"Get out now," she breathed in a tone of urgency. "Hurry, before they come back."

I crawled out from under the bed, dragging my clothes along with me.

"This way, Amir." Eva was at the left corner of her room holding the servants' door open. "Don't stand there. Go! You'll dress later."

I didn't argue. I dashed into the passage completely naked. The door closed behind me and everything went dark.

* * *

Wasting no time, I dressed quickly, then hurried in the direction of the servants' quarters. Two things struck me when I came out of the passage. First, the servants' quarters were boiling with activity. Everyone in here seemed in a state of panic. Second, an out-of-breath Diego waited for me by the door.

Gulping air like a horse after a sprint, he waved a handkerchief at me while gripping his side. "I… I had to… to run. From… from the garden to here… all the way."

I grinned. "I see that."

Diego shook his head. "I have to admit I've misjudged you. You're far more audacious than I gave you credit for. Do you know how close you came to being discovered?"

"I was there, Diego. I know."

Diego produced a devious, yet charming, little smile. "Well, I hope she was worth the risk."

I was about to say yes and praise Eva's wonderful attributes and passionate nature when I realized that this was exactly what Diego wanted. He was fishing for lurid details. That was too bold. So instead of answering, I bowed to him. "Thank you for coming to my rescue with that diversion."

"Actually, about that." Diego grabbed my elbow and pulled me away from the servants' ears. "I intended to throw the king and his men on a wild goose chase, so you'd be able to escape… but it turned out quite differently."

I frowned. "What? You found Thalia?"

"No. She's still missing. We found someone else though."

"Explain yourself better."

"We caught her."

"Who?"

"Isabo. When I came through the garden door, with the king and his guards in tow, Isabo was already in the process of being arrested. Someone else, not me, saw her going out and rang the alarm."

"The alarm—Why? What was she doing?"

"She was leading a giant bear to the forest. I saw the tracks in the snow, Amir. I saw the beast too—its backside anyway."

"Are you sure that's what you saw?"

"In the dim dawn light it looked like a bear, big and dark. I only caught a glimpse of it because it was already entering the forest when we got outside. From what I was told, Isabo sent the beast off before the guards could kill it."

"What about Isabo? Did she try running away too?"

"I don't know. The guards already had her by the scruff of the neck and were leading her to the dungeons to be questioned, when I entered the garden. She fought back all the way to the castle though, and made threats against the queen, the king, the entire royal family really. She said they would all die if they imprisoned her, starting with the queen."

Too shaken by the recent events to make sense of what I was hearing, I asked again, "Are you sure of this?"

"Amir, I witnessed the whole thing, saw it with my own eyes. The woman is a sorceress."

CHAPTER THIRTEEN

Part of that morning was a blur to me. My head was too fuzzy to recall what else Diego and I had talked about. However, I remembered parting ways with him, and after that I somehow managed to shuffle my feet to my rooms.

I'd just gotten to bed after my night's adventure and desperately needed rest, when Milo burst into my bedroom.

"My lord, my lord!" he shouted from the foot of my bed.

Rubbing my eyes, I yelled, "WHAT?"

"My lord, something terrible happened."

"I know," I grumbled. "Thalia is missing and Isabo—"

"No, my lord, not that. It's something else."

I sat straight up in my bed. "Eva! Something happened to Eva after I left?"

"No. It's the queen, my lord."

"The queen?"

"She's dead, my lord. She passed away an hour ago."

"What! She's… no! That can't be true… that's.…" I was too shocked to say anything more. I had expected the queen's health to improve now that Isabo wasn't there to feed her daily doses of poison.… This didn't make any sense to me, none at all. After most of my shock had subsided, I looked up at Milo who was wringing his hands nervously beside my bed. "Milo, have you seen your cook this morning?"

Milo's face became void of all expression. "No. She found someone else."

"Oh—I'm sorry."

Milo shrugged. "Fine by me! It's not like we'd planned to raise a family."

To be perfectly blunt, I didn't know what to reply to that, so I continued as if it hadn't been said. "Milo, when you went out this morning you saw *other* people, servants, guards, all sorts of people. I know I've told you to never spread rumors; however, I think we can make an exception for this time. What did you hear so far about the queen's death? What are the people saying about it?"

Surprised, Milo stared at me silently for a moment, then cleared his throat. "That it's the witch's revenge. It's pretty much the opinion of everyone in the castle. Oh, and there's a mourning ceremony later today. You're expected to attend, my lord. And from what I've gathered, it would be best if you wore dark-colored clothes."

* * *

Fortunately, I had some dark-colored clothes. Dressed in midnight blue from head to toe, I made my way to the throne room where the mourning ceremony was being held.

Although I arrived there with very little time to spare, the tense, gloomy atmosphere of the throne room felt so tangible that I found it hard to actually cross the entrance. It was as if I had struck a solid wall of despair. Right now, entering the room wasn't an appealing prospect. Choosing to delay my entrance, I just stood in the doorway and surveyed the dark gathering of nobles clustered at one end of the room. They resembled a murder of crows in their black garments. All those nobles bore solemn expressions, except for Baron

Molotoff. The man's expression never changed, it seemed. He still had the same stoic cold air as always. Apparently the queen's death left him unmoved. I turned to Diego, who was standing nearby. His handsome face was disguised by a mask of sorrow. Considering what I knew of him, I couldn't help wondering if his grief was an act. Had he known the queen well enough to be this affected by her passing? Was he mourning Thalia? I knew Diego wished to be free of her; therefore Thalia's disappearance should suit him just fine. So why the long face then? That was strange, I thought.

I directed my attention to the other end of the room, more specifically to the small raised dais. There stood the royal family... or what was left of it. Only three members remained: the king, Eva, and Lars. I observed that the king and Lars both wore broad black armbands over their dark purple coats. As for Eva, she was dripping in black lace. Even her head, which hung low, was hidden under a veil of black lacy fabric. The sight of this decimated family brought some unpleasant memories to my mind, memories of my own family, and how it had been decimated by an evil curse.

Reluctantly, I made my way to the small dais and bowed in front of the mourning group. "You have my deepest condolences, Your Majesty. I do share your grief."

To my utter disbelief, the king smiled kindly at me, and then he came down the dais and approached me. "I know you understand our pain. You've lived through something similar to this yourself."

I thought it best to speak as little as possible. So I just nodded.

The king shook his head. "I cannot believe that we nurtured that viper in our midst for all this time. And to think that if she hadn't been caught, I might have married her." Fists clenched, the king bared his teeth in a rictus of ire and disgust.

"Were there signs of her evil nature?" I asked.

The king regarded Countess Ivana, now standing at Eva's side consoling her as best she could. Regret darkened the king's face. "We were warned. But we didn't listen."

Hushed murmurs coming from the assembled mourners made me turn. The two barbarians were entering the throne room. They marched directly to the king. Stopping right in front of him, the barbarians raised praying hands to their mouths then foreheads and finally pointed their hands toward the king's heart. Although the gesture was done in total silence, it was clearly an act of respect and empathy. I watched the pair as they walked in front of Eva and repeated the same gesture. Once it was done, they just turned around and withdraw from the throne room.

I brought my attention back to the king. "What will happen to Isabo now?"

"Now? Nothing. For the next three days, all activity in the castle will cease as we mourn the queen. Even Isabo's execution is being delayed. The witch will burn after our last farewell to the queen."

Supported by Countess Ivana on one side and by Lars on the other, Eva slowly made her way to us. She extended a pale, trembling hand to me. I gripped it in mine. Her palm felt cold, her fingers icy.

"Why?" Eva sobbed. "Why hurt us? We've only been kind to her."

This fact was bothering me too. I looked at the king. "I'm asking myself the same questions. Why would Isabo attack the princesses? What did she want to accomplish by committing those crimes? What was her goal?"

Lars snorted. "Pf, stupid question! Evil doesn't need goals."

I thinned my lips. "Evil always has a goal—always."

"You're right, Prince Amir. It does," agreed the king, which made Lars red with anger. "Think I know that goal. I was the goal, or more exactly the Sorvinkian throne was the goal."

I waited for the king to say more, but he stayed silent. I turned to Eva. She was clutching my hand so tightly, it was as if she feared losing me if she let go. She had lost so much already. My eyes met Countess Ivana's. Her gaze was tired and empty; clearly those were the eyes of someone who hadn't slept for days.

"I should have figured it out," The countess said in a remorseful tone. "If only I had put it together before, the princesses would still be with us. I knew Isabo heard the king tell our beloved queen that he would only remarry if he had no children. But as he had beautiful ones, he saw no need to remarry. I knew Isabo heard this because I was there too."

The king emitted a bitter chuckling sound. "The worst in all this is that my dear departed wife had finally convinced me to remarry. I consented to it two days ago. Isabo didn't need to harm Thalia. She had won."

Lars blanched. He had just realized how close he had come to losing his position as the heir to the throne. Because if the king had remarried, chances were good that he might have had sons.

Straightening himself, Lars approached the king and snapped to attention like a good little soldier. "Have no fear, Uncle, as long as I breathe the Anderson name will rule Sorvinka."

Grasping Lars by the shoulders, the king kissed his nephew on both cheeks. "Yes. You're right. I do have a son in you, Lars."

Now feeling secure in his position, Lars beamed at us. And when the king returned to his throne, Lars trailed behind him like a puppy.

My thoughts turned to Isabo. Obviously, she didn't know about the king's decision to remarry. Otherwise she would still be free and Thalia would be with us. This brought a new question to my mind. Where were the kidnapped princesses? Perhaps they were still alive and held captive somewhere.

The chances of that were slim, yet I thought I should look into it. But first I tried to comfort Eva. I wished I could do more than just hold her hand. I wished I could take her in my arms and gently rock her to sleep. I stayed with her as long as conventions permitted me, and then I left for the garden where Isabo had been arrested.

* * *

The ground around the castle and its courtyard had been trampled by too many feet to provide any valid clues. However, once I reached the edge of the forest the bear's tracks became clear and undisturbed. I followed them to the collapsed shelter Eva and I had visited a few days ago. By the quantities of tracks visible in this area, the bear had wandered in and out of the shelter several times. I also noted that a group of people had gathered here and held some sort of meeting. At least six different footprints marred the snow. *So, Isabo has accomplices.* Now it all made sense. Isabo had led them inside the castle with their trained bears. While the bears created diversions, the accomplices abducted the princesses. Yes, it had to have happened that way. Isabo simply couldn't kidnap the twins all by herself. Neither could she subdue Thalia, who was much bigger than she was.

I peered inside the half-collapsed shelter. The bears had gone on quite a rampage in there. Fir branches were strewn about, the heavy stone cup was toppled over, and ashes from the fire were scattered on the snow like black rain. The destruction was so complete, I questioned if the beast had not turned on its master.

"This animal was enraged," I said aloud. I wondered why. Then again, I shouldn't be surprised that an animal behaved like... well, an animal. I shrugged and returned to the castle's ground.

I might not have learned much by following the bear's

tracks, but what I did learn was very important: Isabo had accomplices. Now, I just needed to find who and where they were.

* * *

I was approaching the stables when I heard the shrill neighs of horses in distress. Sure enough, Lars and his friends were inside the enclosure, tormenting the wild ponies. I couldn't say I was surprised by what I was witnessing; however, I was certainly annoyed by it and rather aggravated. Their behavior was despicable.

March on, Amir. This is none of your business. March on. Of course, that's not what I did. I let out a heavy sigh, and despite the voice of reason in my head telling me I was a damn fool to meddle in something that didn't concern me, I walked up to the horse pen anyway.

"LARS!" I shouted. "LEAVE THOSE HORSES ALONE!"

Shocked by my commanding tone, he and his friends nearly seized up. Quite frankly, I was shocked too. That wasn't how I should have addressed the situation, or Lars, for that matter. I shook my head. I used to be so careful about those things. What was happening to me? Was I losing my head or just my manners?

Regaining his countenance, Lars glared at me. "What is it to you? These horses aren't yours."

"True. But they're not yours either, Lars. And why are you scaring them like that? Surely you and your friends can find a more dignified activity to distract yourselves."

Folding his arms over his chest, Lars raised his chin. "You're right, Prince Amir. We need something more entertaining. Your people are known as great horsemen, and your desert breed as the fastest of all horses, isn't that a fact?"

I winced. I could smell a trap from where I stood. But I had no idea what direction I should take not to get caught in it though. "Yes," I risked. "Our horses are known for their speed and agility."

"Would you care to test this knowledge?"

Aha, there it was! That was a poor trap; the setup was rather clumsy too. Then again, Lars wasn't a genius. "No thank you. I have other things on my mind at the moment."

Lars grinned like a monkey. "Uh-huh, that's what I thought. It's a tale. Like the ones you told at dinner."

"My dear duke, I know what you're attempting to do. And believe me, I won't let myself be caught in your argument."

"Pf, pitiful excuse! You're just afraid your horses won't be able to run in the snow."

"If our horses can run in sand, they can run in snow."

With a side-glance to his friend, Lars declared, "Then the fault rests in your ability as a rider."

"I'm an excellent rider."

"Prove it."

Lord, why won't he stop, I thought, rubbing my temples. Lars was like a dog on a bone with this. I was wondering what was wrong with that boy, which was a lot in my opinion, when I noticed the subtle glances Lars kept throwing at his friends and how these young noblemen where watching him with semi-bored expressions. It was then that I realized that Lars was trying to impress them. I winced internally. *Not a good sign for a future king.* Kings should never behave that way; it was the nobles who should try to impress the king, not the other way around.

I looked at Lars, and despite myself I felt pity for that insecure, *and oh so tenacious,* boy. Perhaps I should just accept his challenge and get it over with. It's not like those heavy-footed Sorvinkian horses of his could beat mine in a race anyway. In addition, losing face might do Lars some good. I smiled. "How do you suggest I prove this, Lars?"

"By competing in a Sorvinkian race against me."

"Fine! All right then, I'll do it."

Lars's friends cheered loudly, while Lars rubbed his hands together in jubilation as if he had just played me a good trick.

A sudden anxiousness came over me. Maybe I should have thought this through before accepting. At the very least, I should've asked what was involved in a Sorvinkian race. I shook my head. Here I was, worrying again over nothing. All races were more or less alike. This one couldn't be that much different—it just couldn't.

CHAPTER FOURTEEN

After Lars and I had both agreed to delay the race long enough for us to change out of our mourning clothes, I hurried to my room. Choosing my most comfortable riding clothes, a loose-fitting, dark tan ensemble, I changed rapidly, then grabbed my coat. I was ready to return outside when I heard someone knocking at the door.

Milo rushed to see who it was, then came back. "It's Prince Diego. I can tell him that you're not here, if you wish," he said, sounding very eager to do just that.

I thought about it briefly, and said, "No, let him in."

Milo's shoulders sagged. With a grim look on his face, he opened the door.

Diego marched in like a man on a mission. "Amir, I heard a disturbing rumor. Is it true that you're going to race against Lars?"

"It's not a rumor. I'm on my way there right now."

Clutching his head with both hands, Diego lamented loudly, "OH, for the good graces of the gods! Have you completely lost your mind?" Normally, I tend to ignore Diego's emotional outburst, but I had to admit that the look of distress on his face scared me a little. Then I recalled the mourning ceremony and thought this was just another one of his acts.

I stared at him coldly. "Diego, you can stop your charade. I know you care as much for me as you did for Thalia. Your acting might fool the king—doesn't fool me though. So stop it!"

Diego recoiled in shock. "How dare you question the honesty of my feelings? I do care about Thalia's well-being."

"Really? Two days ago you were ready to break her heart."

Diego's eyes narrowed to thin slits. "And I still would do it. I'd break her heart ten times over if you'd let me. But hear this, Amir, no matter what people say, nobody has ever died from a broken heart—that's a fairy tale. However, what kidnappers can do to a young innocent girl is another story. Thalia cannot withstand such abominable treatment, Amir. She's not like your Eva. She's not strong."

I watched fear replace anger in Diego's eyes, then anger return with a vengeance. "That witch, that evil witch. Oh how I would love to strangle her." Raising clawed hands in front of him, Diego mimicked strangling someone—Isabo I presumed.

I had to say that if Diego was acting, it was the best performance I'd ever seen. He certainly had me convinced. Even Milo, who openly disliked Diego, seemed to believe him.

"Diego," I began, "I'm sorry for having doubted your feelings. I apologize."

Diego waved a hand around in a dismissive manner. "I've played a role for so long that sometimes I don't know when to stop. Honestly, Amir, Thalia's kidnapping affects me more than I'd like to admit. There, I said it! I, Diego Del Osiega, Prince of Pioval, have grown fond of that fat little brat."

Brat? I wrinkled my nose in confusion. That was an unusual way of speaking about a loved one—again, Diego was an unusual man.

Diego produced a sad smile. "Not many people here like me. As you know, I have very few friends." He paused and gently placed a hand on my shoulder. "It upsets me when one of them goes and puts himself in peril without reason."

"I'm not in peril, Diego. It's only a race. I—"

"It's a Sorvinkian race."

"And?"

"You will lose."

"Why? I'm an excellent rider. Why is everybody questioning my riding skills? That's becoming insulting."

Exasperated, Diego let out a long hissing breath. "You won't be riding, Amir."

"OH—what will I do then?"

"Drive a troika."

The corners of my mouth dipped downward. "What's a troika?"

"Come, follow me. I think it's best if I show it to you."

* * *

A small crowd was gathered outside the stable. By their sparkling eyes, excited demeanors, and animated conversations, one could hardly believe they'd just come from a mourning ceremony.

"What are those people doing here?" I asked Diego, who was walking ahead of me.

"They came to see the race. News travels fast in the castle. And a Sorvinkian race is always an event."

An event! I didn't like the sound of that.

"Ah, there it is!" exclaimed Diego, pointing ahead. "Your troika!"

I frowned, puzzled by what I was seeing. "Are you serious? That strange contraption?"

The thing in front of us looked like an open carriage with no wheels. It was set upon long strips of metal that curled up at the front end. Strangest of all was the harness: three thick, bell-covered horse's collars lined side by side. A large inverted U-frame, garishly decorated with multicolored geometric motifs, stood above the central collar.

Diego threw an arm over my shoulder. "As you see, Amir, a troika is a sleigh drawn by a team of three horses abreast. Sorry yours is such an ugly shade of yellow."

Speechless, I watched stable boys attempt to harness three of my Telfarian horses to the sleigh. I began worrying immediately. Unused to this type of drawing arrangement, the horses were rearing, kicking, pulling left and right; their erratic behavior seriously threatened to topple the troika, if not controlled soon. Concern now tightened my stomach. Clearly, handling a troika wasn't an easy task. I glanced over my shoulder and saw that the crowd had left.

"Where did all the people go?"

"To the lake east of the castle to watch the race."

"We're racing around the lake?"

Diego's left eyebrow rose. "Amir, you're racing *on* the lake."

"On the lake?"

"It's frozen."

"Oooh—OOOH! We're racing on a frozen lake."

Diego nodded his head slowly.

I signed. *Hell, this is getting worse by the minute.*

* * *

Well, I was right about the situation getting worse. First, riding in a troika felt rather like riding on a bar of soap. The damn thing kept slipping and sliding all over the place, and I wasn't even on the frozen lake yet. Second, when I arrived at lake and saw Lars's troika and team of horses, I immediately knew that I would be lucky if I only lost the race (and face), and not a limb, or worse, my life. (According to Diego, Lars was a vicious driver. He had a reputation for bumping into his opponent, toppling their sleigh, and then running them over with his horses.) *Great! I have all that to look forward too. Lovely, just lovely.*

Lars's troika was bright blue and so was the U-frame—which, thanks to Diego, I now knew was a duga—rising above his central horse. This duga, however, wasn't garishly painted like mine, but adorned with dozens of dangling red tassels. Lars's three brown horses were great muscular creatures with powerful round rumps and deep, broad chests. Those horses were built to pull. With a growing sense of doom, I watched them move in perfect union. They were also well trained.

Not yet resigned to lose, I inspected Lars's horses and gear once more, hoping to find flaws in it. When one of the horses raised his hoof to strike the ice, a metallic glare caught my eye. His horses had spiked horseshoes.

"Cheater," I mumbled under my breath. As if he needed this advantage. I glared at Lars with resentment.

Firmly positioned at the front of his troika, Lars held his horses' reins with expert hands, his eyes fixed straight ahead. I stared at the crowd spread along the lakeshore. Two figures attracted my attention. They stood out against the pristine white snow in their dark garments: Eva, clad in a black coat, and Countess Ivana in a red one. Both women were huddled together as if for warmth or support. I knew Eva enough to figure that she didn't approve of my involvement in this race. I shook my head at my own stupidity. What was I thinking? Actually, a lack of thinking was at the heart of the problem, really. Since I'd gotten here I had been unable to think things through.

My attention returned to Eva and Ivana. What I saw then made me uneasy. The two Anchin warriors now stood right behind them.

"EEE—YAH!" Lars shouted. His troika took off, taking me totally by surprise.

"YAAH—YAH!" I yelled, urging my horses ahead. My

troika leapt forth. That starting jolt was so abrupt I nearly fell backward in the sleigh; fortunately the seat broke my fall. While struggling to regain my balance, I dropped the reins. Left without guidance, my horses slowed to a walk. After a frantic search at the bottom of the troika, I found the reins. Once I had them firmly in hand, I was able to regain control of my horses. But by then Lars's sleigh had shrunken to a small point in the distance.

"Damn! YAAH—YAH!" My horses took off again. They tried galloping. Their legs were moving fast, but we were not going anywhere. They were slipping! Their hooves had no grip. Then my gray mare found a patch of rough ice and was able to pull the sleigh away from the starting line. Now my horses were running as fast as they could on the ice, or as fast as the sleigh permitted them. The back of that cursed thing kept skidding sideways, left and right, so much so, I feared it might flip over at any moment, crushing me under its weight. As if this wasn't enough, maintaining the three horses in line was nearly impossible. The two on each side wanted to turn in different directions. After a short battle with the reins, I bent the horses to my will, and they began working as a team and pulling straight. By then Lars had already reached the end of the lake and turned around.

Grinding my teeth, I watched his troika come toward me at great speed. I pushed my horses to run faster. Lars's troika was now near enough to allow me to see the hot breaths of his horses. Expecting some foul play on his part, I braced myself. Our troikas were now so close we could see each other's faces clearly. Lars's was stiff with concentration. We passed each other. Then he was gone.

Stunned, I looked over my shoulder at Lars's troika. I had expected him to attempt to overturn me... or at least give me a lash of his whip. Nothing. Lars had done nothing. I wasn't worth the trouble, I supposed. He didn't need to do anything to win this race anyway. He won it the moment I agreed to participate in it.

As I drove my horses forward, a loud cracking sound resounded in the air. A second cracking echoed right after. This one, however, was followed by a series of popping noises. All those sounds I realized were coming from behind me. Again, I looked over my shoulder. I saw Lars's troika gliding away, then an explosion of *pop, pop,* and *crack* rang out. The ice broke and Lars's troika fell into the lake's icy waters.

I gasped in horror. Meanwhile Lars's brown horses fought to climb back onto the ice sheet, but the weight of the sleigh was dragging them under. Lars's small figure was still visible on the left. He was holding on to the edge of the ice for dear life while desperately trying to stay away from his panicked horses' hooves.

Turning my troika around, I went to Lars's aid. Through the huffing and puffing of my galloping horses, I could hear the crowd screaming on the lakeshore. I peered in that direction and saw Eva, Diego, and the Anchin warriors running toward us. I then spotted Baron Molotoff and his sons. I was certain they would come to our aid, but they didn't move an inch. They just watched. Countess Ivana, for her part, had dropped to her knees, presumably praying for our safety. Her cohort of pretty friends soon joined her in prayer.

Bringing my attention back to the hole in the ice, I stopped my troika at a safe distance from its edge, jumped out, and ran toward Lars. As I got near, I sensed something unusual. I lowered my eyes and saw a huge shadow darkening the ice under my feet. I looked toward the hole. Lars's horses had vanished. "Lord, they sank! Oh no, Lars!"

In panic, I scanned the area at the edge of the hole where I had last seen him. To my relief, I found Lars still hanging on to the ice sheet, but he wasn't going to stay afloat for much longer. I could tell just by looking at him. Frost covered his face. His hands were two white frozen claws clutching the ice and, despite his violent shivering, his eyes appeared sleepy.

He was on the verge of going under. There was no time to waste. I hurried toward him.

POP-CRACK-POP, the ice complained under my feet.

I froze. "LARS!" I yelled.

His eyes regained some focus.

"Look at me, Lars. Keep your eyes on me." I lay down on the ice and crawled to him. Stretching as much as I could, I reached out to him. "Take my hand. Hurry!"

Now fully awakened, Lars began kicking the water and stretching forward. I did the same. Our fingers touched. I learned forth and grabbed his hand. The ice on which I lay suddenly darkened, as if some somber creature was underneath it. Then this dark shadow swam past me. Lars abruptly jerked backward; I nearly lost my hold on his hand.

Lars stared down at the water, eyes wide with terror. His mouth opened, and just as he was about to speak, something ripped him out of my grip and pulled him under the ice.

On all fours, I followed his voyage under the clear icy sheet as he fought with a dark green form. A big fish, I first thought. Then a long green veil, like flowing hair, fell into view. *A hairy fish! No, that cannot be,* I thought, dumfounded. I had never seen anything like this before.

THUD.

I heard Lars hit the ice with his fists.

I forgot the fish. "HANG ON!" I screamed at him, and began jumping on the ice. On my fourth landing I went straight through. The frigid coldness of the water shocked me so that I was nearly paralyzed, and for a terrifying moment I truly believed that I would never be able to move again and that my heart would stop beating from the cold. Then I resurfaced.

No time—get him, I told myself. Filling my lungs, I dived under the ice. Through the murky water, I spotted Lars floating motionless a short distance from me. Was I too late already? I questioned. I swam to him nonetheless.

Scanning the water of the lake for its strange inhabitant, I took hold of Lars's arm and, dragging him along, I swam back to my hole in the ice. The trip up seemed to take forever. I thought my lungs would burst, yet I went on swimming as fast and as hard as I could, my legs kicking and kicking. I could see the hole now; it looked like a shiny white moon right above my head. Pushing my body to its limit, I sped up and broke the surface, gasping for air.

"I made it! God, I made it," I spat, suddenly overwhelmed with feelings of relief and accomplishment. But those feelings didn't last long. Within the space of a couple of breaths, I started panicking. I had no strength left in me. I could barely hang on to Lars's limp body, let alone climb up on the ice with him. Maybe if I let go of Lars, I would have a chance, but that was out of the question. If only he would wake up. I looked at him. As soon as I saw his face I knew he wasn't going to wake up. Lars was dead. That was plain to see. His eyes were fixed. His mouth hung half-opened. His head wobbled loosely from side to side. But the biggest clue of all was that he was blue. *Leave him. Save yourself,* a voice whispered in my head. I couldn't do it. I couldn't let go. My hands refused to obey me.

"Too late," I whispered. "It's too late for both of us." I was exhausted and sleepy. My eyes closed. I was so tired, and Lars was so heavy, too heavy. We began sinking. Just as the icy water was covering my face, something hard closed around my shoulders. All of a sudden, I was dragged onto the ice with Lars's lifeless body still frozen in my clutches.

"Amir! Amir! Say something!"

I recognized Diego's voice. "C… c… cold," I stammered through disabling shivers. More voices touched my ears, strange, incomprehensible voices. Then I felt someone pulling my hands apart and Lars's lifeless body was taken out of my grip. I opened my eyes. The two Anchin warriors were here too. I watched them drag Lars away from me.

Eva fell to her knees in front of me. "Oh, you're alive. I thought I had lost you." As she was covering my face with kisses, Diego draped his coat around me.

Eva then abruptly pulled away from me. "Where's Lars? Where is he?" Her tone was abnormally biting.

"Lars," I said in a small voice. "Lars is dead. I couldn't save him." I looked around, seeking Lars's corpse. Instead I saw the warriors a few paces on my left, crouched over someone. They were frantically pushing, twisting, and punching that person as if they desperately wanted to subdue it. Confused, I watched them for a while before realizing that they were beating on Lars's body.

"STOP!" I yelled. "STOP RIGHT NOW!"

Eva ran to the warriors. Seizing the man by the scruff of the neck, she tried tearing him off Lars. Instead of fighting her off, the man calmly turned around and, displaying the kindest smile, indicated something to her. Something on the ground between them, something I couldn't see because Eva was hindering my sight. I watched Eva lean forward and look at what the man was showing her. She froze and let out a small cry of surprise. I heard coughing coming from the space between the warriors. The sound of someone vomiting soon followed. Eva then melted down on the ground. Now that she was no longer obstructing my view, I could see Lars curled up on the ice, retching water. Once he was done, he rolled over on his back, gasping.

Dumfounded, I rubbed my eyes; I couldn't believe what I was seeing. *This can't be!* I kept thinking, still reeling from the shock. *This can't be!* He was dead. Moments ago Lars was dead. I would have sworn to it.

Now the warrior woman was staring at me. I saw that she was clutching something in her fist, something she'd picked off Lars's clothing. I tried focusing on it, but couldn't see anything. Then too many people had made their way to us, and this newly formed crowd was hindering my sight. What happened next was all clouded in my mind. Only a few details remained vivid to me. I remembered that Diego made the trip to the castle with me, while Eva chose to travel with Lars. That particular detail was seared in my memory. Of all the horrible things that had happened to me today, this, for me, was without a doubt the most painful.

CHAPTER FIFTEEN

This morning I awoke feeling only slightly cold. Gone were the bone-jarring shivers and the headache-inducing teeth chattering of the previous day. Then I had thought I would never be warm again and that my blood would remain forever as cold as ice, just like the lake's icy waters.

Huddled in my bed, I tried to recall yesterday's events. That stupid race; I remembered Lars going through the ice, and me, plunging in behind him. Diego had pulled me out of the frozen water; he had also brought me back to the castle using my troika. Lars and Eva went with someone else, the Anchin perhaps; this part remained cloudy in my mind. Other things were clear though. The fact that Lars was still alive astounded me. He should have been dead. Damn, he was dead—dead as a rock.

The Anchin warriors had done something to Lars, but what? I had difficulty remembering that part. Maybe because all I could see at the time was Eva falling on the snow in shock at seeing Lars breathing again. Eva's last words to me had been harsh and resentful. Was she blaming me for this accident? If she was I needed to clarify the situation. The race was Lars's idea, not mine.

With this purpose in mind, I dragged myself out of my

bed and, *oh surprise,* landed flat on my face on the cold stone floor. I heard a flurry of footsteps and then Milo was beside me, lifting me to my feet.

"My lord, are you hurt?"

"No. I'm fine. My knees gave way under me, that's all. Bring me my clothes, Milo."

"CLOTHES! My lord cannot go out in his condition! Not after such a terrible incident. My lord nearly died."

"I believe I can manage."

"NO!" protested Milo. "My lord is still too weak. My lord should stay in bed. Come, lie down."

I felt a sudden surge of anger rising up in me. Why was this servant discussing my orders? I stared at Milo with the firm intention of reprimanding him for his boldness, but at the sight of his deeply concerned expression, my anger evaporated. If I had died, Milo would've been left alone here. Without my protection, I doubted he would've lived very long—unless Diego took him in his service. Thinking of this now, I believed Milo might have feared that more than death itself.

I patted his hand in a reassuring manner. "Stop worrying, Milo, I'm fine. I am perfectly healthy. Weak perhaps, but healthy nonetheless. Now, go fetch my clothes and help me dress."

* * *

With Milo in tow, I made my way to the castle's new wing where Lars's rooms were located. I threw a resentful glance at Milo as I walked. The eunuch had pleaded and begged to accompany me with such zeal that I had found it impossible to say no. I hated being coerced like this. It angered me that he'd succeeded, and it angered me even more that I didn't have the heart to be more firm with him. Maybe that was another reason why I never had servants before. I didn't

possess the cold, unmoving nature necessary to be a good...
hm, good was the wrong word, an *effective* master. I was still
mulling over this when we arrived at the new wing.

I was shocked to see that the corridor was packed with
people. Many among those present were well-wishers, here
to show support for Lars. But most of the bystanders, however, were just curious people gathered here to find fuel for
new gossip.

As I passed through the assembly all conversations died,
and as if this wasn't intimidating enough by itself, I could
feel dozens of eyes following my progress toward Lars's
apartments. I did my best to ignore this improper scrutiny
and soldiered on.

The door was open. "Stay here," I ordered Milo before I
entered.

Lars's receiving room was crowded, the bulk of the space
was mainly taken by the king and his large entourage.
Slumped in the corner of a long couch, King Erik was a
shadow of himself. Once strong and full of vitality, he was
now worn down and lifeless. The man looked devastated.
Worse yet, he looked beaten, which was dangerous for a
king, because it made him seem weak and vulnerable. To my
knowledge, a king who gave that impression never stayed
king for long.

A scan of the room showed me a wide range of attitudes
among the king's men. Some of his advisors looked worried,
while others bore neutral expressions. Some were talking in
low voices, some praying in silence. The presence of Baron
Molotoff and his sons in the room surprised me. Positioned
together along the back wall, they all displayed similar blank,
stony expressions. The baron's piercing gaze connected with
mine. Although there was no hostility in his eyes—nothing
flagrant anyway—I always had the impression that this man
was constantly evaluating me. As for why he would be doing
so, I had no idea. Holding his gaze, I respectfully saluted him,

then turned to King Erik.

I was debating if I should approach the king or not, when Diego poked his head out of an adjacent room and waved me in.

"How's Lars?" I asked.

"See for yourself." Diego motioned over his shoulder with his thumb.

I stepped inside the room—it was Lars's bedroom. I looked at all the people crowding it. The number of physicians assembled at the foot of the bed was a bad omen, I thought. Then I spotted Eva seated in the corner with her head hanging low. She didn't see me. Countess Ivana, who was kneeling at Eva's foot, did see me however and acknowledged my presence with a kind smile.

"Come on," said Diego. "Let's move in closer."

I followed next to him. Cutting through the sea of physicians, we approached Lars. Tucked in a majestic four-posted bed, the young duke was in a poor shape. His skin had an unpleasant greenish hue, and his breathing was so labored and raspy just hearing it made me wince—or maybe it was that white foam oozing out of a corner of his mouth that did it. Either way, Lars looked terrible.

"He's stuck between life and death," Diego murmured.

"I thought he was dead when you pulled us out of the lake."

"He was," said Diego. "I'm quite sure of that."

"Me too. The Anchin warriors did something to him. Did you see what it was?" Our eyes met. I could see that he was as disturbed by this as I was.

"They punched him in the stomach… I think that's what they were doing." Diego rubbed his forehead vigorously. "Amir, in all honesty, I'm not sure of what I saw."

I nodded. Neither was I. Turning to the nearest physician, I asked, "What are your thoughts concerning the duke's condition?"

"Yesterday, we expected him to be better this morning.

Now, we fear that he may have breathed in too much water."

"What can be done to solve this problem?"

"We did all that could be done. Prayer is all that is left."

My eyes flew back to Eva and Ivana. The countess was praying. As for Eva, she just sat there, staring into empty space. In all evidence, her mind was elsewhere. I took a step in her direction.

Diego grabbed my arm, stopping me. "I wouldn't if I were you."

Roughly tearing my arm out of his grip, I approached Eva. "My love," I whispered softly.

She blinked, and regained her focus. Raising a stern face to me, she said, "Why did you have to race, Amir? Couldn't you just say no? Why do you always feel the need to prove yourself?"

I gasped, backing away in shock. If she had stabbed me in the heart, it wouldn't have hurt me more. "I…" My throat was too tight; I couldn't speak. I swallowed, breathed deeply, then started over. "I did refuse, but he kept insisting. I was also led to believe this was a rider's race." I kneeled in front of her. "Eva, I would never do anything to hurt you, or your family."

She sighed heavily. "I know. I know. Pardon me, Amir. My nerves are frayed to their limit. I'm not myself. I need rest and tranquility… and for this I need to be alone. Therefore, I think it's best if we distance ourselves from each other for a while."

I felt as if all my innards had abruptly dropped to the floor. This was a totally new level of pain I was experiencing now, the kind that started with a shock-induced numbness, but would soon turn into horrendous torture.

"As you wish." I bowed, and rejoined Diego.

In silence, we walked to the other room.

"The ice shouldn't have broken," the king argued with

one of his advisors. "It never does. Not this early in spring. NEVER!" The king put his head in his hands and mumbled in a broken voice, "Have I not suffered enough loss already? Must I also lose my heir too?"

Rising to his feet, the king paced around the room like a tiger in a cage. As his speed increased so did his furor, until it suddenly erupted into a destructive rage. The king kicked a side table, toppled a chair, threw a painting on the floor; his rampaging outburst went on until nothing was left unbroken around him. Panting from exertion, he lowered his head. "I'm cursed."

"Oh, Your Majesty cannot be cursed," ventured a panicked advisor. "Your Majesty is far too powerful for curses."

The king gave a cynical laugh. "Then it must be a sign, a sign from the gods."

I waited for the king to say more, but nothing came. He just let himself fall back on the couch and remained quiet.

"He's gone mad," Diego whispered from the corner of his mouth. "Amir, I think it would be best if you leave before he sees you."

I didn't argue.

* * *

I intended to go to my rooms, yet for some reason my feet brought me elsewhere.

"Why are we here?" Milo asked once we stopped at the foot of the staircase leading up to the tower. "Are we visiting the alchemist again?"

I shook my head. There was another place I needed to see. A place I should have inspected earlier. Determined to correct this mistake, I climbed the steps. I passed Countess Ivana's door and soon reached my destination, the second door, the one leading to Isabo's rooms. As I stepped onto the landing two things became apparent to me. For one, the door was cracked open, and second, someone was inside.

The sound of glass bottles being tossed about echoed to us.

Pulling my rapier, I carefully pushed the door, widening its opening. The *clink-clank* increased in volume. I tiptoed inside and scanned the surroundings quickly.

The room was sparsely furnished and in perfect order. In the far left corner a shadowy figure was bent over a long worktable. The urgency in which this individual was searching through the hundreds of ampoules and bottles neatly stored on the table neared panic. The tremors in his hands were so severe that he was struggling just to hold the small bottles still.

"Thief, what are you doing? Stop!" I shouted.

Startled, the individual turned around.

I was stunned to see that it was Auguste Ramblais, the alchemist.

Clutching his chest, the old man gasped for air. His lips, I observed, had a bluish tinge to them, same for his fingers. "Help me, please," he muttered between struggling breaths.

"Help you how?"

"My tonic. I need my tonic. The damn witch's gone and... Gah." Grimacing in pain, the alchemist grasped the edge of the table for support.

I rushed to his aid and caught him before he could hit the floor. Milo fetched a chair and I lowered the man into it.

"All right, where's the tonic?" I asked.

He pointed at the table with a trembling knobby finger.

Upon seeing the quantity of containers assembled there, I knew that finding the one containing his tonic would not be an easy task. I went to work. After having gone through fifty bottles, I turned to the alchemist. "Sir Ramblais, I don't see any prepared potion or tonic of any kind here. All these bottles contain only ingredients."

"No more…" mumbled the alchemist. "The book. The recipe book." His one-eyed gaze darted to a section of the table.

There set a bowl, a burner, and a mortar. *Isabo's workstation.* When I moved the heavy granite mortar aside, my eyes fell on what could only be her recipe book, a square piece of brown leather folded in half and tied with a piece of string. To me, this looked more like a folio holder. Wasting no time, I hurried to open it. Inside the leather folder were dozens upon dozens of loose sheets of parchment, each holding a different recipe written in tight, neat print with no flourishes or embellishments whatsoever. Apparently, Isabo's plainness extended to her handwriting as well.

The recipe in front of me was titled WARTS AND BOILS REDUCING OINTMENT. *Well, that's clear enough.* I looked at the alchemist. "Which one is your tonic recipe? Does it have a name?"

"The… the queen's… settling heart tonic."

I frowned. "What! You mean she gave you—"

"Hurry. Please hurry."

"Oh yes." I flipped through the folder's pages until I found the recipe then rushed to collect the ingredients. But when I read the recipe I saw that its last ingredient was digitalis. "I can't make this," I said. "There's poison in it."

"Garhhh, just do it," the alchemist grumbled through clenched teeth, while once more clutching his chest in agony.

I hesitated only briefly. With the alchemist's laments echoing in the background—which I must admit played an essential part in my decision to make the potion—I began mixing the ingredients in a beaker. Taking my time, I inspected, measured, and weighed all the ingredients with great care, before adding each one to the potion, especially the last one, the deadly digitalis. Two drops it said in the recipe. That wasn't much… but it was still poison. I glanced at the alchemist—he looked about ready to die—then at the potion again. My mind made up, I let two drops of the syrupy liquid fall into the mixture, and stirred. Beaker in hand, I approached the alchemist.

The man's labored breath and tortured expression were hard to behold.

"I followed her recipe to the letter," I said, raising the beaker.

"Please." Auguste Ramblais extended a shaking hand toward the beaker. "I beg of you... I can't bear this pain any longer."

"What if she was making a different tonic for you? One without poison in it. Have you thought of that?"

The alchemist stayed mute; perhaps he didn't have the strength to speak anymore, I thought.

"Master Ramblais, if I'm right, this potion will kill you, and I—" All of a sudden, I decided that I couldn't let that man drink this brew. I couldn't be responsible for his death, not this way.

By some tremendous effort, the alchemist managed to murmur a few coherent words. "I will die... if... if I don't drink... it."

I looked at Milo who was kneeling beside the old man.

"He has a point, my lord."

I nodded, and gave the tonic to the alchemist before I could change my mind again. With an intense feeling of guilt, I watched the old man drain the three gulps of potion I had made. *Lord, I think I've just killed that man.*

CHAPTER SIXTEEN

To my total amazement, within moments of having drunk the tonic not only was the alchemist still alive... but in fact he was doing much better. His breathing was less arduous, the bluish tinge coloring his lips and fingertips had subsided, and his heartbeat had returned to a steady pace.

I dragged a chair in front of him and sat down. "You should be dead, Master Ramblais. I've just fed you poison."

"Isabo never told me what was in her tonic. All I knew was that it helped steady my heart and the queen's." The alchemist went on to say that the queen's condition, however, was far worse than his, and that to his knowledge, she had had this heart problem long before Isabo's arrival at the castle. But he conceded that the queen's heart worsened shortly after.

"Do you think Isabo was the cause?"

The old man rubbed his bulbous nose. "Can't say. I never understood the woman's mind. Still, this seemed unlikely to me." He shrugged. "But who knows. At the time, no one paid much attention to her. She was just another orphan or widow of noble birth seeking refuge at the castle. The country was in much turmoil then."

"Really—why? What caused this unrest?"

"Three powerful noble families were fighting over the

ownership of a piece of land. To tell you the truth, they were fighting over an ancient temple dedicated to Mirekia, the goddess of war and patron of the soldiers. The temple was a sacred pilgrimage site. Each family claimed the rights to it, and nearly brought the country to war over it."

"What happened?"

"The king stepped in and stopped the fighting. But by then the nobles had almost all killed each other. So to prevent any other conflict of the sort, King Erik had all the deities' temples destroyed throughout the country. Later, he declared that Oledon, the god of the wind, would be Sorvinka's only god. As Oledon doesn't possess any temple, statue, or icon of any kind, there won't be anything to fight over."

Although the king's decision seemed like a logical and simple solution, I knew this was a problem that couldn't be solved this easily. "Surely some people opposed the king's decision to destroy the gods' temples."

The alchemist laughed. "After the destruction and death caused by those noble families, the peasants were too glad to see peace return to the land to protest. The same can be said for the remaining nobility. Only the discarded gods' priests and priestesses were discontent. And the most vocal of those soon filled the Sorvinkian gibbets. Thus, the problem didn't stay one for very long."

I grimaced. This was a drastic way of solving a problem. And although I couldn't deny its efficiency, I didn't care much for it. No wonder the village's peasants were so uneasy when I questioned them about their faith. They were breaking the king's law by worshiping their old gods. *And they're not the only ones,* I thought, recalling the room I had discovered, the one with all the statues. Those people in dark robes were also worshipers. Maybe I should visit that room again—later.

Milo and I stayed with the alchemist a bit longer. While Milo helped him return to his rooms, I remained behind to make more tonics for him—at least three more doses in case he had another attack. After that was done and I'd given the tonics to the alchemist, I tucked Isabo's recipe book under my arm and, with Milo at my side, I proceeded in the direction of the dark corridor where I had discovered the secret entrance to the statue room.

"Are you sure it's here?" asked Milo as I probed the wall.

"Quiet!" I replied. My fingers had just sensed a change in texture on the wall; from rough it had become smooth. "Found it," I said, pushing the door open.

Without making a noise, we both slipped into the room. I heard Milo gasp beside me as he spotted the numerous statues surrounding us. "Shhhh," I blew, scrutinizing the room.

The room wasn't as dark as I remembered it, and also not as cluttered. There were still an incredible amount of statues and religious artifacts piled up throughout the room, but I could swear some statues were missing. There were gaps everywhere. One in particular held my attention. I vividly recalled having seen a towering form covered by a silk drape. Now all that was left was a rumpled mass of silk piled on the floor.

I took a few careful steps further into the room and immediately spotted the man prostrated on the ground in the far corner. Five candles were burning on the small table beside him. So that explained why the room had seemed brighter to me. Indicating the individual to Milo, I motioned for him to be silent. After exchanging nods, we tiptoed close to the praying man.

"Who are you and what is this place?" I boomed at the prayer's back.

The man leapt to his feet in panic. But upon seeing us, he threw himself on his knees and began begging for mercy. "Please, good lords, please forgive this mistake. It won't happen again. I promise. I swear. Please have mercy on me.

Please. Please."

Taken aback by the man's reaction, I found myself short for words and wound up just staring at him for a bit. In his mid-twenties, he was of a slim build, with a long narrow face and thinning red hair. By examining the man carefully, I saw that he was a servant. A porter, I deduced, by the characteristic square-shouldered red coat of his uniform. I tapped his shoulder. "Rise up, porter. You have nothing to fear from me. All I want is a few answers."

The porter looked so relieved and grateful that for a brief moment I feared he might try to kiss me. "Oh thank you, my lord. Thank you, thank you. Yes, my lord, I'll answer. Anything my lord wants."

"What is this place?"

"This is the old gods' room, my lord."

I frowned. "I was told the old faith had been abolished and the temples destroyed."

The porter lowered his head. "It is all true, my lord. However, the statues and icons were spared and brought here. No one dared break them for fear of the gods' wrath. As for the worship, the nobles are free to do as they wish… as long as they're discrete." The porter bit his lower lip. "It's more dangerous for commoners to do so."

I nodded. "I see. Which god were you praying to moments ago?"

"Torvel." The porter indicated a painting depicting a bent, skeletal old man carrying a huge load of firewood on his back and two buckets of water in each hand. The expression painted on his angular face was a combination of agony and stubborn determination. To me, this frail old man looked like he was about to be crushed under the weight of his chores. Not the picture I had in mind for a god.

"Who is Torvel?"

"Oh, he's the patron of hard-working people. He keeps them healthy and free of injury, so they can do their tasks.

He's mostly favored by servants."

"Why?" asked Milo. "Are you not treated when injured? In Telfar, servants are taken care of when sick or hurt. So they could later return to work."

The porter shook his head. "Not here, my lord. Here, an injured servant is always dismissed, which often means being condemned to starvation."

Milo looked horrified. "Oh, how I miss Telfar."

I surveyed the open space behind the porter. That was where I had seen that black robed group. "What's in the other room?"

"More gods and space to pray."

"Show us."

We moved into the other room. I did a quick inspection of the area; I found the pedestal and the small statue the black robes had been worshiping. It represented a battleaxe-wielding woman warrior riding a hellish-looking beast. The creature was neither wolf nor bear nor lion, but a mix of all three it seemed. Bending over the statue, I examined its every detail. Done in a rudimentary chip-carving technique, this old wooden statue, with its stylized look and slightly askew proportions, had a certain naïve charm. "What's this one?" I asked the porter.

"The goddess of war," murmured the porter. He sounded a little bit frightened, I noticed. "She's a powerful god, that one. All the soldiers pray to her. She's their patron."

"What's her name?"

"Mirekia," a resounding baritone voice answered behind me.

I turned around.

The baron and his three sons stood in the room's entrance. They were rather impressive in their military uniforms, with their tall, gray fur hats and matching coats elegantly hanging over their shoulders. They looked angry. Then again, those thick grown-together eyebrows of theirs made it appear as if they were perpetually frowning.

The baron approached us. "If you wish to know more about my god, you'd do well to ask me and not a servant." The man's tone couldn't be more commanding. His deep booming voice was perfectly suited for his rank of army general. It was a voice that demanded obedience.

"I agree, Baron," I said. I turned, intending to dismiss the porter, only to discover that he had already fled. *Of course.* I sighed, and after a respectful bow to the baron, I said. "Please, will you enlighten me, Baron?"

"Mirekia is far more than just the goddess of war, patron of soldiers. She's the dispenser of justice and protector of the righteous. It is this aspect of her that I worship."

Well, he certainly sounded righteous enough to be in his god's favor, I thought. I wasn't sure if I liked it though.

An awkward moment of silence followed, during which we all stared at each other ill at ease. This would have been the perfect time for me and Milo to leave, but too many unanswered questions were still swarming in my mind for me to do so. Gathering my thoughts, I cleared my throat and asked, "Aren't you afraid I might tell the king about this... worshiping?"

The baron smiled. "No, because you won't do such a thing."

"You sound very sure of yourself."

"Because I am. I've watched you since you arrived at the castle, and you don't behave like the sort of man who tells. Plus, the king already knows about it. But you figured that out already."

I nodded. "Why are you watching me? Am I that interesting?"

"As a suitor for the king's daughter, you certainly are. Anything that may affect Sorvinka's future interests me. However, I must admit that my interest in you has waned."

"Why?" I asked even though I had a strong feeling I

wouldn't like the answer.

"I greatly doubt the king will allow you to marry his daughter."

I felt my stomach drop. "I suppose one of your sons would make a better suitor."

"Absolutely!" The baron expelled a long breath. "Sadly, that's not likely to happen. Our king isn't known for his good decision-making skills." He waved a hand at the statue-filled room. "This proves it." He shook his head. "This was a terribly misguided decision."

"I'm sure the king could be convinced to change his ruling."

"I wouldn't presume to tell the king what to do, or try to influence his judgment one way or the other. It's not my place to advise him in politics. After all, I am but a humble soldier."

Sure, the more mistakes the king makes, the better you look and the closer you get to the throne. I had to admit the baron's tactic was devilishly brilliant. It was also underhanded—I didn't care much for that aspect of it. I wondered how patient the man was. Did he covet the throne for himself or would he be satisfied by setting the stage for one of his sons. The baron's stony face gave me no hint of an answer either. Finding no other subject of conversation, I bid him good day and left.

"Where are we going now?" Milo asked once we were in the corridor.

"My rooms, where else."

We were entering "Draft Alley," the corridor leading to my rooms, when a guard came running behind us with the news that someone outside the gate was asking for me. After a brief halt in my rooms to fetch our coats and hide the recipe book, Milo and I hurried to the gate.

A young peasant boy wrapped in a thick sheep pelt, his head hidden under a black wool cap, awaited me. A look of extreme excitement illuminated his cold-reddened face.

"Prince Amir, Dimitry sent me," the boy said, while dancing from foot to foot. "We caught it! The bear! We caught it in your trap."

"When?" I asked.

"Some time ago." The boy pointed in the direction of the village. "I came right away—on foot."

On foot! That meant a fair amount of time had passed since the beast was caught. I stared at the snowy horizon. Perhaps if we hurried, there might still be a chance that we could see the animal alive.

* * *

We rode into the village at break-neck speed, me in the lead on my gray mare and Milo behind on a Sorvinkian bay horse with the peasant boy hooked to his back. I halted my horse in front of the temple's ruin and leapt down. The place was deserted. I had expected to see people around the area where we had dug the trap. I could see that the ground had been churned by a small army of feet, but there was no one near. I was walking toward the trap when Dimitry came out of his house. A group of men followed behind him.

"I got your news, Dimitry," I shouted. "Where's the beast?"

Dimity's expression turned as sour as a rotten turnip. "The cursed animal got out of the trap."

I furrowed my brow. "How?"

"It climbed out. The thing was twice the size of a normal bear. The trap wasn't deep enough to keep it in. Come see for yourself."

I followed Dimitry to the edge of the trap. There was no need asking questions anyway. Claw marks told the story of the bear's escape. They were so clear that I could easily follow the animal's progress from the bottom of the trap right to its top. I then tracked the bear's steps to the altar. The snow all around the altar was flattened and speckled with red dots. Fresh blood by the look of it. Obliviously a battle had been waged here.

"Dimitry, whose blood is this—the bear's?"

The corners of Dimitry's lips dipped downward; he shook his head. "Ours. We tried to stop the beast, but the thing was too strong and too big. We couldn't hold it."

Crouching beside the trap, I peered down at its black bottom. How could this creature climb out of this deep hole so easily? How tall was that monster? I felt the sudden impulse to climb down the trap and touch its bottom. I didn't know why I needed to do that, only that I had to do it. "Can I get a rope?" I asked.

Dimitry snapped his fingers and within moments a rope was let down the side of the trap.

Losing no time, I grabbed the rope and began my descent to the bottom of the trap. I reached the end of the rope quickly enough and my feet made contact with the ground again. It was cold and dark within the trap, far more than I imagined it would be.

Dimitry's head appeared over the trap's edge. "Do you smell it?"

"Smell what?"

"The bear odor."

I took a deep breath. I caught the scent of dirt, snow, and blood, nothing else. I raised my face to Dimitry. "There is none."

"I know." Dimitry's face took on an air of worry. "A horse always smells like horses. A sheep like sheep. But a bear with no smell... I don't care for that."

"We believe it may be a trained bear. Could that affect its odor?"

"Maybe. I know nothing about trained bears. The wild ones are the only kind I know."

Nodding, I brought my attention to the dirt walls surrounding me. *Why did I have the urge to come here?* I asked myself. *The urge to step where the beast had stepped.*

Seeking one paw print after another, I began stepping into them. Slowly, I traveled along the trap in a circle and back to my starting point. Then the bear had climbed out on the left side. I inspected the dirt wall closely.

"Oh," I blew, placing my hand in a long scratch mark in the frozen dirt. His first attempt had failed. "He fell down."

I looked at the ground where the bear had tumbled, and frowned. I thought I saw something shiny in the dirt. Kneeling down on that spot, I began sifting through the soil. Soon my fingers met with something hard. I brought the small pebble up to my eyes and stared at it in disbelief. Resting in the palm of my hand wasn't a pebble, but one of Thalia's blue diamond earrings. The ones I had given her as a gift. *Why is this here? Has the beast eaten Thalia, and for some reason the earring stayed caught in its jaw... until the bear fell down, jarring it loose?* This was a dreadful thought. A more optimistic one came to my mind soon after. *Maybe Thalia attached her earring to the bear, to its collar perhaps, in hope it would lead someone back to her.*

I closed my fist around the earring. No matter how much I wanted to believe this, I just couldn't fathom how someone could attach an earring to a bear—trained or not—without being mauled to death. That was a stupid idea. *What then? What is the earring doing here?* Unable to come up with a plausible explanation for the earring's presence in this hole, I climbed out of the trap feeling more confused than when I'd gotten in.

CHAPTER SEVENTEEN

After discovering the earring in the bear trap, Milo and I returned to the castle. This time we successfully made it to my rooms without disturbance. I spent most of that night and part of the following morning studying Isabo's recipe book. By noon it had become obvious to me that this book was nothing more than a volume of remedies. Although I was disappointed not to have found any spell in it to prove her guilt, I had to admit that Isabo was a very gifted healer and an expert potion-maker. I wondered where she had learned her craft. Moreover, I now questioned her implication in these crimes. Was she really guilty? Doubts riddled me to the point of driving me mad.

What if the queen's death was due to the fact that Isabo wasn't there to provide her with a tonic, and not the other way around? *But if Isabo isn't guilty, who is then? And what about the princesses' kidnappings? Isabo was seen leading the bear, so she has to be guilty. Then why heal the queen? That doesn't make sense.* So many questions, so many strange events, this entire affair seemed unsolvable. I didn't know what to think anymore.

I stared at the window. The bright midday light made its colored glass sparkle like jewels. Today was the queen's funeral, which meant that Isabo's time was numbered. I had two days at best to find out if she was guilty or innocent. But first, I had the solemn duty to attend the queen's funeral.

* * *

Even though dozens of people surrounded me, I felt alone and depressed. Funerals had that effect on me. Also, I believed that my state of mind was made worse by the fact that Eva was so close and yet so far from me.

Draped in a dark fur cap, Eva clutched her father's arm as they both solemnly walked behind the black troika carrying the queen's casket. I wished I could have held Eva's hand, supported her in this painful time. Sadly this wasn't permitted. *I'll have to wait,* I thought, watching the royal family—now reduced to only two people, Lars still being bedridden—enter the stone crypt to bid the queen a last farewell. According to Sorvinkian tradition, only they were allowed in. So I and the rest of the mourners just stood by, waiting for them to exit this small, stone building. Although most Sorvinkians were buried, I was told that noble families often opted for crypts as their last resting places because in winter the frozen ground hindered one's burial. This was why Sorvinkian cemeteries were made up of a combination of tombstones and crypts. This cemetery, situated on the north side of the castle and near the forest, was no exception. I cast an eye down. The nearby headstone was too close to me for my taste and I quickly walked away from it. I strongly disliked this place. There was something in the air here, a presence, an unnatural one at that, not truly dead like a ghost, yet not really alive either. Whatever it was, its essence made me jittery.

In desperate need of distraction, I studied the other mourners assembled in the cemetery. I spotted Diego standing a few paces ahead of me. He looked so different in those dark brown clothes. Gone were the lace and bright colors he usually favored. I almost missed his exuberant flamboyance. Beside him was Countess Ivana dressed in a simple marine gown with a long gray cape thrown over her shoulders. She was as beautiful as ever. Her only artifices were the four raindrop pins she wore in memory of her mother. I smiled. Ivana was remarkable. Few women of her rank and beauty would wear such trinkets.

Motion coming from the crypt caught my attention. Shadows were stirring near the entrance. Then the king and Eva stepped into the daylight. His eyes puffy and reddened, the king walked in front. He bore the tortured expression of one who just had his heart wrenched out. As for Eva, her face remained hidden under a veil of black lace; therefore I couldn't see her tears. But I had no trouble hearing her quiet sobbing though. It was then that I became aware of a strange, new sound mixed with the loud crying of the mourners.

Tilting my head to the side, I listened attentively and tried to isolate this new sound from the ambient noises. Ah, there it was again. The sound was like a sort of grumbling... or more exactly growling. And... and it came from the edge of the nearby forest. I scrutinized the area. At first, I saw nothing but trees, bushes, and boulders. Then the big brown boulder on the left moved. I gasped. That wasn't a boulder. It was a bear, a huge brown bear, running straight toward us.

My head spun in the direction of the small group of people the bear seemed to be aiming for. The king and Eva were at its center. Ivana and Diego were there also.

"Run! Hide!" I shouted. "Move, get out of the way!"

Instead of sending people running, my warning produced the opposite effect. They all froze in place and stared at me with bemused looks on their faces.

I opened my coat and pulled out my sword, which brought appalled exclamations from the crowd of mourners. Weapons had been prohibited from this ceremony. But I had felt compelled to bring mine anyway—being unarmed always unnerved me.

The king was furious. Fists closed and lips thinned, he glared at me through narrowed eyes. "Prince Amir, you have now committed an offense that I cannot overlook. For this—"

"AAAHH! A BEAR!" rose from the back of the assembly. Screams and yells followed as people began running in all directions in panic.

Struck in the chest by the fleeing mob, I fell to the ground, and I would've been trampled to death if not for the headstone that protected me. Huddled against the worn, pitted granite block, I waited for the horde of runners to thin. When it did, and I finally was able to rise up, I saw that the bear was already in the cemetery. Worse yet, this raging mass of shaggy brown fur was rapidly approaching the royal group, which had been pushed to the back of the cemetery by the fleeing mob.

Petrified, the king just stood there with wide-opened eyes, staring at the irate animal. Then patting his side, he began a frantic search of himself—for a weapon, I presumed. Without further delay, I ran toward them.

Meanwhile the bear was rapidly closing the gap separating it from the group. I stared at the king standing in front of the women like a target. *Brave but useless*, I thought and ran faster.

As the bear reached the group, Countess Ivana, seized by panic or imbued with heroism, dashed past the king and ran madly through the cemetery's central alley.

Attracted by this fleeing prey, the bear changed course and chased after her. I immediately pursued them. With a glance behind me, I saw the king embracing Eva and, to my consternation, Diego running away.

"Coward," I hissed, and returned to my pursuit. There was no time to waste. The beast was almost on Ivana. I tried running faster but the deep, wet snow slowed me down.

I looked ahead and saw that Ivana had reached a crypt.

She tried entering it, but the door was locked. When she turned around the bear was right in front of her. The giant beast rose up on its hind legs. Growling ferociously, it then leaned forward.

"Aiii!" Ivana screamed.

The bear was about to tear poor Ivana to pieces, when a tall silhouette with long flowing black locks burst out from behind the crypt and pushed Ivana out of harm's way.

"Diego!" I shouted. The dark-haired prince had not run away as I had believed, but had taken the side alley where the snow wasn't as deep. Because of this clever move he'd reached Ivana first. As I stared at my friend bravely facing the enraged beast, a terrible reality dawned on me. Diego was unarmed, hence defenseless against the bear's attack.

Brandishing my sword, I ran as fast as my legs could manage in this snow. But I knew it wouldn't be fast enough. There was no way I could get to the bear in time to save Diego. The beast was already lunging toward him.

To my astonishment, the bear didn't maul Diego. Lowering itself down on all fours, the bear stuck its long muzzle in Diego's hair and ran its big black nose along his cheek and neck. Diego cringed as the animal sniffed him thoroughly. The bear then backed away, as if confused by something. Well, Diego's perfume was, to say the least, distracting. For an animal, with a sense of smell as acute as a bear's, it was probably off-putting, if not downright repulsive.

During that time, Ivana had managed to crawl amidst a cluster of tombs. She gripped one of the weather-beaten headstones to pull herself to her feet. A piece of it broke off and fell down with a clunking noise.

The bear's head swung toward the noise. The beast's muzzle wrinkled, exposing long, murderous teeth. By then I had reached my friends and was able to step in front of Ivana.

With it small round ears pinned back, the bear stood up

on its hind legs again. Almost twice my height, the beast towered over me while growling loudly.

I thrust my sword forward, aiming for the bear's exposed belly, but fell short of hitting the target. To strike the beast, I needed to move closer to it. In fact, I literally needed to walk into its clutches. For the first time in my life, I wished I had another kind of weapon in my hand instead of my trusty rapier. A pike would have been perfect. I shook myself—wishing was useless; I would have to make due with the rapier. Perhaps I could attack low, as I usually did when fighting taller opponents.

Without further thinking, I rolled left of the bear, rose up, and aimed a blow at his hind leg. My sword bit deep into the bear's flesh, leaving a bloody gash across its thick brown fur. The bear roared in pain, pivoted, and swiped my sword right out of my hand with its giant paw.

The impact knocked me flat on the ground, and before I could rise again, the bear was on me.

I was raising my arms in front of me, in a pitiful attempt to protect my face from the incoming fangs, when an arrow pierced the bear's chest. The animal jerked backward. A second arrow sunk deep in its shoulder while a third one plunged into its neck. The beast let out a gasp of agony, then dropped dead beside me.

Still in shock, I remained sprawled beside the animal. From the corner of my eye, I saw Khuan and Lilloh, the barbarian warriors, approach with caution. They both had their bowstrings drawn ready to send more arrows into the bear… in case it wasn't dead.

Meanwhile Diego had made his way to Ivana, who was curled up against the broken headstone, crying hysterically. Placing an arm around the countess's waist, Diego helped her stand. Turning to me he called, "Amir, are you hurt?"

I sat up. "No. I'm fine, just… just shaken."

Diego breathed a sigh of relief. "Good. I'm glad." On this,

he gently led Ivana out of the cemetery.

The sound of a whispered discussion in a foreign tongue brought my attention back to my saviors. Khuan and Lilloh had made their way to the bear. I watched Lilloh give her bow to Khuan and kneel beside the animal. She closed her eyes, and her lips began moving, mouthing silent words, as if she were praying. Once she was done, she bowed her head. Opening her eyes, Lilloh then touched the bear's fur. A startled yelp escaped her mouth and she rapidly recoiled from the beast. I watched an expression of disbelief twist her small exotic features. Swallowing hard, she touched the animal again. This time her hands went to the bear's broad forehead. A barely inaudible whimper filtered through Lilloh's lips. It was so faint I believed that if I had been a step further away, it would have escaped my knowledge. But the horrified look now drawn on her face couldn't be missed though.

"What's wrong?" I asked.

Lilloh didn't answer; instead she covered her face with her hands and shook her head as if she had just uncovered something terrible.

Bending down to the shaken young woman, Khuan whispered kindly to her in a language I didn't understand. She nodded as if in agreement. Raising her head, Lilloh looked at me, then at the bear, then at me again.

I didn't need more to comprehend what Lilloh wanted me to do. She wanted me to touch the beast. For some irrational reason, I was afraid to do so. I hesitated. I even contemplated the idea of refusing. *I can walk away. This affair is not my problem.* This thought was so seductive to me I almost agreed to it. But something stopped me. Maybe it was my love for the truth and for problem solving. Maybe it was for Eva. Or maybe I just wanted to know why I was afraid to touch this dead animal. Frankly, I didn't know which one was the strongest persuasion… and that surprised me a little. Filling my lungs in one deep breath, I leaned forward and placed my hands squarely on the bear's forehead. At once, all the hairs on my body stood up.

The tingling of magic was there... just as I had feared. Maybe that was why I didn't want to touch the bear, I thought. Oh, but there was more, there was something else under the tingling, something was trapped inside this magic whirlwind. Grinding my teeth, I focused all my effort on piercing this spinning magic shell. Finally, I broke through the shell, and as I did, a strange sense of calm invaded me. I could now detect what was trapped inside the magic circle. It was a lovely shimmering essence, as fragile and as vaporous as the thin plume of smoke one gets after blowing out a candle. I tried concentrating my mind on it, but it was fading too quickly and the magic encircling it was becoming too strong. I had to pull back for fear of fainting.

This was no ordinary bear. I had known that for a while, yet there was more to this animal than just the fact that it was enchanted. I couldn't put my finger on it though. I probed the creature's head with swift little pokes. I didn't want my hands to linger too long on its pelt. I wanted to remain in control of myself.

While I was busy examining the animal, I noted that Khuan and Lilloh were busy examining me, as if I was more intriguing to them than the bear. Ignoring their intense scrutiny of my person, I continued my inspection of this animal. When my hands glided over the bear's ear, my fingertips bumped against something hard and pointy. I tried to see what it was, but couldn't because the bear's head was twisted to the side, partly covering that ear. Taking handfuls of fur, I pulled on the bear's head with all my might. It was too heavy; I couldn't move it.

Khuan then came to help. And once he added his strength to mine, the head finally rolled to the side exposing its ear.

Upon seeing that ear, my breath stayed caught in my throat. The bear wore a blue diamond earring. Thalia's earring.

"No! That's impossible!" I said. I rubbed my eyes, hoping I was wrong and that the earring would disappear. It didn't. Resigned, I slowly extended my hand toward the bear's head and plucked the earring from its ear.

Nestled in the middle of my palm, the sparkling jewel glimmered in the sunlight like a crystallized drop of water. There was no doubt in my mind; this was the other earring I had given her. I closed my fist around the blue diamond and stared at the dead bear. How did one put earrings on a bear? This didn't make any sense. I didn't understand.

Yes you do, a small voice whispered in my mind. *You know all to well what this means… or could mean.* I touched the bear again. The beautiful shimmering essence was almost gone now, her essence, Thalia's essence. My inner voice was right; I knew what the earring meant. I knew the answer, but thinking about it was too painful because… because—I sighed and closed my eyes—because I didn't want to, because it meant that by killing the bear we'd killed a princess. *NO! This is insane. This is exactly the kind of thoughts my crazy brothers had. I will not become like them. I refuse to.*

"I want no part of this!" I declared, then stood up and left the cemetery.

CHAPTER EIGHTEEN

I ran all the way back to the castle, then went straight for my rooms. I spoke to no one along the way, purposely ignoring all questions thrown at me. I wanted to forget what had just happened; I wanted to bury it in the darkest corner of my mind to never recall it ever again. Sadly, it wasn't to happen. That fact became clear the moment Khuan appeared around the corridor's bend ahead of me.

Alarmed, I stopped my trotting. The sound of another's footsteps coming to a halt nearby reached my ears. *Damn!* Someone was behind me. I didn't question who it was—I knew perfectly well who it was. I peeked over my shoulder. And of course, there was Lilloh, blocking my exit. Trapped between those two, I had no other choice than to ready myself for combat.

I pulled out my rapier.

A look of consternation flew across Khuan's face. He raised his hands in front of him, showing me that he was unarmed.

Oddly enough, he wasn't the one that worried me the most: Lilloh was. With her piercing gaze that always seemed imbued with an unnatural intensity, she appeared far more dangerous than her male counterpart, who, to me, seemed to possess a more calm and restrained nature than hers. This woman unnerved me like no other ever had before. That was somewhat troubling. When I glanced at her I thought I saw a similar distrust in her eyes. Apparently we shared the same feeling toward each other. Well, the dirk in her hand was also a clue.

My gaze returned to Khuan. His smooth, high-cheekboned face was impossible to read. And so was his enigmatic little smile. Was it friendly or threatening… I couldn't tell.

Khuan flipped his long black hair over his shoulder and took a step in my direction.

I brandished my rapier.

He sighed. "We mean you no harm, Prince Amir. We only want to speak with you."

"You… you speak our language," I said, quite shocked.

Smiling sheepishly, Khuan nodded. "Yes—indeed."

"But…" A sudden burst of anger filled my belly with fire. I felt tricked. I hated that feeling. I hated tricksters too. I glared at him. "I have nothing to say to you."

"We must talk," insisted Khuan.

"Enough!" I roared. "Let me pass!"

Khuan's gaze then settled on a point behind me. He shook his head *no*.

I swiftly turned, and jumped back in surprise.

Lilloh had sneaked up on me; she was now close enough to, well, stab me in the back. Hell, the woman was as silent as a cat. I raised my rapier and was relieved when I saw her back away. Fighting a woman didn't appeal to me.

Keeping my eyes on the pair and my back against the wall, I inched my way along the corridor until I judged I had put enough distance between us to risk turning my back on them.

"Prince Amir, you know there is evil in this castle." said Khuan behind me. "I know you can sense it."

"You're wrong! I sense nothing."

"It's unfortunate. That means the last Sorvinkian Princess

is condemned to suffer the same fate as her sisters."

This statement brought me to a dead stop. I turned and stared at them, hard.

"Hear us out," Khuan suggested in an extremely reasonable voice, which I thought didn't fit *at all* his wild appearance. "That's all we ask of you."

I sighed. Feeling resentment at having my hand forced, I reluctantly agreed to listen to what they had to say.

* * *

Seated on the couch adjacent to the fireplace, Khuan and Lilloh were quietly sipping tea in crystal glasses. They seemed totally at ease in my receiving room. I must say I found it rather surprising, because when I stipulated the conditions in which I would agree to speak with them, I was certain that they would refuse to submit to these: my rooms, no weapons—for them—I, evidently, would keep my sword. And lastly Milo would have to be present. No sane person would agree to that, I had thought then. Amazingly, they did, and gladly at that. Khuan, to my dismay, was not carrying any weapon at all. Lilloh, on the other hand, had so many concealed on her person that I lost count after her seventh blade hit the floor. Yet, the most mind-boggling instance was when she pulled out a long swordlike weapon from behind her back. From what I understood, the weapon had been strapped against her spine under her chain mail, its ebony grip perfectly hidden amidst her long, silky black hair.

I eyed the weapon pile she had left by my door. This woman was a walking arsenal. I could hardly believe those were all hers. Not to mention that some of the objects on the floor were totally unknown to me... and I knew weapons. I picked up a metal star with four sharpened points.

"To throw," clarified Khuan.

"Ah!" I dropped the star back on the pile. I glanced at

Milo. Our eyes met briefly. A nervous energy inhabited Milo's gaze. I could tell he wasn't fond of having these two here. Like me, Milo had been shocked by Lilloh's collection of weapons. Since then, he had kept a close eye on her. Milo's instinct as a trained bodyguard was an asset to me right now. I didn't need to tell him to stay alert, or to be on guard, he just did it by himself. Now if only he could carry a weapon… oh well.

"Excellent tea," Khuan said in near-perfect Sorvinkian. His mastery of this language was as good as mine, if not slightly better.

"Yes—tea—very excellent," added Lilloh in her light girlish voice, which I thought poorly suited her dangerous nature. Contrary to Khuan, her fractured Sorvinkian left a lot to be desired. She often confused, misused, and over-enunciated words, and at times her accent was so thick that it rendered her speech incomprehensible, forcing me to constantly say, "Pardon—" to have her repeat herself. This, needless to say, infuriated her.

"Emissary Khuan," I began, "your Sorvinkian is beyond reproach. So why did you let everyone in the castle believe you didn't master this language."

Khuan smiled. "People wouldn't speak as freely around us, if they knew we understood what they were saying."

"Isn't it a tad dishonest?"

"Yes, it is. However, Lilloh and I were sent here to learn about these people, about their culture. About the way they think. How can we do this if everyone lies to us? If they knew about our ability to understand them, they would never show us their true faces."

"Hmm…" I gave. No matter how I looked at it, he was right. And by having admitted that their stratagem was dishonest, he'd closed the door on that argument. I nodded and changed the subject. "You said you were sent here. By whom?"

"The Emperor Tomi Cho'tang sent us. We are his

emissaries and loyal servants." Placing their joined hands under their chins, Khuan and Lilloh bowed in reverence to the emperor.

I snorted. "You, Sir Khuan, I believe are an emissary. But your companion…" Sensing Lilloh's piercing gaze on me, I hesitated to continue. The truth was I suspected that she might still have a weapon hidden on her person. *Tread lightly, Amir. Insult that woman and you'll discover a knife sticking out of your chest.* With this in mind, I continued with prudence. "Your companion is… well, not the image one has of an emissary."

Lilloh's dark smoldering eyes narrowed.

My stomach tightened in response.

As if he was sensing a dangerous change in his companion's temper, Khuan patted her hands in a calming manner. "Lilloh and I have been together for years."

"Oh, she's your wife," interjected Milo. "For some reason, I thought she was your sister."

"She's neither," Khuan replied. "We are a shal-galt khos, a shal-galt pair."

I felt a sudden spike of interest. *Shal-galt.* Lilloh had said that word to me before. "What are shal-galts?"

"The most accurate Sorvinkian translation I can find is seeker."

"Seeker of what?"

Again, I observed the return of that enigmatic little smile on Khuan's lips. "Seeker of truth. Seeker of all that is unworldly and esoteric."

My eyebrows rose and I stared at him in disbelief. "Seeker of ghosts? Are you mocking me?"

"Certainly not. Perhaps I should start over." Khuan set down his tea glass. "Shal-galts are born with the gift, or the curse depending on how one sees it, to sense what most people cannot. It can be the world of spirits, the remnants of magic, or the presence of demons and ghosts. Lilloh and

I both possess such a gift. However, being gifted isn't enough to make one an emissary. All shal-galts are trained from a young age, not only to use and master their gifts, but also to be experts in many other disciplines such as combat, diplomacy, medicine, philosophy, and logic, to name a few. No true emissary can efficiently perform his duty without knowledge of those skills. In our culture, shal-galts are highly regarded and are usually at the service of the emperor."

"You mention being a pair. What does that mean?"

"Most shal-galts are born with one gift. They can either sense magic or detect the presence of demons and ghosts. Few can do both. This is why Lilloh and I have been paired together. We complete each other. I can detect demons, spirits, and ghosts, while she can sense magic, spells, and enchantments." Khuan's eyes met mine. "And so can you."

I stayed mute. There was no use denying it anyway.

"The bear," said Lilloh, "It was enchanted—you felt too, yes?"

I did not care for this line of questions. Deciding not to answer, I folded my arms tightly over my chest in a resolute manner.

"You do sense magic, you cannot deny that fact," insisted Khuan.

"I'm hardly the only one," I admitted.

"What do you mean by this?" asked Khuan. He looked quite intrigued by my reply. "Can you explain it further?"

Not seeing any harm in it, I told them about the curse that had decimated my family, and how everyone in the palace had been able to sense it and see its ghostly apparitions, even the servants.

Khuan nodded. "So that is what awoke your gift. A curse this powerful, encompassing over a hundred people, can't be concealed. Others however are so subtle that even the most sensitive of shal-galts cannot detect them."

I shook my head and looked away.

"I see that you're struggling with this," said Khuan. "You cannot escape it. This gift is as much a part of you as your brown eyes."

I shook my head again. "Why should I believe anything you're saying? For all I know, you could be behind everything that happened recently."

I went to a nearby desk and came back with the metal loop I had discovered in the servants' passage. "Is this what you were looking for in the passage leading to the princesses' room," I said, chucking the loop into Lilloh's lap.

The shal-galt pair looked at each other, then looked at me as if they didn't understand what I meant.

"Oh please," I said. "Obviously, you went there to pick up that loop she lost. So there wouldn't be any traces of your presence in that passageway… and the princesses' rooms."

Khuan gave me a chagrined look. "Why would we want to harm these young ladies?"

"To get to the king, I suppose. Your people are known as invaders. If the king is distraught and not in his right mind, it might make matters easier for an invading force."

Khuan leaned forward, resting his elbows on his knees. "Prince Amir, we have an agreement with the king, a pact, one we intend to respect. So it is to our advantage that this kingdom remains stable. And what's happening here threatens this pact." Khuan leaned back in the couch and sighed. "Yes, we were in that passage. But we were there for the same reason as you. We were trying to solve this mystery. As Anchin's emissaries it is our duty to see that the emperor's interests be protected."

Although his explanation made sense, something else remained unexplained. I pointed to Lilloh. "Why did she follow me in the wood that day and attack my friend… and me too?"

"I attack nobody!" Lilloh protested vehemently. "If I attack, you dead now."

Oh, I had no trouble believing that.

Lilloh glared at me. "I follow traces in snow like you. Bear and man traces. Then I follow you and smelly prince." Lilloh pinched her small nose with her fingers and stuck out her tongue, as though she could still smell Diego's overwhelming perfume.

"So you admit following us! Tell me why?"

It was Khuan who answered. "Lilloh was curious about you. She insisted that you possessed some gift and was determined to prove her point." Khuan paused and cast a sly glance at his companion. "She can be very headstrong, you know."

I would not argue that point. "Why did she kiss me? I don't understand that."

Khuan chuckled behind his hand. "We shal-galts can sense a lot through touch... any kind of touch. So why did she choose to kiss you, you've asked? Simply because a kiss is far more disarming than a punch. Generally, one stops struggling when kissed."

That was true. When it happened I was so stunned that I stayed frozen in place like an idiot. *Damn!* I looked at Khuan. Everything he'd said so far sounded logical—besides that ghost seeker part, that is. Perhaps I could trust him... for now. "What did you find about this mystery, Sir Khuan?"

"That something foul is roaming this castle, and I fear it isn't finished doing misdeeds. Let's not fool ourselves; we all know who will be its next victim."

My hands balled into tight fists. "I know. But what am I supposed to do about it. I don't know who's behind this. Do you?"

"Not yet," said Lilloh. "With one more shal-galt we may—"

"Stop right there!" I snapped. "I'm not like you. I'm not a shal-galt. I'm not trained in whatever it is you do."

Lilloh and Khuan exchanged glances. Then Khuan's

patient gaze came to rest on me. "Will you permit us to test you, to see what capacities you have and how far they extend?"

A sudden storm of emotion engulfed me. And I found myself stuck in a mix of terror and excitement. I truly feared what I might discover about myself. But for Eva's sake, I urgently needed to know if my capacities could be of any help saving her.

Sitting down in front of Khuan, I asked in a small voice. "What does this testing involve?"

Khuan gave a reassuring smile. "Only your willingness to participate."

"Hmm... I feared that much."

* * *

The shal-galt pair led Milo and me on a long promenade through the castle, where I was asked to touch all kinds of things, like walls, doors, and such. It all seemed a bit random to me. And after a long period of this touching exercise, where nothing happened, I began doubting the stability of their minds. Maybe following them was a mistake. Maybe those two were just as crazy as my brother Jafer had been.

Our next stop was in the open area, near the stairs leading to the alchemist's tower, where the indoor well was located. I thought we were going to climb the stairs, but instead we went to the well.

"Here—touch here." Lilloh stabbed a finger on a dark spot marring the well's rim.

"No! I have had enough of this. I'm returning to my rooms." Before I could make a move to leave, Lilloh seized my hand and pressed it on the dark spot.

A sharp jolt of energy shot through my arm at the speed of a lightning bolt.

"Aaaah!" I shouted and jumped back in shock. I rubbed my

arm, trying to chase away the tingling sensation left behind by the jolt. "What was that?"

Khuan indicated the dark spot. "We found this *Point of Power* several weeks ago."

"What! If you knew it was here, why did you waste my time by dragging me all over the place?"

Khuan sighed. "We had to make sure that you were truly able to sense magic. For this, we had to test you on empty points first. Some people try too hard and will often declare sensing something where there is nothing."

Lilloh snickered sarcastically. "He tries too little, I say."

"Woman, your remarks and persistence aggravate me," I said as I approached the well. I was still a few steps away from its edge when the tingling reappeared in my extremities. "You call this a *Point of Power?*"

"Yes—" a feminine voice blew near my ear. I flinched; Lilloh had once again sneaked up on me. I sensed her body pressing against mine. Then I felt her breath warming my ear. "When point gets strong… bad things happen to princess."

I swallowed hard. "It's strong now."

"Very strong."

I cringed, wishing she had not agreed. I backed away from the well and from Lilloh's disturbing closeness, and looked up at the stairs. This was the path to Isabo's room. For a moment, I debated if I should share my knowledge of her potion-making with them. Yes, I decided, and told them all I knew. Khuan listened with great interest.

"See, if it wasn't for the digitalis, I would almost be tempted to believe that she's innocent. But poison is poison no matter how I put it."

"Di-gi-ta-lis?" Khuan frowned. "Describe the plant to me."

I did.

"AH—chi'gotank!" they both exclaimed simultaneously.

"You know this plant?"

"Yes. A powerful heart remedy."

"It's poison!"

"Most medicine if given in too large a dose can be poison-ous. Some far more than others. Chi'gotank, or digitalis as you call it, belongs to these and has very strict usage rules. Two drops you live, three you die, that's the rule."

"Two drops... that's exactly what goes in the queen's tonic. So Isabo wasn't poisoning anyone after all. Well, that complicates things. Because now I have absolutely no suspects." I looked at Khuan. He appeared to be lost in his thoughts. Apparently, they were of an unpleasant nature because his forehead and brow were deeply furrowed. With his hands joined behind his back, he began pacing around while mumbling in his native tongue.

"He thinks hard now," Lilloh commented. "Men have harder time thinking than women."

"Pardon!" I said in a vexed tone.

Lilloh produced a half-pout, half-smirk smile. "Khuan," she called. "We have suspect. The student innocent... but teacher—the teacher can be guilty."

"Yes!" he said, coming to a sudden halt. "That could be the solution."

Well, now I was lost. And by the dazed look on Milo's face, so was he. "What are you talking about? What teacher?"

Lilloh pressed herself against me and in a purring voice said, "The teacher of potions."

"Yes! That's it!" I exclaimed! Putting some space between me and Lilloh—the woman was again too close to me for my taste—I pondered over this new development. I came to a quick decision. We should search for the person who taught Isabo how to make those elaborate remedies. I figured she might have an accomplice. Why didn't I think of it before? It annoyed me that I had not thought of it, but it annoyed me even more that it was Lilloh who had figured it out first.

It was then that a sudden and rather disquieting realization dawned on me.

From the beginning, I had assumed that Khuan was the smarter of the two. Now, I thought that maybe he was just the most reasonable one, and that made Lilloh... well, far more dangerous than she already was, which was a lot. However, there was one detail she failed to mention. I folded my arms and asked. "And how are we going to find that teacher?"

"We could ask Isabo," suggested Milo.

Khuan shook his head. "We tried seeing her after she was arrested but were denied access to her cell."

"Unfortunately, I don't see who else could help us besides her."

The pair exchanged glances, and although their eyes only made contact for the space of a few breaths, I had the feeling that they had had a long conversation. Those two shared a strong bond. They possessed a complicity only achieved through years of companionship.

Khuan hugged himself and stayed in that position for a long period. Then his arms fell to his sides and, as if it pained him to do so, he said in a grim voice, "There is someone else that might be able to help us... or at the very least answer some of our questions."

"Who?" I asked.

"The ghoul."

CHAPTER NINETEEN

From the couch of my receiving room, I watched the sun go down with growing apprehension. After Khuan, Lilloh, and I had made the decision to go looking for the castle's ghoul, it was also decided that nighttime would be best to conduct this *affair*. According to Khuan, ghouls were notoriously shy during the day and tended to hide.

Milo approached the couch. "Are you sure this is a good idea?"

"I thought you *wanted* me to chase monsters," I replied with humor.

"I'm not questioning that part, my lord. I meant going out at night with those two. I don't mind Sir Khuan. The woman… that's a different story. You've seen how many weapons she carries. Worse, one cannot tell she has that many on herself."

"True. She conceals them rather well." I watched Milo fidget beside the couch. Obviously, something else was on his mind. "Speak."

"Hm… I was thinking that maybe we too should carry concealed weapons of our own… just in case."

"Forget it, Milo. I'm not giving you a sword. You'll be in more danger carrying one than without. Think of what would happen to you if you get caught with a sword."

Milo's shoulder sagged and his chin lowered to his chest. "Yes, my lord," he said in a disheartened voice.

I sighed, feeling sorry for Milo. "Listen. If it were my choice, I would gladly give you a sword. You're more useful to me with one. But I cannot take that risk here, though. Don't worry, Milo, you will carry a sword again, I promise."

Milo nodded. Yet I could tell by his long face that he placed little faith in my promise. Maybe it was for the best. I shouldn't have made that promise in the first place, because I had no way of keeping it, and it wasn't fair to him.

Three sharp knocks sounded at the door.

"They're here," I said, pulling myself to my feet.

Grabbing our coats, Milo and I hurried to join the pair in the corridor. Both wore pointy fur-rimmed hats, heavy leather capes, and fur boots.

"Where shall we go first?" I asked Khuan.

Baring an enigmatic expression, he answered, "I don't know, you decide."

"I thought you knew where the ghoul was?"

"I know where it is. But I want to see if *you* can find the ghoul."

"Me?"

Khuan nodded. "For all we know, you may have both gifts. I think we should verify if that is the case."

I shrugged. "Fine."

As I had been assigned the chore of searching for the ghoul, I took the lead. In my opinion, this exercise was meaningless. First, everybody knew that ghouls roamed cemeteries—as they fed on corpses—no need being a shal-galt or a seeker to figure that out. Second, how could we trust a ghoul to give us reliable information? Those were vile, deceitful creatures. Frankly, I wouldn't believe a word coming out of a ghoul's foul mouth.

As we made our way through the castle's corridors, an upsetting detail floated to the top of my mind. I stopped and glared at the pair, and said in an accusing tone, "Lars! Lars was dead. And you… you beat him back to life. What sorcery was that?" Uneasy, I distanced myself from them.

In a soft, calm voice, Khuan began explaining the technique he had used to revive Lars. The whole process consisted of emptying his lungs of fluid then filling them with air, while pounding on his chest to awaken his heart.

"And that works?" I said, skeptic. This *technique* sounded complicated and, to be perfectly honest, far fetched, yet plausible too… in a bizarre way.

"Perfectly!" said Khuan. "I'm surprised that no one here knows about this ancient technique."

"Pf…" sneered Lilloh. "And they say we savages."

I smiled. "And they call us savages, you should say."

Lilloh became very serious.

Mmm, that was a mistake. I bowed to her. "I apologize, Emissary Lilloh. I shouldn't have corrected you."

Lilloh grinned, and then she gripped her throat with both hands as if she wanted to strangle herself. That wasn't the reaction I had expected from my apology. "Er… I don't understand that."

"Lars," she said, "Lars… green grass… squeeze throat. I ripped off… help breathe."

I scratched my head. "Green grass? Oh—algae! There were algae wrapped around his neck."

"Yes. Yes. Long, long… like." Lilloh grabbed a handful of her long, silky black hair. "Long," she repeated.

"Yes," I said, "like long hair." I remembered seeing something like that when I was underwater; it was tangled around a fish—and here I thought I had seen a *hairy* fish. Apparently these algae were wrapped around Lars's neck too. I could comprehend that ripping these green strings from Lars's neck could help him breathe. That made perfect sense to me… certainly more than Khuan's story about that old technique he told us earlier. What a fable that was.

Now that my question had been answered, and this matter had been settled, we continued our search. When we reached the courtyard door, I stopped at the guards' station located at its entrance to borrow four torches. Then we set out from the castle.

The sky was clear, the moon and stars shone brightly, the air painfully icy and dry. It stung my cheeks and made breathing as painful as if I had glass shards in my lungs.

Covering my mouth and nose with my glove, to warm the air entering my nostrils, I stopped a moment to orient myself. Then with the snow squeaking under my boots, I walked toward the cemetery. The others followed without question. In no time, we had reached the edge of the cemetery. I stopped and scanned the area. There was nothing here but dark shadows, snow, and tombstones. Still, I decided to inspect every alley regardless.

After having zigzagged across the entire cemetery, I came to the conclusion that there was no ghoul here. If this was another stupid test, where I wasn't supposed to feel anything, I would not take it lightly. We were wasting too much time, far too much, and it was freezing cold outside.

As I turned to ask Khuan about that, a cold shiver ran along my spine that I knew had nothing to do with the ambient temperature. No. This icy sensation on my skin was caused by the sudden eerie feeling that something abnormal was nearby, a presence, and a very peculiar one at that. I had felt it once before, today actually, at the queen's funeral. To my surprise, it didn't emanate from the cemetery or any of its crypts, but seemed to be coming from the castle itself.

Raising my torch, I slowly advanced in that direction. Immediately, the feeling of having cold fingers dancing along my spine intensified. I hurried to the castle and began following its dark stone wall. Within moments, goose bumps covered my entire body. I was near, very near. Just then I saw what I was looking for, the door of a cold cellar dug in the ground nearby the castle's foundation.

Placing a foot on the door, I sensed something unpleasant beyond it. The feeling was so repulsive that it brought to mind the image of maggots feasting on a corpse. I shuddered and turned to Khuan. "The ghoul is in there, isn't it?"

He and Lilloh exchanged forlorn looks. Nodding, Khuan let out a heavy sigh. "So you are doubly cursed." His voice sounded too chagrined for my taste.

"Do you care to explain why you're so saddened by this?"

"It's difficult enough to live a normal life with one gift, to do so with two is nearly impossible. People possessing both sights, especially untrained ones, have difficulty coping with the many visions their gifts impose on them. Many choose to end their lives, or go mad. Being doubly gifted is generally a family curse, one that is passed along through generations. Often in those families more than one person at a time are affected by it."

My thoughts turned to Jafer. "A few of my brothers were mad. Thinking about it now, some might have had that double curse too. At least one did, of that I'm certain."

"You are—rarity," Lilloh said.

I frowned.

Khuan smiled. "Doubly gifted individuals are not that rare. However, untrained ones who remain sane, at your age, and with your level of sensitivity are almost never seen. If you wish, I would gladly share some of my knowledge—"

I raised my hand, stopping him. "No. I appreciate the offer, but I'm not interested." The last thing I needed was to be trained to seek ghosts and demons with more efficiency. In my opinion, the sooner I would forget about this, the better it would be. I didn't care much for the looks they were giving me either, like I was some exotic creature brought in for study.

Kneeling down, I grabbed the cellar latch and opened the

door. A stench of death and decay hit me right in the face. Staggering backward, it took me a moment to regain my composure and move in.

Torches in hand, Milo and I were first to descend the couple steps leading into the cellar. A long, narrow space with a dirt floor and a low ceiling, the cellar stunk of cabbage and vinegar. It was more spacious than I thought and also darker than I liked. Fortunately the darkness didn't last. Because when Lilloh and Khuan joined us, adding their torches to ours, the entire place lit up. The first things I saw were the corpses of the guards and servants killed by the bears. They were all lined up on the floor ahead of us. Then I saw the ghoul at the end of the line.

Crouched over the body of a guard, the creature was too busy gorging itself on the putrefied flesh to notice our presence. The ghoul, I observed, had a basic human form, but there ended the resemblance. This foul apparition was covered with scars, boils, and sores. Even its bald head was a raw mass of oozing sores and red-crusted wounds... *unless they're leftovers from previous feasts.* Utterly disgusted, I brandished my torch toward the ghoul. "Stop, vile monster!"

Stupefied to have been caught in the act of gnawing on a body, the ghoul raised bloody clawed hands, shielding his narrow red eyes, and hissed aggressively at us.

His face wasn't as I had expected. Beastly was how I had imagined it would be. But instead it was, to my dismay, like the face of an old man, wrinkled, twisted, and nearly toothless. Quite frankly, I found it far more disturbing than if it had been beastly looking.

Pulling to my side, Milo lowered his torch toward the creature. The ghoul shrieked, exposing a mouth dripping with blood and smeared with half-chewed chunks of maggot-infested flesh.

"OH—ghastly!" Milo exclaimed just before he bent over and emptied his stomach at my feet. "Pardon me, my lord," he said, rising. "I... I couldn't..."

"Shhh!" I hushed, moving forward.

The ghoul growled and hissed in a threatening manner. Yet it failed to frighten or intimidate me. By the way the ghoul's narrow eyes were anxiously darting around in search of a way out, it was evident that the ghoul was more scared than anything else. Suddenly, the creature's eyes settled on a point behind me. The ghoul's physiognomy changed. From scared it became terrified. Curling up in the corner of the cellar, the ghoul began whimpering like a beaten dog. I peeked over my shoulder to see what could cause such a reaction in the ghoul: Lilloh. She was slapping the flat side of a short blade in the palm of her hand, muted plop, plop, plop sounds accompanied the gestures.

"Good! It remembers me," she said with a proud smirk.

"You've met this creature before?"

Khuan nodded.

"I don't understand. If you've questioned it already, why are we here?"

"Then we thought the ghoul guilty of these crimes. We didn't know as much as now. We didn't ask the right questions. Evil does not volunteer information. One must be clever and precise in his questioning to get the right answers."

"I'll ask." Lilloh advanced toward the ghoul.

The creature reacted by letting out a bloodcurdling shriek and clawing the air in desperation. I must admit that, for the space of a heartbeat, I felt some pity for the screaming ghoul.

Covering my ears, I turned to Khuan. "There must be a better way of dealing with this horrid being."

Khuan aimed patient eyes at me, and I was glad to see that his wise gaze harbored no cruelty whatsoever, only a hint of concern. "This is the proper way, Amir," said Khuan. "Sadly, ghouls need incentives to cooperate; otherwise it would lie to us. Pain, or the fear of pain, is usually what works best."

"Call her back then. This ghoul is clearly ready to talk."

After giving a nod in my direction, Khuan spoke briefly to Lilloh in his native tongue. She cast him a dark resentful look, and then her somber stare switched to me. With her full lips pushed forward in a sign of disapproval, she shook her head. "Too much kindness... bad! Can hurt you. Evil does best work through kind people."

"I agree with her, my lord," Milo snorted. "Let her beat that creature. Better yet, let me do it."

Lilloh bowed to Milo, and before I could tell the young eunuch to quiet down, Khuan squeezed my elbow. "Do not reprimand your valet in front of this creature," he whispered. "When confronting evil, even an entity as weak as a ghoul, always, and I mean *always*, show a united front."

How dare he give me orders! Even though I didn't protest openly and kept my mouth shut, I nonetheless expressed my discontentment by roughly pulling out of his grip.

Seemingly unaffected by my rude behavior, Khuan said, "Come. Let's approach this creature together."

We crossed the distance separating us from the hissing ghoul. As we got close to it, a powerful stench of decomposed flesh engulfed us. The smell was so vile I had to draw air through my mouth for fear that if I breathed normally I would retch uncontrollably.

"Who is behind those deaths?" asked Khuan.

The ghoul didn't answer, it just growled at us.

"Speak, or we will hurt you," Khuan threatened.

For a moment the ghoul looked as if torn by conflict. Finally, its mouth twisted. "They'll hurt me worse if I do," the ghoul said in a gravelly voice.

Confused, I looked at Milo and Lilloh. Did the ghoul mean these two?—somehow I doubted it. "Who will hurt you? Who are they?"

The ghoul spat in my direction. A fat glob of bloody spit

landed on my boot. My dislike for this creature was growing by leaps and bounds. I thrust my torch at the ghoul. I had no intension of actually burning the repulsive creature, but I thought I could make a good bluff of it. The move brought me a disapproving glare from Khuan. The ghoul, for his part, shrieked loudly and leapt back in fear.

"Who are they?" I demanded.

"The disciples," the ghoul snarled. "They'll hurt me if I talk. The disciples will hurt me. The old one is wicked— WICKED."

"The old one," I repeated. "Who's the old one? What's his name? And who are these disciples?"

"Can't—too afraid," the ghoul blurted out.

We tried extorting more information out of the ghoul, but failed to get anything coherent from the terrified creature. We all came to the conclusion that there was no use staying here any longer.

As we were about to leave the cellar, a thought crossed my mind. *Perhaps there are other questions the ghoul could answer, questions that will not frighten it as much.* I turned around. "Ghoul, is there someone else besides you who can answer our questions? Someone who is not afraid of the old one?"

"All that serve the old one, fears the old one."

"Name someone who isn't serving the old one then."

The ghoul became as still as a statue. While it remained in that pose, with its head slightly cocked to the side, it looked too human for my taste. Then its small red eyes rose toward me and the traces of humanity I had thought I saw in that creature moments ago vanished. What was left in front of me was nothing but a demon.

"The witch," hissed the ghoul. "The witch knows." The creature then produced a hideous grimace, which I supposed was his idea of a smile.

I tried more questions but got nothing else out of the ghoul. Short of options, we decided to leave the cellar. Once I was outside in the cold night air, I filled my lungs with much delight. Lord, I was happy to be rid of the horrid stench of the ghoul. Milo stepped beside me and bent down. I watched him rub a handful of snow over his ashen face.

"You bluffed," Khuan snapped. "When you made as if you were going to burn the ghoul with your torch, you were bluffing." Khuan's sharp reproof took me by surprise; he was usually so composed.

"It worked. The ghoul believed me."

"Doesn't matter. Never bluff with evil. If you do something, you better mean it. Otherwise if it sees through your bluff, it will never believe you again, no matter what you try."

"Enough, Khuan!" said Lilloh. "He did well. He got answers."

The tension stiffening Khuan's shoulders eased and soon he was looking calm and collected again. "The witch that the ghoul mentioned, can it be the girl in the dungeon?"

I had come to that conclusion too. Isabo was probably who the ghoul meant. I nodded. "I believe so."

"Then we learned nothing," said Khuan. "Because seeing her is impossible."

"That's not true. We learned about the disciples and the old one. I think I know who they are." I told Khuan and Lilloh about the baron and the black robed group. "It makes sense. The black-robe followers are the disciples and the baron is the old one. It fits."

Khuan rubbed his smooth chin. "Or his god could be the old one. If that's the case, we're doomed. We cannot win a fight against a god."

In a sudden outburst of frustration, Lilloh elbowed her way between me and Khuan and exclaimed, "Men! Blind men! See, Isabo was with bear. Why with bear, if not to do bad things. I think she enchanted bear. She disciple. Teacher of potion is old one."

I sighed. The ghoul had said disciples not disciple. Sadly Lilloh's rudimentary knowledge of Sorvinkian didn't permit her to catch the nuance between plural and singular. But that wasn't the main flaw in her reasoning. "No. You're wrong. The ghoul said that the witch, Isabo, didn't serve the old one."

Lilloh frowned. "No! She guilty."

"I disagree. My gut feeling tells me that she's innocent."

"Gut! Gut know only food."

I moaned and rolled my eyes in despair. "That means something different…" I paused; explaining this to her was an exercise in futility. "Never mind, Lilloh, you can't understand."

Lilloh didn't take my remark lightly. She stepped closer to me and raised her chin in defiance. "You not so smart. Explain bear."

"I can't."

"Then I right."

"No, you're not," I argued. "The baron has something to do with this. I'm sure of it."

"Do you smell magic on baron?"

"Smell? Sense magic on him, you mean—no, but—"

"You *sense* magic on Isabo."

Reluctantly, I said, "Well, yes."

"See, Amir, I right."

"Amir! How dare you use my name this freely! I did not permit you this familiarity. This is highly impolite and rude."

Lilloh's eyes narrowed. "Yes. But I right. You sense fat princess inside bear."

I flinched and stepped back. "I sensed nothing of the sort."

"Liar! You sense. I saw. Isabo with bear. Fat princess in bear. See! I right!" Lilloh stamped her foot down repetitively. "See! See! See!"

"All right, all right. I see your point," I admitted with obvious discontent. Needless to say, I was beginning to dislike Lilloh quite a bit.

"My lord," Milo murmured into my ear. "I'm glad you've agreed with her. Otherwise I fear this she-devil may have stabbed you."

Khuan threw me a sheepish look. "I think Lilloh might be right. Sadly, that brings us back to Isabo and the fact that we can't see her."

Churning the problem in my mind, I came to an obvious solution. "I'll have to ask Eva to help us. I'm quite certain she can convince the guards to let me speak with Isabo."

"If she agree to see you," said a skeptic-looking Lilloh.

"Why wouldn't she? We're trying to help her family, her sisters."

Lilloh pouted. "She won't help you. Trust me, I speak truth. That woman... Pf. She brings you only pain. She worthless."

"Watch your tongue!"

Lilloh raised her chin. "No. I say what I think."

Khuan promptly stepped in between Lilloh and me. "I believe we've wasted enough of your time, Prince Amir. A thousand thanks." On these words, he bowed and left, nearly dragging an unwilling Lilloh behind him.

Good, leave! That was just as well, I thought, because I had seen enough of those two for now. As I watched the glow of their torches diminish, one thought haunted me: What if Lilloh was right? What if Eva refused to meet me? How would I save her then?

CHAPTER TWENTY

The next morning I awoke very early because I had something clear and precise in mind. A special plan of action, which to be successful needed to be set in motion at the earliest of hours.

Fearing that Lilloh might be right to assume that Eva would refuse to help me—or just plainly refuse to see me—I had decided to enter her bedroom without her consent or knowledge. First, I made my way to the servants' quarters. Once I arrived there, I was surprised by the frantic activity of the place. Cooks were hard at work; stewards were busy polishing silverware while valets and maids rushed in and out carrying freshly laundered linen and sparkling porcelain dishes.

"What's the cause of all this excitement?" I asked a maid as she dashed by me.

The maid, a plump woman in her thirties with heavy-hooded eyes, gave me a perplexed look. "But, my lord, we're preparing the banquet hall for tonight's announcement."

"What announcement?"

"Oh, my lord doesn't know!" exclaimed the maid. "The king has decided to remarry. He's announcing his choice tonight!" The maid paused and peeked around briefly before whispering in a tone of secrecy, "It's Countess Ivana.

Everybody already knows about it. Tonight it's gonna be made official though. Now I must go back to work, my lord." On these words, the maid curtseyed and fled through one of the passages.

Although this wedding seemed a bit rushed to me, I was glad the king chose Ivana. I believed she'd make a wonderful queen. My thoughts returned to Eva. Soon, she too would begin preparing for this event, and then maids would swarm around her like worker bees tending a queen.

Knowing that I had no time to lose, I entered the passage leading to her room. I tiptoed to the door and paused before opening it. Maybe coming here was a mistake. It was certainly improper. Chances were good that she was going to be angry at me. If so, what would I say? I sighed. There was no way of predicting her reaction, and staying here was a waste of precious time. And really, the consequence of this action couldn't be worse than the torment of not knowing anyway. My mind made up, I gathered my courage and entered Eva's bedroom.

Standing motionless in front of her window in her black mourning dress, Eva resembled one of the many shadows inhabiting the corners of her dimly lit room.

I cleared my throat.

She didn't move; her eyes remained lost in space. "I don't want anything this morning, thank you," she murmured, believing I was a servant.

I was astounded by the dullness of her voice, by her downcast attitude. "Eva, it's me; Amir," I whispered.

She turned and, for a brief instant, surprise illuminated her red puffy eyes. Then this minute spark of light extinguished itself and her eyes took on a somber air of defeat.

"What are you doing here?" she asked in a voice that was devoid of interest yet still managed to be laced with condemnation. "Don't say it is to get news of Lars's health, which hasn't changed by the way, or to congratulate Father on his decision to remarry. I know you care not for my family."

Her biting tone tore through my feelings as easily as fangs would tear through my flesh. As a result I found myself caught in a storm of conflicting emotions. For one, I wanted to hold her, kiss her, and beg for her forgiveness. But, at the same time, I was angry at her. I had done nothing wrong. Why was I treated so harshly? I didn't deserve it. "Why are you so unkind to me, Eva? You know how much I care about you. You know how hard I tried to gain your father's approval. And why are you blaming me for something your cousin engineered. I… I don't understand you anymore."

Eva lowered her head. I watched her bring her fists to her forehead. "Please, Amir, enough reprimand, enough of your litany of excuses and blames. I cannot quarrel with you today. I don't have the strength for it. So just tell me why you're here and end this meeting."

I blinked. I believed that if she had slapped me I wouldn't be more hurt. For a moment, I debated if I should leave. I could certainly do that. It would be easy, just turn around and walk away. But instead, I stepped forward. "I need your help."

Eva looked up at me, and for the first time since I entered her room, I saw a hint of interest in her eyes. "For what?"

"Solving the mystery of your sisters' disappearances."

Her beautiful, smooth brow became furrowed. "How?"

"Well, I don't know yet. First, I must speak with Isabo, and for this I need you to accompany me to the dungeon. The guards won't refuse you access to her cell."

"No! Isabo can rot there for all I care."

I could tell Eva wouldn't be convinced without knowing more. So I wasted no time and quickly told her all I had learned so far. I recounted my meeting with the baron and the black robed group, with the ghoul, my visit to the Baba's house. I also told her about Isabo's tonic. I told her everything except the fact that I believed Thalia might have been transformed into a bear—a bear which was now dead. Eva was already too broken up. I couldn't deal her that devastating blow right now; it would've been too cruel. No matter how much she'd hurt me, I didn't have the heart to make her suffer more. "Eva, I'm beginning to think that Isabo might be innocent."

"That witch, innocent—NEVER! What you've told me doesn't prove her innocence, Amir."

"It proves that she didn't poison your mother. At the very least, she's innocent of that."

"Are you sure she has nothing to do with Mother's death?"

"Totally," I said, although I wasn't certain, but I needed to convince her, so she would agree to help me.

Eva hugged herself. "If you're right… and she's innocent that means…"

"That means you're in grave danger."

Eva's eyes plunged into mine. "I care not for my own safety. I thought you'd understand this by now. I fear for my father, my family, and the future of my country. Whoever is behind this isn't only attacking us; he's also attacking Sorvinka's stability."

Crossing the space separating us, Eva said, "Come, Amir. We must hurry. Isabo is scheduled to be burnt at the stake in the very near future. So if we want to speak with her there is no time to waste."

* * *

The castle's dungeon was cold, humid, and, despite numerous torches burning against the walls, cloaked in semipermanent darkness. This was probably due to the lack of windows and the dark gray stone used in its construction.

Eva and I stopped in front of the head guard.

"Princess!" he said in a mixture of surprise and reverence.

"Why is Your Highness here? This isn't a place for—"

Eva raised a hand and, in a commanding tone, ordered, "Where is the witch? I demand to see her."

"Yes, Your Highness. This way, Your Highness." The head guard led us to the iron gate of a cell. Its bars were pitted by time and encrusted with rust flakes. After a brief battle with the lock, the guard opened the gate and let us in.

Taking the lead, Eva took a hesitant step inside the cell, then stopped abruptly. She stayed fixed in place, as if paralyzed. I tried to see what was ahead, but she was hindering my sight. Breaking free of her static state, Eva leaned slightly forward. "Isabo…" she said in a strangled voice.

Nothing. No reply came.

"Isabo—Isabo!" Eva called more firmly this time.

Again, no reply.

I looked at the guard standing just outside the iron gate for an explanation.

"She won't answer, Your Highness. She's been like this ever since we brought her in."

Intrigued, I managed to squeeze past Eva and finally got a look at Isabo.

Seated on the straw-covered floor of the cell with her legs spread wide apart and her mouth hanging loosely, Isabo stared at the ceiling without blinking. Her posture was evocative of that of an automaton I had seen years ago. The mechanical doll had looked very much alive when moving, and very much dead when not. I then saw Isabo's chest rise slightly. *She breathes… shallowly though.* I also observed that her face was bruised and swollen in places, and that she was disheveled and dirty.

Again I turned my attention to the guard. "You said she's been in that… trance, (I couldn't find a better word to describe her state.) since she was arrested."

"No," said the guard. "When we arrested her, she screamed, cried, and cursed us. It's only after we threw her in here that she turned that way. She hasn't eaten or drunk anything since."

I stared at the stale loaf of bread and the bright blue bowl of water set in the corner of the cell. The loaf was untouched, the blue bowl, with its cheery raindrop decoration painted on its sides, was still filled to the brim.

The guard shuffled his feet. "We tried to make her speak… without success. She didn't say a word or make a sound, not even a peep. Nothing worked on her. It's as if she feels nothing."

I eyed Isabo's bruised face, her lips were split, her nose bent and bloody. I shook my head. She certainly had been brutalized enough to at least have yelled in pain. "You mentioned that she was speaking when you arrested her. What did she say then?"

As the guard glanced at Isabo, his attitude became one of disdain. For him she was a criminal like any other. "The usual," he said with a shrug. "You know, I'm innocent; you're making a mistake and such. Then she cursed the queen."

"Interesting! Do you recall the words she used, her exact ones?"

"Hm…" The guard scratched his head. "She said that if she was arrested the queen would die. Something like that."

"Did she mention that the queen would die without her care?"

The guard's head bobbed up and down. "Oh yes! That too!" A look of puzzlement wrinkled his face. "Were you there, my lord? I don't remember seeing you."

"No. I just guessed." I turned around.

Kneeling in front of Isabo, Eva was scrutinizing the young woman's bruised face as if hoping she could read something in her features—the truth, I suppose.

I approached them and crouched beside Eva.

"What do you think is the matter with her, Amir?"

One look at Isabo's empty eyes was enough for me to know

what possessed her. Still, I leaned forward and touched her hand to make sure. The jolt of energy that rushed through me was so strong that for an instant I thought I had been kicked in the belly by one of the guards. Gasping for air, I rapidly pulled away from Isabo. Once I had regained my breath, I saw that Eva was examining me attentively. A definite expression of concern was imprinted on her lovely features. *So she still cares a little about me,* I thought, rejoicing.

"What is it, Amir?" Eva asked.

"Isabo—she's bewitched."

Eva's eyes flew to Isabo then back to me. "How... and who did it?"

Shaking my head in response, I stared at Isabo. "I think the important question is why."

I crawled closer to her, and peering deeply into her seemingly dead eyes, I whispered, "You knew, didn't you? You figured it out, so you needed to be dealt with, to be disgraced... but most of all, you needed to be shut up."

Rising to my feet, I began a thorough inspection of the cell. I was determined to examine every speck on the ground, every scratch on the walls—everything.

Eva joined me by the cot at the back of the cell. "Amir, what are you doing?"

"Shhh..." I made, while dusting a suspect spot on the wall.

"Don't shush me! Tell me what's going on instead." By the firmness of her tone, I knew Eva would not give up until she learned the aim of my search. She could be very headstrong at times. Of all her flaws, that one was probably my favorite.

I smiled. "Listen. The guard mentioned that Isabo became entranced only after she was brought here, therefore there must be something in this cell that set it off."

The look of confusion plastered on Eva's face told me that she didn't truly grasp the workings of magic. So I explained in more specific details. "Spells can be set like traps, across doorsteps and thresholds and—" I rushed to the gate and began inspecting every single bar it possessed until my hands were red with rust. I found nothing on the bars. Well, there were quantities of scratches on them but no tingling, no strange sensation whatsoever. So it wasn't the gate after all. Still, it had to be near the entrance. I searched the nearby surroundings for some minute clues I might have previously missed and came up with none. Besides the loaf of bread and the bowl of water, with its raindrop decoration, there was nothing here.

"Amir, come see this," called Eva.

I was surprised to see that Eva wasn't at my side anymore. I looked around and found her once more kneeling in front of Isabo. Eva gently lifted one of Isabo's hands. "Look at this, Amir. Look at her nails."

Actually, Isabo had almost no nails left; they were all broken and worn down to the quick.

"How fast do spells usually work?" asked Eva.

"No idea."

"Can someone fight a spell?"

I stared at Isabo. "Maybe if that person has some knowledge of magic."

Eva stood up and surveyed the cell. "If I was thrown in here, my first impulse would be to hide in a corner." She pointed to the right. "That dark one!"

We both walked to the somber corner and began inspecting it. A small dark line at the bottom of the wall caught my eye. I bent down and after a careful examination saw that it was part of a drawing. Half of it was etched in the stone. The other half was drawn in blood. There seemed to be two separate designs. To me, the first drawing looked like a square with a circle beside it. The other one was made up of three undulating lines depicting water or waves with a stick figure above it.

"Do you understand what these represent?" asked Eva.

"Hard to tell what she meant by these."

"Why not write instead?"

I sighed. "I'm assuming that the spell was beginning to take effect and drawing might have been all she could do." I closed my eyes and tried picturing the scene. *Isabo suddenly finds herself unable to speak. She knows she is being bewitched and panics. She tries to write, but her hand cannot form letters. So she draws what she can—quickly.*

I opened my eyes and stared back at the drawing. I noticed two very pale lines I didn't see before. They were sticking out from under the square... like legs. "Legs? Hmm, a square with legs. What about that circle beside it?" I rubbed my beard.

"A lake," suggested Eva.

"No. Doesn't look right. It looks more like a corral or a fenced enclosure—OH!" The answer suddenly came to me. I knew the meaning of that drawing. It was so simple! In my excitement, I seized Eva by the shoulders and pulled her toward me. "The square with the legs, I know what it is. I do! It's the Baba Yaga's house. The peasants told me that the Baba often stole children. She's the one who kidnapped your sisters. " I pointed at the drawing. "And that's where we need to go."

CHAPTER
TWENTY-ONE

"E va, why are we coming here?" I asked as we entered the conservatory. "The Baba lives in the woods. What we need are coats, not flowers."

In a swirl of black taffeta and frilly petticoats, Eva faced me. "You're wrong, Amir. We do need flowers."

That's it, I thought, *grief has rendered her insane.* "Flowers... really?"

"Yes, flowers! For the Baba. As a gift for her."

"Huh? Witches like flowers, I didn't know that."

Eva cast me a stare so dark it made me wish I had kept my mouth shut. But as she stared at me I watched her frustration and anger wane and an apologetic smile make its way to her lips. "Forgive me, Amir. These last days have been trying for me. Lars's state and Father's urgency to remarry don't help the situation. I fear my nerves are a little frayed."

"No need to worry, Eva. I understand. I heard that your father is going to propose to Countess Ivana. What do you think of it?"

Eva shrugged. "It's a good choice. I'm glad he picked her; I just wish he'd wait a little longer before getting remarried. Mother hasn't been gone a week yet...."

Not finding anything to say on that subject, I just held her hand. "Now, can you explain to me why we need the flowers?"

"First, I need to see if we actually have them." This being

said, Eva dashed across the lush greenery of the conservatory.

I followed without arguing. Soon we were leaving the jungle of exotic plants and entering the rose garden. Eva stopped at its edge and scanned the shrubs.

I pointed to the bush on my left. "Those red ones are stunning. I'm sure she'll like them."

Eva turned around. "No she won't! Worse, she'll kill us!"

"But how can you be so sure of this?"

"Amir, you must trust me on this. I know what I'm doing. I have known about the Baba since childhood. My nanny used to tell me stories about her." She paused and plucked one of the red roses I had shown her. Caressing the flower's velvety petal, Eva said, "As lovely as it is, this rose won't do, Amir. There's only one way of gaining the Baba Yaga's help, and that's by bringing her a blue rose. The legend says that she makes a rejuvenating tea out of its petals. It is also said that the Baba sometimes helps the kindhearted. So I thought that perhaps if I give her the roses, she'd release my sisters."

I nodded, thinking that blue roses were like flying horses, they didn't really exist. Then again, I had seen the Baba's house… and a house with giant chicken legs shouldn't exist either. Feeling a tad more hopeful, I began combing through the garden for the elusive blue rose bush. After having been stabbed and scratched by thorns one too many times, I was on the verge of giving up when I spotted a peculiar colored blossom on my right.

"Eva," I called. "Come see this one."

She rushed to my side and crouched in front of the bush. "It's not blue." Her tone was heavy with disappointment. All right, the rose was pale lavender; still it was an odd and unusual color for a rose.

Brushing back the lower branches of the shrub, I uncovered a small sign planted in the soil at the foot of the rose bush. BLUE LADY ROSE was written on it.

Eva sighed. "I suppose we have no other option." Clipping the only three flowers that were in bloom on the bush, Eva then opened the glass box she had brought along and pinned the roses in the wet sea sponge inside it. Once the roses were safely tucked away in the box, she asked, "Amir, do you remember the road to the Baba's house?"

"No. But I think I know how to find it."

* * *

Our next stop was at Master Auguste Ramblais's place, the alchemist's tower. While Eva talked with a flabbergasted Auguste—obviously he's never been visited by a princess before—I made good use of his telescope. Just as I had expected, I didn't see the house. However, I spotted a clearing in the forest with a thin plume of chimney smoke rising from its center. After taking notes of the diverse reference points visible, I felt confident that I could find the place again without too much difficulty. Next thing I knew, we were outside trotting toward the forest on horseback.

Well, finding my way to the Baba's house proved slightly more complicated than I had anticipated. Twice, I led us in the wrong direction. And when I finally oriented myself properly and we began making progress, the snowdrift became so deep and the forest so heavily treed that we were forced to leave the horses behind. So it was on foot that we neared the clearing where the Baba lived.

"There's the house." I pointed to the log cabin peeking in and out of sight through the trees. "Let's run."

Eva gripped the hem of my coat, holding me back. "No, Amir. We cannot barge in on her like that. We must be respectful. There are rules to follow."

"She's a witch and possibly a kidnapper. I don't see why we should respect her at all."

"Please, Amir, for my sisters' sake let's proceed my way."

After a long period of brooding silence, I agreed to her demand… reluctantly though.

On Eva's order, we made our way toward the front of the house and approached it slowly, following a long, narrow alley. I scrutinized the two skulls atop the house, and, sure enough, the moment we stepped onto the alley, their black empty eye sockets glowed with an ominous red light.

Holding the glass box in plain view in front of her, Eva soldiered on bravely. She looked so stoical in her mourning clothes; her hair simply braided and pinned around her head. At that instant, my love for her was deeper than ever.

Pacing my steps to hers, I walked proudly at her side. Movement at the foundation level of the house caught my eye. One of the giant claws, the only part of the chicken legs now visible, had moved. That worried me because if the house rushed us all of a sudden, I doubted there would be enough time for us to move out of its way—not from this short of a distance. *Look away. There is nothing you can do now, so look away.*

I focused on the house's door. Painted a deep forest green, it stood out against the pale wood logs that made up the rest of the house. As I was staring at it, the green door silently opened.

My body reacted by tensing up.

Beside me, Eva swallowed hard. Yet, without missing a step, she moved on toward the opened door. Well, I thought, it seemed like this time the Baba was home.

Side by side, we climbed the steps leading up to the door and entered the witch's house.

* * *

The welcoming warmth and pleasant glow of the fireplace bathed the entire room.

Immediately I saw the cauldron of brew boiling over the

fireplace. I swiftly diverted my gaze from it, fearing that its sight might bring back some horrible visions. It was then that I noticed the woman seated in the wooden rocking chair in the corner of the room.

She was busy knitting while gently rocking herself back and forth. This woman, which I knew couldn't be anyone else but the Baba, wasn't old—middle-aged was my guess—nor was she ugly. She had a sort of wholesome beauty that was simple and earthy. With her shiny brown braids streaked with a hint of gray, round rosy cheeks, and warm brown eyes, their corners marked with tiny crow's-feet, she reminded me of Kathia, Dimitry's wife. To me, she was the kind of women that perfectly embodied motherhood and was the salt of the earth. Not at all the portrait I had in mind for a witch. She looked nothing like the monstrous hag with stony teeth described by the peasants, either.

While her fingers continued moving the blue yarn around her knitting needles with a sharp *click, click, click,* her attention slowly rose from her work, and she made eye contact with me.

Goose bumps rose all along my spine.

"Greetings, Prince Amir. If I'm not mistaken, you've been in my home before." Her voice was a velvety alto as soft and as rich as Kathia's pudding. Her alert eyes moved to Eva standing just beside me. "Princess Eva, you are always welcome in my home. Very few people know how to properly approach my steps, and rarer still are those who know to bring the proper offering."

Eva squeezed the box against her coat. "Good Baba, I'm afraid my roses might not be of the right shade."

From the comfort of her chair, the Baba smiled kindly. "Don't be afraid my child. Yours and Prince Amir's hearts are good. I know you've meant well by coming here. Now come closer and show me those roses."

We obeyed and approached the rocking Baba.

With trembling hands, Eva extended the glass box forward.

Upon seeing the roses kept inside, my eyes widened in disbelief. They weren't lavender anymore, but sky blue. *They changed color, that's not possible.* Unless it was the unusual warm glow of this room that made them look this color. I couldn't tell.

The Baba let her knitting needles drop beside her chair, took the box, and opened it. Plucking out one of the roses, she brought it to her nose. "Mmm," she gave, breathing in the strong tea scent emanating from the rose. "They are perfect. See, you've worried for nothing."

I watched the tension that had captured Eva's body release its hold on her. Her shoulders relaxed, and she sighed in relief.

The Baba twirled the rose between her fingers. "You know the rule, Princess. Ask."

"My sisters. I want my sisters back. I know they're here!"

The Baba nodded. "Clever! You found a way of asking without wasting a question." She paused, and I noted that a profound sadness now marked her face. "My poor dear child, your sisters are indeed in my care. However, I doubt you'll want them back at your side in their present state."

Eva stepped up. "Why did you steal them in the first place? Why?"

The Baba arose from her rocking chair and, with a gesture meaning for us to follow her, she walked into the adjacent bedroom. "Look," she said, indicating the window.

I remembered that window, it opened to her enclosure. In the morning sun, I could now see the mouth of the cave clearly. A huge brown bear lay in front of it. I spotted another one roaming on the east side of the cave, and the movements in the nearby shrubs were probably caused by a third bear.

Eva turned away from the window and glared at the Baba. "Why are you showing me these bears? This is not what I've asked you."

The Baba looked at me. "You understand but she doesn't." She shook her head. "To answer your questions, Princess, I didn't steal your sisters. It is true that I do steal children who trespass on my ground. But I have never invaded anybody's home to steal their children, or transformed anyone into bears. And I'm showing you these bears because they are your sisters."

"What!" Eva's gaze returned to the animals in the enclosure. "Those aren't my sisters. One of those bears attacked us. They killed that rabid beast, so it cannot be true." She faced the Baba again. "I refuse to believe this. It's a lie. It's not true."

"Princess, you know I cannot lie. These are the rules," said the Baba.

Eva aimed pleading eyes toward me. "Amir, say it isn't true."

"I'm so sorry, Eva. It's the truth; these bears are your sisters. They are victims of an enchantment."

Eva let out a whimper; fat tears began rolling down her cheeks. I tried taking her in my arms. At first, she fought back my embrace, then she became limp and I was able to close my arms around her and rock her gently.

Burying her face in the crease of my neck, Eva sobbed softly. "Noo, noo, noo" she lamented, as reality set in. "The bear that attacked us, the one that was killed— Oh, this means... OH NO!" she cried. "Which one... which one of my sisters died?"

Tightening my grip around her shoulders, I whispered in her ear, "Thalia. It was Thalia."

Eva cried loudly. I had never seen her this distraught before. It was literally tearing me apart inside to see her this way. Worse yet, there was nothing I could do to fix this, absolutely nothing. I hated being this helpless.

Eva turned teary, desperate eyes to the Baba. "Can you free

them? Can you break the spell?"

"If it were mine, yes. But as I have nothing to do with it, I cannot. Only the person responsible for their enchantment holds the key to break it."

"Who has done this then?"

"Ah-ah-ah!" The Baba wagged a finger at Eva. "Three roses, three questions. You know the rules."

"*Pleeease*, oh please," begged Eva.

"Princess, breaking this rule will endanger my life. I will cease to exist. We magical beings are bound to live by strict rules. Very few of us can break them without paying a terrible price. I'm sorry, Princess. I cannot answer any more questions. However, if you're willing to stay a little longer, I can tell you a story."

We agreed and followed the Baba to the front room. Once we were back in its warm bright light, I saw that our host wasn't the vibrant middle-aged woman who had welcomed us at our arrival. Old, bent, and wrinkled, the Baba was now an elderly woman with slow and painful movements.

"Time for my rose infusion," she said in a crackling voice.

I watched her take one rose, pluck out its petals with bony-knuckled fingers, and drop them in a teapot. Then she poured steaming hot water on top of it. A strong rose-tea aroma embalmed the entire room. At the same time a wave of tingling traveled through my entire body, starting down at my feet and ending at the roots of my hair. I found this sensation oddly pleasant, not at all like the brutal jolt of energy I often felt when dealing with magic. This feeling was as light and as delicate as the caress of a feather on one's skin. Intrigued, I questioned why her magic felt so different to me. As I gazed at the Baba's cozy interior, the answer became clear in my mind. *White magic! That's why it feels so... so soft, so benign.*

I looked up at the Baba and gasped. She was young

again—well, middle-aged. For the space of an instant, I was submerged by memories of my father, of his last days, of how the curse placed on him had made him grow old quickly, then young again. These were bad memories saturated with feelings of failure, sorrow and helplessness.

As I struggled to get rid of these emotions, the Baba quietly sipped her rose infusion while observing me with great interest. Lowering the small wooden bowl serving her as a cup, she addressed me: "Prince Amir, I'm sorry. If I had known that witnessing my change of appearance would convey such painful thoughts to you, I would've been more careful."

Stunned, I stiffened. Had she read my mind?

"No, I read your expression." She smiled. "I've promised you a story. Now it's time for me to tell it to you."

The Baba walked to her rocking chair, and after having made herself comfortable, she began her story. "Years ago, a child ventured on my land, an impudent girl, as young girls often are. I captured her and offered her a deal. The same one I offer to all the unfortunate children who trespass on my land. She could either serve me, which would extend her life, or refuse and be returned to the eternal cycle of life."

I frowned. "The eternal cycle of life? I don't—"

Eva poked me in the ribs. "It means she'll end up in the Baba's cauldron," she murmured through the corner of her mouth.

Horror struck. I stared at the cauldron of boiling brew hanging over the fire.

"Life and death are links of the same chain," said the Baba, her eyes staying fixed on me. "Life, death, life, death, it's a repeating pattern that goes on forever. Anyway, to return to my story, the girl chose to serve me. And served me well, she did. So well in fact that after a number of years I felt compelled to grant her her freedom. However, freedom wasn't the only gift I bestowed on her. She returned to her former life with some useful knowledge, knowledge she had learned here, with me. Later, she became a healer."

A light illuminated my mind. "Isabo!" I exclaimed. "The girl was Isabo. She mentioned that she'd been kidnapped when young; and her gift at potion-making, she learned it here. That's… that's…" There was something else, something important I was missing. Something I should know by now. *Oh, could it be this simple.* I looked at the Baba's kind features. "That's why Isabo led the bears here—to protect them."

The Baba nodded. "My clever Isabo quickly recognized the bears for what they truly were. She feared the princesses would be killed. In their enchanted state, they are subject to the beastly nature of their forms. However, some of their original essence remains, and it leads them to seek out familiar ground."

"They see the castle as their home. That's why they kept returning there."

The Baba sighed. "Those bears gave us so much trouble. They kept escaping, forcing poor Isabo to chase them all over the countryside. When she lost one in the forest, she even had to ask for my help to bring it back. Good thing I love riding at night, so I went and fetched the bear. Of course, it had returned to the village… again."

I nodded, recalling the bear's and hunter's tracks we had followed in the woods, the hunter was Isabo and the rider I saw later that evening was none other than the Baba. I shook my head, remembering that peasant who kept insisting that he had seen the Baba leading the bear away that night. I guess he wasn't dreaming after all.

"So I was right. Isabo *is* innocent." A question was burning my tongue. I wanted to know if the Baba had helped Isabo discover the truth. My gaze met the Baba's. Her eyes were warning me to be prudent. Beware your words, young man, they said. Tread lightly, very lightly.

I hesitated. Maybe if I made statements instead of questions. "Isabo… Isabo knows the rules. She knows how to ask questions."

"Yes, she does. Blue roses don't bloom often, so it took her some time before she could gather enough flowers to learn the truth—too much time maybe."

I sighed. So Isabo knew the truth. She knew who was behind this, but didn't have the time to tell anyone. Whoever was guilty of those acts got to her before she could speak, and that person made sure that Isabo would never speak again. Sadly right now, I couldn't see any other way of uncovering the truth.

CHAPTER TWENTY-TWO

I advanced toward the bears' enclosure alone—Eva couldn't bring herself to do so and had stayed at the cabin.

The bear closest to the fence raised its massive head and sniffed the air. A low growl escaped its throat.

"I wouldn't get too close if I were you," said the Baba. Wrapped in a brown shawl, she had suddenly appeared a few steps to my right. "The longer they remain in this form, the more their behavior becomes like bears'. The youngest has already forgotten her former life."

"Thalia was older; her sisters were just little girls. She was also the last one to be enchanted. Perhaps that's why she was so intent on coming back home. She remembered it more vividly than her sisters."

The Baba produced an enigmatic smile. "Yes, that one was determined to fight."

I nodded, recalling how Thalia had attacked us. Blinded by rage, she was then. Still, despite everything, she had managed to regain enough control over her growing animal instinct to rein herself in and spare Diego's life. Thalia had recognized the man she loved. She had stopped herself from killing him.

"Wait a minute…" I stared at the bears. If Thalia could recognize Diego and not rip him to shreds, maybe she could also recognize the person who had enchanted her. Was she, like her sisters before her, roaming the castle with the goal of killing that person, but only wound up killing innocent people instead? Could that be what had happened?

I turned to the Baba. "I think the princesses knew the person who did this to them."

The Baba didn't make a sound.

I continued, "Hm, I just don't understand why they were enchanted in the first place. That part doesn't make any sense."

The Baba let out a bitter chuckle. "On the contrary, it makes perfect sense. It's a means to an end."

I crossed my hands under my chin. "A means to an end? I suppose you can't explain that without breaking the rules?"

She shook her head. "I will say no more on this subject. I can offer you a ride to your horses, however. If you accept my offer, you will gain precious time. And time is now of the essence."

"Then I will accept."

* * *

If I had known that the ride the Baba had offered us wasn't on horseback or in a sleigh, but in her walking house, I would have thought twice before saying yes.

Standing very straight in the center of the main room, the Baba ordered, "Hold on to something."

I gripped the doorframe, while Eva's arms circled my waist.

The Baba clapped her hands three times and commanded, "House up."

In a lament of twisting wooden planks and a *clink-clank* of pots and pans, the house stood up.

The rapidity of its ascension took me by surprise. I felt as though my stomach had leapt right into my throat. My knees weakened for a brief instant before regaining stability again.

"House forward," said the Baba.

The house began rocking back and forth. Regardless of the solid grip I had on the doorframe, I was being thrown about on all sides.

For her part, the Baba remained fixed in the center of the room. She was as unmoving as a tree. After a short period of intense shaking, she ordered, "House stop!" followed by "House down!"

There was a last bone-jarring, stomach-flipping crash downward and everything became still. Only then did I risk letting go of the doorframe, and after having thanked the Baba, Eva and I staggered outside.

Fortunately, our horses were still tied to the tree where we had left them. In a hurry, we climbed on their backs and began retracing our steps in silence. Throughout the trip back to the castle, the Baba's words kept twirling in my head: a means to an end, a means to an end. *What end? What is it? If only I could learn that, I'd know who is behind this. What does that person want? Who has the power and knowledge to cast such powerful enchantments? Who was Thalia hunting that day? Who else was in the cemetery that day—besides everybody? What about her sisters? They too had tried taking revenge on someone. And why were they all attracted to the village?* So many questions, it was overwhelming, I didn't know where to start.

As I massaged my temples an idea came to me. Maybe I should start over. Maybe I should retrace the bear's footsteps inside the castle. I might learn something new this time. Yes, I would do that, I promised myself.

* * *

Once we were back at the castle, Eva left for her apartments right away. I had hoped she would stay with me for a while longer. Yet, I thought it best not to show my disappointment at her departure. I knew how distraught she was at learning of Thalia's death, and I understood her need to be alone. Also, it would've been insensitive, if not reprehensible, on my part to place any demand on her at this time.

So, it was alone that I shuffled my feet toward the junction of the main entrance where so many people had died. I was halfway there when Diego met up with me. "Where were you? I've searched the entire castle for you."

"I was out riding," I answered vaguely.

"Alone?"

I shrugged. I wasn't sure if I should tell Diego anything more.

"Have you heard the news?" Diego asked.

"What news?"

"The king will remarry."

"Yes, I heard that."

"Well, he's making it official tonight at a special banquet."

I nodded. "How's Lars?"

Diego gave a joyless chuckle. "At this point, it's hard to say if he's more dead than alive, or more alive than dead. All that praying people are doing isn't helping much." Diego became pensive all of a sudden. I could tell that something was bothering him. I thought of asking him what it was but he spoke before I did. "You know, Amir, I've been thinking that maybe the savages cast a spell on him."

"I doubt it, Diego, they saved his life."

"That's it. Maybe they didn't save him. Maybe he's still dead. He was dead when I pulled him out of the water."

I explained to Diego the technique used by Khuan to reanimate Lars, even though the entire thing sounded like a fable to me. I had a hard time believing that one could be brought back from the dead in such a fashion. I also told Diego about the green algae Lilloh had pulled from around Lars's neck. And that, in my opinion, was what allowed Lars to breathe again.

"Algae? Sea-hag hair, you mean?"

"I don't know, but Lars seemed to have become entangled in them."

"That's strange," said Diego. "I grew up by the seashore. That sort of algae is common in the sea. I didn't know it could grow in a lake though."

"Really?"

"That's what I thought—apparently I was wrong. Could be something else altogether—hard to tell without looking at it."

I nodded in agreement. If only Lilloh had thought of keeping some of those green strings so we could give it a look. "What else do you know about sea-hag hair?"

Diego stuck out his lower lip. "Old tales. Nothing important."

"Tales. What do they say about it?"

"Mainly, that these strings are water spirits' hairs left behind when they are called upon to do some misdeed. That sort of story."

I scratched my beard, thinking about what Diego had just said. That shadow under the ice, could it have been a water spirit? It sure had looked like a fish to me. "Shall we pay a visit to Lars?"

Diego's eyes narrowed with suspicion. "Certainly. However, you must tell me why you're suddenly so interested in his health."

"Can I do it once we get there?"

Diego sighed heavily, then acquiesced.

Good, I thought. Now I had a bit of time to decide how much information I wanted to tell Diego—because at this point, I trusted no one in this castle.

* * *

We entered Lars's quarters and, ignoring the people

assembled in his receiving room, went straight for his bedroom. The tense atmosphere of the room was suffocating. Right away, I noticed that two groups of people were posted on either side of Lars's bed.

Kneeling on the left side were Countess Ivana's friends, a dozen beautiful young ladies and gentlemen dressed in humble mourning garments. This group had been busy praying in low voices when we entered. They immediately stopped their litany and acknowledged our presence with kind smiles and solemn nods. After a bow in their direction, I turned to the right where the second group stood: Baron Molotoff, his three sons, and a few loyal army officers. This bunch of stiff-backed figures with their dark, hungry gazes reminded me of a gathering of vultures waiting for a wounded creature to die, so they could tear his body apart and rejoice.

My eyes darted from one group to the next. They seemed to be waging some silent war over Lars's inanimate body.

"Intense, isn't it," murmured Diego in my ear. "One party is praying for Lars to live, while the other is waiting and wishing for his passing. I have no doubt on the latter. With Lars dead, the road to the throne becomes wide-open for the Molotoffs."

"Are you serious? Surely the king has other nephews. One of them can take Lars's place."

Diego shook his head. "If Lars dies, the Molotoffs will succeed the Andersons on the Sorvinkian throne. Poor King Erik, the man's unlucky. With the exception of Eva, he has lost his entire family."

I threw a discreet glance at the Molotoffs. Now I knew why the king was in such a hurry to remarry. He needed a new heir... because this one was about to pass. I made my way to the bed and looked at Lars.

His brow was sweaty, his eyes closed and sunken, his face waxy. Lars's condition had not improved since I had last seen him. Actually, his breathing seemed shallower than before. I turned to the prayers. They all bore anxious looks; some even had fear in their eyes. The baron, on the other hand, seemed unmoved. I returned my attention to Lars. I cringed. In my opinion, the greenish hue of his skin was a bad omen. It was the color of pus, as if something was festering inside him. I touched Lars's forehead. A sudden burst of light exploded behind my eyes. It hit me with the swift brutality of a lightning bolt, leaving me blind and dizzy. I was so shaken by this unforeseen attack that I had to grab one of the bedposts not to fall down. I felt a strong hand gripping my elbow, which helped me regain my balance. I didn't question whose hand it was. The strong perfume enveloping me was a dead giveaway.

"Amir, are you falling ill?" Diego asked in a concerned tone.

"No," I managed to blurt out. "Tired, that's all."

Having regained my countenance, I eyed Lars again. He was under a spell, and a strong one at that. The fabric of that spell was unlike anything I had ever felt before. I extended a trembling hand toward Lars and lightly grazed his forehead with my fingertips. A succession of bright sparks flashed behind my eyes again. But as my hand moved down to his nose and over his lips, the sparks diminished in intensity. They only increased again once my fingers reached his chest, taking on an angry red hue. I blinked, then rubbed my eyes to get rid of them.

"Amir, what are you doing?" Diego sounded embarrassed.

"Hush!" I said, placing my hand over Lars's abdomen. Darkness filled my vision. I pulled away my hand fast. In doing so my fingers bumped Lars's right hand. A sharp flash of green light burned my retina. "*Oooh,*" I mumbled, quickly covering my eyes with closed fists.

"What's happening to you, Prince Amir?"

I recognized Baron Molotoff's deep baritone voice. "Nothing—nothing."

"Lies! Clearly something is ailing you."

I shook my head. "It's an old wound. It comes and goes." Using Diego as support, I straightened myself. "See, now I'm well again."

Baron Molotoff sneered at me, and then he lowered his gaze to Lars.

So did I—to his hand actually. The root of the evil that was slowly killing him had to be there. I was sure of it. And after a close inspection of his fingers, I found it. Well, I thought that could be it. A long greenish hair was tightly wrapped around Lars's ring finger. But the moment I tried pulling it off, I was once again struck down by a green flash of light. Except this time the luminous blow was so powerful that I nearly fainted.

"Your old wound again, I presume," commented the baron in a skeptical tone.

Ignoring him, I turned to Diego, who had thrown an arm around my waist to stabilize me. I didn't protest his initiative. Frankly, without it, I would probably be face down on the floor by now.

"Amir, you're truly ill."

"No. I'm fine." I stared at the hair. It needed to come off, but how? I couldn't touch it, well, I could but not without fainting. Surely there must be a solution to this problem. I tried getting closer to the bed. My knees buckled and I nearly collapsed.

"You're too weak, Amir. You must sit down," Diego said in a panic. He nudged Lars a little to the side, making space on the bed for me to sit.

I gasped. I had just found the solution to my problem: Diego. He wasn't a shal-galt or a seeker; therefore he couldn't sense magic, so it didn't affect him as it did me.

"Listen to me, Diego. Look at Lars's hand, at his ring finger.

You'll see a hair wrapped around it."

Before I could explain further, Diego bent down and plucked out the hair from Lars's finger. "This, you mean?" he asked, raising the long hair in front of my face.

"Er… yes."

Just then I heard a strangled, gurgling sound coming from behind me in the bed.

I turned around, and, to my amazement, I saw that Lars's eyes were wide open. In a sudden move, he sat up. With a face contorted by a look of terror, Lars took a few gasping gulps of air, bent forward, and vomited violently. Streams of steaming, putrid lake water shot out of him in quantities that defied all logic. Everyone present in the room either gagged in disgust or gasped in shock.

Finally, after some last forceful retching, Lars expelled a huge lump of green hair.

The green lump hit the bed covering with the most unpleasant wet thud. Seemingly emptied of all strength, Lars collapsed against his pillows. I immediately noticed that his face, although still a bit pale, had returned to a normal color. His breathing was back to normal too.

Baron Molotoff glared at me. "What did you do to him?"

"Break the spell that was on him. You appear rather displeased by this turn of events."

The baron's bushy singular eyebrow rose. "I am indeed. Because of you Sorvinka is doomed to ruin. This stupid calf doesn't have the qualities of a good ruler."

"So you admit putting this spell on him."

Molotoff chuckled. "A spell! How amusing! Prince Amir, I'm a soldier, a man of war. I settle scores on the battlefields. I know nothing of spells."

"I don't believe you. You have too much to gain by Lars's death."

The baron smiled. "The whole Empire will gain by his

death. Personally, I'm not gaining anything."

"You'd gain a clear path to the throne."

The baron's smile broadened. "Young man, if I wanted the throne I could take the throne. I control the army; I have the support and love of the population. And with the unpopular rulings the king's made recently, I could successfully overthrow him if I wanted to."

I frowned, surprised by the candidness of his reply. "Why don't you then?"

"Such an act, no matter how swift and successful it may be, would weaken the Empire; scar it for years to come. And to do it now would be disastrous. With the threat of an Anchin invasion looming over us, I have to place the good of the country ahead of my personal ambitions." Squaring his shoulders and raising his chin, the baron took a stoic pose. "It is my duty, not as a noble or an officer, but as a Sorvinkian. As such I cannot do anything that would jeopardize the motherland's safety."

"But you can kidnap princesses and wish the heir's death."

"Kidnap princesses! Why would I do such a senseless thing? I have three sons, why would I deprive them of potential mates. Prince Amir, you are looking at the wrong person. I have nothing to do with those crimes. As for the heir, I admit that I did wish his death. But as far as I know, wishing is not a crime."

The man had an answer for everything it seemed. I believed none of them though. "Well, I won't apologize for breaking your wish and saving Lars. Looks like he's going to be king after all."

The baron lowered a gaze dripping with contempt toward Lars, his bushy eyebrows furrowed, and his upper lip rose exposing his teeth in a sneer of loathing. "Not necessarily. There could still be hope for Sorvinka's future. Things have changed. Maybe now that the king is getting remarried, to a Sorvinkian woman this time, the situation will improve. Perhaps our king will finally have a son this time. If nothing else, the countess will see that our customs, cults, and traditions are reinstated and respected. At least the gods will be pleased." Looking rather satisfied about it himself, Baron Molotoff saluted us then exited the room with his group.

Moments later, the room became overcrowded with so many physicians, valets, and counselors that there was literally no place left for us. So Diego and I decided to return to my rooms.

"Diego, do you believe what the baron said or do you think he's involved in this?"

Diego didn't think long before answering. "I don't know. Maybe. Maybe not. I don't know."

"Well, you're helpful!" I said.

He shrugged. "Sorry, Amir, I'm not good at solving puzzles. When things get too complicated I usually lose interest."

I smiled. I truly believed that. Just as I believed Diego had nothing to do with this affair. He didn't have the cold, calculated temperament needed to plan such an elaborate plot. *He's as innocent as I am.* My mind made up, I decided to tell him all I had learned so far, starting with Isabo's innocence, my shal-galt gifts, and the princesses' enchantments. I told him everything… even the painful news of Thalia's death.

Upon hearing this sad news, Diego stopped. "Thalia, she recognized me… that's why the bear… she stopped." Curling his hands into hard fists, Diego hissed through clenched teeth, "I want that spell caster dead! Amir, promise me that you'll let me put an end to his wretched life."

"Well, first we must discover who it is." Strangely enough, although my heart kept screaming that it was that devilish baron, my brain said something else: *What about the princesses? Why would he need them gone? Girls cannot rule, they pose no threat to him.*

The Baba's words came floating back to the top of my

mind: *a means to an end*. Was destroying the king's family the means or the end? I sighed. The answer was simple. I knew it was.

"There's something I don't understand, Amir," said Diego.

"Which is?"

"You said that both members of the Anchin pair possess that… gift you have. So why didn't they realize that Lars was under a spell the moment they touched him, right at the lake. Wasn't he covered in that green algae then?"

"Huh, I didn't think about that." Looking back at the incident by the lake, I could see Lilloh ripping the sea-hag hair from around Lars's neck. She should have sensed something… unless. "Lilloh can sense magic but not spirits and demons. So the sea-hag hair did nothing to her because it belonged to a water spirit. Unfortunately, she got rid of it before Khuan could touch it."

"All right," Diego said. "What about the spell you just broke, wasn't it on him back then?"

"Obviously not. Whoever is behind this thought that drowning Lars would be enough. He didn't plan on Khuan and Lilloh bringing him back to life. The spell was placed after, using the sea-hag hair so the illness produced by it would look like a consequence of his dip in the icy water of the lake."

Diego nodded, yet I could tell something was still bothering him. He cleared his throat. "Drowning him… so falling through the ice wasn't an accident then. Fine, I can understand that part, not the rest however. First, where can one get his hands on sea-hag hair? I'm quite sure the creature that owns that hair wouldn't give it up freely. And why kill Lars anyway? Sure, he's a bumbling idiot, but that hardly deserves death."

I nodded silently. It was useless to speak because I couldn't answer any of those questions. No matter how much thought

I put into this matter, I couldn't figure out anything right now. It was like my brain was wrapped in wool. That was so infuriating, I wanted to break something.

We had reached a corridor junction and stopped to let two maids pass so they could go prepare the banquet hall for the king's wedding announcement. Carrying buckets of water, they hurried down the corridor, leaving a trail of droplets behind. As I noticed the glistening trail of water, something in my mind clicked and part of the fog surrounding this riddle suddenly dissipated. I could see part of the solution. I thought I knew the end. Now all I needed was to find who'd engineered it.

"Change of plan, Diego. Follow me. We have no time to waste."

CHAPTER
TWENTY-THREE

W here are we going in such a hurry?" Diego huffed, trotting behind me.

"To find someone who can give us information on Sorvinkian deities."

"Why? Are we going to battle a god?"

"No. Its disciples, a grand priest maybe. I'm not sure." I sighed. What if I was wrong? What if I failed again? *Stop!* I ordered myself. *No more doubts, stop it!* I took a deep breath and continued, "Anyway, I think it might be linked to water."

"There are at least five Sorvinkian water deities that I know of. Perhaps if you can be more specific."

"Well, I think it is symbolized by a giant sea monster."

"A giant sea monster, uh?"

"You know which god that is?"

Diego shrugged. "I have a vague recollection of having heard of it. Nothing useful comes to mind though."

"I was thinking of asking Milo's servant friends to tell me about their gods. To my knowledge, no one knows more about gods than servants."

Diego nodded in agreement. "Good idea. Actually, I personally know a couple of maids who will gladly answer any question I ask them. They might even draw a few pictures for you."

Something Diego said brought me to an abrupt halt. "A picture! I think there is already one. Come, I'll show it to you."

I led Diego to the indoor well. I remembered having seen a carving on its stone rim. But the instant the well fell into view I was faced with a new problem. The *Point of Power* located on the well's rim pulsated with such force it was nauseating. I couldn't get close enough to look at the carving. The waves of energy rushing out of it were just too strong for me to combat.

Diego on the other hand walked to the well without demonstrating any discomfort. He dusted off the flat stone of the well's rim, looked at the carving, then stared at me. "You said a sea monster. That's not a sea monster."

"It's not?" I was sure it was. Dumfounded, I tried to recall the carving. I had seen it only once, and very briefly, when Lilloh had placed my hand on the *Point of Power*. So its image was a little vague in my mind. "Er... Diego, isn't it a carving of a giant scaly fish with the face of a man and long hair?"

"Yes."

"Well, to me, that's the description of a sea monster."

Diego shook his head. "No. That's the description of Samu. Amir, this is a carving of Samu, the god of running water, seduction, and beauty. It's not a priest we should be looking for, but a priestess. A woman is always at the head of the cult of Samu... Oh goodness!" Diego's face became as white as milk.

"What is it?"

"The disciples of Samu must all be young and beautiful."

"All young and beautiful!" I repeated. At once, everything became crystal clear in my mind. "It's Countess Ivana. She's using water as magical conduits." The image of the water pitcher in the princesses' rooms, the bowl of water in Isabo's cell, the lake... oh god, the lake. I could see her dropping to her knees. Back then I thought she was praying for us. If she was praying, it wasn't for us. Now I believed she was calling Samu to her aid. I shook my head. Something didn't fit. "The disciples the ghoul talked about were the disciples of Samu. What about the old one? It's not Ivana. So who could it be?"

"Samu itself maybe," ventured Diego.

"I don't know... I have trouble believing that." Suddenly, I felt confused and unsure of myself. My fondness for Ivana, the kindness she had displayed toward me clouded my judgment and filled my mind with doubts. I looked up at Diego. "I'm not convinced. Perhaps we're moving too fast. Maybe we're wrong about her involvement in this affair. After all, Ivana helped me to enter Eva's room and—"

"And nearly got you caught by the king," interjected Diego. "Ivana knew the king would rush to Eva's room. She wanted him to discover the two of you in bed together, which would've meant death for you and disownment for Eva. No need changing your *beloved* princess into a bear after that."

My jaw dropped. I could've kicked myself for my naïveté, and for having once liked that devious creature. Suddenly nauseous, I closed my eyes. I felt so betrayed and disgusted it was making me sick. How could I have been so naïve, so trusting. I hated myself for it. But I hated Ivana more. My nausea morphed into outrage; I opened my eyes and looked at Diego. "You are right, my friend, she's guilty! We must warn the king before he makes his engagement to her official."

As we turned to rush to the banquet hall, we found ourselves face-to-face with Countess Ivana's friends. I counted eight disciples, all male. I supposed the female disciples were now busy assisting the countess.

Diego rushed to my side. "Amir, these are the prayers we saw in Lars' room. They followed us."

I didn't say a word, I just pulled out my rapier. But before I could step up to meet the advancing enemy, Diego pushed me aside and, screaming like a banshee, charged our attackers.

Taken aback by Diego's flash attack, the disciples of Samu froze. By the time they realized what was happening, two of them had been struck down by Diego's blade. That awakened the others and they started fighting back. Within moments, they were all over us.

Parrying blows coming from two different disciples, I found myself being pushed toward the well. My head began spinning. The periphery of my vision darkened. Struck by panic, I threw myself on the floor and rolled toward the bottom of the staircase. One of my attackers dashed after me. Before I could rise to my feet, he tried stabbing me from above. I twisted to the left and simultaneously thrust my rapier under his ribs. Just as he was falling down, I pushed him against his acolyte. They both hit the floor, which gained me a few precious seconds. Leaping to my feet, I managed to climb the first steps of the stairs before my second attacker rushed me again.

As the action unfolded, I caught glimpses of Diego who was still battling two foes. Then I witnessed an act that was so despicable, so immoral, that it iced my blood. I saw one of Diego's attackers throw himself on my friend's blade. In a last dying effort, the disciple embraced Diego in his arms, holding him tightly in place. At first I was confounded by this behavior, but when the second disciple appeared behind Diego and raised his sword to stab him in the back, I realized the goal of this sacrifice. "Diego, behind you!" I yelled.

Too late. The sword plunged deep into Diego's back.

"NOOO!" I shouted, moving toward my friend. A blond disciple stepped in front of me, hindering my sight of Diego and forcing me to concentrate on fighting. I parried, blocked, and thrust, while climbing the steps in reverse.

A second disciple joined the fight. I recognized him as the one who had stabbed Diego in the back. Now that there were two against me their tactic changed. This wasn't a regular combat anymore, but a sacrificial one. Twice, one of the disciples tried to impale himself on my sword, so his acolyte could finish me while my blade was stuck. To parry this insane maneuver, I constantly had to thrust the side of my blade forward, using it as a barrier between me and them.

The fight drove us up the stairs, and soon I found myself on the tower's last landing with nowhere to go. When my back hit the stone wall, I knew this was going to be my last stand. Bracing myself, I faced my attackers. Just as I had feared, one of them threw himself on my blade the instant it was pointed outward.

Spitting blood and baring his teeth in a grimace of agony, he grabbed me by the shoulders, holding me still while his friend approached for the coup de grâce.

I tried pushing and kicking the disciple off me, but it was to no use. In his last moment, this man was determined to reach his goal. And there was nothing I could do to change it. Pinned between the wall and the dying man, I watched, helpless, as the last disciple raised his sword to my throat.

Just then I saw a bright metallic flash behind the disciple's head.

A loud *bong-crash* rang out in the air, followed by a shower of brass wheels, gears, and wood splinters. The disciple collapsed to the floor. Behind him stood Auguste Ramblais, the alchemist, with the empty wooden frame of his time-device clutched between his hands. He had smashed it on the disciple's head, knocking him out.

Auguste stared at the remains of his device and shrugged. "The damn thing kept terrible time anyway."

My attention returned to the dying man still holding on to me. He was blond, young, and as pretty as a girl. I stared straight into his deep blue eyes and said, "Your friend is dead.

It's over—release me."

His eyes widened, and then the spark of life that had animated them slowly extinguished. I felt his grip on me loosening. The disciple slowly slipped to the floor.

The alchemist kneeled beside the disciple he had struck. "This one isn't dead. Stunned, that's all." He turned the young man over. "I know him… I recognize his face. He's one of the pretty countess's friends."

Auguste's good eye went to the other disciple. "That one too. Prince Amir, why were these noblemen attacking you?"

"There's no time for long explanations. The king is in danger and Prince Diego… Oh lord, Diego!" At the thought of my friend, a visceral fear for him, for his life, ripped through me. I dashed down the stairs at breakneck speed, taking two and often three steps at a time. When I reached the bottom of the stairwell, I looked around for Diego. I found him near the corridor's opening, lying on his side in a pool of blood, moaning. I hurried to him and kneeled down at his side.

He grabbed my wrist with a bloody hand. "Amir, my friend."

"Diego, don't speak. Keep your strength."

A joyless smile stretched Diego's lips. "Thank you for caring." Grinding his teeth, Diego reached out, took his sword, and placed it in my hand. "Give this to Milo—from me. I know he'll use it well."

"Diego, no. You're still alive. You're young and strong."

Movement at the foot of the stairs made me look up. Auguste was limping in our direction. He cast one look at Diego, then raised his good eye to me and shook his head.

"Prince Diego," he said, painfully crouching down.

"Shhh," Diego hushed. "I'm not in this world for long. Let me speak." Diego's hand became like a steel claw on my wrist. "Amir, I have a favor to ask of you… you owe me one."

"Please ask me anything you want."

"There's a small bronze box in my blue dresser. Can you make sure that my father gets it?" Diego smiled. "This is all I ask of you, my friend. Everything else I possess is now yours, Amir. All my treasures, my trinkets too... all my possessions are yours."

"I can't accept."

"Please, this is my will... my last will." Diego moaned. "Mmmm, now leave... Go warn the king before it's too late. But be careful, my friend... she'll be waiting for you."

"He's right," said Auguste. "Go. I'll stay with him. Finish what you began. Rid the castle of these people, whoever they are."

Nodding, I squeezed Diego's hand one last time. So little strength was left in his grip that I feared letting go of it. I feared leaving him. Most of all, I feared this was our last moment together. But I had to leave. Reluctantly, I let go of Diego's hand. To my chagrin, his hand fell limp upon the floor.

I was about to rise when the alchemist tugged on my kaftan. "Take these. They might come in handy," he said, shoving two fist-sized silver balls into my pocket.

"What are those?"

"A new invention of mine. Don't worry, they're easy to use. Light and throw, that's all. Now go."

I looked at Diego one last time. *I will miss you, my friend.* Then rising to my feet, I left.

I was running in the direction of the main corridor when the alchemist shouted at my back, "Light and throw. And don't forget to duck!"

I paid no mind to him or to his last instruction; my mind was too busy worrying about what awaited me ahead. A priestess... and possibly the god she worshiped. I knew how to fight people. But I didn't know how to fight a god—I had no idea how to do that at all. Worse, I wasn't even sure it could be done.

CHAPTER
TWENTY-FOUR

I ran all the way to the banquet hall. When I burst into the vast expanse of the hall, I knew this was going to be a delicate operation.

Decorated for the occasion, the hall was seeded with giant urns overflowing with huge bouquets of fragrant white flowers. Candelabras and chandeliers were lit throughout the room adding their glow to the flickering flames of the dozens of storm lamps dotting the walls like amber jewels. Already nobles and dignitaries from all over the Empire and beyond were gathered in tight groups everywhere. By the look of it, the hall was almost filled to capacity.

Raising myself on tiptoes to see above the crowd, I looked straight at the small dais at the front of the room where I thought Eva would be. The instant I set eyes on her I felt my stomach clenching. She was surrounded by four disciples of Samu. All smiles, the beautiful ladies conversed with my beloved in the friendliest of manners. But when they saw me, those warm friendly manners cooled down as shock invaded their eyes. Obviously, they didn't plan on my surviving their friends' ambush. Good, I thought, and looked for the countess. I found her a few steps to the left. She was hanging on to the king's arm with an air of ownership I didn't like.

Lord, I hope I'm not too late, I thought as I marched across the crowded room.

Gasps of shock and shouts of horror punctuated my advance.

"He's all bloody!" exclaimed a nobleman.

The courtesan beside him fainted.

I stopped and looked down at myself. The front of my kaftan was covered in blood, the suicide disciple's blood but also Diego's. A searing rage burnt its way through me, like a lava flow after a volcano eruption. Glaring at the countess, I continued advancing. "Your Majesty," I shouted, drawing my rapier.

At once, people began yelling in fear around me. "Aaaah! He's armed! He's armed!"

Paying no mind to them, I soldiered on. "Your Majesty cannot marry this woman."

A nobleman stepped in front of me, hindering my progress. Without any hesitation, I kicked him in the groin, and when he doubled over, I unceremoniously pushed him aside. Approaching the dais, I stared at the king. The look on his face held more confusion than anger. However, I saw that he had nonetheless pulled out his ceremonial sword.

Pointing his weapon toward me, the king ordered, "Halt! Don't come any closer!"

"Your Majesty, this woman has deceived you. She's fooled everyone here. You cannot marry her."

"Amir, what are you doing?" lamented Eva. She tried to approach me, but the disciples of Samu held her back, saying that it was for her safety. Meanwhile a dozen guards had sneaked up behind me.

My time was now numbered; I needed to hurry. I stared at the countess. Unintimidated, she stared right back at me. I noted a sly smile curling her lips. The insolent woman was mocking me; it made my blood boil. "She's guilty, Your Majesty," I said.

"Guilty of what?" boomed the king.

"Of everything that has befouled you since she arrived at

the castle, beginning with the queen's illness. It worsened upon her arrival."

"Nonsense! Guards arrest him!"

As the guards moved on me, I shouted, "Majesty, she's a priestess of Samu!"

Loud gasps rose from the assembly of nobles.

Perplexed, the king raised a hand. The guards halted their advance.

Pointing to the ladies encircling Eva, I continued, "These are her disciples. The men attacked Prince Diego and me a moment ago, and he's been mortally wounded. The countess also captured your daughters. The princesses are prisoners of her enchantments."

The king turned to the countess.

Ivana smiled humbly at him. "He's lying, Your Majesty. You know I cannot do any of this." Her voice sounded so innocent that I almost believed her myself. I cringed. I had better come up with some convincing argument soon, otherwise she would win.

"Your Majesty, please listen to me," I pleaded. "This woman came to the castle with the goal of marrying you, so she could have the old faith reinstated. But when the queen convinced you to marry Isabo instead, Ivana made sure that it wouldn't happen. She made everybody believe Isabo was a witch. Ivana is the one who called attention to Isabo's actions. She rang the alarm the morning Isabo was arrested."

"Why should this be of concern to me?" said the king. "The countess did well to denounce the foul woman."

"No, Your Majesty. Isabo was only trying to help your daughters, to protect them. She is innocent."

Taking a step forward, the king glared at me. "You've gone mad, young prince. Isabo was caught leading a beast out of the castle. She's a witch. To proclaim the countess guilty of these crimes is blasphemy. I will see you thrown in the dungeon for uttering such lies."

"NO, FATHER!" shouted Eva. "Amir's right. Isabo is innocent. The beasts are my sisters."

The king's head turned from Eva to me a few times. "Have you both taken leave of your senses?" he said. "The countess saved my life. Without her selfless dash across the cemetery the bear would have mauled me to death."

"Your Majesty was never in any danger. It was the countess the bear was seeking out that day. Or any other day, for that matter; that's why most of the bear's killings in the castle happened in the area near her room." Suddenly another fact became clear to me. I looked at the countess. "The village's ruins—it's an old temple. And one of the gods it is dedicated to is Samu."

I looked up at the king. "Your Majesty, your daughters often accompanied the countess to the village, for charitable purposes. They knew about her status as a priestess of Samu. They knew she celebrated ceremonies in the old ruin. That's why the bears kept going there. The countess used to hold office in that temple. The villagers said priests and priestesses still visited it."

"This is madness," breathed the king, yet I could see that the seed of doubt had been planted in his mind. "Why should I believe such a tale? Why should I take the word of a stranger over those of the countess, whom I know and trust?"

"Because it is the truth!" a gravelly voice declared from the back of the assembly.

The crowd parted revealing the presence of a determined-looking Auguste Ramblais. As the old alchemist limped in my direction, I noted that he was hiding something behind his back. Auguste aligned himself beside me in front of the dais and pointed at the countess with his free hand. "Her men ambushed Prince Amir and Prince Diego at the foot of my tower. They killed Prince Diego. I've witnessed the entire wretched affair."

Shock blew through the assembly like a strong winter

wind. I could see stunned, horrified, or bemused expressions printed on almost everybody's face.

Shadows of concern now clouded the countess's beautiful face. She gently touched the king's arm. "He, too, is a stranger in our land, Your Majesty. They both are intent on deceiving you. I fear they've murdered Prince Diego themselves and are trying to pin this devious crime on me."

"Curb your vile tongue, witch," hissed Auguste. Then turning to the king, he added, "I had an inkling that this young prince would need help. So I broke into the countess's rooms and found this—"

Auguste pulled out the hand he had kept hidden behind his back. A bronze statue of a sturgeon fish bearing a man's face was clutched in his fist.

"SAMU! It's Samu," echoed from the crowd. "It's true, she's a priestess."

"Alchemist," the king began, "a single statue hardly constitutes proof of misdeeds."

"Search her room, Your Highness, and you'll find all the proof you need," said Auguste with a look of disgust toward the countess. "This woman has had a shrine to her god built in one of her rooms. It's far too elaborate to have been constructed in a day for the purpose of discrediting her. The giant statue of Samu in its center must have taken at least four men to move."

"The missing statue!" I exclaimed, remembering the pile of drape on the chamber's floor." That's what your friends were carrying in that rug. They told me they were decorating. Well, they were indeed."

The king glared at the countess. "Is this true?"

She nodded her head, backing away.

"WHY?" roared the king.

The countess flinched, then raised her chin in a gesture of defiance. "How dare you ask me why! You never thought once about the fate of the priesthood when you banned our cults and destroyed our temples, leaving us destitute and without a roof over our heads. The things we were forced to do to survive are unmentionable. Some of us were reduced to begging for food, like dogs." As she spoke, the countess slowly walked to the edge of the dais, where two giant urns were placed.

"What hardship are you talking about, you married a count," said the king.

"Yes," said the countess in a voice rendered deep with anger. "And marrying that disgusting bag of wine was my first step toward my goal. Many more followed."

Suddenly the Baba's words made sense to me. "The queen's illness, the princesses' enchantments, Lars's condition. It was all meant to force the king into marrying you. Those were all… means to an end."

The countess didn't reply. She only smiled. An odd detail struck me. For some reason, I thought her eyes seemed bluer than before. From where I stood they appeared as though they were two dark pools of stormy water. As I was pondering the meaning of such a change, she raised her arms in the air. What followed happened so fast that it took me completely by surprise. First, a rush of energy hit me. Then all the banquet hall's doors slammed shut and the giant urns, spread throughout the room, began overflowing, spilling out water all over the floor. Screams of panic sounded through the room as the crowd dashed to the doors.

"They're locked," shouted a nobleman.

"The water's rising fast," yelled a lady in panic.

"All is lost! We're doomed!" cried another.

My gaze turned to the countess. I gasped in shock. Her skin had acquired the silvery white color of a fish's belly. Scales ran along her neck, and her hair, which was now green, had broken loose from its ties and flew wildly about her head as if animated by a life of its own.

I took a step ahead and was appalled to discover that the

water was already touching my calves. "Someone stop her," I shouted.

Brandishing his sword, the king advanced toward the countess. She aimed white scaly hands in his direction and mumbled inaudible words.

The king flew backward as if he were pulled from behind.

I didn't look to see if the king had survived his fight. I was too worried about Eva's safety to care about his. So I was relieved when, looking through the moving crowd, I saw that she had managed to slip out of the disciples' grip. I tried running to her aid but the water had reached my thighs, making it impossible.

All of a sudden the atmosphere in the hall became stormy. The light dimmed; thunder rolled, wind blew, and the water, which now licked my waist, became a stirring mass of crashing waves.

Grinding my teeth, I tucked my chin down and moved forward. I felt someone pulling me from behind. I turned, facing a distraught-looking Auguste.

"LEAVE HER," he screamed above the thundering storm. "WE MUST STOP THE PRIESTESS BEFORE SHE DROWNS US ALL."

"EVA NEEDS ME," I shouted back at Auguste before moving toward my beloved.

"*Amir, no,*" a firm voice ordered in my head. "*Change your aim, brother. Change aim before it's too late.*" I froze. It was my brother Jafer's voice. Reluctantly, the focus of my attention switched to the countess. She looked more and more like Samu, the god she worshiped. He was taking domicile in her body. That was obvious. If I didn't stop her now, while the transformation was still incomplete, I would never be able to do it after. "Can't beat a god," Khuan had told me. So I had to dispatch her before she became one.

"But how can I stop her?" I asked myself aloud. *The urns.*

Break the urns.

At first, it seemed simple enough, but I soon realized that it was impossible, because I was stuck in the center of a stormy sea and the urns were all out of reach.

I wracked my mind for another plan of action and something came to me. Battling the waves, I approached the old alchemist. "The statue! Auguste, give me the statue."

Fortunately, Auguste still had it. With the statue held firmly in my fist, I gestured for him to follow me. Together, we managed to swim to a tall, marble-top table set against the wall. Gripping the table's side for support, I struck the statue against the table's hard marble surface until its head broke off.

Well, my plan didn't work. Nothing happened. Actually, that wasn't quite true. The storm, raging furiously in the room, worsened. Moreover, now it was raining. The water was now at my chest.

From the corner of my eye, I saw that the royal guards had managed to climb atop the dais where the water was only waist high. Filled with hope, I watched them approach the countess.

She emitted a throaty laugh, as if welcoming their approach. Then I saw the guard at the head of the group vanish underwater. Another guard followed, then another. One by one, all the guards were pulled under the waves as though by some invisible hands. Howls of terror rang throughout the banquet hall as more and more people were being dragged under the angry surf.

In panic, I grabbed Auguste and lifted him onto the table. Then I climbed up beside him.

"We must break those cursed urns," said Auguste.

I nodded. "How?"

Auguste pointed to the two storm lamps hooked to the wall above us. Protected from the rain and wind by glass casings, their flames were still burning. "Light the balls I gave you."

I shook my head. "It's no use; the moment I lift the glass casing the rain will extinguish the flame. We have to look elsewhere for a solution." That's exactly what I did. I looked. From this high standpoint, I could see the entire room. The urns were now underwater. Perhaps I could swim to them. I began a search for the urn nearest to me. In this process, I discovered a small object set atop a tall bookshelf. A clay bowl decorated with a raindrop pattern. Not only was it out of place in this hall, but it was very familiar to me. I could swear I had seen a similar bowl in Isabo's cell. This had to mean something. It just had to.

Removing my kaftan, I plunged into the stormy water and swam with all my might in the direction of the bookshelf. Finally, my efforts paid off, and my hands made contact with the bottom shelf. I grabbed the shelf above it and hauled myself up.

I was halfway out of the water when I felt something grabbing my ankles. A violent tug downward followed. I held on to the bookshelf. Again something pulled me down. This time, however, one of my hands slipped and I felt myself being dragged underwater. In desperation, I tightened the one hand that was still gripping the bookshelf. Another brutal tug shook me and I went down, bookcase and all.

The massive piece of furniture hit the water with a huge splash, nearly drowning me, and whatever was pulling on my ankles let go.

Freed, I swam up, took a gulp of air, and plunged down again. Through the dark murky water, I spotted the bowl; it was resting on the floor right below me. As I reached out to grab it, my fingers got entangled in some green strings. Before I could pull my hand back, a green veil of those strings had snared my arms and engulfed my face. Soon they were circling my throat. I felt a cold body pressing itself against my back. Icy hands seized my waist. It was the countess, I realized. Damn, she had me. Those strings surrounding my neck, that was her hair, and it was now crushing my windpipe, choking me. In panic, I kicked and thrashed as hard I could... to no effect.

Regaining control of myself, I slipped two fingers under the rope of hair. I tried tearing it off, and I would have succeeded if the countess hadn't twisted her snarling face around and bit my hand.

I gasped; a mouthful of water entered my lungs. I coughed, and it made my situation worse. The edge of my vision darkened. I felt myself sinking to the bottom of this makeshift lake. My back hit the floor. The countess's face suddenly appeared above mine. I tried gouging her eyes out. She easily brushed my hand away; it struck the floor, and my fingers made contact with the rough surface off a rounded object. I turned my head and looked at it.

Through an increasingly thickening haze, I saw bright blue raindrops. The bowl was right under my fingertips. With my last strength, I seized the bowl and smashed it on the countess's face.

A bloodcurdling shriek pierced my eardrums and catapulted me out of the water and high up into the air. When I hit the water again the shock of my landing, which felt very much like a giant body slap, revived me.

Gasping for air, I stared around in dismay. The rain had stopped, the storm had dissipated, and the water level was coming down. I could see the urns again. I could stand up. After an anxious survey of the room, I discovered Eva hanging from the dais's drapery. She had climbed up the velvet panel to escape being dragged underwater. I was so relieved I almost fell to my knees. "My clever princess," I whispered with pride.

Then I spotted the countess. A shiver ran down my spine. Caught in mid-transformation, she was helplessly flapping around in the now knee-high water like, well, like a fish—except that she still had arms that ended in webbed hands.

Surprisingly her face remained as beautiful as ever, even with her mouth twisted into a rictus of rage. Her expression then softened, and Ivana took on an air of intense concentration. Her lips began moving. Her voice rose. *"Wak me akiros Samu ikiv mahoke."* She repeated these words over and over.

I recognized this language; it was an archaic form of Sorvinkian. As a wave of tingling ran up my spine, I knew without a shred of doubt that she was reciting an incantation. Sure enough, the urns began spouting water again.

Oh no, I thought. Not again! Determined to wring the priestess's neck and get this over with once and for all, I ran toward her.

"Skah," she hissed at me.

An invisible fist struck me in the chest. I sailed to the other end of the hall and hit the wall with force. Dizzied, I staggered to my feet. "All right, that won't work."

"THE BALLS," Auguste yelled from his spot on the table-top. "LIGHT THE BALLS BEFORE IT STARTS RAINING AGAIN."

I dashed to the nearest storm lamp, lifted the glass casing, and then pulled out the silver balls from my pocket.

A small bit of wick was sticking out of their top-ends. But when I tried lighting one, all it made was a series of crackle and pop sounds—and some smoke. I cursed the futility of it all, yet I persevered, and after a nail-biting period of time, the flame of my lamp dried the wicks enough for them to light.

My first impulse was to throw the balls at the urns, but at the last moment I hesitated. I wasn't sure if this was the best move anymore. I stared at the countess's hissing face. Perhaps *she* should be my target.

"THROW! THROW!" shouted Auguste, while pulling at his hair. "THROW THE DAMN BALLS."

Urged into action by Auguste's urgent cries, I pivoted around and threw one ball at the countess, then the next.

Before I could do anything else, a terrible blast shook the entire castle and a strong gust blew me off my feet. Once more I was projected against the hall's back wall. My head struck its hard stone surface and everything went black.

When I regained consciousness, I saw that the doors of the hall were open and that only a thin film of water remained on the floor. The next thing I saw was Auguste's concerned face hovering over me.

"Prince, are you hurt?"

"I don't think so."

With his help, I rose to my feet. Together we made our way to the center of the room where the broken, lifeless body of the countess lay amid a large circle of rubble.

To my astonishment, I saw that Milo, Khuan, and Lilloh were already there, waiting for me. My thoughts went to Eva. Seized by panic, I looked at the dais. All my fear vanished as I watched the king help Eva come down the drapery. I smiled, glad that the king had survived too. Eva had suffered enough loss as it was.

Milo rushed to meet me. "Oh my lord, I was so worried," he said, his voice cracking with emotion. By the look on his face it was relief. "My lord, do you need help?"

I shook my head *no*, but that didn't stop him from grabbing my elbow to straighten me up. I didn't protest; instead I smiled and asked him why he and the Anchin were here. Milo explained that Auguste had sent them word to come help us. Unfortunately, they didn't arrive quickly enough and were stuck behind the sealed doors.

Having regained my balance, I approached the circle of rubble. Pointing to the countess's corpse in its center, I addressed Khuan. "I thought you said gods couldn't be defeated?"

Khuan smiled. "Gods can sometimes be tricked, but never beaten." He cast a cold eye to the countess's dead body. "By no means was this thing a god. It was a minor water spirit, at best, worshiped as a god, which isn't unusual. I've seen it one too many times. Most supposed deities I've encountered turned out to be spirits in the end—that's when they were not demons in disguise. Real gods are much rarer."

"How can you be sure?"

Khuan shuddered violently. He looked positively frightened. "I felt the presence of a real god once. Trust me, that *thing* wasn't it. That creature wasn't powerful enough to be a god. That's why you won over it." Khuan paused, studied the ravaged room then added, "This thing was powerful nonetheless." His inquisitive eyes met mine. "Killing the countess was the right way to end this… the only way actually. She was the spirit's vessel, his conduit. With her death, this spirit lost all means of exercising its power here and was forced to flee. Good thinking on your part."

I shrugged. "I hardly had the time to think about it, really. It just felt right."

I looked down at the countess's body. A woman again, she still wore her dress and signature raindrop aquamarine pins. Three pins. I frowned. She had four at one point. I could swear she did. At the queen's funeral, just before the bear's… before Thalia's attack, I thought she had four then. And when I had first met the countess she wore only one pin in her hair. Then, only one princess was missing.

I kneeled down and touched the pins. They were pulsating with magic.

"Lilloh," I said.

"Yes. I can feel it from here," she answered, anticipating my question.

"One pin per princess… hm?" I looked up at Khuan. "What should I do? The wrong move on my part may end the princesses' lives."

"Do what your instinct tells you to do."

Carefully unhooking each pin from the countess's lapel, I laid them delicately on the floor; then I looked up at Khuan again. "You're sure about this?"

He nodded. "Follow your instinct."

I rose and stared at the neatly lined pins. Taking a deep breath, I slammed the heel of my boot down on the pins over and over until each stone had been crushed into bits.

As I stepped back and contemplated the sparkling dust and broken bits of gold attachments scattered on the floor—all that remained of the pins—doubts began tormenting me. Soon, I feared for the worst. *Lord, what have I done? What if I was wrong?* I shut my eyes. Then I would have the death of those young, innocent princesses on my conscience for the rest of my days. I knew I couldn't live with such a weight on my mind. I knew it all too well.

CHAPTER
TWENTY-FIVE

S lowly strolling through Diego's empty rooms, I inspected each one carefully to verify that nothing had been forgotten. I was glad to see that the chore had been well done and that everything had been packed and stored away… well, except for the small bronze box in my hands. The one I had promised to deliver to Diego's father, the King of Pioval.

As I stared at the empty rooms one last time, a heavy feeling of loss weighed on my heart. Although several weeks had passed since Diego's death and my battle with the priestess of Samu, it still felt like yesterday to me. I kept expecting to see Diego come out of his bedroom at any moment. He had been so vibrant and exuberant when alive that it was hard to imagine him gone. Yet he was gone, gone forever.

I sighed heavily and walked to the window. I looked outside, amazed by the landscape's metamorphosis. Spring had finally arrived in Sorvinka. Green grass now replaced the snow on the ground and tender leaves dressed the previously naked trees.

My gaze fell on the three princesses, the twins Olga and Mesa and little Aurora, playing in the garden under Isabo's watchful eyes. My instinct had been right. Crushing the pins was the right thing to do. Later that day, the princesses had come running to the castle, with tales of the Baba and her walking house. Strangely enough, none of them remembered having been transformed into bears and their time spent in animal form. It was for the best, I supposed. Soon after the princesses' triumphant arrival, I rushed to the dungeon and broke the water bowl, freeing Isabo from her trance.

Poor Isabo was so weak that it took her days to regain her strength. As for the princesses, they were in perfect health—although, if you asked me, they seemed a bit... wild. It was as though they were now imbued with some animalistic qualities, which they previously did not possess. Then again, maybe it was just me, imagining things.

Shy knocking on the door behind me pulled me out of my thoughts. I turned and saw Khuan standing in the doorframe.

I bowed. "Emissary Khuan."

"Prince Amir," he replied, bowing too.

"So, you're leaving today, I hear."

Khuan nodded. "Yes. We have, *it seems,* worn out our welcome."

"The king didn't take your deception lightly, concerning your ability to understand Sorvinkian."

Khuan smiled. "It's understandable." His expression darkened. "What isn't understandable is Lars's official nomination as heir to the throne. It is a very questionable decision."

I agreed with him. In my opinion, this was a wrong move on the king's part. Lars had not come out of the lake incident whole. Part of his mind, I believed, had been lost in the icy water of the lake. Mind you, the boy wasn't brilliant to begin with, but he certainly wasn't a simpleton either. Now, however, there was a troubling emptiness in his eyes and a slackness in his jaw that didn't bode well for any man, let alone a future king. Furthermore, the boy was easily confused and disoriented. The words *addled mind* always came to the tip of my tongue every time I saw Lars. It wasn't all bad news though. If Lars's intellect had deteriorated, his temper, on the other hand, had greatly improved. The duke was now a polite, likable young man.

I placed a hand on Khuan's shoulders. "It's not for us to judge, my friend. The king is determined to see his dynasty remain in control of Sorvinka. And as he has officially proclaimed that he would never remarry, *ever,* that leaves only Lars as successor."

"In the condition he is in right now, he won't stay in power for long. The Molotoffs will see to that."

I shrugged. "There's nothing we can do, my friend. Sorvinka isn't our kingdom."

"True. It isn't our kingdom—yet." Khuan smiled. "Let's not linger on this subject any longer. Politics isn't what I came here to discuss with you. I came to remind you that my offer still stands; you can come with us if you want. Auguste Ramblais, the alchemist, is coming."

I smiled. "Thank you for the offer, Khuan. But as appealing as your invitation is, I must decline. My heart is here, so I'm staying."

Khuan's optimistic demeanor changed. His smiled faded and his shoulders sagged a little bit. He sighed. "You're a gifted shal-galt, Amir. It saddens me that you refuse to seek training."

"Training for what? Seeking ghosts and talking to ghouls? Those are the last things I want to do. What I want is to quiet the voices in my head and halt those horrible feelings from invading my senses. That's what I want."

"This is exactly why you should come with us. Part of a shal-galt's training is devoted to the art of shutting one's mind. There are specific techniques one can use to build mental barriers against the assaults of the spiritual world that surrounds us. Without this ability you may go mad."

His offer was tempting. Madness had been the downfall of many of my brothers. Jafer had been plagued by it. But I couldn't leave. I didn't want to.

"I can't, Khuan. The king likes and respects me now. He's indebted to me and cannot refuse me anything. He told me so himself. So when I ask him for Eva's hand in marriage, he will consent to our union." I felt my heart soaring, as it always did when I talked about marrying Eva.

With his hands joined together under his chin, Khuan bowed. "I wish you the best. However, if you ever change your mind, ride east."

On this, we bid each other farewell.

* * *

Later that day, after having spent a few more hours reminiscing about my time with Diego, I returned to my room carrying the small bronze casket with me. I was pleasantly surprised to see Eva waiting for me in my reception room. Lately, she had been so devoted to her cousin Lars that we hardly spent any time together. Although her selfless dedication toward Lars's rehabilitation was admirable and should be commended, I didn't like it. For some reason, her devotion to her cousin made me nervous and jealous… and also a little ashamed of myself for having those feelings, so I kept them hidden from her.

"Eva!" I said, beaming. "I'm so glad to see you."

"Me too, Amir, I'm pleased to see you," she said, rising from my couch. Although her words were joyous ones, the flat tone of her voice and the solemn look on her face indicated that she felt otherwise.

"What's troubling you, Eva?"

She came to me. I opened my arms, but she stopped a short distance from me, refusing to enter my embrace.

I felt a sudden tightness gripping my throat. "Eva?"

Her head lowered, and she began wringing her hands. "Father is calling all the noblemen to the castle for an announcement."

"Really," I said, grinning like a monkey. "Is it for our wedding?"

"Amir, please, let me finish." She paused as if to gather her courage; then raising an oddly pale face to me, she began, "I thought... I thought it best if I came here in person and tell you myself." She paused again. Her eyes were all misty. After swallowing hard several times, Eva continued with evident torment. "I thought it best if you knew beforehand. I didn't want you to learn it there... surrounded by strangers... and... and..."

"What is it?"

Burying her face in her hands, she breathed, "I'm marrying Lars."

I gasped. For a brief instant I couldn't breathe at all. My head was spinning. I stepped back. "You're jesting. This isn't true. Say you're jesting."

Eva shook her head.

"But... but, your father said—"

"I know what my father told you, Amir," she interjected. "My marrying Lars is my idea. I suggested it to Father, and together we agreed that this was best for Sorvinka. The stability of the Empire has to come first."

I stared at her, wide-eyed. Right now, I thought my heart was going to stop from all the pain. I just couldn't believe what I was hearing. I didn't want to believe it. "Eva, you can't. We love each other. We've lain together. You... you love me, you said so."

"My feelings toward you haven't changed, Amir, nor will they ever," Eva said in a quivering voice, as tears streamed down her cheeks. "Lars cannot rule. His mind isn't sharp enough. Therefore, I decided... that... that I will have to rule for him. If I don't do it, our dynasty will perish. No matter how much I love you... I cannot allow that to happen."

Perhaps it was the pain talking, I wasn't sure, but I found myself saying hurtful things to her. "No. That's a lie. You're just like your Aunt Livia—power hungry. You want to rule more that you want me. That's the reason behind you choice, nothing else!"

Eva raised her chin. "Maybe you're right. Maybe I always wanted to rule and now is my chance."

I felt as though a knife had plunged into my chest and was being twisted around and around. I couldn't speak. I had nothing to say anyway. I knew Eva well enough to know that when her mind was made up, nothing could be done to change it. Obviously, my love for her would not do it, no matter how strong it was.

Eva took a hesitant step toward me. The hard, determined look she had displayed moments ago was now replaced by one of deep regret and sorrow. "Please don't hate me, Amir. I never meant to hurt you. If it wasn't for this disastrous affair, I would've gladly married you. You know this... you know I'm not lying."

I didn't reply. I was too hurt to speak, too hurt to believe anything she was saying anymore.

Eva expelled a long, broken sigh. She bit her lower lip; then, with her brow furrowed in apprehension, she leaned forward to kiss me.

I turned my face away, so her lips met nothing but empty air. Undeterred, she moved closer, letting her tear-streaked cheek brush mine. I stepped back, jaw set, and arms tightly folded against my chest.

"You don't need to be cruel with me, Amir," she whispered. "I didn't hurt you on purpose."

I closed my eyes. "Leave."

"Amir."

"Leave I said. Go! Get out!"

"As you wish!" Her tone was bitter.

I kept my eyes shut, somehow, not seeing her made this torture a tad less painful. I listened to the diminishing sounds of her footsteps, and then I heard the door slam. Eva was gone, gone from my room and gone from my life.

I opened my eyes and wiped tears off my cheek. Eva's tears, which she had left behind when she had tried kissing me. Maybe she did love me after all. For all that was worth, it didn't make me feel any better. Actually, I felt worse, much worse. The pressure encircling my chest was such that I feared it would crush me like a nutshell.

Raising my face to the ceiling, I stared at the crude wood beams supporting the old slate roof. I felt so lost in this foreign land, in this castle. I had no purpose for being here. My purpose was gone. What was I supposed to do now? I couldn't stay here. *I must leave this cursed place at once… but for where?*

Forcing myself to breathe deeply, I directed my attention to Diego's box still clutched in my hands. Gently, I ran my fingers on the lid.

* * *

Regardless of the cold breeze whipping my face, I felt better. My pulse—my heart—was still painfully throbbing in my throat, but my head was clear. Leaving the castle had been the right thing to do.

I brought my gray mare to a stop and waited for Milo, who was driving the first wagon of our two-vehicle caravan, to catch up with me. He was doing well, considering that the second wagon had no handler and was just attached to the first.

At this time of the year, the road crossing these vast steppes was muddy, slowing down travel. Still, I thought we were making good time.

"WHOOAH!" Milo pulled on the reins, slowing his team of sturdy Sorvinkian draw horses to a trot. I guided my mare close to the heavy wagon, so we could talk while riding.

"My lord, I'm afraid that going at this fast pace on such a

broken road may have damaged many of our goods. I heard breaking sounds coming from inside the wagon." Milo poked a thumb over his shoulder.

"The time we've gained far exceeds the damage we may have suffered," I replied, eyeing the road ahead. A dark silhouette was now visible on the horizon. It was another caravan; I had no doubt of that. Smiling, I pointed to the growing shape. "See, Milo, there they are. I knew if we rode hard enough, we would catch up with them before nightfall."

A furrow of concern wrinkled Milo's forehead. "Are you sure going east is our best option?"

"Yes," I answered. For me, joining Khuan, Lilloh, and Auguste was the least painful option. I had seriously considered going west and fulfilling Diego's last wish. But too many painful memories were linked to this obligation—I wasn't ready to go there yet. It would have to wait. I knew Diego would understand. Thinking about the promises I had made to my friend brought an important detail to my mind. There was something else he had wanted me to do.

I looked at Milo. "I believe we're far enough from the castle for me to give you this."

I pulled out Diego's sword, which I had packed on my horse alongside mine, and gave it to Milo.

His eyes widened in disbelief. He gripped the sword with all the reverence due a weapon of such a magnificent quality. "That's the sword! The one I liked. My lord, I cannot take it."

"It's yours, Milo. Diego wanted you to have it."

"I'm not allowed swords."

"We're not at the castle anymore. And what use is a guard to me, if he cannot carry a sword?"

"Yes. My lord is right. Thank you, my lord." Beaming with delight, Milo fastened the sword to his belt.

I was glad for Milo. Having a sword and being able to fulfill his guard's duties again meant a lot to him. At least one of us was happy, I thought, staring ahead.

Khuan's caravan had stopped moving and I could see my friends clearly now. They were all waving at us, Khuan and Lilloh from the back of their ponies, and Auguste from the seat of his wagon.

We waved back.

Look to the east, Jafer had told me in a dream. Maybe this was indeed the right option for me. Meeting the emperor and seeing the traveling city were interesting prospects to me. Also, I could learn to build mental barriers to block the spirits' voices, learn how to ignore the presence of magic. *And maybe forget Eva,* a voice whispered in my mind.

The lump in my throat swelled to a choking size. I would never forget Eva. This I knew. The best I could hope for was to learn to live without her.

With this thought in mind, I spurred my horse into a gallop and hurried to join my new traveling companions, Khuan, Lilloh, and Auguste.

DEATH IN THE TRAVELING CITY
[AN EXCERPT]

CHAPTER ONE

My mind was calm and peaceful, my breathing slow and easy. I raised my imaginary hands; they looked so much bigger and rougher than my real ones. These were the hands of a worker, not a prince. They were good and strong, exactly what I needed. I flexed them a few times, making fists, then opening them up again until, finally, I felt ready to build my protective mental barrier—my *wall*, as I called it. As usual, I began by conjuring a brick, a simple red brick. It slowly started to take form. I could see it growing; I could feel its weight increasing between my hands. Then it all went wrong, and I wound up holding a misshapen red lump of muddy clay. I felt my shoulders sagging. Why did I have so much trouble focusing today? I leaned against the tree trunk; maybe more shade would help me concentrate. All I needed was to conjure up the bricks, then the rest would come easily; after that I could relax and watch the wall take shape. *Focus Amir! Think about the wall, the barrier, think of nothing else besides the barrier.*

According to Khuan—my friend and teacher in these matters—these barriers were different for everyone. For instance, his was a transparent sheet of glass that only slightly clouded his perception of the spirit world, which only "shalgalts" could sense, that surrounded us all, allowing him to rest his senses while remaining aware of his surroundings. My barrier wasn't nearly as sophisticated. Actually, to be honest, mine was pretty crude. Not that it mattered to me; I loved my wall regardless of its rough appearance: my thick, opaque, red brick wall. To learn how to build this barrier, this wall, was the reason I had decided to accompany Khuan and Lilloh, both emissaries of the eastern emperor, to the famous traveling city—well, it was not the only reason, but definitely the most important one.

I was a shal-galt, they had told me: a ghost seeker, a demon killer, a sorcerer hunter. I should have been relieved to know that the voices in my head were in fact echoes of ghosts' whisperings *and not* the product of a deranged mind, as I had previously feared. And that the strange and disturbing sensations my body was often experiencing, like tingling, stomach pain, nausea, and sudden cold, were caused by either the proximity of a demonic creature, or the effect of some residual magic lingering in the air, and not by shattered nerves. So, I wasn't crazy after all. Oddly enough, I gathered very little joy from this knowledge. I despised magic. I loathed it, really. As for demons and ghosts, needless to say I'd rather do without them, hence the wall. The thicker the better. I didn't want anything to seep through—anything at all. I found ghostly voices, demonic presences, and magical auras highly upsetting. I didn't want to be a seeker, shal-galt, or anything associated with the supernatural world. I wanted to be normal, ordinary even. I wanted peace of mind.

I concentrated again. Once I had successfully eliminated all thoughts from my head, I focused on erasing the outside interferences: the gurgling sound of the river lazily running beside me was the first to vanish. (I was seated close enough to its pebbly shore that if I stretched my hand I could touch its icy water.) Next to go was the feel of the breeze on my skin, and then the rustling of leaves from the tree under which I sat. When my mind reached that relaxed state of blissful numbness, I began building my wall, starting with the foundation, just as Khuan had taught me. First, I conjured the image of my hands, then bricks, and finally a bucket of mortar. My imaginary hands grasped a brick and laid it on the ground rather clumsily, a second brick was set beside the first, then another and another until I had made a long row. A copious layer of mortar was then applied. Slow at first, this process soon sped up. My movements became easier. I could see my hands placing each square lump of clay one atop the other, each one making my wall stronger, taller, bigger—slowly enclosing my special senses, my shal-galt senses, within its protective circle and sheltering me from the assaults of the supernatural world that surrounded me.

Amir, no! Please don't lock me out, Jafer begged in my head. As usual the ghost of my dearly departed brother was trying to stop me from building the wall; however, his attempts were now less frequent and much weaker than they had previously been. Like me, Jafer had been a shal-galt—a ghost seeker able to sense either magic or spirits and demons or, in our case, both. And after his death, Jafer had kept appearing to me... to council me, I suppose. Although my brother meant well, I found his constant whispering in my mind and impromptu apparitions in my dreams quite disturbing. But thanks to this mental-barrier building technique things were now bearable.

"He's a strong spirit," my friend Khuan had said of Jafer. "But with time, your brother will eventually cease coming to you. He should go to rest, that will be best for both of you. What he's doing is dangerous. It puts you and him, his immortal soul in particular, at risk."

I hoped Khuan was right in saying that Jafer would at some point go to rest and leave me alone. I wanted to be at peace. I wanted to forget the past, to forget Jafer's death, and, most of all, I wanted to forget Eva's rejection. A couple of months had passed since I had left Sorvinka and joined Khuan, Lilloh, and the old alchemist, Auguste Ramblais, on this journey toward the Anchin's traveling city. Hard to believe, but it was almost summer now. Time might have passed since the day I left Sorvinka—the same cursed day Eva had rejected my marriage proposal and announced that she would instead marry Lars, King Erik's heir to the throne—but little else. I still felt my gut wrench every time I thought about it. I still hurt just as much as if it had happened yesterday; the wound remained just as deep. One thing had changed though. My anger toward Eva had subsided. Now I just wanted the pain to go away as well.

The sound of voices reached my ears. I looked over my shoulder and spotted young Milo, my trusty eunuch guard and servant, and Khuan chatting together beside the camp-fire. Those two made a very peculiar pair. Milo was tall, blond, and slender to the point of gauntness, and, more or less, the total opposite of Khuan, who was short—well, shorter, he only looked short in comparison to the tall, lanky youth—solidly built with long, silky black hair tied into a braid. His facial features were small and delicate: he had well-defined high cheekbones, a rather small nose for a man, and inquisitive, dark, slanted eyes. Milo's eyes, on the other hand, were wide, round-shaped, and a soft mossy-green, and his features, aquiline nose and square jaw, were pronounced and highly masculine.

My focus gravitated to Milo's smooth, beardless cheeks. I rubbed the coarse hairs of my own chin. It felt wrong. I leaned over the river's edge and gazed at my reflection, and sighed. My beard was a little crooked, shorter on the left than on the right side. Besides the poor grooming job, something else in my appearance struck me. The tan-skinned young man staring back at me in the water, with his angular cheek-bones, his square chin and jaw, looked nothing like a prince. Sure, I still possessed the straight nose and flawless profile of my family, the warm brown eyes and thick dark hair of my kind. But nobody could ever tell that I was Prince Amir Ban, second in line to the throne of Telfar, land of sun and sand, after my beloved brother Erik, the ruling Sultan.

No. Right now I looked like an ordinary man, a simple

traveler, nothing more.

An outbreak of boisterous laughter disrupted my reverie; I turned my gaze to my friends again. Their sight brought a smile to my face. I liked them both. And more importantly, I trusted them. Trust was new to me. *Better hurry up and finish this wall,* I decided, anxious to join them.

I sat straight and fixed my eyes on the vast, empty plain stretching to the horizon. Taking a deep breath, I tried to forget my surroundings: the sound of the wind rushing through the leaves of the tree's canopy stretching above me, Milo's laughter as he helped Khuan and Auguste clean up our camp after breakfast, and Lilloh's constant critiquing in the background. I frowned, gritting my teeth. Her voice grated on me—not because its timbre was unpleasant, but because her know-it-all or know-it-best tone certainly was. Worse still, she had the attitude to match. Women should never be so... so bold. And this particular one certainly didn't know her place.

Forget her, I ordered myself, *forget everything.* It worked. My concentration recaptured, I started the barrier-building exercise over from the beginning. Again, I envisioned a brick, a rectangular red, hard lump of dried clay, then conjured up the image of my hands. I watched them work, applying the gray, muddy mortar over my foundation. It spread easily. The bricks followed. I could feel their weight in my hands. Slowly, brick by brick, row by row, the wall rose. And as it did, Jafer's voice, my doubts, my insecurity, my fears, and my pain were locked behind it. I felt lighter. I felt at peace.

"You shouldn't do that," Lilloh said behind me.

I winced, and at once my wall crumbled. I tore up a handful of grass and threw it at her in frustration. "*Arghh,* Lilloh! Now I have to start all over again."

"No you don't," she argued, which didn't surprise me one bit; arguing with me seemed to be Lilloh's favorite pastime. However, I had noticed that our arguments had steadily gotten worse lately. As a result, I regretted having let Milo give her all those Sorvinkan lessons. (Lilloh was now perfectly fluent in this language, while my Anchin left a lot to be desired—a fact she took pleasure in reminding me.) Teaching Lilloh Sorvinkan was a mistake, I thought. She was more sufferable when she had less vocabulary.

"You need to accept what you are, Amir, and learn to live with it. Not hide behind a mental wall like a coward."

"Watch your tongue, Lilloh!" I warned, glaring at her.

She held my stare, her dark, piercing eyes riveted to mine. "I have the habit of speaking my mind, and I'm not going to change that on your account!" One of Lilloh's eyebrows rose as she paused. When she spoke again it was in a different language. "And from now on I will speak to you only in Anchin. You would do well to answer in the same language. You need to practice, Amir. You're accent is too thick. If you want to be understood by our people, your Anchin needs to improve!"

I shook my head. Lilloh might have been more articulate in her own language, but, sadly, she remained just as rude.

She made her way under the tree and rested her back against its trunk. It was then that I noted that she wasn't wearing her usual rough leather garments and chain mail. Instead, she was clad in a pale brown, loose-fitting, linen shirt over matching pants. A wide yellow belt tightly circled her waist, accentuating its narrowness. Her jet-black hair, as lush and shiny as mink fur, which normally flowed freely around her heart-shaped face, was now tied into one long braid that fell to the middle of her back. This new hairstyle exposed every detail of her face like never before. Her high cheekbones, dark almond eyes, and her full lips were particularly striking. And in the soft morning light, her skin appeared more golden and moist than a freshly baked bread roll. The new clothes and hairdo suited her well, in my opinion. This was an improvement. Lilloh looked more polished, more civilized, very unlike the savage creature I had met in Sorvinka, the one who always seemed on the verge of gouging my eyes out.

Lilloh wrinkled her small, low-bridged nose. "What's wrong with you? Why are you looking at me as if you've never seen my face before?"

"Don't be silly! I've seen your face far too often if you ask me. It's the clothes I'm curious about. What's with the new outfit?"

Adjusting her belt, Lilloh said, "Summer clothes. Soon it will be very warm, too warm to wear leather."

I nodded. I too had abandoned my thick kaftans in favor of light cotton tunics and comfortable linen pantaloons. I looked at Lilloh again and saw that she had grasped the tip of her braid. A leather hair tie with two jade beads dangling at its ends held her braid together. I watched her roll the beads between her fingers as an uncomfortable silence settled between us. It was Lilloh who broke it first. "You're still going to build that mental barrier regardless of what I say, aren't you?"

"Yes!"

"Then I won't subject you to the sight of my face any longer."

"Good!" I said, staring directly ahead. Moments later, I heard her leave. By the brisk stomping sound her feet made, I knew she was angry—yet again. I sighed. For some reason, Lilloh and I couldn't have a discussion without seeing it turn into a heated argument of some sort. I guess some people were just not meant to get along no matter what. Shaking my head, I tried to banish Lilloh and her unpleasant, arrogant attitude from of my mind, and I started rebuilding my barrier—once more.

I was just beginning to make progress when the sound of galloping horses broke my concentration. I saw two riders racing toward our camp. Khuan and Lilloh had already mounted their shaggy brown ponies and were trotting out to meet them. I gathered the small rug on which I had been kneeling, and hurried toward the camp. By the time I had rejoined Milo and Auguste at the campsite, Khuan and Lilloh had met up with the riders. All four now stood some distance away from us and appeared to be talking.

"Who are those newcomers?" I asked Milo.

"Messengers from the Anchin emperor."

"Here? Are you sure?"

"Yes," said Auguste. The old alchemist limped beside me. Stroking his long gray beard, he aimed his good eye at the group; crossed by an ugly scar, his other eye was white and dead, the disastrous result of a failed experiment. Auguste pointed a knobby finger at the riders, or more precisely at the red and gold banner the man on the right was carrying, and explained, "See the gold lion at the center of the banner? That's the emperor's emblem. Khuan told us so before riding to meet them." Auguste rubbed his red bulbous nose, then his fingers traveled to his scar, where they lingered. "What do you think their sudden presence here means?" he asked.

I surveyed the group. Khuan's and Lilloh's stiff, formal posture didn't bode well. "Nothing good, my friend. Nothing good."

* * *

The messengers didn't stay long. Shortly after my exchange with Auguste, they turned their horses and rode off in the same direction they had come, and Khuan and Lilloh rejoined us.

"What's going on?" I asked as they reached the camp.

"The emperor summons us to the palace," answered Khuan.

"Why?"

His brow furrowed for a brief instant. "I can't say." He

paused, and shot a hesitant side-glance to a very pale and distraught-looking Lilloh before adding, "It wasn't fully explained to us."

How bizarre, I thought. If I didn't know Khuan as well as I did, I might have been tempted to believe that he was lying to me right now.

"Let's hurry and break camp," Khuan said in an upbeat tone. "We must be there before sundown."

"Before sundown—that's impossible!" I exclaimed. "You said the city was two weeks of travel away."

"Not anymore," said Lilloh. "The city has moved to the Sanksiki province. If we make haste, we can be there this afternoon."

"Oh yes! Yes! Wonderful!" cheered an enthusiastic Auguste. "Let's hurry to the traveling city! I can't wait to see this marvel. What about you, Prince Amir?"

I smiled. "Oh yes! I am looking forward to seeing this city, too. I'm sure Lilloh and Khuan are also impatient to return home."

Khuan replied with a series of nods and a broad grin.

Lilloh, however, looked so glum that it took me aback a little. The expression on her face was a blend of shock and sadness; I thought she looked as if she had unexpectedly lost something very precious to her and was still in shock.

I felt my stomach knotting. *Lord! Something's up, because this woman doesn't upset easily.* Clearly the news they received from the emperor's messengers was troubling her. I must say that filled me with apprehension.

* * *

We had been riding hard for most of the morning, when the first sign of the city appeared on the horizon: smoke, huge plumes of it.

Rising on my stirrups, I peered ahead. The city had to

be farther away because all I saw was the flat grassy steppe stretching to infinity, like a wind-swept undulating green ocean. Just as I was slowing my gray mare, Khuan pulled beside me on his shaggy brown pony.

"We're almost there, Amir. It's just ahead."

"Where? I don't see anything."

"You can't see it now, but there's a ridge in front of us. It leads down to a valley. That's why you can't see the city. It's in the valley."

As we progressed, the edge of the ridge became visible. I could now distinguish a second ridge rising in the distance and the beginning of a dip between both.

"This way!" shouted Khuan, turning left along the ridge.

Before chasing after Khuan, I looked over my shoulder to make sure that Milo and Auguste, who were both driving wagons, were still following us. They were moving along without too much difficulty. Reassured, I swiftly caught up with Khuan, who had stopped at the edge of the ridge. Khuan pointed down to the valley. "There, Amir! Look!"

Stretching in my saddle, I gazed down at the city with amazement. A flow of red buildings ran along the bottom of this valley as far as the eye could see. At first glance, it looked like a river of blood. Every house, every tent, every construction in this city was of one shade of red or another: it went from the palest, nearly pink hue, to vibrant carmine and the darkest of maroon. If the color was the first detail to strike me, the sheer size of the city was a close second. It was enormous—so much so, I couldn't see where it ended. By the look of it, this city numbered at least a couple hundred thousand habitants.

"It's so big," I whispered.

"It's home to so many people, it has to be huge," replied Khuan. "People belonging to dozens of different races call Ulahn Gazar home. Three races form its core, though: the Anchin, the Chechow, and the Taiko, which is, as you know, the race I belong too."

I nodded, absentmindedly. Frankly I was not paying attention to anything he was saying. I was too absorbed by my examination of Ulahn Gazar. "How can such an immense city be moved? And why?" I whispered to myself. That was beyond my comprehension. I directed my attention to the heart of the city where the largest buildings were nestled. This particular cluster of imposing constructions appeared to be surrounded by some sort of wall, and at its center was a huge house with a glossy green roof. "What's that one with the different colored roof?"

"That's the emperor's palace," said Khuan.

I scanned the portion of the city neighboring the palace complex. It was the most densely constructed area of all. The houses, tents, and all sorts of buildings in that sector seemed almost piled one on top of the other. But as my gaze traveled away from the city center, the space between the houses widened. Yet, in spite of this, I was left with the suffocating impression that this city was too crowded.

A sudden tightness gripped my chest. *Could the thought of entering such an impressive city be the cause of the oppressive feeling now growing inside me?* I wondered. I felt uneasy, nervous, and jittery. I looked around, seeking the source of my discomfort, but found nothing tangible. As I spurred my horse to the very edge of the ridge, I sensed an unusual energy floating in the air, like a heat wave on a hot day... but not quite. This energy was like nothing I had experienced before, and it was radiating upward. To my dismay, I realized that it was coming from the city. It was as if this place were alive, as if this city had a spirit of its own. What at first had begun inside me as a vague uneasiness hadn't ceased intensifying; it seemed to be mirroring the flow of energy that kept rising up to us in strong bursts like waves hitting the shore at high tide. It climbed and climbed, up and up, until in one final leap it touched the tip of my feet. My entire body tensed as tingling sensations danced along my limbs making me shudder, raising goose bumps all over my skin.

"Magic! So much magic!" This city seemed to be constructed entirely of magic, as if conjured out of nothingness. This was so shocking to me that it literally took my breath away. After a brief struggle, I managed to catch my breath again and was able to hiss through clenched teeth, "Why didn't you tell me about this, Khuan?"

Looking sheepish, he said in a small voice, "Knowing how much you dislike magic, you wouldn't have come if I had."